Three Times Buried

Jane Smith

Prologue

St Cyrus Poor-house

Winter had set in: the bleak, bone-deep chill of a Scottish December.

The old man huddled upon a wooden chair, as far from the door as he could get to escape the draught that was fingering in through the cracks. He'd have liked a pipe, but it was a long time since he'd been able to afford tobacco. He breathed onto his chapped hands. Arthritis and too many winters had stiffened his hands and hips and knees into rusty hinges – just as it had done, decades ago, to his mother's. He tucked his claws into his armpits and thought about his long-dead mother. He assumed she was long dead.

The other men were shuffling about in the deflated way of poor-house folk. They were crooked, toothless, hair-thin, like him. Wheezing, sighing with every movement. They sat together, as if huddling would warm them, but it didn't. He found no pleasure in their company; they were fellow inmates – nothing more. Like him, recipients of the kirk's grudging charity. Forty years in the parish, and he was friendless.

It had been better when he could work. The rhythm of toil had sustained him then. The routines: getting up at dawn, ploughing, cutting hay, singling turnips, yoking the workhorses, feeding the cattle, going to bed with the sun. It was easier to live when the routines of labour had carried him through the hours and days and years. Now – nothing. Too frail to work, and no use on the farm. Nothing to look forward to. Nothing much to look back on either, if he thought about it.

He'd grown querulous with age. He griped about his aching bones, but his companions had troubles enough of their own. His grumbling set off a fit of coughing and his neighbour told him to cut the racket. He wiped the mucus from his lips with his sleeve and muttered a curse – quietly, so it wouldn't reach the ears of the kirk.

It was five o'clock in the afternoon, and darkness had set in. He struggled to his feet and said to no-one in particular that he'd have an early night. No reaction. He shuffled off to bed. He sat on the edge of his narrow cot, reached into the small cabinet beside it and withdrew a razor. Then he lay down, looked up into the darkness and, with a swipe of the razor, laid open his throat.

Part One

Chapter 1

12 November 1826

Futteret Den

A figure emerged from the morning fog down on the turnpike road: a young woman, strolling as if she had all the time in the world.

Widow Lovie saw her from the door of the cottage, where she stood wheezing, just returned from the well. She grunted as she lowered the buckets of water to the ground, one eye on the girl. Worn out already, and the sun was barely up. The girl waved but did not quicken her step, and the widow tucked frozen hands into her armpits and waited.

The figure came into focus. It was the McKessar girl, poor Henrietta's youngest but one. What did she want?

The girl made her way across the frosty field and stopped at the cottage door.

'I'm Margaret McKessar,' she said, puffing clouds into the bitter morning. The wind had planted roses in her rounded cheeks; they looked as if they would dimple when she smiled.

'I know who you are.'

'Your son John hired me yesterday,' Margaret McKessar said. 'At the feeing market.'

So: the new servant. The tip of her nose was red with the chill, but her eyes were merry.

'Where are your things?'

'My brother will bring my kist this afternoon.'

Margaret McKessar smiled, and the widow saw she was right about the dimples. The girl lived only half a mile away and would, no doubt, be forever running back to her family. A servant from further afield would have been better – a hungry quine without distractions. And a plainer girl, too: that would have been better. Still, she looked strong and healthy, and that counted for a lot.

Widow Lovie nodded. 'All right, then.'

She bent to pick up a bucket, flexing her knuckles painfully. These icy mornings played havoc with the rheumatism. The early days of winter were the worst, when the dense sky heralded months of gloom, and no respite in sight.

Margaret McKessar made no move to help, and so she said, 'Take one, will you?' and the girl hoisted the other bucket from the ground. The water sloshed, and Widow Lovie clenched her teeth to hold back a reproof. The girl's good cheer might be worth a lost drop or two.

They turned to the cottage, each with a bucket in hand. A robin flitted above the door – a gorgeous splash of red against stone. *A sign of ill luck. An omen of trouble with the law.* Widow Lovie raised her free hand and touched the wooden door frame. Best to take precautions. She met Margaret McKessar's eye, and the girl nodded. So: she understood the old ways.

'They call you "Meggy", don't they?'

'Aye.'

They ducked inside, into the short, shallow passage that opened to a room on each side. She shut the door to trap the warmth in, and the two women paused to let their eyes adjust to the gloom.

Meggy glanced towards the room on her right, but Widow Lovie ushered her leftwards to the kitchen. She had already got the fire blazing, and the kitchen smelled warm and peaty. They placed the buckets on the earthen floor, and she watched with satisfaction as the girl gazed with open pleasure at her new surroundings. Seen through a stranger's eyes, she thought, it *was* a charming room: bigger than the neighbours' homes, but still cosy.

Meggy took a step deeper into the dim kitchen, and a wintry ribbon of light fell from the small window onto her patched woollen skirt. She slipped her wrap from her shoulders and slung it onto the seat of the long carved deece under the window. The deece was far finer than the settle in the McKessar home, which the widow knew the gravedigger Brown had knocked up out of driftwood for them. They were charity cases, the McKessars.

Meggy strolled to the hearth and held her hands out to the flames. In the silence, John's clock measured time in sleepy ticks. Meggy turned her head towards the tall mahogany clock on the far wall, and the widow felt another small swelling of pride. She shuffled past Meggy, lifted the lid of the tea kettle on the ledge by the grate and peered inside.

Meggy ambled back towards the deece. The hinge of the folding table creaked as the girl flipped it up flush with the seat's back.

'Will I sleep on the deece?' she asked, testing the table's mechanism, up and down, up and down.

Widow Lovie shook her head. 'Nay.' She nodded towards the closet set into the corner, against the partition between the two rooms. 'You'll sleep in there with me.'

Meggy strode to the closet and pulled the door open to study the box bed. When she turned back, she was smiling. 'Am I the only servant?'

'For now,' Widow Lovie said. 'But my grandson helps out with the cattle at times. John says he'll take him on and a farmhand as well at Whitsunday.'

The girl wandered back to the passage by the front door and peered into the other room, but Widow Lovie said sharply, 'That's John's room.'

Meggy took the hint and turned back to dimple at her. 'Where *is* John?'

'Your master? He's out threshing the corn.'

John had slept late that morning and woken with a sore head. Too much carousing after yesterday's feeing market, she supposed. John wasn't much of a drinker, God bless him; a dram or two before bed was enough for him. Unlike his father – now there was a slave to the bottle, George. He'd been a strong man, for all that, could drink the farmhands unconscious and still get behind his plough at dawn with all the power of a pair of workhorses. John wasn't like that. Still, he *had* staggered home late last night, noisy, and with the stink of whisky on him. *Oh, John.* Her heart shifted, thinking of him.

The girl was filling the room, touching things, prodding, sniffing.

Lucky girl, she thought, though Meggy showed no sign of awareness of her good fortune. The widow wondered if the new servant had taken part in the post-fair revelry. She seemed too bright-eyed to have spent the night drinking and flirting. Then again, she was young. But she was fit for work today, and that was all that mattered.

The widow waved a hand at the wooden armchair. 'Sit, then. Have some tea.'

The girl drew a chair closer to the fire. Widow Lovie placed her shawl on the small round table – it was warm in the cottage – and picked the tea kettle up from the ledge. It was still hot from John's breakfast. She poured a mug for the girl and another for herself. There was much to do, but the girl's lightness made her feel reckless. She put a mug in Meggy's hands and sank with a sigh into the other armchair, facing the fire. She took a gulp of tea, closed her eyes to savour it all: the tea, the warmth, the stillness.

When she opened her eyes, Meggy was smiling at her. She had straight teeth and neat crinkles around her eyes. She'd thought the girl might be a chatterer, but – thank God – she wasn't. They sat and slurped in silence. There were things she could have said – pleasantries, instructions, rules – but they could wait. She was too tired for small talk.

'My son will give you your instructions later,' she said. 'Today you can help me clean the kitchen and settle yourself in.' She rested her head against the back of the chair. There would be rules ... but what *were* they? She would have to make some, she supposed. She peered sideways at the girl through slitted eyes. Would Meggy follow rules anyway? She didn't seem the submissive type. She'd be trouble; young women always were. But the widow was too tired to worry about that.

There was a knock, and before she could creak to her feet, a slanted rectangle of pallid light gusted into the cottage. Meggy started and spun around, alert, bright-eyed, dimpling. *Expecting John.* Widow Lovie exhaled slowly. *So that's how it is.*

But instead of John, in marched his sister Elspet in a whirl of briny ice-wind.

'Och!' Elspet said, thrusting her jaw at her mother. 'You've got company.'

Elspet was ten years younger than John, but you'd never guess it from her face; she already sported deep lines from nose to jaw. She'd put on weight lately, and it didn't suit her.

'You know Meggy McKessar,' the widow said, tilting a cheek for her daughter to kiss.

'Aye,' Elspet said, not looking at the girl.

Elspet stomped to the fire and poured herself a mug of tea. She frowned at Meggy, waiting for the girl to vacate the armchair for her. Meggy smiled behind a cupped hand and remained seated. Widow Lovie felt a twitching at the corners of her mouth.

'How's William?' Widow Lovie said, with a pointed glance at Elspet's swollen breasts.

'William is well,' Elspet replied coldly, still standing, her back to the fire. Elspet was due to wed in two weeks; she really ought to be livelier. If a woman couldn't be cheerful on the eve of her wedding, then whenever could she be? But jauntiness wasn't Elspet's way. She had the knack of turning autumn to winter.

Elspet looked down her nose at Meggy and said sharply, 'I thought Mr Scott wanted you on *his* farm.'

'Oh, aye,' Meggy said. 'He did.'

'Your mither said she favoured *him*.'

The widow's stomach dropped at that. So the rumours were still going about, then? The whispers about that awful business with the Chessor girl, the liar?

Meggy shrugged and laughed. 'Cranky old Scott? *I* favoured John Lovie's offer.'

The widow gave a short, sharp laugh. Let mothers warn their daughters all they liked. Mothers wanted their daughters to work for old, worn-out men who would keep themselves to themselves – but would daughters ever listen to their mothers?

Elspet reddened. Meggy rose lazily and took her mug to the dresser, her hips swaying. The maid was showing off! No wonder Elspet hadn't taken to her.

'Meggy,' Widow Lovie said, smiling. 'Go and look about the farm. Acquaint yourself with the dairy.'

Meggy nodded and sashayed to the door. A blast of cold air and light washed in, and then the widow was alone with her daughter in the gloom again.

Elspet flung her a dark look as she lowered herself into the vacated armchair. 'She'll be trouble.'

'Phhht,' she said, with a flick of the wrist. She was feeling – unusually – playful. 'Don't fret yourself.'

'Don't say I never warned you.'

Chapter 2

13 November 1826

When Widow Lovie awoke, it was still dark. It took a moment to register that there was a body in the bed beside her, and that it belonged to the new servant. She sighed, threw off the wool blankets and creaked out of bed, not bothering to be quiet, but Meggy didn't stir.

She slipped her feet into boots, pulled on a black blouse and black wool skirt over her shift, tied an apron about her waist, tucked her wiry hair into a mutch cap and wrapped a black shawl about her shoulders. She padded out into the kitchen, where embers smouldered in the hearth. She tossed a chunk of peat onto the dormant fire, prodded it and waited for the flames to flicker to life. When the blaze was strong and bright, she turned, picked up a bucket and made for the door. With a hand on the latch, she braced herself, bending her head to greet the outdoors.

She pushed the door open and emerged into the frosty morning. The pre-dawn sky was grey and raw.

Shivering, she hurried across the corn yard. The cattle were lowing, deep and sad, from the byre attached to the end of the cottage. *Give me a moment!* Always so many chores, so many things needing attention. Maybe it was a good thing, after all, that John had hired a girl.

Trying to avoid the worst of the wind as she crossed the corn yard, she kept close to the outbuildings – the cart shed and corn kiln – that formed an 'L' shape with the cottage and byre. Opposite the house, she passed the washtub and the small yard, sheltering briefly behind the high stone wall that obscured the property from the turnpike road. Then out past the wall, she blinked against the wind and trudged across the frosty ground to the well, a hundred yards away, the empty pails swinging from the yoke across her shoulders.

At the well she attached a bucket and worked the well handle, her breath coming out in misted puffs as she laboured. Her fingers were stiff, iced over and aching with the fatigue of age. She grunted as she heaved the full buckets up and hoisted them onto the yoke. Taking care not to splash the frigid water onto her skirt, she carted it back to the cottage, where she wriggled free of the yoke with a deep groan.

With the bitter morning at her back, she opened the door and was plunged at once into the sensual pleasure of warmth and light. Meggy was up and holding white hands to the fire. Widow Lovie slammed the door, shutting out the dawn. Meggy blinked and yawned.

'Sit down,' the widow said, planting a pail on the earthen floor. 'I'll get your brose.'

The girl flopped onto the deece.

'You'll cook from tomorrow,' she said, 'but today I'll make it.'

Meggy nodded mutely, still yawning and rubbing her eyes. She'd dressed but her hair was tousled and her cheek criss-crossed with lines from the chaff in the mattress. The widow fussed about in the kitchen. She poured boiled water from the kettle into a bowl of oatmeal and stirred, eyeing the girl on the deece. It was oddly pleasing, having a girl here to pamper. She would have to take care not to indulge her; Meggy *was* only a servant.

'How is your mither?' she asked, handing over the warm brose and easing herself into an armchair. It still stung to know that Henrietta had urged her daughter to go to old Scott instead of John, but she was willing to be charitable. She understood a mother's protectiveness as well as anyone. Besides, poor Henrietta was a woman it was hard to resent: a skinny, crooked figure to be seen daily trundling along the turnpike road to and from the shore with her handcart.

'She's well enough,' Meggy said through a mouthful of brose. 'She has a cough.'

'And your sister, Jean?'

Meggy shrugged and swallowed, licked her lips, wiped a sleeve across her mouth, muttered, 'I suppose she is well.'

'You *suppose*?'

Meggy rolled her eyes extravagantly. 'Jean wanted me to work for old Scott too.'

'Did she?' Her heart slowed again with that familiar ache. 'Why?'

'Oh – Jean. What would she know? Twenty-seven and plain and nobody wants *her*.'

The widow opened her mouth to retort, but she didn't know where to start. She didn't like the implication; did the foolish girl imagine John wanted her for more than her labour? Surely not. John must be twenty years her senior, though of course he was still a strong and handsome man. John had no need for a change of that sort – Heaven forbid it. And then, there was Meggy's disrespect to her sister. She should not let that go without reprimand, but why bother? She didn't much like Jean either. She pitied Meggy's mother, who was withered beyond her years, but Meggy's prickly older sister left her cold. Meggy had always been the pick of the McKessars.

'Where's the master?' the girl asked abruptly.

John had scarcely shown himself since Meggy had arrived the previous morning. When he'd finished threshing the corn, he'd gone to the Broch – Fraserburgh – for some business or other and not returned until evening to take his supper. The widow had almost felt sorry for Meggy, who wasn't used to the waiting yet – not like *she* was. Meggy had grown quieter all day until John had stood in the doorway with the gloaming behind him and said, 'Meggy McKessar, I hope you are settling in.' *Then* she'd been all smiles.

'John's working,' she said.

'Oh.'

She gathered up Meggy's empty bowl and spoon. 'He'll come in for tea soon.'

'Well, then,' the girl said, leaning back on the deece. What an ability she had to sprawl – even on a straight-backed settle! 'What do you want me to do?'

The maid's directness was refreshing, though how long it would take to become annoying was anyone's guess. John had clearly chosen her for her looks, not her manners.

'Are you a good worker?' she asked sharply. The girl laughed and shrugged, and the widow sighed. *No, then.* Meggy's posture screamed a lack of discipline. But her giggle, bubbling freely now that she was fully awake and sated, was irresistible.

'You'd better be,' she said dryly, but not unkindly. 'In the spring you'll help with the hay-making. For now, you'll be in the house and yard with me. The cooking and cleaning, and the knitting of course. You'll yirn the milk and fetch the water, and you'll cut moss in the spring and give a hand with the milking when it's needed.'

'Aye,' said Meggy, and her eyes, suddenly bright, darted to the rattling door. 'Here's John.'

Chapter 3

A Sunday in December 1826

M ist, clingy and dense as cobwebs, muffled the tolling of church bells.

'Hurry!' said the widow. Meggy snorted, the clouds of her breath mingling with the fog. It was near impossible to stir the wretched girl. 'Hurry, or we'll miss the service.'

She bustled ahead, forcing Meggy to quicken her step.

The winter so far had been harsh. For weeks, rain and snow had trapped them in the snugness of the cottage, while gales hammered the doors and whistled through cracks in the window frames. Tramping out to the village was a herculean task, and one they had avoided through the long, squalling season. But in the last few days the rain had eased and Meggy had nagged her for an outing.

'I'll go mad,' she'd said, hands on hips, pouting, threatening, as if sanity was a choice.

'Go mad, for all I care.' Through the glass of the tiny window, she could see that the rain no longer slashed, but the air was a white pall. Why venture out? Inside was stillness and warmth. The widow closed her eyes, listening to the rattling of the door, the purring of the fire, the ticking of the clock.

But Meggy wouldn't budge. She was stubborn, that one.

'All right.' Annoyed, she surrendered. 'We'll go to the kirk, then.'

It was a compromise, and a cunning one; Meggy couldn't refuse. Besides, it was weeks since they'd attended a Sunday service, and their absence made the widow uneasy. God might give some leeway on account of the weather, but he would surely draw a line. And if God didn't, the neighbours would.

'The kirk,' Meggy sulked, eyes rolling. But she wrenched her apron off, flung it onto the settle, and snatched up her shawl.

***

The morning was bleak and soggy, but it felt good to be out. Widow Lovie inhaled deeply. The freshness of the air! After the peaty odours of the cottage, it was glorious. Then she coughed as the chill stung the back of her throat.

Ahead, the spectre of a stone church slipped in and out of view, wraith-like, through the fog. The belfry emerged, clear through a break in the mist, its bell keening from within its birdcage mount. The widow cut across the wet grass of the kirkyard, dampness dragging at the hem of her skirts. Meggy followed.

The girl had proven, on balance, to be a worthwhile addition to the household. She went about her chores well enough, though no-one would call her industrious. Neither was she especially skilled; she spilled milk and dropped stitches, and she left lumps in the porridge. But Meggy's faults had their compensations. This outing, for instance. The widow glanced back at the dawdling maid. They'd still be trapped in the soupy air of the cottage if Meggy hadn't pushed to go out.

Besides, what choice did she have but to humour the girl? Meggy shrugged off her rebukes and John let her get away with it, so what else could she do? Meggy was demanding, but hard to refuse. It was easiest to give in; she hadn't the energy to resist. There was even a perverse pleasure in watching Meggy taking advantage. The girl behaved like a daughter, taking indulgences for granted. She wasn't a daughter, though.

16

And her actual daughters couldn't put John in a good humour the way Meggy did. She bowed her head against the mist and smiled. *John.* Lately, when she'd thought of him, her heart had been lighter. But a woman couldn't love a son the same way she loved a daughter. The rewards were fewer. The love for a son was looser, more helpless, lonelier.

But there was no room for loneliness with Meggy in the home. Meggy was everywhere.

'Oh!' Meggy said, interrupting her thoughts. 'My fingers are frozen.'

'It was you who insisted we go out.'

'Not across this soggy field, not to the kirk.'

'Where else, on a Sunday?' Almost daily, she was tempted to slap the girl. But she didn't, for she remembered what it was to feel the sting of an angry palm on a cold cheek. 'Stop your sulking.'

Meggy laughed, giggles spilling from her damp lips, and hugged her shawl close. The widow smiled in spite of herself.

Trouble, Elspet had called her, and Elspet was right. There was no peace when Meggy was about; she was impossible to ignore. Then again, Meggy made peace seem like a poor substitute for life.

Through the mist, crooked rows of graves huddled like the fair-folk of her own mother's stories. George's grave was amongst them. *How much would be left of him down there?* Little enough, she suspected. There would be bones.

The last of the congregation were filing into the church as they approached. Red-nosed with the cold, shawl-shrouded women nodded and smiled, rubbing hands and breathing fog. Meggy beamed at them.

They clamoured in, eager to escape the bitter air. She dropped a coin in the collection box at the door. Meggy was breathing sharp and shallow by her side. This was a novelty for the girl, despite her complaints, for Meggy's folk attended the new kirk in Fraserburgh. The widow watched her gaze about, drinking it in: the smell of oak, the shining pews, the unfamiliar faces. She was all eyes and lips and hips. It was miraculous to see how the icy air freshened Meggy – coloured her cheeks, quickened her breath, burnished her hair. The winter's effect on Widow Lovie was altogether different; it dragged her down, made her heavy and brittle.

She shuffled down the aisle, Meggy at her elbow. Mary was already in their usual pew, an impatient frown upon her pasty brow. The lines around her eyes relaxed when she saw her mother. 'Here you are!'

The widow slid in beside her, smiling at Mary and nodding at her son-in-law and grandson. The little boy swung his legs and blew a kiss at his grannie.

Meggy slipped in beside her, and they shuffled along to make room for old Mrs Scott, who had followed them in.

The old woman leaned across Meggy to whisper to the widow. 'John not with you, then?'

A blade across her throat could not have hurt more. 'As you can see.'

The old lady clucked and shook her head. The widow calmed her breathing. Mrs Scott was still cross because Meggy had chosen the Lovie household over hers; that was all.

The vestry door opened and the precentor emerged, carrying the Bible and psalm book. The congregation fell silent as the robed official mounted the steps to the pulpit and placed the books reverently in position. The widow's breathing settled, soothed by the routine. When the precentor had retreated, the minister laboured up to the pulpit.

'Let us worship God,' he said. 'Psalm 1.'

The precentor led the singing, his rich voice sparking a delicious charge through the congregation. Voices all around the widow rose to accompany his. She joined in mechanically; the psalm was as familiar as breathing. Her attention wandered.

George should have been sitting on her left, where Meggy was now. After all these years, she still missed the size of him: the broad shoulders, the long legs, the calloused hands. She missed his smell – the smell of sweat and earth and horse all mixed together with sea air. Time had not distorted her memory of him; he'd been a hard man, a hard husband, a hard father. Men *were* hard here in the lowlands; they had to be.

Meggy was singing loudly beside her. *She'd* never known a father, but if the lack had harmed her, she didn't show it. The girl had never known the blow of a fist the way John had. What would George have made of this mess of John's – this business with the Chessor girl and her child? It was better that he was gone; he'd never understood John the way she did. He'd done his best, though, George had. He'd always provided, even through the winters; he'd given John everything he needed: food, shelter, and the skills to run a farm. To know when to plough and sow the neeps, how to manure the ground, to make hay and tend a sick beast and keep vermin at bay. John's father had given him all those skills.

But *she* had given him love.

Meggy's voice pounded out the melody, hearty and slightly off-key, turning the hymn into a public-house ditty. The widow was conscious of the dryness of her own croaking. She used to have a pretty voice. When had it shrivelled up? It seemed that age was simply a process of shedding – of losing vigour, teeth, memories, hopes, husbands. Souls. She closed her eyes and said a quick prayer for John. *Keep him safe, God. Save him. Save him for me.*

Meggy sang beside her, '*... the way of godly men unto the Lord is known: Whereas the way of wicked men shall quite be overthrown ...*'

The singing finished and the congregation stood for prayer. The widow wriggled her toes, trying to pump warmth into her feet without drawing attention to herself. Her eyes flickered up to the loft above the nave where the heritors sat. It was richly carved oak, grand and canopied and sombre as befitted those benefactors of the church –

the landowners, the gentry. She sensed the congregation flagging as the minister droned on. People shifted from one foot to another, slumped upon the backs of pews, breathed warmth surreptitiously onto their fingers when they thought no-one was watching. It was hard to keep one's mind on God when knees were aching and chilblains were swelling.

'Our Father,' said the minister, 'Who art in Heaven ...'

With George, thought the widow. In Heaven. She supposed that was where he was. It would be warm in Heaven. The minister finished his prayer and began the Bible reading. At last it was time to sit, and she folded herself back onto the pew. She leaned closer to Meggy; the girl radiated heat. They sang again.

The sermon was about faithfulness – or perhaps charity; it was hard to tell. The minister rambled in language too grand for her ears. No wonder John hadn't been tempted back to the kirk. Weighed against the discomfort and tedium of the service, endangering the immortal soul might seem a risk worth taking. Still, she found reassurance – if not comfort – in the church. The smell of oak, the rituals, the rhythm of song, even the droning of the minister's voice: all these were soothing. The sense of God's presence – whether wonderful or dreadful, she could not tell – moved her.

At last, the prayer of thanksgiving and intercession – another twenty minutes of aching knees and frozen feet – and then a song. *As long as life its term extends / Hope's blest dominion never ends / For while the lamp holds on to burn / The greatest sinner may return / Life is the season God hath giv'n / To fly from Hell and rise to Heav'n / That day of Grace fleets fast away / And none its rapid course can stay.*

The greatest sinner. Unease lodged in her throat. Would John ever return to the kirk? Would he rise to Heaven? *That day of Grace fleets fast away.* Lord, she would stay its course if she could. She surely would.

'At last,' Meggy whispered when the benediction was done, and the widow pretended not to hear her. Old Mrs Scott scowled. The widow looked down at her hands to hide her smile.

They filed back out into the mist. Then it started up: the glances in her direction, the whispers behind hands. The peace of the service evaporated, leaving in its wake familiar dread.

Dear Lord, would they never give up? It had been years since John's alleged transgression. She should come oftener to the kirk, she supposed; maybe the scandal would lose its fascination for them over time, with familiarity. If only she had the heart. In the spring, she promised herself. In the spring the harvest would be plentiful and the beasts would fatten up, and John ... perhaps John would repent. In the spring things would be put right.

Clumps of the congregation milled about in the kirkyard: the fisher-folk and the farmers. Two disparate tribes. They stamped their feet and breathed upon chapped hands, hunching and nodding at each other. Mourners drifted about the mossy headstones, bowing heads and kneeling to brush weeds and rubble from graves. Winged souls, death's heads and hour glasses stared back at them. She didn't go to George's grave. She couldn't see the point.

The beadle and gravedigger, Mr Brown, moved amongst the people, doling out smiles and laughs that echoed in the mist.

'Meggy, love,' he said, taking the girl's hand in his massive paw.

'Gweed day tae ye, Mr Brown,' Meggy said. She leaned in to him like a conspirator. Brown had been good to the McKessars in their need, so it was no wonder the girl should feel affection for him – but the presence of a man so intimate with death made the widow's insides curdle. God alone knew how he kept his spirits up. He was jolly and red-nosed as always, and he appeared to be sober; he usually managed to abstain on a Sunday. She didn't blame him for the drinking; most folk around here were fond of a dram, and anyone who had buried as many as John Brown had the right to find his comfort somewhere.

'Mrs Lovie.' Brown breathed sourly into her face – not *quite* sober, then.

'Fine service, Mr Brown.'

Brown drifted away and the neighbours, old Mrs Scott and old Mrs Urquhart, tucked in close to gossip.

'How is Elspet?' Mrs Scott asked.

'She is well,' the widow replied.

'Was she pleased with the wedding?'

She bit her lip. Mrs Scott's downturned mouth told her – if she hadn't already known it – that *she* was not pleased with the wedding. It had been a low-key affair. Elspet wouldn't have had it otherwise, even had the circumstances been different; she wasn't one for frivolity.

'Of course,' the widow replied loyally. 'It was just as it should have been.'

Her last remark was a lie, and an unconvincing one at that. Elspet had observed the most basic customs – the foot washing for the bride and the smearing of the feet with soot and cinders for the groom – but had refused a procession. The neighbours had been put out by the lack of ceremony, though God knew that the season and Elspet's nature would have made a grim affair of it anyway. The neighbours' displeasure was no concern of hers, though the widow did fret about ill luck. It seemed rash to tempt fate.

'In any case,' Mrs Urquhart said, 'she is wed.'

It was true: Elspet was wed, and that was something. Her child would have a father, and a steady one. No-one thought ill of a couple for testing whether they could make a child before the wedding – not even the kirk. *But the kirk won't turn a blind eye to a man who won't follow through on what he's started.* That's what people whispered, she knew it.

Meggy's elbow dug her in the ribs. Her eyes were wide. 'Isn't that—?'

The widow and her neighbours followed her gaze. Meggy was cocking her head at a woman emerging from the kirk. A red-haired ghost, wending her way through the mist. She was holding the hand of a small child.

'The Chessor girl!' Mrs Urquhart whispered.

'And her bast—' Mrs Scott began, but the widow, furious, snapped, 'Mrs Scott! Remember where you are!'

Meggy was studying the young woman with undisguised curiosity. Good God, the Chessor girl was making directly for them. The widow turned away, but the girl wouldn't have it. She stood squarely before the huddle of women, her red hair a bright slash in the mist.

'Mrs Lovie,' she said. She was thinner than she used to be. She'd grown a small vertical crease between her brows, and her lips were pale and taut, but she was still pretty.

The widow cleared her throat. 'Helen. I'm surprised to see you here.'

Her eyes were drawn to the boy who tugged on Helen's hand: a bonny, round-cheeked child. His eyes were sky blue, like John's.

'I come to the kirk often,' the girl said. 'I want to be reconciled.'

'I wish you well,' the widow said, her cheeks burning, and tried to turn away, but Helen grabbed her arm.

'I beg you to speak to John.'

She pulled her arm from the girl's grasp. Meggy was standing goggle-eyed beside her. Mrs Urquhart's skirts rustled as she moved closer.

'Leave John be,' muttered Widow Lovie. 'You have no claim on him.'

'No claim?' The young woman's laugh was bitter. 'John admitted being in my father's house with me after the other folk had gone to bed. He *admitted* it.'

'He admitted to being there – that is *all* he admits!'

Three years on, and that fool girl was still accusing John, as if she'd ever wear him down. The widow turned again and made to step away, but the swift movement and the damp heaviness of her skirt made her stumble. Mrs Urquhart caught her arm and steadied her. She leaned on her neighbour and her breath came in quick, foggy gasps.

'Please, Mrs Lovie,' Helen's voice was tearful. 'For the sake of his soul. Urge him to repent!'

'For the sake of his soul? Not for the sake of *your* reputation?'

'There's little left of my reputation.'

'You want to save John's soul?' the widow said. 'Retract your statement to the kirk. That is the only way the kirk will take him back. *Retract your statement!*'

'And what of my son? What of John's son?'

'He is *not – oh!*' The mist was settling on them, seeping into her bones, making her shiver. 'John denies all guilt with you. Go back to the kirk. Tell them he is blameless!'

The widow picked up her skirts and pushed past the girl and her blue-eyed brat, down the path to the road.

Helen's voice came at her as the mist closed behind her: 'What of the *truth*, Mrs Lovie?'

Mrs Urquhart trotted to her side. She could hear old Mrs Scott panting as she tried to keep up. Meggy skipped beside her, breathless, open-mouthed. The kirk was hidden behind a shroud of mist.

Mrs Scott was indignant. 'The hide of her.'

'She only wants to do the best by her child,' Mrs Urquhart wheezed. She slipped her hand in the crook of the widow's arm and gave it a gentle squeeze. 'Take pity on her. A woman will do anything to protect her son.'

Aye, she thought grimly, snatching her arm away and gripping Meggy's instead. Aye, that she will.

Chapter 4

January 1827

The bellowing of starving cattle echoed long and loud from the byre.

The widow ushered little John Yule inside the cottage and slammed the door against their moaning. Her grandson had just finished shovelling manure from the byre and dumping it on the dung-heap, and he was shivering and streaked with filth. Meggy pinched her nose and flapped a hand in front of her face as he trotted to the hearth.

The boy was often at the farm. 'John will take him on as a cowherd in the spring,' Widow Lovie had told Meggy. 'He's old enough.' She could have added: *if the cattle survive*, but left the words unsaid.

The winter seemed endless. Months of sleet-streaked winds had buffeted the cottage and turned the fields to mud. Feed for the cattle was all but gone, and the beasts had been reduced to upholstered skeletons. It was the usual way of things; there was no sense in complaining. The cattle suffered and starved in the stinking byre through the winter, and by the time spring came, they were half-dead wretches, barely able to stand. If the winter was not too long or too cruel, John would help the feeble creatures out of the byre in the spring. Otherwise, he would carry out their carcasses.

This winter had been harsher than most. Outside, the weather raged; inside, Widow Lovie waited for the spring. The encounter with Helen Chessor had unsettled her. Three years, and the woman persisted with her lies. The sheriff had ordered her son to pay the child's maintenance, though the boy wasn't his. The business kept her awake at night. It wasn't the thought of the money, though that was worry enough; it was John's soul that was at stake. The kirk would hold him at arm's length until he accepted the boy as his own and paid his dues. He couldn't partake of communion. He couldn't be buried in the kirkyard with his father. His neighbours would continue to distrust him. God help him, he couldn't marry.

What was to be done? Every day that Helen Chessor accused John, she damned him for all eternity. She must be persuaded to recant; in the spring, John must persuade her.

The winter had been cruel, but today there'd been some respite. The sky was milky and wan, but the wind had dropped and the rain had subsided. They'd all taken advantage of the lull in the weather: she and Meggy had brought in extra water from the well and cleaned the cottage, and John had mended roofs, sharpened tools, groomed the horses.

As little John Yule brought the stink of the manure of penned-in cattle and the still fouler stench of the midden into the kitchen, Meggy shook her head and laughed. The widow moved towards him, but Meggy cut in. She put her hands on his shoulders, brought her face down to his and frowned. 'Look at you, all covered in muck and blood like twice-buried Mary.'

Meggy clasped his hands and turned the palms up to inspect them. His fingers were cracked and bleeding with chilblains. Tut-tutting, Meggy dragged a creepie stool to the hearth and patted the seat. Obediently, the boy sat upon it.

'Who's twice-buried Mary?' he said, gazing up first at his grannie and then at Meggy, the firelight red-gold on his grubby face. The peaty warmth intensified his smell, and the widow put a hand to her nose. *Dear God!* But Meggy, smiling, poured warm water from the kettle into a wooden bowl, dragged another stool closer to the fire and sat before him, placing the bowl in her lap.

'You'll spoil the poor loon,' the widow said, but she didn't really mind. She settled herself into an armchair and waited. A story was coming, and where was the harm in listening?

Meggy dipped a corner of her apron into the bowl. 'It was a long, long time ago, in a place called Inverurie, fifty miles from here.' She wrung the apron corner out over the bowl and dabbed it on the boy's outstretched hand. 'A girl called Mary fell in love and married a handsome man.'

'What was his name?'

Meggy shrugged and glanced at the widow. 'James,' she said.

'Alexander,' said the widow.

Meggy smiled. 'Or Alexander. It doesn't matter. Anyway, her husband loved her, and they had lots of bairns.'

Meggy wiped the blood gently from John Yule's swollen fingers. 'But one day, Mary fell ill, and before you know it, she was dead.'

The boy watched as Meggy stroked his hands with the cloth. The widow rose from her armchair to toss a peat brick on the fire, and the flames sizzled, casting quivering shadows about the room.

'The poor man was beside himself with sorrow. He laid his dead wife out in her bridal dress and put a ruby ring on her finger. It was a special ring, see, that he had given her with love. They buried her in the kirkyard, and he went on home to mourn. But the townsfolk went to the inn to have a drink for Mary, and when they were there, they talked about how beautiful she'd looked in her wedding dress with the big ruby ring on her finger.'

Meggy put her hands around the boy's and curled his little fingers into a fist. 'The ruby on her finger was almost as big as your fist!'

'Oh!'

'Well, a stranger was at the inn, and he heard tell of poor dead Mary and her huge ruby ring. And he thought, *What luck for me!* Mary would have no need of that ring anymore. So off he went, in the dead of the night, to the graveyard to steal the ring.'

Meggy rinsed the cloth in the bowl, wrung it out again, and dabbed at a streak of muck on the boy's cheek. 'It was a dark night, but the moon was out, and it was easy to find the grave, for it was fresh dug. The man took a spade to the grave, and by the light of the moon, he dug and he dug and he dug. And all the while, the owls hooted about him, and the ghosts danced about the gravestones.'

She sponged the soft cheek gently, tracing the little boy's jawline. The widow watched Meggy's tenderness through lowered lids. The night had wrung the colour from the girl's face, and it glowed white in the firelight. Like a ghost herself, she was. Her voice low and whispery. *Trouble*, Elspet had said. The widow shifted in her armchair, told herself not to be such a fool.

Meggy leaned forward. 'And then his spade struck the coffin. And he unscrewed the lid, and then by the light of the moon, he saw her: Mary, pale and beautiful in her white wedding gown, with a big fat ruby ring on her finger.'

Meggy dropped the damp cloth and took the boy's hands in her own. His hands were clean now, but still swollen with chilblains. Meggy fiddled with the ring finger of his left hand and whispered in his ear, loudly enough for them all to hear. 'And the man took hold of the ruby ring and tried to slip it off her finger. But the ring wouldn't budge! He pulled and twisted, but he couldn't get the ring off.' The little boy stared at his own hand as if he could see the ring upon it. 'And the man was getting nervous out there in the dark, dark graveyard, with the moon shining upon him and the dead woman in the coffin there in the pit below him. And so he took out a knife and put it to her finger. He was going to cut her finger off! But when he pressed the blade into her skin'—she dropped the boy's hand—'Mary sat up and SCREAMED!'

John Yule yelped, and Meggy shrieked with laughter. The widow jumped, shook her head and grunted.

'Was she a ghost?' the little boy said, when Meggy had stopped laughing.

'Nay, she was no ghost,' she replied, wiping tears from her cheeks. 'You see, Mary wasn't really dead. She was only in a trance, and they'd buried her too soon. When the knife cut her, it woke her from her sleep.'

'What happened to the man?'

'He ran away in fright. And Mary went back to her husband and her bairns, and they lived happily until she was an old, old woman.'

The little boy thought for a moment. 'And is she dead now, Meggy?'

'Oh, aye, she died a long, long time ago. They buried her back in the pit where she was first planted. They say that if you put your ear to her grave and listen close, you will hear a knock-knock-knocking, and it's twice-buried Mary trying to get out again!'

'You'll frighten the wee boy.' The widow creaked to the fire and took the bowl of muddied water from Meggy's lap. 'Off home, grandson. It'll soon be dark. Your mither will worry.'

Meggy smiled and waved, and the boy scurried to the door. The widow shooed him away before the darkness could consume him.

Chapter 5

February 1827

Rain hurled itself against the tiny windowpane. By the fire, Widow Lovie sat and knitted. Even hampered by rheumatism, her fingers were nimbler than Meggy's. The girl perched on a creepie, sighing, the *tick-tick* of her needles beating a half-rhythm to the widow's *ticker-ticker*. The widow bit back on her irritation.

John shifted his pipe from one side of his mouth to the other, raising his eyes heavenward. Fretting about the thatching, she guessed. She had no such worries; John's work was sound. He had never let her down. He lowered his eyes, met hers, smiled shyly to have been caught worrying.

Meggy tossed her knitting aside and stood, stretching. She ambled to the hearth, taking care to brush her skirt against John's leg on the way, and squatted to prod the fire with the poker.

'Have a care!' the widow said as sparks danced from the hearth.

'Will the winter never end?' Meggy said, ignoring her.

'It'll end when it's ready.'

The girl rose again, brushing her hands on her apron and leaving a smudge of grey behind. She flopped onto her stool and picked up her knitting, but let it rest idle in her lap. The evenings were long and dull; the widow understood that, but the girl's restlessness got on her nerves just the same.

The clock chimed, the sound flooding her with a familiar rush of pleasure. A sound roof, enough peat for the fire, and a clock that regularly proclaimed her good fortune: these were the blessings to count.

'Time to rest these old bones,' she said, and Meggy nodded.

Her joints popped painfully as she stood and put her knitting neatly in its basket and set it on the earthen floor beside the armchair. She said goodnight to John and made her way to the closet with Meggy following, holding the candle. The girl helped her out of her skirt. The intimacy bothered the widow. She was glad of the dimness and the worn flannel of her slip that hid her sagging, papery flesh from Meggy's young eyes. She draped her black skirt and blouse upon the kist and, shivering, turned to Meggy to help with her undressing. Meggy bent, stepped out of her wool skirt, handed it to the widow while she wriggled out of her blouse.

The skirt was still warm from Meggy's body when the widow placed it on the kist with her own discarded clothing. In her white slip, Meggy glowed: young, fleshy, animal. The widow tried to imagine her as an old woman. The fullness about her shoulders would swell into a dowager's hump, and her heavy breasts would stretch and sag; her dimples would set into vertical lines from cheek to jaw, and her bright eyes would grow red and rheumy. Her belly would be slack and webbed with the marks of childbirth. Her languor would no longer be charming. She would let herself become grubby and rank, and her moods would mark her as a querulous old hag. It was inevitable, and she pitied Meggy for it.

She sagged into bed with an audible whoosh from her weary lungs. She pulled up the coarse blankets; Meggy snuffed the candle, and it was dark. She felt the girl slip in beside her and shuffle into position. They lay back-to-back in the darkness, silent, listening to the rain and the wind and each other's breathing.

Despite her deep-etched, bottomless fatigue, the widow couldn't sleep. She told herself that it was the usual worries of winter keeping her awake: the cows starving in the byre, the depletion of the potato and grain supplies, the fear that a bad season would put them behind in their rent. It was always the same; life never got any better. Meggy – the poor fool – saw a well-thatched roof and a clock and thought she was in clover. Oh, for the ignorance of youth.

Meggy was awake too; the widow could sense it in her stiffness. Listening out for John, she guessed. She could hear him moving about in the kitchen. She shifted, struggling to find a comfortable position for her aching knees. She edged closer to Meggy's warmth; her own feet were frozen. *Will the winter never end?* They were Meggy's words: words that had annoyed her by giving voice to her own frustration. It was so much easier to be stoic if you were silent. Once you started complaining, there was no end to misery.

The girl's voice came in the darkness. 'What's it like to be old?'

She thought for a moment, surprised but not offended by the question. She thought of the years she had accumulated – of the knowledge that she'd be better off without. Being old meant stiff joints and tiredness that never ended, and it meant the shrivelling of her flesh and the wasting of her muscles. Age meant loss. But did it? No, not only loss. There were her daughters, grown to womanhood, and little John Yule, and her sons ... there was John. She was ashamed of her ingratitude.

'Cold,' she said at last. 'It's cold.'

Meggy barked with laughter. 'Cold?' The bed rattled with her mirth.

A smile forced the widow's lips apart, despite her best efforts to suppress it. 'Always cold,' she confirmed with a wheeze that passed for a laugh.

Meggy shifted her legs away, leaving a pool of heat in the bed where they had been. 'Put your feet there,' she commanded, and the widow obeyed. The warmth seeped deliciously into her feet.

The girl chuckled again and turned over, and her breathing grew slow and deep. The widow lay awake and listened to Meggy's breathing, and the patch of warmth slowly grew cold under her feet.

Chapter 6

Whitsunday, May 1827

Spring was late in coming. Winter ended with a storm that surged in from the sea, violent winds hurling the ocean ashore to claw at the sand. Great pellets of rain pounded the beach. In the harbour, the masts of fishing boats danced. The old folk would be muttering fearfully about the goddess of the winds, and the seafarers whispering that someone must have killed a pig on board, for such a storm to have stricken them. Like them, Widow Lovie threw salt over her left shoulder and – to cover all bases – mumbled prayers.

After three days the storm blew over and the sun rose into a freshly wrung-out sky. The shore was strewn with dirty foam and old women collecting sea-ware for their crops. The ocean receded. The farmers set about mending roofs and doors, and the sounds of their hammering and sawing echoed across the fields.

John led his starved and trembling cattle from the byres into the blinking sunlight. They had survived – almost every one. Widow Lovie breathed again. Her aching joints began to torment her less, and she looked forward with hope to the lengthening days.

She had sent Meggy out to fetch the water, and she'd stood at the cottage door watching the girl flouncing across the muddy yard, the empty buckets swinging loudly from her yoke. It was Whitsunday, and spring was in full bloom. John had gone out early to the Broch for the hiring fair to find a loon to help out through the summer. All around the county, labourers would be washing their faces and flexing their biceps. Dairymaids would be pinching their cheeks, mending their boots and sponging mud from the hems of their skirts. Fiddlers would be tuning their instruments and hawkers gathering up their wares.

But Meggy wouldn't be amongst them. John had asked her to bide for another term, and of course she'd readily agreed. The widow had raised no objection. Meggy was part of the household now, part of the rhythm of Futteret Den. This Whitsunday she'd be spared the humiliation of having to spruik her services at the hiring market; she was safe for at least another half-year. And after that? Who could tell?

The widow left the door ajar and turned back to sweep the kitchen. The thawing air swept in, full of promise. John expected a good harvest, so he'd sorely need another pair of hands. The idea of having a young man about the farm would be exciting for Meggy, she supposed, and the girl did need a distraction after the long, dull winter. An old woman wasn't company enough for a maid like Meggy; she was under no illusions about that. If the sighs and eye-rolls and shrugs didn't convey the girl's irritation with her clearly enough, the backchat did. At twenty or so, Meggy would be looking for a mate soon enough. Better a young farmhand than John.

She paused for a moment in her sweeping. What if the Chessor girl didn't give up? If both of them held fast to their positions, John was as good as damned. The kirk would not let him back unless he admitted to fathering that child and repented. And yet he wouldn't repent, she knew it – not unless he had reason to. Not unless, say, he wanted to marry.

Oh, she'd seen how Meggy looked at John.

She resumed her sweeping. The idea was absurd. A poor McKessar quine for John? Never. Besides, she'd seen, too, where John's gaze fell: on the cattle or the newspaper or the thatching or the clouds. Poor Meggy: she could brush her hair, wash her face and neck and hands, rub the stains from her skirt and pinch her cheeks all she liked – for the new farmhand, whoever he might be, for John would never notice.

***

Jean McKessar trudged along the turnpike road, enjoying the morning sun's timid warmth on her face. The salt air was bright and crisp.

Her mother trotted beside her, two quick little steps for Jean's every one. Jimmy frolicked ahead, tossing stones, skipping, cartwheeling – romping with the joy of a day off. Her brother's good cheer was infectious, even for Jean. Watching him, she laughed and put an affectionate hand on her mother's bent back, feeling the stiffness of her, the wiriness. Henrietta's bowed head bobbed as she trotted in comfortable silence.

The crunching of footsteps made Jean half turn and frown. Their neighbour, John Lovie, was gaining upon them.

'Gweed day tae ye,' he said, smiling and falling into step beside Henrietta.

'Aye, aye,' Henrietta replied.

Jean nodded. Jimmy, up ahead, dropped the pebble he had been preparing to toss and waited for the trio to catch up.

'Off to the feeing market?' John Lovie said.

'Nay,' said Jean.

'I already have a position,' Jimmy boasted. 'William Duffus has asked me to bide at Nethertown.'

'Good for you.'

'We're paying a visit to my sister-in-law,' Henrietta said.

'Give Mrs Will my regards.'

Jean shrugged. She had no heart for idle chatter with John Lovie. Let her mother call her churlish; she didn't care. If Henrietta refused to see what was plainly before her eyes, it wasn't *her* fault.

'How is my daughter Meggy?' Henrietta said.

Lovie smiled broadly. 'Meggy is well.'

Jean turned away. There was lechery in his smile and it made her insides cold. She would not have a bar of his glib charm. She knew too well what Meggy's appeal was for a man like John Lovie.

'The master's good to me,' Meggy had said on her last visit home. 'The mistress, too.' So full of herself, so cocky. John Lovie and the widow had fed her and housed her and kept her warm through the winter, she said. They didn't beat her or threaten her or make unreasonable demands. She was allowed to visit her family often. Meggy was doing well for herself, and she scoffed at Jean's disapproval.

And yet ... Jean clenched her jaw and marched in silence. Meggy was too trusting. She was the youngest girl – the little quine who had grown up fatherless. Her family had protected her too much. They'd cosseted her. They'd let her view the world through a child's credulous eyes long after she should have grown up. How love had led them astray! Now, Jean could do nothing to save her sister. Meggy had launched herself into the world without a thought, without a plan, like a shooting star. There was no knowing what trouble she'd get herself into, though Jean could make a fair guess. She worried for her sister, and worry made her bad-tempered.

'You're a sour old maid,' Meggy had sneered, and she was right. Jean worked the fields and churned the butter and cut the moss, and she grew daily more brittle. It felt, sometimes, as if there were decades between her and her sister.

'Bye, bye, then,' Lovie said, having fulfilled his neighbourly duty and, it seemed, grown bored with it. 'I must be at the fair early to get the best of the hands.'

'Aye,' Jean said quickly. 'Bye, then, John Lovie.'

He touched his cap and strode on. Jean clenched her teeth. Such a rare moment of lightness she'd been enjoying, and John Lovie had spoiled it. She took her mother's hand and tucked it into the crook of her elbow, enveloping Henrietta's knotted fingers in her own.

Chapter 7

After Whitsunday, May 1827

Next morning at dawn, Alex Rannie tramped along the turnpike road towards Percyhorner. The wheel of his handcart squeaked like a puppy, companionably, and Rannie whistled along. A timid morning sun sparkled on dewy grass. The spring air was fresh and sharp. He hadn't far to go. He would be early. Still, in his eagerness, he couldn't help but hurry.

Futteret Den was a good farm, they said. The job would keep him fed and warm right through the summer. No more sharing a bed with his younger siblings, no more taking food from his mother's table. His father's farm at Pitullie was too small to need another pair of full-grown hands; besides, at seventeen, Rannie had his own life to make.

Ahead was good, honest work; ahead was a dry home and a regular income.

Ahead was John Lovie. He slowed at that. But no, he wouldn't give his misgivings another thought; they were firmly behind.

John Lovie. The previous day, Alex Rannie had set off to the feeing market with high hopes; he was young, sober and strong, and he had a good name in the district. He'd arrived at first light, but already the place was abuzz. The fiddler was warming up, starting and stopping with a disjointed screech that set his teeth on edge. The men were lining up on one side of the road, the women on the other. He joined the throng, squeezing his bulk between the forest of elbows. He'd rather have made himself invisible, but that would have defeated the purpose.

The men were rolling their sleeves up despite the morning chill to display their ropey forearms, shouting and bragging. The racket hurt his ears. Rannie's boot sank into the boggy field and he stumbled and collided with a broad back. The man turned and swore at him, spit spraying from his mouth. Rannie righted himself and edged away from the man's fists. The fiddler was getting louder and faster, worse than a beast giving birth. But it didn't drown out the shouts of the men, all seeking the attention of a fair master. Any master, really. He didn't blame them. A man needed work, or he'd starve. If he didn't have work through the summer, then he'd have Hell to pay through the winter.

Somehow, Rannie found himself at the front of the throng, on the edge of the road that the farmers strode along, looking to hire. They were stopping to size up the men on one side, the women on the other, as if inspecting stock. A familiar figure lurched and wove between them. It was Brown: the beadle, the gravedigger. What business had he here? He wasn't hiring, that much was for sure. Rannie knew why he was at the fair, though; he could see it in the redness of his nose, in the looseness of his grin. At this hour. But he wasn't the only one; the fumes were strong in the crowd.

On the other side of the road, the women were facing Rannie. Shawled and bonneted, noses rosy from the morning breeze, they jockeyed for position. It was embarrassing to see them. In a few years, his sisters would be amongst them, flirting, haggling, casting modesty aside. A woman caught his eye – a girl, really, surely not more than fifteen. His neighbour's daughter, Fiona. She'd spruced herself up for the occasion, scrubbed the dirt from her face and neck. Her boots were too big – probably her sister's. Rannie raised a hand in greeting, but the girl turned away. Shy, he supposed, ashamed. And no wonder; it was madness here.

At that moment a man stopped before him. He was about forty, hair dark with streaks of grey, broad-shouldered, blue-eyed, smiling. Rannie stiffened; he knew the farmer by reputation. When the man spoke, Rannie leaned in closer to hear him.

'You look an earnest chiel,' the man shouted.

'Gweed day, Mr Lovie.' Rannie said. It was true, what the man had said; Rannie knew he had neither a handsome face nor a remarkable one, but diligence and honesty were written plainly upon it. 'I'm a hard worker,' he forced himself to say.

'I'm sure of it.' John Lovie's smile broadened.

Lovie gestured at his arms, and Rannie rolled up his sleeves to let the farmer prod the muscles. Lovie nodded distractedly, almost apologetically, as he jabbed. At least he didn't ask to check Rannie's teeth – although, if he had, he would have found them sound.

'I know of your family name,' John Lovie shouted into Rannie's ear. 'It's a good name.'

Lovie nodded.

They haggled a little over the fee – another noisy, tiresome ritual – and, with relief (on Rannie's side, at least), settled the deal. Lovie sealed it with a token penny and offered Rannie a dram. He swallowed the whisky reluctantly and felt it burning all the way to his stomach. And then they shook hands and parted. Alex Rannie bolted back to Pitullie to share the news with his father.

John Lovie had referred to Rannie's reputation, but Rannie had not spoken of Lovie's. Though what, after all, did he really know of the man? Rumour, his father said. It's only rumour. Rumours weren't always true. And if Lovie had failed to see a promise through – well, he was only a man. All men had vices, or so it was said. Who was he, Rannie, to judge? And besides, who could afford to refuse an offer of work? Work was hard enough to come by. It was every man for himself out there. Rannie would rather have laboured for a man with a more wholesome reputation, but he hadn't the luxury of choice.

Maybe something better would come up at Martinmas.

***

A well, set back from the road, told Rannie that he was getting close. A little further on was a high stone wall, beyond which smoke rose from a hidden chimney. This would be Futteret Den, the Lovie farm. He turned off the road and strode towards it with the handcart, leaving footprints in the dewy grass. He trundled further, following the line of the wall until he came to a break that opened to a small yard. At the far end of the yard was a cottage: small, gabled and thatched.

As he turned to enter the yard, a young woman emerged from the cottage carrying a yoke and empty buckets. They stopped, facing each other.

'So you're the new labourer?' she said, placing the buckets at her feet and planting a hand on her hip. She tilted her head and squinted up at him. Rannie blushed and pushed his cap back from his forehead. The woman was pretty in a way that was hard to define. It wasn't so much in the regularity of her features as in the arch way she arranged them. He nodded and cleared his throat.

'What's your name, then?'

'Rannie,' he said. 'Alex.'

'Well,' the girl said. 'You'd better get on with it.'

She picked up her buckets and made as if to go around him, but he stepped aside to stop her, suddenly bold. 'Have *you* got a name?'

The girl raised an eyebrow. 'You can call me Meggy,' she said. Then she ducked around him and trotted towards the well.

He turned and pushed his cart the last few yards to the cottage. The door was ajar, and he peered inside. The room to the left of the entry passage was dim and smoky. An old woman, straight-backed and shrouded in black, stood at the fire, poking at something in a pot. Rannie rapped on the wall and the woman turned and stared at him. Her face was deeply lined, and white hairs sprouted from her chin, but her cheekbones were high and proud, and her pale eyes sharp and bright.

Rannie started to speak, but before the words could come out, a small boy hurtled past him into the kitchen.

'Grannie!' he squeaked. 'Who's this?'

'Mind your manners,' the old lady chided. The boy giggled and turned round eyes to Alex.

'Alex Rannie,' he said, annoyed. 'I'm the new labourer.'

The old woman nodded. 'Welcome, Alex Rannie.' Her tone was businesslike but not unkind. 'I'm Mrs Lovie, John's mother. The loon is my grandson, also John.'

'John Lovie's son?' Rannie was surprised. Lovie was unmarried, and the only son Rannie knew of was one the farmer refused to acknowledge.

But the woman shook her head. 'John's nephew, John Yule. Son of my daughter Mary Yule. He starts work today as my son's cattle-herd.'

'How do ye do,' he said awkwardly, and the old woman gave a half smile.

'Bring your things inside and leave them in the corner.'

'It's just a kist with a spare set of clothes.'

Widow Lovie nodded. 'All right, then. You'll sleep here in the kitchen, on the deece,' she said. 'My grandson sleeps in here too, on the floor. You'll find it comfortable,' she added, as if daring him to find it otherwise.

It did seem comfortable. The fire was merry, and the kitchen smelled of burning peat and the herbs that had been hung to dry from a hook on the wall. A tea kettle sat on a ledge and a cast iron pot bubbled over the fire, making Rannie's stomach growl. The little cowherd sat upon a creepie stool by the hearth, humming and trying to fashion something out of a forked stick.

'I sleep in there'—the woman gestured with a spoon to the closet in the corner of the kitchen—'with the servant girl, Meggy. You've met her already?'

Rannie nodded, blushing; the old woman must have heard them talking. Why that would make him blush, he could not say.

'Aye,' she answered her own question. Her face creased into a thousand folds, as if the thought of the girl amused her. 'And through there'—she waved the spoon at the other room—'in the but, is where John – your master – bides.'

She turned back to her cooking, and Rannie took it as his cue to settle himself in. He went outside and hoisted his kist onto his shoulder, pushed the handcart aside, and returned to the cosy kitchen. He placed the kist in the corner as instructed, then stood, arms dangling, waiting for orders.

'Sit,' Widow Lovie told him with a sigh, pointing to the deece.

He sat. He watched as she fished a potato from the pot, dropped it onto a plate, and plodded across to him. The sight of her stiff gait flooded him with guilt. He shouldn't let her wait upon him. But he clasped his hands in his lap and didn't get up. The old woman flipped the table of the deece down beside him and planted the plate upon it.

'You can start work after you've eaten,' she said kindly. She went back to her chores as he ate. They didn't speak, and that was fine by him. She moved about quietly, throwing occasional sideways glances at him with her sharp eyes.

Mrs Lovie was a widow, that much Alex Rannie knew. Everyone knew everyone else's business in the parish, or thought they did. He knew that Mrs Lovie's husband had died years ago, and that not many in the parish regretted his passing. He knew that her eldest child, her unmarried son, John, looked out for her. That he had helped to raise his younger siblings, that he shared the lease on the farm with his mother and that he worked hard to keep her in comfort. They were all points in the master's favour.

'You'll find my son a fair master,' she said, as if reading his thoughts again.

Rannie nodded, chewing.

'He's with the horses,' she said. 'You'll find him there.'

This pleased Rannie; he had feared that his master might still be in bed, nursing a sore head from the post-fair revelry. If the master was disciplined with regards to the drink – or, at least, if he could hold his whisky well – it was a good sign. He devoured his potato, pushed back his chair, thanked the widow and emerged from the dim cottage into the brisk morning.

He found John Lovie in the stable, shovelling manure into a cart. The master had rolled up the sleeves of his grey flannel shirt, despite the bite of the early spring air. He nodded as the farmhand approached. Rannie saw that his eyes were red-rimmed and his mouth downturned. He hadn't come through the evening's festivities unscathed, then.

Rannie breathed in the warm horsey air, closing his eyes, relishing the smell. Beasts of all kinds were so much easier to understand than their masters.

'I'll manage them,' he said to his master. 'If you want to go in for your tea.'

'Aye,' John said. He stood, spat on his palms and wiped them on his breeks. Grasping the handles of the cart, he wheeled it out to dump the manure on the dung-heap outside the byre.

Now he was alone with the horses, the tension in Rannie's shoulders eased. The beasts were huge and muscled, clear-eyed and well fed. Already recovered from the winter. He sidled up to the nearest of the pair and placed a hand on its neck, feeling its heat seep into his fingers.

He hummed and the horse snuffled as he stroked its muscular hide from neck down to shoulder. The master had already fetched clean hay; Rannie stooped to gather armfuls of it to spread about the stable, enjoying the fresh, sharp scent of it.

He found the brushes and settled in to the rhythm of grooming, sweeping the flanks smoothly and firmly. The horses twitched and harrumphed their pleasure. Rannie hummed as he fetched the corn and hand-fed the beasts, smiling at the feel of the wet, rubbery lips.

He savoured it all: the new day, alone in the stillness with the beasts in the balmy, muted, peaceful morning. It felt like a promise. It felt as if life were opening up, and it was going to be glorious.

Then a beast blinked its glossy eye at him, and its long lashes made him think of Meggy. His joy faded and was replaced by an uneasiness he could neither explain nor define.

Chapter 8

Mid-May 1827

Widow Lovie rose at dawn. Rannie heard her moving about the kitchen: the scraping of her poker in the fire, the sloshing of water in the tea kettle. He lay still, eyes closed, clinging to a few minutes' more sleep. The widow was humming, and her voice was surprisingly sweet.

The room lightened and the door creaked; the widow had gone out into the dawn. Rannie sat and swivelled upright on the deece, yawning. The master would already be out threshing the corn or tending the neeps. The wee boy, John Yule, was sleeping on a mat on the floor, open-mouthed and drooling. The pair of them slept like the dead after a hard day's labouring. Rannie got up and nudged John Yule with his foot, and the boy woke instantly.

'Where's Grannie?'

'At the byre, I suppose,' Rannie said. He didn't know why the boy asked; the routine was the same every day.

Wide awake now, Rannie hurried out into the lightening morning. He wanted to be out of the cottage before Meggy was up, because Meggy was a terror in the early mornings. She'd stomp out of her closet bed with her face all creased up from the bedclothes and her hair in a mess. She'd be full of complaints: the kitchen was too cold, or the fire wasn't stoked, or the water wasn't boiled, or her hands were raw from the washing, or the bread was dry. There was always something.

He sucked in the morning air: crisp, but with a promise of warmth to come. The sun was beginning its ascent from the sea. He was pleased with himself for managing an early escape, for he was always the one to bear the brunt of Meggy's ill humour. She'd be in a better mood by the time he returned for breakfast.

He trotted to the stables to greet the horses and put them out to grass. They snuffled as he approached, glad to see him.

'Come on, my lovelies,' he said as he led them from the stable.

Rannie spent an hour or so with the horses, as he did every morning, and then he got to work on the chores about the cottage and outhouses: mending ropes, fixing gates, cleaning the stables. By eight o'clock he was ravenous, and it was safe to go back to the kitchen.

By this time, as he'd expected, Meggy was in a good mood. She had done her first chores and shed the last remnants of sleep. She was at the fire, stirring the pot, and the flames lent her face a pink glow. She tossed a smile over her shoulder at him, and he grunted and pulled up a chair at the table.

John Yule was perched on a creepie stool by Meggy's side, chattering. 'But *why* are they ugly?' he was saying.

Meggy put a finger to her lips. 'Hush. We mustn't offend *themselves*.'

'Stories again?' Rannie said sourly, but secretly he was pleased. He liked Meggy's folk tales, and he liked the sound of her voice when she told them. She often told them at night, when they sat by the fire and the widow knitted and John Lovie smoked his pipe. Meggy was a great one for stories of broonies and ghosts and magic and long-ago romances, though he suspected she made some of them up.

Rannie frowned, remembering. Last night Meggy had been in full flight with her stories. John Lovie and his mother had sat in their armchairs, while Meggy and Rannie perched on creepie stools beside them, and wee John Yule sat cross-legged at their feet. Like a little family, they were. The women had been knitting, although Meggy's knitting had spent most of the evening sitting idle in her lap. Meggy had started on some story or other, and John Lovie had set aside the newspaper he'd borrowed from his brother-in-law so he could listen. The master was the only one of them who could read; Rannie thought it an affectation for a farmer. Some evenings Lovie read stories from his newspaper aloud: reports of politics and laws and other things that Rannie didn't care for. He liked it better when Meggy told *her* stories.

Last night, all eyes had been on Meggy. The widow had lowered her knitting and tipped her head back to watch her warily, as if the stories frightened her. And John Lovie? It was impossible to know *his* mind. He'd leaned back in his armchair, puffing on his pipe, smiling, eyes fastened on Meggy. Rannie didn't like that look. Predatory – that's what it was.

He put the memory from his mind. John Lovie's thoughts were no concern of his. And stories were for night time, not the morning when there were chores to be done.

Meggy slapped bowls of brose into John Yule's and Rannie's hands – not angrily, but carelessly, as if she had better things to do.

'Brose,' John Yule said. 'Again! I'd rather have pottage.'

'Count yourself lucky.'

The boy sighed dramatically and dug his spoon into the bowl. He kept up a stream of chatter as he ate, chirruping through mouthfuls of mush. Rannie ignored him; he was distracted by Meggy, who was glancing repeatedly at the door.

'Where's Mrs Lovie?' he said.

'Gone to her daughter's.'

But it wasn't the widow that Meggy was looking out for – he knew that. It was the master. Meggy was always making eyes at him.

Rannie watched her as she made the tea. She half turned, saw him watching, curled her lip in a sly smile. 'What're you staring at?'

'Nothing.'

She came to the table with a bowl in her hand, swaying her hips, and brushed her skirt against his leg as she passed him. Rannie blushed, flattered and embarrassed. She meant nothing by it. She was only exercising her charms – practising skills that she might need later, when she was with someone worth impressing. She sat with Rannie and the boy and shovelled her own brose into her mouth.

When she was done, she wiped her lips with the back of her hand, still keeping an eye on the door. Most days after breakfast, Meggy went into the but to drink tea with the widow – and with Lovie, if he had come in from the fields. Meggy's boldness embarrassed Rannie. He rarely went into the but; the best room wasn't his place.

On this day, though, the widow was out, and the master hadn't reappeared for his tea. Meggy wouldn't bother going in there.

Rannie went out to the fields, where John Lovie was fetching the horses for yoking. The master was tall, and his movements slow and fluid. Rannie glanced down at his own sturdy frame. No wonder Meggy looked at Lovie the way she did, and not at him.

The master greeted him with a nod, and together they yoked the horses. Over the previous days they had harrowed the fields, breaking up clods formed by the harshness of the winter to loosen up the soil. Now it was time to cross-plough the earth, get it ready for the summer.

'Good harvest ahead, I'll warrant,' Lovie said, and he agreed.

The sun was rising fast, softening the bite of the air. Rannie's spirits were high. He had been working side by side with Lovie for almost two weeks now, and he was mostly reassured. The master had a firm grip on the plough and an eye steadily focused on the land, just as a farmer should.

Rannie urged the horses on, and they began their plodding. Behind, Lovie steered the plough.

'How much land is there?' Rannie asked.

Lovie waved a languid hand at the fields and smiled. 'Seventy-one acres.'

Rannie whistled. 'My father has less than half that.' He looked down at his own broad hands and stumpy fingers, reddened and caked with dirt.

Lovie said, 'Hi there!' to the horses, which were starting to slow their pace. At the sound of his voice, they quickened their step.

'You're clever with the horses,' Rannie said admiringly.

Lovie smiled. 'Off with you. Go and clear the ditches ahead while I handle the plough.'

Rannie did as he was told.

When the sun was high, Lovie called to him and they hitched and fed the horses and went together to the house for dinner.

The widow was back from her daughter's. She was sitting in her armchair by the fire with a pile of mending on her lap and looked up as they trudged into the kitchen. Her eyes were identical to her son's: cool blue – a wintry sky.

Meggy was bending over the pot on the fire. Rannie saw the way she straightened up and tucked a curl behind her ear, and he felt bad for her.

'The new hand is a good worker,' Lovie said, with a nod to Rannie. 'The beasts like him.'

Rannie coughed, embarrassed. Lovie and his mother talked a little about the weather and the harvest, but Rannie wasn't really listening. He was still tongue-tied from the master's praise.

It would have been better, he thought, if he'd never heard that gossip about the Chessor girl. It wasn't fair to judge on rumour.

Chapter 9

Late May 1827

Jean McKessar was at her spinning wheel when the scuffling of boots warned her of Meggy's approach. She looked up and saw her sister in the doorway. She sighed and stopped the wheel as Meggy flounced in.

'What's wrong?'

Meggy flopped onto a creepie stool and folded her arms. 'Why should anything be wrong?'

Jean shrugged. So Meggy was in a mood, then. She placed the wool into a basket and moved to the hearth to pick up the tea kettle, prickling under Meggy's critical gaze. She was conscious of the dirt beneath her fingernails and the looseness of the blouse that sagged from her shoulders. As she poured, she couldn't help seeing the kitchen as Meggy must: small, dark and dirty, crudely furnished. The creepies were fashioned from old fish boxes, and every surface suffocated under a film of soot. There was no time for cleaning, and no reason to either. The cottage must seem dull and plain compared with the Lovie home, with its panelled deece and box beds and mahogany clock.

'I have a headache,' said Meggy. 'That's all.'

Jean handed her sister a wooden cup of tea and sat opposite, nursing her own cup. 'This will help.'

She watched Meggy as they sipped. Her face was pale and dull. Meggy closed her eyes, savouring the tea.

'You're tired,' said Jean. 'They're working you too hard.'

Meggy's eyes sprang open. 'You dinna ken what you're talking about.'

'All right,' she replied. 'What, then?'

'Don't pester me,' Meggy sulked. 'Where's my mither?'

'Taking pottage to old Mrs Scott.'

'That old hag!'

'Meggy! *You'll* be old one day,' Jean shook her head, frowning. 'And you'll be glad of kindness from a neighbour.'

Meggy waved a hand in dismissal. 'Mrs Scott's a mean old thing. She doesn't like me.'

'She thinks you're a fool for turning down Scott's offer – that's all.'

'Huh.' Meggy raised her chin. 'What would *she* know?'

There were voices, and Henrietta's stooped figure appeared in the doorway. Her eyes creased into smiles when they lit upon Meggy. 'Meggy!'

'Mither.' Meggy rose and kissed her. Then, to the old lady who hovered behind Henrietta, she said wearily, 'Gweed day tae ye, Mrs Urquhart.'

Mrs Urquhart nodded, looking Meggy up and down. 'The Lovies are feeding you well.'

Meggy coloured. 'They look after me,' she said coolly.

'So I hear,' Mrs Urquhart said, her voice laden with innuendo.

Jean rose and drew an armchair closer to the hearth for the guest. The old lady groaned as she lowered herself into it. Henrietta bustled to the fire and poured tea into the last remaining cup. She handed it to Mrs Urquhart, pulled up a creepie and sat beside her.

The old lady slurped loudly. Jean and Meggy caught each other's eyes, and Jean had to bite her lip to stop herself from smiling.

'Beware of that John Lovie,' Mrs Urquhart said, and the moment of lightness died. 'Remember the Chessor girl—'

Meggy huffed. 'Oh, not *that* again.'

'People are talking!' Mrs Urquhart's voice rose. 'Looking at you, wondering what John Lovie has in mind.'

'Let them talk.'

'Meggy,' Jean warned.

'I don't care for gossip,' Meggy retorted. She stood and stomped to the fire. She picked up the tea kettle and poured the last dregs into her empty cup. There were beads of sweat upon her forehead, from the fire or indignation, or both, Jean supposed. Meggy turned back to her mother, dropped to her haunches, and placed the warm cup in Henrietta's chapped hands.

'Drink up, Mither,' she said. She kissed her mother's cheek and straightened up.

Jean followed Meggy to the door. They stepped out into the pallid sunlight and wandered towards the road.

'Don't judge her harshly,' Jean said. 'It's concern for you, that's all—'

'Concern! The old gossip.'

Jean bit her lip. 'Six months you've had at Futteret Den,' she said slowly. 'Six months you've been hoping and making eyes at him, and not a word from John—'

'Oh, stop it!'

Jean sighed and took her sister's arm. 'Don't be angry.'

Meggy scowled. Jean tugged her gently to a halt and kissed her cheek. 'Pity me,' she said. 'I have to go back and listen to more of Mrs Urquhart's grumbling.'

Meggy laughed and squeezed her hand. 'Aye, aye, bye then,' she said, turning away with a smile. Jean watched as Meggy trotted towards the Lovie farm. Then she trudged back into the cottage.

Chapter 10

Early June 1827

'The weather has turned,' said John Lovie, raising his face to the sky.

His brother didn't look up. James Lovie's eye was focused upon the yoke, his brow furrowed in concentration, tongue protruding slightly as he tugged the fastenings tight.

'Aye,' James said absently, 'And just in time.'

Rannie watched as John Lovie turned his gaze fondly from the glorious sky down to his brother. It was more the gaze of a father than a brother – and no wonder; there must be twenty years between them. James Lovie was about Meggy's age, Rannie guessed. He often thought of people and things in relation to Meggy. It was a habit he had fallen into; it bothered him, but he couldn't help it.

'All right,' James said, standing and brushing his hands together. 'Yoke's firm.'

James stepped back from the pair of horses and inspected his work. His scrutiny was businesslike, impatient. His eyes flickered to Rannie and away again. James Lovie's eyes weren't steady like his brother's and mother's; they were constantly on the move. He shifted his weight from one foot to the other, flexed his fingers, pursed his lips. He was like a beast that had been too long in the yoke.

Rannie nodded and stepped closer, placing his palm against the neck of the nearest horse. He'd noticed the way James handled the animals – as if they were tools. That wasn't unusual amongst farmers, but it wasn't Rannie's way. Neither was it John Lovie's way; that was one of the things Rannie admired in the master. John Lovie had a feel for the animals, for the land, for the weather. Rannie sensed it.

'The rain has kept the frost away,' the master went on, tearing his eyes away from his brother and turning them to the sky again – blue against blue. 'If this sun keeps up now, the harvest will be good.'

James nodded. 'Late,' he said, 'but good. Better than last year.'

There it was: business. James had a nose for business, so people said. Always poking about, looking to see where he could profit. 'He'll go far,' was what folk said about James Lovie. 'The world's too small for him,' they also said. They said it in an admiring way, but Rannie couldn't for the life of him understand why.

'I hope so, brother,' said John Lovie. 'I *hope* so.'

Rannie glanced at his master with surprise. It was a rare thing to hear such passion in Lovie's voice. The master's eyes were still raised to the sky as if seeking answers. If Rannie didn't know better, he'd have guessed John Lovie was praying. Rannie ran his hand down the horse's neck, eyeing him curiously. There was nothing strange in a farmer's worry; all men who lived by the land lived on the edge of disaster, forever at the mercy of the weather. The harvest last year had been poor, and most in the district had suffered; they looked to the future with equal measures of hope and dread. But the Lovies? Rannie had thought them, with their seventy acres of fertile land, their pair of horses and their half-dozen cattle, to be above the troubles of humble folk like his kin. The Lovies enjoyed none of the luxuries of their landlord, but neither did they want for milk or tatties; their fire was always burning and there were blankets on the beds.

Foolish, though, to think anyone was safe. Fate would do what it chose; no-one could rest easy. Why should the Lovies be any different? But if even the master had cause for worry, what of Rannie? What of Meggy?

Rannie sighed and shook the fears from his head. Worry wouldn't make the neeps grow. He crouched beside his master's brother at the plough and watched as James attached it by long chains to the yokes. 'Folk say you're a fine carpenter,' Rannie said, noticing the deftness of James's fingers.

'Do they now?'

'They say you'd rather be behind a saw than a plough.' Try as he might, Rannie couldn't keep the resentment from his voice; it seemed wrong for a man not to love the work that was his fate.

'Yet here I am.'

Rannie blushed. He always felt wrong-footed around men like James Lovie.

The master's brother was tugging the chain, testing that it held fast. He was smaller and sharper than his brother, finer in the features. You had to work hard to dislike James, he supposed, and if *he*, Rannie, didn't like him, it was likely due to some fault in himself.

'What's news in town, brother?' John Lovie asked, rocking on his heels.

'They've arrested Malcolm Gillespie,' James replied, springing to his feet and wiping his palms on his breeks. 'It's in all the papers.'

'Have they, now?' The master raised his brows heavenward.

Rannie hated to show his ignorance, especially before a clever man like James Lovie. But curiosity got the better of him. 'Who?'

'Gillespie,' James repeated. 'Exciseman. Sworn enemy of the Highland distillers.'

'"King of the Gaugers", they call him,' the master said.

Rannie pondered. 'Why is he arrested?'

'He's accused of forgery,' James replied.

'And burning down his home for the insurance money.'

'I wouldn't like to be in his shoes,' said James. 'They're holding him in the Tolbooth at Aberdeen. He's to be tried in the autumn.'

'Then he'd better hope the law is merciful,' said John Lovie, 'or Gillespie's a dead man.'

Chapter 11

June 1827

A warm morning in early summer. It was good to be outside. Alex Rannie and Meggy were at the dung-heap by the byre, churning the mixture of moss and manure over with their hoes. The exertion and the heat radiating from the fermenting mass made them sweat. Rannie didn't mind. It was honest work – hot and smelly, but useful. The stuff was turning dark and moist and friable, just as it should, and it would soon be excellent compost for the neeps. He liked the rhythmic swing of the hoe – swing, plunge, lift, swing, plunge, lift – and the regular flexing and easing of his muscles. His efforts were nurturing the earth; his labour would put food into his belly. That was a good feeling.

Meggy didn't seem to see it that way. 'The stink,' she grunted, stabbing at the dung-heap with her hoe. 'I'll never get it out of me. That's enough, isn't it? It's done.'

'It's not done.'

Meggy sighed and speared her hoe into the heap. Rannie turned away. He'd rather have worked alone than have Meggy souring his mood. He'd have told her so, but there was too much work to be done and he needed the help.

A curl clung to Meggy's damp cheek. The sight of it made Rannie hotter. As if sensing his discomfort, she stood and put a hand on her hip, smiled sideways at him. Rannie blushed and stabbed the dung-heap with his hoe. Meggy kept watching him, smiling. Her chest rose and fell from the exertion, and a trickle of perspiration trailed down her neck into her blouse.

Rannie clenched his teeth. 'We haven't got all day.'

Meggy shrugged. She took her hand from her hip, lazily, and placed it back on the hoe. Rannie tried not to notice the curve of her buttocks under the heavy skirt as she bent over the dung-heap.

When the sun was high, the widow appeared in the yard, black-shawled and bonneted and clutching a bundle. She caught sight of Rannie looking at her and waved. He raised a hand, and she turned and limped across the yard, away towards the road. Visiting her daughter, he supposed.

When the black speck of the widow had disappeared from view, the master came in from the fields. He had finished the first yoking of the day and his cheeks were ruddy from fresh air and labour. He was panting and lightly sprinkled with sweat. As he passed them at the dung-heap, he exchanged a furtive glance with Meggy. Rannie saw it and tightened his grip on the hoe. There had been something urgent and sensual in that glance. Lovie strode to the cottage, opened the door, cast hot eyes at Meggy again, vanished inside.

Rannie watched Meggy as they hoed in silence. After five minutes, she stood, scraped a curl from her cheek and tucked it behind her ear.

'Enough,' she said.

He'd have liked to keep her there longer, but he had no reason to give. They *were* finished. They put the hoes away and Meggy wiped her hands on her apron. She ambled to the cottage and Rannie trailed behind her. They went into the kitchen, and the dimness, as they came in from the bright morning, made them blink. There was no sign of Lovie, but the creaking of furniture from the other room gave away his presence in the but.

Rannie sat, glad to rest his feet. Meggy prowled about the kitchen. She was making him twitchy, so he moved to the hearth to peer into the cooking pot. A rustling behind him made him turn back. Meggy's skirt flared out as she dashed through the passage from the kitchen into the other room.

A hot blush rose in Rannie's cheeks. A prickle of anger. He grasped the back of a timber armchair and dragged it away from the suffocating heat of the fire. He sat down heavily and waited, straining his ears. Meggy and Lovie were in the master's room together – alone. The master's bed was in there through the short passage. Rannie wasn't born yesterday. *That fool girl.*

He waited.

About a quarter of an hour later, Meggy reappeared. The lushness, the warmth of her. Nostrils flaring, she tilted her head at Rannie.

'Is that how you do?' he hissed.

Meggy laughed. 'What?'

'Going to bed with folk.'

She bent over him, cocking an eyebrow. 'I'll go to bed wi' *you!*' she said, hot breath on his cheek.

He turned away. 'I don't want you,' he spat.

Chapter 12

Mid-June 1827

'Rannie.' The master's head was silhouetted in the doorway. 'Come help me with the dung.'

Rannie followed Lovie to the dung-heap and took up a spade to help his master shovel compost onto the cart. The compost had fermented nicely and would be a rich treat for the turnips. Rannie shovelled in silence; since the incident between Meggy and Lovie, he'd been tongue-tied around his master. If Lovie minded or even noticed, he didn't show it.

When they had loaded up the cart, Lovie hitched it to his mare.

'She's restless today,' he said. The workhorse stamped its great hooves and snorted. Rannie sidled up to the horse's head and stroked its nose, murmuring. It jerked its head away and huffed.

'Aye,' said Rannie, keeping his hand on the mare's neck while Lovie finished fastening the cart. He knew how the mare felt: unsettled, resentful. Distrustful.

'Right,' Lovie said when the cart was ready, and swung himself up onto it.

Rannie stepped back as his master urged the beast into action. It took off and the cart jerked into motion. The wheels creaked and rumbled. The workhorse squealed and bolted – too fast. The cart groaned and rocked, and Lovie, perched upon it, lurched. He strained at the reins; the beast tossed its head and shrieked. It leaped forward, tearing the reins from Lovie's hands, charging full pelt. The cart bucked over the uneven ground, swayed and hurled Lovie through the air.

With an *oof!* he thudded to earth.

Rannie sprinted. The horse lumbered away, dragging the reeling cart over ditches and mounds and spilling the precious dung in its wake. Regretfully, Rannie watched the cart go as he hurried to the body crumpled up in the field. The master was inert.

Heart racing, Rannie put a hand on his shoulder and squeezed it lightly. 'Master!'

Lovie groaned.

Alive, then. Rannie sighed.

Lovie rolled onto his back and swore. 'My shoulder!' He hauled himself up to sit, shaking his head as if to clear it. His shirt was torn, and blood oozed down his back and shoulder.

'Will I fetch a doctor?' Rannie asked, but Lovie shook his head.

Rannie stood and gave his master his arm, and Lovie staggered to his feet. He dusted himself off and the pair inspected the damage. Lovie's hand was bruised and skin was torn from his back and shoulders.

'It's bloody,' Rannie said, 'but it could've been worse.'

'It'll mend,' Lovie said, gritting his teeth against the pain. 'Damn!'

Rannie hovered, uncertain.

'Well, get on with it,' Lovie snapped. 'Fetch the mare.'

He nodded and jogged after the renegade beast. It was lucky that Lovie's wounds were minor. Any worse and he'd have been laid up, and Rannie would've had double the workload on his hands. And if he'd died … well, Rannie might have found himself without a job at all. He was dependent on Lovie; there was no getting around it. Whether he liked it or not – and he didn't, not since the business with Meggy – John Lovie was his master.

The mare had exhausted herself a hundred yards or so distant. The cart had come away and lay listing in a ditch. Rannie cursed; he would need to fetch a shovel to salvage the dung that had spilled onto the ground. The wretched beast had just added hours of work to his day.

He jogged across the field to the horse. Lovie hobbled behind him.

'Are you all right?' Rannie asked when his master caught up.

Lovie nodded with a grimace. 'Let's just get this done.'

Rannie agreed; of course Lovie hadn't the luxury of lying abed until he was healed.

'When we're finished,' Lovie went on, 'Meggy can tend to my wounds.'

Chapter 13

Mid–Late June 1827

'**A**re there any rats about the farm?' Alex Rannie worried as the master knelt to open the sack of seed. The seed was precious; the farm depended on it. If vermin had destroyed the seed, they would struggle to feed the cattle through the next winter.

They'd laboured hard over the preceding weeks to prepare the land – ploughing and cross-ploughing, pulverising and manuring the fields. John Lovie's injuries had not prevented him from working, though now and then he would pull up short with a sharp intake of breath, as if gripped by pain. Meggy had proven to be a poor nurse, but he'd been healing well since the widow had taken over the washing and dressing of her son's wounds.

Now they were ready to sow. Preparing the fields had been hard work, but Rannie didn't mind it. It was honest labour, and if he kept his mind away from the memory of Meggy emerging from the master's bed, he could almost enjoy working alongside John Lovie. The man was easy company. For all his faults – and Rannie hadn't forgotten them – Lovie was mild-mannered and fair. Even better, he was a good farmer: stoic, cool-headed, pragmatic.

I'm lucky, Rannie told himself every time the bile rose. Lucky.

But that business between Lovie and Meggy had poisoned things. The heat between them; the sway of Meggy's hips. It made him blush to think of it. Her hot breath on his cheek, teasing: *I'll go to bed wi' you.* The shock of her carnality. The vileness of John Lovie – the thought of that middle-aged farmer's hands upon her sweet young flesh. It made him sick.

In his mind's eye, Rannie saw the widow's black-swathed figure flap down the turnpike road, unknowing, while the lovers waited like a pair of dogs for the chance to paw at each other. How could a fellow trust a man who would take advantage of his mother's absence to sneak about with a young maid? It wasn't right; it just wasn't.

And worse, though Meggy and the master had taken care to hide their lust from the widow, they hadn't bothered to hide it from *him*. They'd flaunted it before him. Rannie knew what that meant: he didn't matter; his opinion counted for nothing. That stung.

But he wasn't paid to uphold the moral standards of Futteret Den. He did as he was told, and he would not dwell upon the goings-on around him. Lovie was an amiable master, and he was, after all, the master.

'Don't fret, chiel,' Lovie smiled and clapped a hand on Rannie's shoulder. 'There are no rats.'

Rannie shrugged off the hand, stood, and turned to John Lovie's brother James, who was running a finger along the struts of the sowing machine he had borrowed from a neighbour.

'How does it work?' Rannie asked. His father had always sown by hand.

He listened with half an ear as James launched into a lecture. James's enthusiasm for modern technology was marvellous – at least, so his brother appeared to think. Rannie watched the master watching his brother. His arms were folded, and he smiled with the indulgence of a father, as if James was some kind of miracle.

Well, he wasn't a miracle. Rannie tried to ignore his irritation, but it wasn't easy. He might be a lowly farmhand, but he was no less of a man than James Lovie or his brother. Rannie mightn't be acquainted with modern sowing equipment, but he could calm a fretful beast. He knew nothing of politics or laws, but he understood cattle and turnips and the moods of the seasons. And as for honesty and decency, he knew more about that than his master ever would.

'Did you hear news of the *Dundee*?' John Lovie interrupted his thoughts.

He was addressing his brother, but Rannie cut in. 'What news?'

'The whaling ship.' Lovie turned to him. 'It was given up as lost, a year or more past—'

'I know that,' said Rannie. The *Dundee* had set off from London and vanished, somewhere in the strait west of Greenland. It had been much in the minds of the fishing folk, right up and down the coast. In the absence of news for months past, it was widely believed that the crew had abandoned the ship to seek shelter upon the islands and perished there. Rannie shivered, thinking of it; he'd never been to sea, though he had lived all his life in the sight of it. He'd never been on the islands or even outside of Aberdeenshire. The horror of those wind-lashed nights the men must have suffered upon a frozen ocean, trapped – he could hardly bear to think of it. 'I know that. But what news is there?'

'She made it to Lerwick,' Lovie said, scooping seed from the sack.

'Lerwick?' Rannie straightened, surprised. 'They made it through the winter, after all?'

'Aye. Safe and sound.'

He smiled. 'Good news, then.' The ship and her crew were nothing to do with him, but it made him glad to hear that fate could be kind. Good luck stories were rare. Too often, human life proved to be no match for adversity. Rannie bent down to the sack of seed and mouthed a quick prayer of thanks. He kept his face turned away from his master; John Lovie made him self-conscious about his own piety.

'Aye, good news then.'

***

Widow Lovie was at her knitting and Meggy was kneading dough when a thundering at the door startled them. Meggy wiped her floury hands on her apron and strolled to the door.

'Mr Brown,' she said to the figure listing in the sunlight. 'Come in.'

'Aye, aye, Meggy, love,' the beadle slurred, lurching into the kitchen. Meggy threw an amused glance at the widow, and she sighed and put her knitting in the basket.

'Would you like some tea, Mr Brown?' Widow Lovie asked, unfolding herself from the chair.

'Tea?' the beadle repeated, licking his lips.

'Or whisky,' Meggy said. She smirked at the widow's frown and took the bottle of whisky from the dresser.

'Och,' said Brown with a wave of his hand and a greedy eye. 'Would your master mind?'

The widow sidled past the visitor to the door. She glanced out at the fields, at the distant figure of John, before shutting the door. *Would John mind?* His relationship with the kirk being uncomfortable, he might not welcome a visit from the beadle — but no-one liked to be seen as inhospitable to a guest.

'Have a seat, Mr Brown,' she said, flicking a hand at John's armchair. 'Meggy will pour you a cup.'

'But have ye not had enough already?' Meggy teased, raising an eyebrow at him as she poured whisky into a horn cup.

The beadle affected hurt. 'I've been calling on parishioners all day,' he said. 'I canna help it if they offer me a drink. It would be rude to refuse their kindness.'

67

'And yet I've never seen the minister in your state,' Meggy said, handing him the cup. 'And *he* calls upon his parishioners oftener than you.'

The widow frowned at Meggy.

Brown winked. 'Aye, but the minister's nae so popular in the parish as I am.'

Meggy let out a bark of laughter. A smile tugged at the widow's lips as she settled back into her chair.

The beadle took a swig from the cup. 'I've been to see your mither,' he said, and wiped a hand across mottled lips.

'Oh?' said Meggy. 'How is she?'

'She worries about you,' Brown replied, his glance flickering sideways at the widow. Annoyed, she bent to pick up her knitting.

The girl rolled her eyes. 'She has no need.'

The door creaked open, and John stepped into the passage, framed by the light. The sight of him, haloed, stopped Widow Lovie's breath.

'Mr Brown!' John said, sauntering into the kitchen. His brother and Alex Rannie trailed behind. 'Welcome to my home.'

'Aye, aye, John Lovie.' The beadle struggled to stand.

'Doing your pastoral duty?' John asked.

Meggy put a hand up to her mouth, and her eyes creased in merriment above it.

'Aye,' Brown replied. He licked his lips and glanced from the widow to John and back. She studied John's face, curious. How far did his resentment of the kirk extend? The beadle was probably wondering the same thing.

But John said, 'Please, sit,' and Brown sank back into the chair.

'Meggy,' she said. 'Get on with it.'

Meggy fished out three potatoes from the pot: one for John, one for his brother, another for Rannie.

'Will you dine with the men, Mr Brown?'

The beadle held up his hands. 'Nay,' he said. 'Thank you, Meggy, love. I dined at your mither's.'

The widow resumed her knitting while the men ate. She kept a wary eye on John. He'd not set foot in the kirk since the business with the Chessor girl. How must he feel, playing host to the beadle? If he was bothered, he didn't show it. If there was tension in the room, it came only from some unspoken grievance that Rannie seemed to be harbouring – but then, that chiel always had his nose out of joint about something.

Meggy, as usual, seemed to be enjoying herself. Pounding the dough to the rhythm of her own humming.

'Meggy!' she said. 'Stop that noise. We have a guest.'

Meggy rolled her eyes again and folded her arms. The widow turned back to the red-faced beadle, who was still trying to make sober conversation with the men.

'I heard Gillespie is in the Tolbooth Gaol,' he slurred.

'The exciseman? Aye, so I heard,' said John. 'There'll be rejoicing in the Highlands.'

'Rejoicing amongst the smugglers,' James said.

'Haha!' Brown said. 'Aye, aye. They say he's got no less than forty-two wounds on his body from his run-ins with smugglers.'

John Lovie snorted. 'Who says? Gillespie himself?'

'Whether true or not,' Brown went on, 'his past bravery won't help him now. Forgery! Huh!'

There was a murmur of agreement. 'What will become of him?' Meggy asked as the men chewed their potatoes.

James swallowed. 'If they find him guilty, he'll hang.'

Hang! The words fell heavily on the widow's ears. The cottage was warm and crowded, thick with the smells of sweat and whisky and smoke. Meggy wiped the perspiration from her forehead with a still-floury hand, drawing a white streak across her brow.

Brown rose unsteadily to his feet. 'Will I see you at the kirk, John Lovie?'

Her heart rattled so loudly in her chest that she put a hand to it to stop her son from hearing.

John didn't look up. 'I doubt it.'

James blushed deeply. He was embarrassed! Well. Embarrassed by his own brother.

She stood, joints creaking, stabbing her knitting needles into her ball of wool and dropping it into the basket by her chair. 'Thank you for your visit, Mr Brown.'

The beadle paused and steadied himself, ignoring her and turning back to John. His complexion was ruddy, his eyes bloodshot and his nose bulbous, but there was gentleness in his voice; even she couldn't help but notice it.

'Think on it, John,' he said. 'Think on it.'

Then he nodded at the widow, winked at Meggy, picked up his cap and staggered out of the cottage.

Chapter 14

Late June 1827

The hay harvest had begun early; warm and bright weather through the spring had brought the grasses to flower by mid-June. The morning dew was long gone, and the grass was dry, green and ripe for cutting. The field was dotted with the bobbing and swaying figures of men.

Alex Rannie worked through the field, sleeves rolled up, scythe in hand, sweeping the blade in a wide, clean arc, watching the grass tumble to the earth. He'd been up for hours, since the first timid glow of sunlight had dragged him from his bed upon the deece. Now he was shining with sweat.

John Lovie worked a few yards behind. Further down towards the road, James Lovie was also helping with the mowing. The women – the widow and some local girls – were coming out with their rakes to spread the grass. Rannie stood and stretched his weary back. His arms were starting to tire. He wiped the sweat from his face with a greasy forearm and watched the women. John Lovie, seeing Rannie pause, stood also, rested the scythe by his leg, and lifted a hand to his brow to squint into the sun.

The women fanned out, following the paths that the men had mown. They swept their rakes across the fresh-hewn grass, strewing it evenly upon the earth, exposing it to the sun. The widow led the small party.

'Your mither's too old for this,' Rannie said. The widow, head down, moved slowly and carefully as if protecting fragile bones. 'She should be indoors.'

'She likes to help.'

'Likes to please you,' Rannie corrected, and the master smiled.

'Where's Meggy, then?' asked Rannie. 'Why isn't *she* working?'

John Lovie inspected his calloused palms, spat on them, and grasped the handle of his scythe. 'Meggy's not well.'

'*Again?*' Rannie shook his head. The second day of hay-making, and Meggy was already shirking. She was too sure of herself, that one. The lazy way she looked at a man, as if she was staring right into his thoughts. Well, she couldn't see into *his* thoughts.

'Is Meggy abed then?'

'Nay.'

'What's the matter with her?' Why should *he* have to work all hours of the day when that girl rested up whenever she felt like it?

Lovie shrugged and swung his scythe through the syrupy air.

'She's always slacking,' Rannie grumbled. 'If she can't work, she ought to leave service.'

Lovie sighed. 'Aye.'

Rannie's pulse quickened. He hadn't really meant what he'd said. He didn't want any harm to come to Meggy; all he wanted was for her to do her fair share.

'Well,' he said, 'maybe she'll come out after dinner and help make the windrows.'

'Aye. Maybe she will.'

They stood side by side and surveyed the field. They'd made good progress. Behind them, the women raked and turned the hay; ahead, walls of grass stood green and thick, waiting to be mown. Above, the sun blazed high in a dome of China blue.

'Another hour to dinner?'

Lovie nodded and rubbed his sore shoulder. The skin had healed since the accident with the cart, but the joint still troubled him at times.

'Did you hear the story of that poisoning at Dundee?' Lovie asked, rolling his shoulders.

'Mary Smith? Aye, I heard about it.' The case was a notorious one, the talk of the town. Back in February, Mary Smith of Dundee had stood trial for murder. 'That woman who poisoned her servant girl with arsenic.'

The story was heard all over Scotland; even the *Aberdeen Press & Journal* had run a report. Anyone who could read knew of it, and most who couldn't.

'They say she didn't mean to murder. They say she was trying to rid the girl of a bairn,' the master went on.

'Aye, so I heard. They say the bairn belonged to Mary Smith's son.' Now that he had stopped work, the sweat was drying on Rannie's back and brow. His muscles were starting to tighten, and he flexed his fingers. The second day of cutting was always the hardest. He'd toughen up soon enough. 'They say that Mary Smith thought her son was too *grand* to have a bairn with a *servant* girl.'

John Lovie threw him a sidelong look. Rannie clenched his jaw.

'Hmm,' Lovie said.

'The girl was a fool,' Rannie said, working himself into a state of indignation. 'Did you hear it? She already had a child and didna ken who the father was.' Much as he disliked the idea of a woman like Mary Smith setting herself so far above a servant girl, he disapproved of the servant girl just as much. It was one thing for a quine to confirm her fertility with a man she meant to wed – that was common practice, whether he liked it or not – but it was quite another to lift her skirts for any man who looked her way. It was going against God. Not that she deserved to be murdered, he told himself hastily. She didn't deserve *that.*

'I wonder,' Lovie mused, 'what would cause a woman to part with a child.' He spat on his palm, picked up his scythe and swished it through the air again. 'I'll warrant that Saty, or someone like him, could clear a woman of a bairn.'

'Saty? You mean Foreman? That prophet at Crimond?'

'Aye.'

Rannie was doubtful. 'I dinna ken.' Foreman was a healer of the old type: a man of strange herbs and incantations. It was said he could cure anything if he had a mind to. His cures were spoken of in whispers. 'They say he can cure a man of fitting by getting him to drink water at dawn out of the skull of a suicide victim,' he said, shuddering. 'I wouldn't want to trust a man like that.'

'You're right,' Lovie said. 'My mither talks about his cures for her aching bones, but I dinna ken. What physic causes purging, do you think? Jalap?'

'Aye,' Rannie replied, puzzled. John Lovie's face was turned skyward, eyes closed, soaking up the sun's warmth. 'I suppose it does.'

'Do you ken what quantity of jalap would cause purging … and what would cause death?'

'Nay,' Rannie replied, and then added, 'It's dangerous, messing with physic like that.'

'Aye,' said Lovie, smiling, opening his eyes and fastening them on Rannie. 'My mither ought to see the doctor for her cures, not that fool prophet in Crimond.'

Rannie nodded and hefted the scythe in his hand. If he rested too long, his muscles would protest when he resumed work. There was too much mowing to be done to stand about gabbing. The master followed suit, squared his shoulders, planted his feet wide, poised his scythe.

'Mary Smith,' Lovie mused before turning his back to Rannie and lining himself up with the bank of grasses. 'The jury couldn't prove the case against her, did you hear? She got away with it, didn't she?'

Chapter 15

Early July 1827

'Where are you going?' Alex Rannie lumbered into the kitchen.

Meggy was all scrubbed up and looking purposeful. She was in her best skirt and wore a shawl with a pretty frill about the neck.

'To visit my aunt in the Broch.'

'Here, take some bread for her,' the widow said.

'That's kind of you, Mistress.' Meggy took the warm loaf, sniffed deeply, wrapped it in a cloth and placed it into her basket.

'She has troubles enough,' the widow said. 'We might as well try to ease them.'

'Aye,' said the girl, closing her basket and slipping her arm through the handle. She raised her eyes to Rannie's. 'Her son – my cousin – is ill.'

'I'm sorry to hear it,' he said. 'Shall I walk with you?'

Meggy looked surprised. 'On your day off? Aren't you going to visit your father?'

'Aye. I'll go through the Broch.'

''Tis a long way round.'

Rannie shrugged. 'I don't mind.'

'All right then,' Meggy said, hoisting her basket from the table.

'Let me take it,' he said. Meggy threw him an amused glance and handed the basket over. 'You're not making love to me, are you, Alex Rannie?'

Rannie's face burned. 'Of course not.'

'Don't tease the boy,' the widow said with a smile. 'Go on, then.'

They emerged into the sunshine, blinking. The smell of freshly baked bread mingled with the scent of hay. Rannie sucked the wholesome air deep into his lungs. They cut through the yard down towards the turnpike road, Rannie plodding with the basket swinging from his arm, and Meggy strolling beside him. She flicked Rannie's arm with a corner of her shawl. 'Don't mind me,' she said. 'I'm only teasing.'

'I wish you wouldn't.'

'I won't, then,' she replied. Rannie pursed his lips and Meggy sighed. 'If you're going to be sour, you might as well go your own way. I can carry my own basket.'

After a moment he said, 'I won't be sour.'

'Good.' She skipped ahead and turned back to watch him. 'There's the widow Lovie, looking at us from the door.' She waved back at the black-shrouded figure.

'It's bad luck to look back at the house when you're leaving,' Rannie warned.

'Phhht! Bad luck? There never was a luckier girl than me.'

Rannie laughed.

'It's nice when you laugh,' Meggy said. 'Your whole face looks kinder. You should do it oftener.'

He blushed and cast his eyes down. 'What makes you think you're lucky?'

'Well,' she said, counting off on her fingers. 'One: I am in fine health. Two: I have a kind master. Three: it's a beautiful day!'

Rannie laughed. 'Is that all?'

'And I'm taking fresh-baked bread to my aunt, and she's sure to share it with me.'

'You're a goose!' he said, chuckling, and she honked in reply.

On each side of the turnpike road, the long grasses swayed, ripe for cutting; their fresh scent on the sea breeze was warm and clean.

Meggy's eyes were bright and her lips full and pink, and the sun washed gently over her complexion.

At length, Rannie said, '*Is* he a kind master, then?'

'John Lovie?' Meggy turned to him in surprise. 'Aye.' She hesitated. 'Don't you think so?'

'*Too* kind, to *some*,' he said darkly. How could he express the growing unease he felt in his master's presence? 'I don't think he treats you the way he ought,' he said at last.

'Oh?' said Meggy, her tone growing cool. 'He treats me well enough. Days off when they're due, all the food I want, and never a harsh word. Some would say that was fine treatment.'

'You know what I mean.'

'Oh, not *that* again.' Meggy shook her head. Rannie scowled and kicked a stone along the road. 'And you needn't be so disapproving.'

'No good will come of it,' he muttered. The image of John Lovie's wolfish eyes upon Meggy burned in his memory. The heat that had stirred the air between them. The vision of Meggy, hot and rosy and animal, fresh out of John Lovie's bed.

'And no good will come of your *meddling* either,' Meggy snapped. 'If you want to talk wi' me, talk of pleasanter things, or hold your tongue.'

Rannie kicked stones along the road, aggrieved, while Meggy strode beside him in silence. In the distance, the hunched outlines of Fraserburgh's buildings came into sight.

'All right, then,' he said. 'Tell me about your home.'

'My *home* is at Futteret Den,' she replied, still sulking. 'I went there at Martinmas last, and the master asked me to bide again at Whitsunday. So you see, I am quite at home there.'

'But your real home – your home before that.'

'It's only a half-mile from the Lovies', as you well ken, where my mither and sister still live.'

'Where is your father?'

Meggy smiled wryly. 'I have no father. He went to India with the regiment long before I can remember. Eighteen years ago, must be. We've heard nought of him since.'

Rannie walked in silence for a moment as he took it in. 'Nothing at all?'

'Nothing.'

'Is he dead, then?'

Meggy sighed. 'I suppose so. Honestly, Alex Rannie, have you nothing more cheerful to talk about?'

'Like what?'

She slipped a hand into the crook of his arm. 'Oh, I dinna ken. Do you have a sweetheart?'

'There you go again, teasing me.'

Meggy laughed. 'Sorry. Only, you're so serious, how can I not?'

'Well, you could try—'

'Shush! Here's your road to Pitullie. I'll say goodbye.'

'I can walk you to—'

'I'll take the basket from here,' Meggy said firmly. 'Cheerio now, Alex Rannie.'

They stood at the intersection, where the road to Pitullie led off from the turnpike road. Rannie turned his gaze to Pitullie, but his feet remained firmly planted on the turnpike road.

'Meggy,' he said, his voice thick and low, 'I've noticed ... you won't like me to ask, but—'

'Then don't ask!'

Her right hand was upon her hip, her left hooked through the basket. She strained against its weight, thrusting her left hip forward. The sea breeze lifted her curls and scattered them across her brow. The sun was high now, and cast harsh light upon her features. Her skin was sallow, her eyes cold, her pout wanton. Irritation burned through him; why had he ever thought her pretty?

'Only I've noticed things about you,' he accused.

Meggy narrowed her eyes. 'What things?'

Chapter 16

Mid-July 1827

Rannie thrust his fork into the cole of hay and hoisted it skyward. Golden threads rose and sailed high, soared, and drifted back to earth. He plunged again, lifted and tossed. The sweet scent thrilled him. John Lovie worked further down the row, turning his separate cole over to the sun and air. They had worked through the morning, heaping hay into bigger coles that would later form the ricks. Prickly shreds and grit clung to the sweat on Rannie's forehead and neck.

John Lovie whistled as he worked. The melody drifted pleasantly across on the warm breeze to Rannie.

'I had a strange dream last night,' Lovie called to him, pausing for a moment to rest upon the handle of his pitchfork. 'I dreamed that you gave me two cups of whisky and one of laudanum.'

Rannie tossed the last forkful of hay onto the cole. He was pleased with his work; the hay had dried nicely. He stood back to admire it. Soon, they would rope the base of the coles and use the horses to drag them together, then they'd form the ricks by the corn yards. The same routine, year after year. Just how he liked it.

'Now, why would I ha' dreamed such a thing?' the master went on.

Rannie straightened, shrugged, and wiped the sweat from his brow with a dirty sleeve. 'I dinna ken.' He had no time for his master's cryptic conversations; they tired him. Talk of politics and law and strange happenings was all very well for folk who were interested in such things, but it didn't make turnips grow.

John Lovie spat on his palm and gripped the handle of the scythe. 'I wonder how much laudanum it would take to put a person to sleep,' he mused.

What could a man reply to that? Nothing, and so he made no reply. He strode further down the row to the next cole of hay and stood back to size it up. The weather was holding out nicely. Plenty of hay-making hours left in the day. He raised the fork, hefted it in his calloused hands, swung, and plunged it into the hay. There was no time to stand around gossiping.

Chapter 17

A Sunday in July 1827

Jean leaned into the wind. Beside her, Meggy tugged at the damp skirt that flapped about her feet in a vexed attempt to keep the hem out of the mud. Jean felt dowdy beside her sister, who was in her best attire: a blouse and dark blue wool skirt, almost clean, and a warm wrap with a frill at the neck. The wrap was frivolous, but Jean envied her for it; the weather had turned unusually cool. The briny wind blew needles of mist against her face. Her hair would be a mess by the time she got to her aunt's place, but she supposed Mary Will wouldn't mind. Poor Aunt Mary.

They were almost there, at the cottage where their cousin lay dying. Jean drew her thin shawl tightly around her shoulders, head down, and charged along the track, but Meggy dawdled behind. Jean stopped and tapped her foot. Meggy caught up and grasped her arm, holding her back. The shooshing of the sea grew louder, and Meggy closed her eyes to listen. Jean calmed her breathing. The sound wasn't soothing so much as compelling.

'Let's go down to the shore,' Meggy said.

What did a few more minutes matter? They turned off the track and picked their way across the grassy slope down to the shore. The beach swept in an arc off to the right. It was deserted but for the distant hunched figure of an old woman. Collecting sea-ware for the crops, Jean supposed, watching the figure dip and rise as it swept along the high-water mark. The sea was grey, stirring like a fractious, half-wak-ened beast. Jean shivered; she wouldn't like to be out on a skaffie today.

They stood for a while, looking out to sea. The horizon was spiked with the masts of the fishing vessels pitching and swaying in the bay. The sky sagged dark and heavy. Beside her, Meggy was silent and dull. Jean knew better than to ask why. She put a bony arm around her sister's waist, taking pleasure from her fleshy warmth. Meggy stirred and tipped her head against Jean's.

To the left, cliffs rose from wave-lashed rocks. On the hill sweeping back from the verge, Kinnaird Lighthouse perched above the tower of the old castle. And there, right on the edge of the cliff, looking as if it was about to leap off – as it had done for 300 years – stood the wine tower: a grim, grey cube of stone. There were legends about that tower; all the townsfolk knew them. The story went that a daughter of the old noble family of Frasers had fallen in love with a common piper. When her father had found out, he'd locked his daughter in the tower and had the piper imprisoned in a cave below it. When the tide had risen, it had flooded the cave and drowned the piper. His lover, the young Fraser girl, had thrown herself from the tower onto the rocks in despair.

'That old legend of the piper and the Fraser girl,' Jean said. 'Do you think it was true?'

She imagined it had happened on a day like this – when the clouds bulged so heavy and low that they were almost sinking into the white-tipped sea. What had the Fraser girl (what was her name? Iso-bel?) thought about as she gazed down at the rocks where death waited to swallow her? Had she tried to imagine the freefall, the shock of impact, the agony of her body breaking apart upon the sea-slicked rocks? Surely not. Surely she had closed her mind to the horror of the act and thought only of the misery she was escaping. Otherwise, how could she have jumped?

Meggy shrugged. 'Do you think she regretted it? As she was falling, might she have changed her mind and begged God to save her?'

'Meggy! What an awful thought.'

'Better to fall peacefully, I suppose, looking forward to the release of death.'

Jean paused, shivering. 'I suppose. Such a terrible thing. I suppose she must have thought that life without her lover would have been too empty to bear.'

A light chuckle rippled through Meggy's body beneath Jean's arm. 'What a romantic you are!' Then, more seriously: 'Could love really be so desperate?'

She was thinking of John Lovie, then; Jean was sure of it. 'How would I know?'

'You wouldn't,' Meggy said.

Oh, that stung!

'Why love John?' Jean said, bullish. 'He won't do right by you.'

Meggy snorted and pulled away, leaving Jean exposed to the cold. 'Look at you, a dried-up old maid. Always looking for disaster.'

'I don't need to look for it; it's there whether I look or not.'

'And so willing to find fault where none should be found.'

'Meggy—' Her sister was picking her way across the sand, moving quickly now. 'Remember Helen Chessor!'

'You refuse to see the good in him.'

'What good?'

They stopped and faced each other. Meggy's face was flushed, her eyes watering in the wind. She counted on her fingers as she rattled off his praises. 'He's good-natured and dutiful to his mother. He's handsome. He's ... he's a hard worker, and clever. So clever! His farm makes a decent living too. And he's got a long-term lease and a good home—'

'What's that to you? If he never makes you an offer—'

'Why wouldn't he?'

'He's above you—'

'Not so far above! Sooner or later he'll want a wife ... and there will be plenty who won't have him, not after the Chessor woman—'

'But *you* would, only he's not offering.'

Meggy sighed and looked so downcast that Jean felt sorry for her words. She reached out to grasp Meggy's hands. They were cold and calloused, like her own.

'In any case,' Meggy said. 'You needn't fret. You can't die for love. The folk we know die of hunger or cold or fevers or childbirth. They don't die for feelings.'

She was right. Romantic notions were luxuries for rich folk like the Frasers: the lairds, who didn't have to wonder about where their next meal was coming from or whether they had enough peat for the fire. To throw away one's life for something as intangible as love seemed a terribly frivolous thing to do. And yet ... the thought weighed Jean down. Was love really so feeble?

The clouds rolled deep and threatening over the jagged cliff. 'Some folk say you can still hear the mournful tunes of the drowned piper on a stormy day,' Jean said. 'And that the Fraser woman's ghost can be seen drifting between the castle and the tower.'

'I don't believe it,' Meggy said, and her lip curled up in a smile. 'If there was a ghost, she'd be lurking below outside the cave, looking for her lover.'

Jean laughed softly. Meggy was never ill-tempered for long. She tugged Meggy's arm and steered her away from the sea, back towards the road. 'Come on. Aunt will be waiting for us.'

Chapter 18

Late July 1827

'What's the matter?' asked Alex Rannie.

John Lovie was coming out of the byre with a frown. 'It's the houk,' he said, gesturing to the cow with a jerk of his head. 'I've sent the boy to fetch Alex Milne. Come and see.'

Rannie followed him into the byre. It was cool and dim inside and smelled of cattle and straw. John Lovie led him to a brown cow in the corner. She lowered her head and blinked at him. Her eyes were crusted and inflamed. Rannie spread his broad fingers against her neck and greeted her with a soft *hello*. John glanced at him, amused. Rannie blushed. He liked cows. Most farmers saw them merely as useful objects, but he didn't view them that way. Neither, he sensed, did the master, though *he* kept his feelings close.

'See,' John Lovie explained, resting a hand upon the beast's back and gently massaging it. The cow lowed and backed up in alarm. 'Hide-bound.'

'Shhh,' Rannie soothed. Lovie shifted aside so Rannie could feel it for himself. He placed a hand on the cow's back and massaged as his master had done. The cow's coat was rough and inflexible and clung to the muscles beneath.

'Here he is,' said Lovie, and Rannie turned to see a broad-shouldered man approaching, carrying a sack. 'My brother-in-law, Alex Milne.'

Rannie nodded, and Lovie said, 'If he can't help the beast, no-one can.'

'Your boy says it's the houk,' Milne said, by way of greeting. Little John Yule trotted in after him.

'Aye,' said Lovie.

Rannie moved aside to let Milne examine the cow. All the attention was making the beast skittish. Rannie calmed her with a song, his voice low and tuneful.

'The bonniest lass in a' the warld, I've often heard them telling. She's up the hill, she's down the glen, she's in yon lonely dwelling.'

'Can you mend it?' John Lovie asked.

'Aye,' said Milne. 'I'll bleed it. Rannie, stop courting the beast and hold its head for me.'

John Lovie chuckled. Rannie shrugged and did as he was told, wrapping his arms around the cow's head and pressing it against his chest. One day he'd have cattle of his own, and he'd sing as often as he liked. Milne put his sack on the byre's floor and withdrew a fleam and bowl. He gave the bowl to the boy. With his left hand, Milne prodded the cow's neck until he found the vein. In his right, he held the fleam. John Lovie stood back, watching the proceedings with folded arms. John Yule loitered beside him and stared, his eyes wide.

The cow moaned and tried to wrench her head from Rannie's grasp. He held firm and hummed *the bonniest lass in a' the warld* into her ear. Milne transferred the fleam to his left hand and gripped it with his index finger and thumb, while pressing hard upon the vein with his other fingers. Then, with a flick of the wrist, he slammed his right hand into the fleam and pierced the vein. The cow bellowed and Rannie struggled to keep it steady. Blood streamed along the fleam, down the cow's neck and onto the earthen floor. Milne held his hand out for the bowl, and the boy Yule scurried closer to give it to him. Milne held the bowl against the cow's neck to catch the blood. They all waited in silence as the dark liquid poured into it.

'Enough,' Milne said at last, and withdrew the fleam. The boy Yule took the bowl of blood from him. Rannie sighed and pressed his face against the cow's cheek. Milne drew the edges of the wound together and pinned them up. 'The wound should have healed enough to remove the pin tomorrow. Keep an eye on it. I don't expect trouble, but send the boy to fetch me if there is any.'

John nodded.

'She's up the hill, she's down the glen, she's in yon lonely dwelling,' Rannie sang to the moaning beast.

John shook his head at Rannie and laughed. Rannie didn't mind. Let them think he was mad; so long as he could work alongside the beasts, he would learn to tolerate the humans.

***

Alex Rannie and his master ambled with their hoes between the rows of turnip seedlings. Singling the new shoots was a delicate job that demanded concentration. It was not heavy work, but all the bending was wearying. The tender shoots lined up neatly and sturdily, having responded well to the warmth of the season. The men prodded the clumps of new plants, separating them out and carefully distributing them along the ridges of earth.

'The butter is fetching a good price,' Lovie said.

Rannie nodded. 'The mistress will be pleased.'

'Aye,' Lovie said. 'If the summer keeps on this way, we'll make up the rent from last year's deficit.'

Rannie was surprised. 'It's in arrears?'

John Lovie shrugged. Rannie studied his master, and Lovie's eyes slid away. 'All the tenants are in the same position. Last season was a poor one.'

'This one will be better,' Rannie assured him, hoping his words were true.

Lovie smiled. 'I wonder,' he said, after a few minutes' silence, 'Do you know the name of a poison ... a white kind of stuff?'

'Poison?' He was thrown by the sudden change of topic. He thought for a moment. 'D'you mean arsenic?'

'Aye,' John Lovie replied, gently disentangling roots from a clump of earth. 'That's it.'

They worked for a moment in silence. Rannie's thoughts turned to the harvest; it would be bountiful, he expected. There would be turnips enough to feed the cattle right through the winter if they were lucky.

'I suppose Mr Officer in the Broch keeps it for sale,' John Lovie interrupted his thoughts.

For a moment, Rannie struggled to follow him. Then: 'Oh!' he said. 'The arsenic. Aye, I suppose so.'

Lovie nodded again. 'I suppose so.'

Rannie glanced at him curiously. His master was an odd one; he had a habit of bringing up strange notions. And then as soon he aired the strange idea, he would abandon it for another. At first the struggle to keep up with John Lovie's thoughts had troubled him – he knew he was no scholar, but he didn't like to be thought stupid – but it didn't bother him anymore. The master's musings were better humoured than understood. Lovie tended to think aloud; he could safely be ignored. And it was better to hear him speak of politics or poisons than of Meggy.

Rannie's thoughts returned to the turnips. The seedlings were plentiful and robust. He took pleasure in the sight of the dainty green shoots and the scent of the earth. While John Lovie chattered on about the abundance of herring and the benefits that a good season would bring to the town, Rannie knelt and marvelled at the miracle of the turnip.

Chapter 19

Friday 3 August 1827

FRASERBURGH

The town of Fraserburgh lay a couple of miles to the east of Futteret Den. From the northern limit of the town, a great narrow neck of land curved outward and formed a harbour in which the seas had been tamed by three separate piers. Further north, the lighthouse – pride of the town – gazed down from its position on top of a squat tower. The masts of fishing vessels spiked the harbour like needles in a pincushion.

Summer – herring season – had transformed the town. Fishermen, rope-makers and fish-curers swarmed. Salt breezes, alive with the cawing of gulls, swept in from the harbour and chased the busy townsfolk along the streets.

Close to the shore, the roads were lined with low-set homes of mud and stone; inland, towers and steeples traced the skyline. Industry abounded: butchers' and bakers' stores, chemists, millineries, draperies, banks and pubs. The parish school trilled with the singing of children. The town hall looked across the market square – past the cross mounted upon a stepped pedestal – to the grand Saltoun Inn.

Tucked in amongst these neat, busy streets was John Officer's drugstore. His shop boy, William Massie, stood behind the counter. His master had stepped out of the shop, leaving the youth in charge. The eighteen-year-old smoothed his moustache, cleared his throat, puffed up his bony chest to prove he was equal to the task. He cast a critical eye about the shop, taking mental notes: the bandages wanted tidying, the powders re-stocking, and the shelves behind the counter were in need of dusting.

Massie took up a feather duster and had just begun applying it to the shelves when the bell tinkled, and the opening door let in a whoosh of warm breeze and the chatterings of the street. Massie turned and saw a tall man in the doorway, backlit by the summer afternoon. The newcomer strode in with the rolling gait of a farmer.

'How d'you do, Mr Lovie?' William Massie said.

John Lovie nodded. He strolled about the shop, glancing right and left, picking up bottles and putting them down. His eyes flickered to the boy's and away again.

'Can I help?' Massie asked.

Lovie cocked his head, considering. He strolled to the counter and rested an elbow upon it. 'An ounce of jalap,' he said.

Massie nodded, turned and unlocked a cupboard behind the counter. He withdrew a box and placed it between them.

'That'll be a good dose,' Lovie murmured.

'For a beast, you mean?' Massie asked. 'Such as a horse?'

Lovie shook his head. 'No – for a person.'

Startled, Massie put a hand on the box. 'That dose would kill any person,' he warned, heat rising in his neck.

'Then I'll give a different dose,' Lovie said, smiling. 'For a purgative.'

Massie nodded and opened the box. As he measured out the jalap, Lovie said, as if in afterthought, 'Is it the strongest purgative you have?'

'Galoniel is stronger.'

Lovie paused briefly, then shook his head and reached out a hand for the jalap. He paid, turned away, stopped, and half turned back again. 'What's the best poison for rats?'

'Arsenic,' Massie said, his chest slowly deflating.

'Is there anything else?'

Massie paused to think. '*Nux vomica* would poison rats, but not anything else.'

Lovie considered. 'I would prefer something ... no, never mind. I'll think on it.'

Massie nodded, tugging on the sparse wires of his moustache. The customer's manner was odd. At first glance he seemed still and steady, but a closer inspection revealed a mass of tiny movements – darting eyes, fluttering fingers, shallow breaths. Massie was relieved when his customer took the package of jalap and turned away. Lovie sauntered to the door, and the bell rattled, and the hubbub of the street intruded again, and then there was silence. Massie was left alone with his bottles and tubes of ointment and tonics and poisons, waiting for his master's return.

Chapter 20

Friday 3 August 1827

FUTTERET DEN

Widow Lovie was stirring pottage over the fire when a knock sounded at the door. She sighed and limped across the kitchen. Her knees hurt. There was talk in the village that Saty Foreman could cure sore knees with seaweed. She'd half a mind to try it out, in spite of the whispers against the healer of Crimond. John had told her to see a doctor, but what could a doctor do? What could anyone do? Looking for cures – it wasn't worth the bother. Nothing was right since George died and even long before that. John did his best by her, but it wasn't enough. Everything was an effort.

Even the brightness of the girl, Meggy, that had so amused her through the winter, failed to lift her spirits now. Why, she couldn't say. Maybe she was just getting too old.

Maybe the girl was herself less radiant than she had been in the winter, now that she thought about it. The widow wondered about that. What reason had the girl to be sour? She was treated well at Futteret Den. The girl was young and flighty; maybe she thought she could do better. She clenched her jaw.

God, she was tired – aching and tired.

She wrenched the door open and let in the bright evening light. Elspet stood in the doorway, tapping her foot.

'Elspet,' she said. 'You don't need to knock.' It was an affectation; now that Elspet was wed, she refused to treat Futteret Den as her home.

'Mither,' Elspet replied, kissing her cheek.

She opened the door wider, and her daughter marched inside. Elspet was looking sallow and puffy, severe with fatigue. There was a wrapped bundle in her arms that squirmed and grunted. The widow peered at the bundle, lifting the edge of the swaddling cloth with a finger to expose more of the blinking little face beneath it. She couldn't help but smile. 'Och, wee one.'

The baby squirmed in its mother's arms, its wet lips pursed. Elspet brushed past her mother, hoisted the bundle onto her shoulder and strode towards the fire. The baby, startled, opened its eyes, burbled, blinked, its head wobbling on its tiny neck. The widow resisted the urge to snatch it from her daughter and bury her face in its warmth.

Elspet was nosing about the kitchen. The widow breathed deep to suppress her irritation; such a meddler, her eldest girl.

'Will ye sup with me?' she said.

'Aye,' said Elspet, planting herself upon the deece. She peeled the baby from her shoulder and cradled it in her lap.

The widow flipped the folding table down beside Elspet on the deece and slapped a wooden bowl of pottage onto it. She handed a bone spoon to her daughter and took one for herself, then sat beside Elspet on the deece, the folding table between them. Elspet reached awkwardly over the infant in her lap and dipped her spoon into the steaming soup. The widow waited for her daughter to taste it before she took a spoonful from the same bowl. A minute or two passed in silence, punctuated by Elspet's slurps.

'Where's John?' Elspet asked, a string of pottage dripping from her lip.

John was making the most of the lingering summer light. 'At his neeps,' she said.

Elspet nodded. 'And the loons?'

'Rannie's out with John,' she said. 'And the boy is at his father's.'

Elspet lowered her head, glanced side to side with sly eyes. 'Where's the girl?'

She frowned; Elspet's dislike of Meggy was getting tiresome. Forgetting her own dissatisfaction with the maid, the widow shifted her irritation to her daughter. 'Meggy's visiting her mother,' she said – adding, with a surge of protectiveness, 'like a good girl.'

Elspet huffed. 'You ought to get rid of her.'

'Meggy?' She blinked. 'Why ever?'

Her daughter scowled but made no reply. She took another slurp of pottage.

'Mind your business,' the widow said.

'Have you forgotten the trouble with the other one?' Elspet persisted. 'The other girl John took a fancy to?'

'Oh, I haven't forgotten,' her mother said darkly. 'And there was no fancying on *John's* side. But I haven't forgotten.'

How could I forget? The Chessor girl herself wouldn't let anyone forget. She paraded that boy around the district as if he were a trophy. Named him *John Lovie* after the man she accused of fathering him. Four years old now, and such a bonny boy. He'd be the widow's grandson if what the girl said were true. But it couldn't be true. She wouldn't think of it.

'That bairn's not John's,' she muttered. 'She'll admit the truth soon enough.'

The Chessor girl was a troublemaker. An unwed mother, looking to accuse the nearest man. John should have known she was bad luck, with that red hair of hers. The widow touched the wood of the table, just to be safe.

Elspet snorted.

'You're a fine one to judge,' the widow said. 'Producing a wean barely five months after getting wed.'

Elspet ignored her. 'The Chessor girl repented, did ye hear?' she said. 'In the spring, she did. Paid the penalty and the kirk took her back.'

'I know it, I know it.'

Elspet took another slurp of pottage. 'They say it's because she wants to marry. She's got her eye on one of the Chalmers men.'

Her heart puttered. Marry? So her course was set, then.

'Whether the bairn's John's or not, my brother's still under church scandal,' Elspet went on. 'He canna wed your Meggy, you know, even if he wants to. Not 'til he repents and pays the kirk.'

'I *know* that. But he's no mind to wed Meggy,' she said bitterly, but her mind was racing. If John did have his heart set on marriage, he would have no choice; he would have to admit to the child, repent and pay the kirk. Meggy wasn't much, but if she could lure John back to the fold …

'He tells you his mind, does he?' Elspet taunted, and her mother pressed her lips together.

'Enough,' she said, placing her spoon upon the table – too firmly – and wiping her narrow lips with her apron. John had his troubles, but why must she think of them? The bairn being bonny and dark-haired didn't make him John's. John had admitted being in the girl's house with her alone at night, aye, but he'd denied all guilt with her, and that was an end to it. She wouldn't ask him to lie. They all mistrusted her John: the girl, the kirk – and even his own sister, it seemed. But *she* wouldn't side with them against him. She wouldn't speculate about his guilt. John was her son. Her *son*. God alone would be his judge – and hers. God would find an answer.

Elspet wouldn't leave it alone. 'Meggy has to go.'

'We canna let her go,' she snapped. 'She's been fee'd again 'til next Whitsunday.'

'Pay the fine and let her go,' Elspet said. 'You ought to get rid of her, no matter what the consequences. Else there'll be trouble.'

'What trouble?' John was at the door.

She pushed the bowl towards Elspet and stood. She hobbled to the fire to fetch a fresh bowl of pottage for her son. John smelled of sweat and horse. He smiled his thanks, and her heart lurched. He was so handsome, so vigorous. Why dwell upon his flaws? What good would come of it?

'Meggy,' the widow said, throwing dagger eyes at her daughter. 'Elspet thinks you're too fond of her.'

John laughed and shook his head. He spooned the pottage into his mouth. He wouldn't talk about it. He wouldn't be bullied by his sister, God bless him.

'You wait,' Elspet said, rising awkwardly. 'You wait and see.'

Chapter 21

Saturday 4 August 1827

When Alex Rannie came in from tending the horses, he felt something amiss. The air in the kitchen was thick with summer warmth and cooking fires and body odour. Meggy was chopping something at the dresser, and she kept her back turned when he clattered in. The widow was sitting, silently sewing. Rannie made his way to the deece and sat. The folding table had already been set down and there was food upon it: a bowl of half-eaten pottage and a wedge of bread.

'Eat,' Meggy said, without looking up. 'I've had my share.'

Rannie watched her curiously. Meggy's voice sounded phlegmy, as if she was ill or weeping. He tried to look at her eyes, but she wouldn't raise them; in any case, after the brightness of the outdoors, it was too dim in the kitchen to see if they were red.

He picked up a spoon and scraped the bowl, watching Meggy. Her head was bowed and her shoulders slumped. There was nothing of her usual jauntiness about her. He waited for her to turn and tease him with a sidelong glance or a saucy quip, but she didn't oblige.

'Meggy?' he prompted, and she said, 'Mmm.'

He shrugged and ate some more. Serves her right, he thought. Whatever it is.

Then Meggy stiffened and put a hand to her belly. When she turned around, Rannie saw that her face was white and studded with perspiration.

'Meggy!' he said again, as she buckled, both hands now at her waist. He stood and she pushed past him, burst into the passageway and through the door into the yard. He hung around the doorway, hesitant. Grunting noises, so loud they reached him all the way from the midden by the byre, made him blush. Meggy was easing her bowels. He came back in and shut the door.

The widow glanced at him. 'She's not been herself.'

'Will she be all right?'

'She's a strong one, that girl.'

Rannie sat down to finish his dinner. Meggy's discomfort was none of his business. The widow continued with her wordless mending.

When Rannie was done, he pushed the bowl aside and stood. 'I'm going to my father's house,' he said, and the widow replied, 'All right, then.'

He met Meggy coming in as he went out. Her face was pale and grim, and there was a sour stink about her. But she lifted her chin so she could look down her nose at him as usual. She bade him a good evening in a raspy voice.

Rannie set off across the field to the turnpike road. It was a mile and a half to his father's house at Pitullie. The twilight was fresh and golden, and he whistled as he walked. A mile down the road, he caught sight of Fiona, the neighbour's girl; she was returning from an errand at the Broch. He hailed her, and she stopped to speak. Last time he'd laid eyes on her, only months before, she'd been a skinny child in her sister's boots, frightened and ashamed at the feeing market. She'd been fee'd to a farmer not far distant, she told him. The work must have suited her; she seemed taller, prouder.

He passed a pleasant few minutes in conversation, and then they said their farewells. The girl was barely out of his sight when Rannie's step faltered. A cramp seized his guts. He tried to ignore it and push on. A hundred yards further, and his insides were twisting in knots, fit to burst. He panted and sweated. He looked around in desperation. He had to void, or he'd soil himself. There was a bush a few yards back from the road; it would screen him if he could make it in time. He jogged to the bush, trying to run smoothly so as not to jolt his bowels. He made it just in time, lowered his trousers, squatted, and groaned as his guts exploded onto the ground.

He sighed and wiped the sweat from his forehead. The pain had eased a little, but the nausea remained. If he could make it the last half-mile to his father's house, he'd take some salts and rest up for the night.

Poor Meggy, he thought ruefully, as he stood and fastened his trousers. They were in for a long night, the pair of them.

Chapter 22

Sunday 5 August 1827

Meggy had spent the next day with her Aunt Mary Will, whose son had lately passed away. When she slouched back into the kitchen that evening, the widow felt almost sorry for the girl; she looked hollowed out and weary.

It wasn't just the sorrow of loss. The girl had been up half the night before, purging. She'd tossed and turned in the bed, gripping her belly and doubling up in pain. Every time the widow had started drifting off to sleep, the girl had bolted upright and scrambled from the bed to run to the midden and relieve herself.

They were *both* tired, then, though the wretched girl could not be expected to spare a thought for *her* state. Meggy slumped onto the armchair by the hearth and sighed.

Widow Lovie eased her stiff bones into the chair opposite. 'How is your aunt?'

The girl's eyes were red-rimmed and puffy. 'My poor aunt. Her son lies in a fresh-dug grave at Kirkton. How do you *think* she is?' Her tone was so defeated that the widow let her rudeness pass.

'Did your mither and Jean go with you?'

'Nay. She wouldn't want a visit from my sister. Jean would curdle your cow's milk just by looking at it.'

The widow snorted.

'My aunt asked after you,' Meggy said, raising a defiant chin. 'She asked if my mistress treated me well.'

'Oh? And what did you tell her?'

'I said that you were good to me, but you were old and cranky.'

'You never!'

'I did.'

'Cheeky girl. And did she ask about John? Did she ask if *he* was good to you too?'

The girl rubbed her nose and said in a small, distant voice, 'Aye. I told her he was a fine master, but ...'

'But what?'

'But his farmhand Alex Rannie sings to the cows.'

The widow *tsked*. The girl's attempt at levity wasn't convincing. Her eyes were dull, her mouth sagging. She wouldn't look the widow in the eye. What fool complaints had she been pouring into Mary Will's ears? There would have been complaints, for sure; the girl couldn't help herself. She'd been surly lately, and ungrateful for all the kindnesses she'd been shown at Futteret Den all these months. Or was it Elspet? Had word of her nagging reached Meggy's ears? Meggy wasn't stupid; she must surely know that Elspet wanted her gone. *But didn't I speak up for her? And at Whitsunday, didn't I let John keep her on for another term?* The girl would have work until at least November, and probably longer if John still favoured her by then.

Ah. Was that why she looked so sour – because John didn't favour her as she'd have liked? Her eyes were always upon John, but *his* still gazed elsewhere. A thousand things claimed John's attention – the cow that was poorly; the threat of rain during the hay-making; the rent payments; the wounds to his shoulder; Alex Rannie's moods; the accusations of the Chessor girl; the demands of the kirk – a thousand things, but none of them was Meggy.

The girl might complain all she liked to her aunt, but none of her complaints would make John love her. And God knew where that would leave them all.

Chapter 23

Thursday 9 August 1827

'They say it will be a good season for the herring,' said John Officer, patting his paunch and gazing with satisfaction about his shop.

William Massie, the shop boy, paused with his feather duster in hand and glanced through the window out onto the street. Fraserburgh was bustling with the traffic of seasonal workers – fishermen who chased the herring through the summer. The shouts of the salty, rough-edged men carried into the town every evening at dusk as they secured the nets to their skaffies and set out into the darkness of the harbour. Every morning, the stink of the fish rolled in from the sea as they hauled their loaded nets ashore. By day, the beach was laced with their nets drying in the sun.

'Aye,' said Massie, fingering his moustache. 'So I've heard.'

The fishing trade kept the town alive, it was true, but the fishing folk were a breed apart. Hard-drinking, swearing, superstitious types. They rarely patronised Mr Officer's shop. The druggist and his apprentice were better acquainted with the townsfolk and the farmers. Still, a good herring season was good for the town and good for business.

Massie flicked the duster over a picture that hung on the wall and his knuckle caught its corner; the picture tilted, swung and fell from its hook. He flung out a hand to catch it just as the picture hit the floor.

'No harm done,' he said, crouching to inspect the picture.

John Officer nodded, unperturbed, rocking on his heels. 'The fishermen would doubt it,' he said with a smile. 'A falling picture precedes a death.'

'Superstition.' Massie shrugged scornfully. He rose, dusted off the picture and re-hung it on its hook. The bell rattled and the stink of the fish-curing houses washed in as the door opened.

The farmer strode in, smelling of horse and earth and hay.

'Good day, Mr Lovie,' said John Officer from the counter.

'Aye, aye,' Lovie replied, not looking at the druggist but addressing his gangly apprentice. 'Give me some of that stuff,' he said.

'What stuff?' said Mr Officer.

Chapter 24

Friday 10 August 1827

'Eat your pottage,' said the widow, placing a dish in John Yule's hands.

He swung his legs and hummed as he ate. She turned to watch her grandson from the dresser as she kneaded the dough. *Like his mother*, she decided, admiring the curve of his cheek and the roundness of his forehead. She smiled as his little tongue flickered across his pottage-oiled lips. He was a good wee fellow: uncomplaining, mostly, and a hard worker for a seven-year-old.

'Grannie,' said the boy, smearing pottage from his lips across his cheek with a dirty sleeve. 'Why is Meggy still abed?'

'She wanted more sleep, that's all.'

'Why does my uncle let her lie abed when she should be working?'

She paused to wipe the smudge of pottage from the boy's cheek with a corner of her apron. 'Because he's a kind master.'

'Alex Rannie says it's not fair.'

'Alex Rannie should mind his own business.' She picked up the dough, slapped it onto the floury surface and pressed the heels of her hands into it.

'He says my uncle should let her go if she canna do her work.' The boy scraped his bowl and went on. 'I don't want him to let Meggy go.'

'Meggy can do her work,' she said, irritated. 'Eat your pottage.'

'Alex Rannie says my uncle lets her get away with murder because he is too fond of her.'

The widow paused, chilled. 'Alex Rannie gossips like an old woman.'

The boy slurped the last of his pottage. 'Is my uncle too fond of Meggy, Grannie?'

The widow pointed a floury finger at her grandson. 'Enough!'

'Is that why he kissed her behind the byre, Grannie?'

The blood drained from her head. Kissed? 'John Yule,' she cried, snatching up a spoon. 'I will tan your hide! Gossip is for old women.' She dropped the spoon onto the dresser, her mouth dry, hands shaking, heart thundering. 'The cows are waiting. Go!'

Chapter 25

Monday 13 August 1827

At six o'clock, the evening was bright and mild. A breeze rolled in from the shore, bending the hay. The widow put a hand on the door to shut the air out, for the draught would soon turn cool. John was outside, strolling towards her from the stable. He'd finished his work for the day and fed and unyoked the beasts.

She stood in the doorway and watched her son. She never tired of watching him. His broad shoulders, his long legs, his fluid gait.

She was lucky to have a son who looked after her so well; many women didn't. After George had died, it was John who had provided for her. It was John who had helped her raise James, the youngest. James had been only a bairn when his father had turned up his toes. He'd adored his older brother; they all had.

She'd once believed that John would marry and fill the house with children. She'd even – at one time – looked forward to his marriage. She'd speculated about his future wife, sized up the young women in the neighbourhood for the role. All had fallen short. She'd lowered her standards, made suggestions, even engineered meetings with potential daughters-in-law. John had resisted.

But they'd grown into a rhythm together through the years, she and her son: a comfortable rhythm. John had had no need for marriage. Meanwhile, her other children had peeled away. Jean had slipped off to marry Alexander Milne. Their farm was only down the road – she could see the thatched roof from the well – but Jean rarely came to call.

They saw her husband, who helped out when the beasts fell ill, more than they saw Jean. And then Mary had wed George Yule, and Elspet had wed William Scott. Her other son, George – named for his father – had settled at Hillhead with his wife and little ones, but seldom came to Futteret Den. Then, of course, there was James: still unwed, but he'd deserted the farm anyway to hire himself out to whoever would serve his interests. Restless James.

There was only John now. John and her, his mother. Without knowing it, how happy she had been! John's desires were so simple and so few. A tattie in the evening, a pipe and a dram, and time spent in his own company. He asked for so little. How foolish her efforts to find him a wife had been. How lucky that no wife had been found!

When the Chessor girl had sought John's eye, she'd known there would be trouble. The girl was ambitious, looking to trap a hardworking farmer with a steady lease. A pretty girl, but uppity. She would never have done. The widow had worried, back then, that the Chessor girl might try to lever her out of John's life, but she needn't have. To think that *Helen* could have snared a man like John. The girl had presumed too much, and she'd paid for it.

And now there was another. She saw now what she should have seen all along: John would never marry Meggy. The girl had no power to save him. He would kiss her behind the byre the way he had with Helen Chessor, and she would only drag them all closer to ruin.

John was striding towards her with the kindly evening light upon him. There was no hope for him in the next life, but *this* life still had to be lived. The best she could hope for now would be to keep him close. And that was enough – of course it was! No mother was as lucky as she, to have such a son.

A smile lit John's face, and she smiled back at him; but then he waved, and she saw that his grin hadn't been for her. A straw-haired neighbour was passing up the road towards the house. She watched as

John altered his course, veering off to greet the passer-by. She watched the men nod and rock on their heels in conversation, and then stroll shoulder to shoulder through the hayricks towards the house.

'Meggy,' she said, turning around, the dimness of the kitchen momentarily blinding her after the glare of the outdoors. 'Seems William Park will be joining us for supper.'

'Not enough tatties,' the girl replied, peering into the pot that bubbled over the fire.

'I'll have porridge then,' she said irritably. It made no difference to her what she ate – potatoes or porridge, it was all the same.

Meggy nodded, looked up and dimpled; without turning around, the widow knew that John must be behind her. The way Meggy straightened up, thrust out her chest, dipped her chin, glanced sideways through lowered lashes.

William Park greeted the women and followed John into the kitchen. John nodded at his mother, sliding onto the deece and avoiding Meggy's eye. The widow plodded to the fire and put oats and water into a pot. Meggy was beside her, smelling warm and yeasty. The girl turned and swaggered to the deece where the men sat either side of the folded-out table. She pulled up a creepie stool beside John and sat so that their knees were almost touching.

The widow threw her a sharp glance. 'Where's Rannie?' she said, adding crossly, 'Meggy! Get the tatties.'

'Gone to the shoemaker's,' said John. 'He won't be back till later.'

Meggy shrugged and sauntered back to the fire, dropped a potato from the pot onto a plate with a piece of bread, and slapped it into the visitor's hands. He grunted his thanks. Meggy piled up another plate and gave it to John, who nodded without looking at her.

'Meggy, pour the milk, go on,' the widow snapped, sighing and rubbing her aching neck as she stirred her porridge. There was a splash as the girl poured the milk from the ceramic pitcher on the dresser. The widow scraped the gluey mess of porridge into a bowl and plodded noisily to her armchair. Meggy had put all the milk into one bowl, for Heaven's sake. The two men were drinking from it in turns. She could have fetched another for the guest, she thought. We *do* have another. The girl was getting too lazy, too sure of herself. She sighed again.

Meggy fetched a potato for herself and turned towards John and his guest on the deece, hesitating with her plate in hand. Normally she would sit by John, but he wasn't paying her any heed. Despite everything, the widow felt a stab of pity. Meggy pulled an armchair across to the round table on the other side of the kitchen.

'I heard you had trouble with a hummel,' said William Park.

'Aye,' said John. 'It's well again now. Alex Milne bled it for me.'

The widow yawned. Meggy hunched over the table, chomping noisily and throwing occasional glances John's way. The widow couldn't blame the girl for making eyes at John. Who could help it? He was a good catch, for all that he was almost twice her age. The girl had taste, even if she had no sense. But she overestimated her charms. Others had tried to snare John before her, and look what had happened to them. Even if John had a mind to marry, he could do better than the poor McKessar girl.

But of course, he had no mind to marry – and nor should he. She saw it clearly now. She and John were fine just the way they were. And even if John lied and said the Chessor boy was his, he'd have to pay the kirk, and then where would he be? How could he ever afford to marry? How would he meet the rent? Nay, the idea was absurd; she should never have considered it. Elspet was right. Meggy was nothing but trouble.

Close to eight o'clock, William Park was still in the kitchen. The men had talked all evening of their neeps and their cattle, and the widow's lids were heavy. At last, their neighbour got to his feet and made for the door with John at his heels. Meggy smiled up at John, rising, dimpling. John seemed eager to get out of the cottage.

'I'll walk a way with Park,' he said, skirting around Meggy, who was already by the door.

When they'd been gone a little while, she heard voices outside, and then Rannie was at the door, bringing the evening chill in with him.

'You'll want supper,' Meggy bustled, chin up, all smiles. She shepherded Rannie to the deece and gave him a tattie. While he ate, she clattered about the kitchen, glancing now and then at the door. The widow knew what she was looking for, and so, she was sure, did Rannie. They both knew it, but they didn't want to speak. It was embarrassing. The girl was pining, like a puppy, for her master.

Chapter 26

Tuesday 14 August 1827

Widow Lovie awoke at six. Meggy was asleep in the bed beside her, snug and warm; the widow could make out only her outline in the dark closet. It was tempting to stay in. There would be work to do the instant she arose; too much work for sixty-seven-year-old bones. How nice it would be to stay in bed, listening to the easy breathing of the girl.

Meggy was a good sleeper, and getting better every day. She was also getting fat. It hadn't escaped the widow's notice – how could it, when they slept side by side every night? The girl was eating too much, taking advantage of her master's generosity.

She sighed and creaked out of bed, put cold toes to the earthen floor and gasped as her bunions sent pain shooting through her feet. Meggy didn't stir. Let her sleep, she thought, with a faint resurgence of almost-forgotten affection. She could let herself feel pity now – now that she had given up on the girl. She sat on the edge of the bed and pulled woollen stockings up her bony legs, wriggling her toes to warm them. She picked up her heavy widow's weeds and grunted with the effort of donning them over her shift. She thrust her stockinged feet into her boots, grasped her long plait, deftly twisted and pinned it to the back of her head, enclosed it in a mutch cap and tied the ribbon under her chin.

She padded out of the closet into the kitchen. The cottage was quiet; the boy, her grandson, had slept at his father's the previous night and was yet to arrive for his working day. Rannie was sleeping upon the deece. He stirred as she moved about the kitchen, then yawned, grunted and swivelled himself upright. She shuffled to the but end of the house where John slept; the scent of his pipe lingered, but he wasn't there. Out putting the horses to the grass, she guessed. She stood for a moment, breathing in the scent of John's pipe. Then she trudged back to the kitchen.

A rustling from the closet disturbed her peace, and Meggy emerged, scowling, warm and stale-smelling with the aftermath of slumber.

'The fire needs stoking,' the widow said, and Meggy grunted.

Meggy stoked the fire and then slipped out to fetch more water from the well. The pot boiled and the widow braced her shoulders to lift it from the hook and pour water into the tea kettle. Wincing as her fingers and shoulders protested, she made a mental note to add tea-making to Meggy's list of chores. She was getting too old, too weary.

Meggy came back in with the bucket, nudging the door with her hip to open it wide so she could slosh her way into the kitchen. There were dark splashes of water on Meggy's skirt; sloven, the widow thought, frowning, but she said nothing.

Rannie was thumping about the kitchen in the graceless manner of a labouring loon more at home in the fields. He lingered longer than was necessary, and the widow wondered if he was waiting for a smile from Meggy. Then he muttered something about fetching a drill plough, pulled on his boots and lumbered out into the dawn.

Meggy went out to the dairy to yirn the milk. The widow waited for the tea to draw, then poured herself a cup. She sat, eyes closed, and raised the steaming mug to her lips. How good it felt: solitude, a moment of rest, hot tea.

It must have been twenty minutes or so later, though it seemed as many seconds, when Meggy came back in, flushed with the effort of yirning, her face lightly oiled with perspiration. The widow tipped back her head and drained the cold dregs from her cup.

'The cows are waiting,' she said, rising from the chair regretfully. Meggy shrugged.

She stepped out of the cottage's stony dimness into the fresh morning. The air was still and thin and sharp. She paused to breathe it in, feeling her spirits rise. She might have been all alone in the world but for the muffled lowing and shuffling of the cows. 'I'm coming,' she murmured.

In the byre, the cows mumbled at her, and she grunted back. Squatting on the milking stool, she rested her head against the cow's side. Her fingers found the teats and tugged. Jets of milk squirted with tedious rhythm into the bucket. It was work she could have done in her sleep. Four cows later she was done, and the bucket was full.

She unfolded herself gingerly from the stool, groaning as she lifted the bucket. She carried it gently – awkwardly – back to the cottage, careful not to spill a drop.

John Yule had arrived and was in the kitchen, wolfing his breakfast. She gazed tenderly at his narrow neck, his tufty golden hair.

Meggy put a hand upon her stomach and turned to the widow with a frown.

'I feel sick.' She didn't look well. Her face, which only minutes ago had glowed with health, was pale and damp. 'It's strange,' she mumbled. 'It came on all of a sudden.'

'You slept well?' the widow asked, knowing the answer; she slept lightly herself and knew the girl had barely stirred through the night.

'Aye. I was well when I woke ...'

The widow sighed. There would be more work for her if Meggy were to have another attack of dysentery.

Meggy groaned. 'Ohhh,' she said. 'I feel sick.'

'Go out,' the widow told her. 'Go and take some air.'

Meggy stumbled to the door. She was gasping and clutching her belly. The widow turned a grim face back to her grandson and snapped at him to get to work. She would have lectured him further, but her heart wasn't in it. Meggy had looked dreadfully poorly. It was only ten days since her last stomach upset, and this one looked as if it would be worse. What could it mean? She refused to speculate about the signs of late: Meggy's growing chubbiness, her reluctance to work, her malaise. Her distraction, her moodiness. It wasn't her business, and she wouldn't think about it.

She left Meggy to her own devices while she busied herself in the kitchen. She had work to do, and the boy was getting under her feet, but she didn't mind; it kept her thoughts from dwelling too heavily on the ghastly noises coming from the yard. After a while, the retching and groaning stopped, and there was silence. The widow and the boy looked at each other and said nothing. She kept an eye on the door, expecting Meggy to darken it again, but the girl didn't come.

She wiped her hands on her apron and strode out into the yard. It was some time after eight o'clock now, and the freshness of the early morning had staled. Meggy was lying face-down at the far end of the corn yard. There was no movement or sound coming from the body lying rumpled in the dirt. Heart quickening, she trotted to the girl and squatted. A filthy smell hit her. The girl's skirt was stained, and her face was pressed into the earth. Widow Lovie bent an ear to the maid; she was panting light, foul puffs of breath.

'Meggy,' she said. Except for the slight rise and fall of her chest, the girl showed no signs of life. 'Come in to the house!'

Meggy groaned.

'Meggy!'

The girl mumbled, 'In a minute,' or something like it.

'Oh!' The widow struggled to her feet. Her knees were killing her and now there was mud on her skirt. There were chores to do; she had no time for Meggy's dramatics. Still, the girl seemed in a bad way. 'All right, then. Come in soon. Come in and rest.'

Troubled, the widow trudged back to the house. She didn't look behind; Meggy would follow when she was ready.

But Meggy didn't follow.

Chapter 27

Tuesday 14 August 1827

Alex Rannie came in at half past eight. He'd been out at a neighbour's farm to borrow a drill plough for the neeps and was ready for his breakfast. Widow Lovie was in the kitchen alone. She put his oatmeal in a pot with a dollop of butter and a little hot water, stirring it as Rannie eased himself onto the deece.

'Meggy's ill,' she said. 'She won't be able to hoe today.'

Rannie, annoyed, grunted. 'Is she abed?' he asked, but the widow did not answer. She handed him his brose and he began to shovel it into his mouth. The girl's illness was nothing to do with him. She paid no mind to him; why should he care about her? He ate quickly and rose; there was no time to linger. He left the bowl on the dresser for the widow to clean up, and lumbered back out into the morning.

Rannie found John Lovie out near the well with his horses. He'd been shearing the grass for their supper since dawn and was flushed and shining with sweat. Beyond Lovie, trudging along the turnpike road, was a hunched woman pulling a handcart. It was Henrietta McKessar, Meggy's mother. She was on her way to the shore, Rannie guessed, to fetch seaweed for the crops.

Lovie nodded a greeting to Rannie. 'Where's Meggy?' he asked. 'Why isn't she out yet?'

'She's sick,' he said.

'What's the matter with her?'

Rannie shrugged. 'She's sick.' The ruddiness in Lovie's cheek deepened but he said nothing. He glanced across to the turnpike road, where the stooped figure of Meggy's mother trundled closer. The squeaking of her handcart wheel grew louder as she drew level with the men.

'Morning,' Henrietta called out as she passed. Up closer, she seemed less ancient than she'd appeared from a distance. Her back was bent and her hair grey, but her eyes were clear and her cheek still plump like her daughter's.

'Morning,' they replied in chorus.

Rannie waited for his master to mention Meggy's illness to her, but he didn't. Instead, Lovie turned back to him. 'No time to waste,' he said, rubbing his hands.

That's how it would be, then: business only. That was fine by Rannie. Now that they had the neighbour's drill plough, they could get to work preparing a catch crop of white turnips, seeding on stubble between the rows of established plants. It pleased him to see that not an inch of the land was to be wasted. Lovie hitched the plough to the horses while Rannie grasped the handles and steadied the cumbersome frame. Before long, the horses were lumbering through the fields and Rannie had fallen into step behind, and the rhythm of the task had erased the problem of Meggy from his mind.

Chapter 28

Tuesday 14 August 1827

It was almost nine o'clock and Meggy still hadn't come in from the yard. Widow Lovie was worried. She sent her grandson out to the cows and ventured back to the yard to find Meggy. The girl was still lying face-down on the ground.

'Come in, Meggy,' she insisted. Meggy moaned, rolled over and pushed herself upright. Her face was smeared with dirt: dark stains against chalk. The widow didn't wait or help the girl to her feet. She turned and scuttled to the cottage. Meggy, bent almost double, followed her in. She seemed a little revived.

'I have a pain within,' she gasped.

'Where?'

Meggy shook her head and wrapped her arms around her belly. 'I'm thirsty,' she whispered.

Widow Lovie sent her to bed and Meggy stumbled off without protest. She put the kettle on the fire and brewed up a cup of strong tea. She took it into the bed closet, where Meggy lay in the dimness and moaned and wept.

'Drink,' the widow said, and the girl took the cup with shaking hands. She took a deep swig from the cup, then cast it aside, sat up abruptly, and hurled the contents of her stomach onto the floor. The widow picked up the cup, lifted her skirts, and stepped over the pool of vomit, out of the fetid cavern and into the warm, peaty kitchen to fetch a bucket for the girl. There was nothing more she could do; nature must take its course.

John came in for breakfast a little while later. He faltered in the doorway, creasing his brow and raising a hand to his face. The whole kitchen was rank with the stench of vomit. From the closet came the sounds of Meggy groaning and retching. John's eyes flickered towards the closet and away again.

'Meggy's ill,' the widow said.

John frowned and took his tea into the other room. It was his custom to breakfast there, but need he really escape so hastily? Must he leave her alone with those animal noises coming from the closet? The sounds would be less urgent in the but, away from the kitchen. She bit down on a small twinge of resentment. Alone in the kitchen, she listened to Meggy and fretted.

***

Rannie, who was out amongst the neeps working the drill plough, looked up as John Lovie emerged from the cottage and tramped back across the field to join him.

'Meggy's nae well,' Lovie said.

Rannie shrugged. 'She might soon get better.'

Lovie slowly shook his head. 'If she goes on long in this way, she'll not be in the way to grow better.'

Rannie turned back to the drill plough. It was just like Meggy to shirk again. He was fed up with her malingering; if she couldn't keep up with her work, then her master should show her the door. There were plenty more who'd take the work if it was offered. The saucy cow. Making eyes at the master, she ought to be ashamed. Giving the place a bad reputation.

Still, unease settled upon him. He thought of Meggy: her teasing, arched brows, her plump cheek, her hand on his arm on the day they had strolled together towards the Broch. The warmth of her. His insides turned cold. Sudden illness could sweep you away without notice. God could snatch life away on a whim, and He frequently did. There was no knowing whose turn it would be next.

The squeaking of a wheel, faint but growing louder, made its way into his consciousness. It was Henrietta McKessar, returning from the shore with her load of sea-ware. Rannie, sweating with the effort of pushing the plough, watched the lonely figure grow nearer. He straightened and wiped the perspiration from his brow with his forearm. His master noticed the direction of his gaze and frowned.

'Don't tell her that Meggy's ill,' he said.

Rannie raised an eyebrow.

'It will prevent a clamour among them,' Lovie said with a shrug. 'And prevent them running back and fore to the house.'

Rannie nodded, but the order didn't sit easy with him. What if Meggy's illness was grave? The girl would want her mother, and the mother would want her daughter. *I have no father*, Meggy had told him. *He went to India with the regiment ... we've heard nought of him since.* Mother and daughter were close, he guessed; they had to be. Hardship and suffering and loss had dogged them all their lives, and kinship was all they had. Maddening as Meggy was, she shouldn't have to suffer alone.

But the master had turned back to the plough. Rannie held his tongue.

They worked until past noon. When Henrietta trundled her handcart back along the turnpike road towards the shore again, neither of them spoke. Rannie settled his lips into a grim line and kept working. It wasn't his business.

At one o'clock, hunger and fatigue drove Rannie from the field into the cottage. The kitchen was dim and warm and stewing with the stink of sweat and vomit. The widow's brow was pleated into a thousand lines. The boy, John Yule, was playing in the kitchen, but his grandmother seemed too distracted to respond to his childish chatter. An animal moaning came from the closet: panting, rasping, heaving. Rannie met the widow's eye, and his stomach lurched. It was worse than he'd imagined.

The widow gave Rannie a plate of tatties, and he ate them to the music of Meggy's retching. He bit down upon his growing dread.

Then Meggy's ragged voice rang from the closet. 'Rannie!' she cried. 'Go and fetch my mother or my sister! Oh! I was never so unwell before!'

The widow had been gazing out through the door to the road. At Meggy's words, she spun around and grabbed her grandson's arm. 'There's Meggy's mother, coming up the turnpike road,' she hissed. 'Go, boy; go and get her.'

The boy sprang out through the door, out of the stuffy, poisoned air of the cottage.

'Water!' Meggy cried from the closet.

Chapter 29

Tuesday 14 August 1827

The air in the closet was foul. Widow Lovie tiptoed into the gloom with a cup in her hand, leaving the door ajar. Meggy was fussing on the bed, whimpering. When the widow had fed her tea an hour ago, the girl had drunk greedily and kept it down, and she had thought her settled. Now she saw that her hopes had been misguided; Meggy had fallen into a terrible state.

'Oh, what shall I do?' Meggy panted.

She hesitated by the bedside. 'Fly to Christ,' the widow whispered. 'Fly to Christ.'

She was sorry for the quine, but what could she do? There was nothing to be done. A prayer might be in order, but – much as she loved and feared her God – she didn't hold much stock in the results of prayer. Lowland folks died young all too often, and no amount of prayer would save them if God had made up His mind. He never seemed to pay too much heed to people like them. The only thing a woman like her could do was to harden her heart a little; she'd had practice at that.

'Will you have a sip of this?' she said. She wasn't sure the girl had heard her, but then the writhing form on the bed unfolded itself into an upright position. She placed the cup into Meggy's shaking hand, and Meggy took it and gulped. Then the hand dropped, and the cup tumbled, and the tea dregs splashed onto the widow's skirt. The girl's mouth fell open and she slumped back onto the bed.

The widow listened for a moment. There was no sound. Meggy was still. The widow fumbled in the bedclothes for the girl's hand and found it cold. She wrapped her own hands around the girl's tender cold hand and thought that *now* would be the time to pray, if she could only find the words. Her heart ached and pounded.

Rannie was thumping about in the kitchen.

'Rannie,' she cried. 'Get John. I think Meggy's dead.'

There was a grunt from the kitchen, and his boots thudded out the front door. She sat in the cold stinking gloom with the girl, fidgeting.

Then the closet door darkened, but it wasn't John who appeared. It was a woman, thin and ragged and smelling of sweat, much older than her fifty-three years. Motherhood, thought the widow. It's motherhood that ruins us. The woman was out of breath from running.

She felt her throat tighten with panic. 'Henrietta.'

'Meggy!' said Henrietta, ignoring the widow and scuttling to the inert girl's side. She trod in something that squelched: vomit.

Henrietta leaned over her daughter and tried, awkwardly, to gather her up in her arms. Meggy lay limp and unresponsive. Henrietta drew back, took her daughter's hand and grasped it with her own. 'Her hand is cold.'

The widow watched as Henrietta bent her ear to Meggy's lips and frowned. If any breath came from Meggy, it was too soft even to stir the wisps of grey hair that fell across her face.

'I think she's dead,' Henrietta said.

'I am afraid of it,' the widow replied. And she *was* afraid; dread was lurching through her, threatening to cut loose and drive her to hysteria. She tried to drown it in a torrent of words. She babbled on about the morning – about how she had found Meggy lying in the yard, how Meggy had complained of sickness and pain and thirst, and how she had given her tea; about how Meggy had been sick with purging two weeks ago and had recovered, and how she, the widow, had expected her to recover just the same this time. She'd had no reason to think the girl wouldn't recover. No reason at all; she was young and healthy, wasn't she? How could they have known she would turn so rapidly?

John cut her short. He'd run in from the field and was loitering beyond the door to the closet, where he must have had full view of the two older women but not the stricken girl on the bed. She heard his breathing – heavy and ragged from the running – and half rose in a panic. She told him that Meggy was dead or fainted, and John made a pained noise far back in his throat. His face was in shadow and his expression impossible to read.

'Tell Rannie to fetch her sister,' Henrietta said. 'She's working up in the moss, a mile away.'

Then she turned cold eyes to the widow. 'It's a strange thing, for no doctor to be sent for,' she muttered. 'Whether she be ill or dead.'

'John,' the widow said, trembling, 'fetch a doctor.'

'Aye,' John said, and retreated from the cottage.

The women sat together in the dim closet, with the knowledge lying heavily between them that no doctor on Earth could help Meggy now.

Chapter 30

Tuesday 14 August 1827

Jean burst in, breathless, just before three. She'd run a mile from the field where she'd been cutting moss. Rannie had fetched her, luring her back to the Lovie farm with the news that her sister was ill.

The cottage was crowded with women. Old Mrs Scott was there with young Mrs Scott. Mrs Urquhart was emerging from the closet, beetling, head bowed, towards the door. She brushed past Jean, shaking her head and muttering as she scuttled from the gloom of the cottage. Jean pushed her way through the women into the closet. Her mother and Widow Lovie were perched on the edge of the bed, and Meggy lay still upon it.

Jean's eyes were sharper than her mother's. She saw the pool of vomit on the floor before she could step in it. Someone had covered it with sand, but the stench still infused the tiny space.

'Meggy!' she cried, trying to wake the crumpled form, though it was clear she was dead. Her mother and Widow Lovie were staring at her, as if looking for answers. What answers could she give? She was a nobody; a pathetic, weather-beaten spinster of twenty-seven who spent her days toiling in the moss. She was powerless. Her sister's master hadn't even shown her the respect of telling the truth. *Meggy is ill*, was what he'd said. *Ill*. Not dead. Although, truth be told, she'd known that it must have been bad. Lovie wouldn't have sent his farmhand a mile down the fields to fetch her for a head cold.

Jean edged closer to the bed, and Widow Lovie stood to give her space to sit. John Lovie's clock struck, loud and solemn: *one, two, three.* Jean sat on the edge of the bed and plucked Meggy's hand from her mother's. She turned the cold fingers over and saw that the nails were blue. She'd held those hands when they stood on the shore talking of the legend of the Fraser girl and the piper. They'd been cold then, too, but fleshy and alive. Now they were limp.

'She was complaining of sickness,' the widow babbled, 'and pain in her stomach.'

Jean leaned in and laid her cheek on Meggy's breast. It was still warm, but silent and still. Meggy was dressed in a crumpled slip and could have been alive but for the silence and stillness of her. A handkerchief lay on the bed beside her. Jean picked it up; it was heavy and slimed with vomit. She kept hold of it; the vomit would wash out, and there was no sense throwing away a good handkerchief. It wouldn't bring Meggy back.

Jean bowed her head and wept.

Chapter 31

Tuesday 14 August 1827

A t four o'clock John came back with a young man in tow.

'Where's Dr Jamieson?' the widow cried.

'The doctor was out,' John replied curtly.

The young man in the doorway grasped a brown leather bag awkwardly in both hands. 'I'm Thomas Bisset,' he said. 'I'm a student of Dr Jamieson's.'

The widow muttered that Bisset was just a boy, but she ushered him to the closet where Meggy lay in the care of her mother and sister. It was crowded in there: three women – one of them unconscious – and now the pretend doctor, while John and old Mrs Scott loitered in the kitchen by the door to the closet. Bisset sidled up to the bed and the widow slipped into the closet behind him. They looked at the body briefly in silence.

Bisset placed his bag on the edge of the bed and fumbled about in it, drew out a candle and handed it to the widow while he struck a match. He held the flare to the wick, and the candle's sickly glow flickered upon the walls of the box bed. Bisset shuffled closer to the patient, slipped an arm beneath her shoulders and propped her higher on the pillows. Her head lolled. He withdrew his arm and cupped her head in his right hand. Silently, he held out the other hand to the widow. She gave him the candle.

The women leaned forward as Bisset held the flame close to Meggy's lips. It turned her face orange and ghastly with shadows. No-one breathed. They waited for Meggy's breath to trip the flame up, make it dance. Breathe! Widow Lovie thought. Breathe! But the flame remained straight and steady.

'There's no breath,' Bisset said.

He put his fingers to her wrist and to her neck, searching for a pulse. He touched her cheek, her forehead, her hands. She was slick with cold sweat. He lifted the blanket from her and placed a hand lightly upon her chest.

'The warmth has gone,' he said. 'Gone from every part of her except here, her left breast.'

John, lingering in the doorway, cleared his throat. 'I think it's a heart colic,' he said. 'You should open a vein.'

Bisset shook his head. 'It's too late for that. The girl is dead.'

Chapter 32

Tuesday 14 August 1827

I t was said that if a body was not watched for every second between the moment of death and the burial, the Devil would carry it off. But Alex Rannie was in no mind to sit with Meggy. All he wanted was to flee. As the day faded into twilight, Rannie took his leave from the place of horrors and scampered down the road to his father's house. He left the widow sitting by Meggy, the candle's shadows making hollow sockets of her eyes and caverns of her cheeks. It was hard to tell, at a glance, which of the women – Meggy or the widow – was the corpse.

Rannie had deserted, more than willing to leave the task of protecting the girl's soul to the widow. He wanted no part of it. The whole business gave him the creeps.

It wasn't as if he'd never seen death before; too many times, he'd sat through a flickering candlelit night guarding a corpse. Death was no stranger to poor lowland folk like him. It came to them in so many ways. Young women perished through giving life, and their underfed bairns followed them to Heaven; the fogs of winter chased old folk to the grave, and the ocean swallowed the fishermen. It was the way of nature.

But it was hard to see the hand of nature in Meggy's passing.

Death had snatched her so violently. There had been no warning, no unexplained knocking to predict it, as the lore would have it. *I was never so unwell before,* she'd cried. The sounds of her retching and keening in the closet still rang in his ears.

The late afternoon sky was drained of colour. Rannie took a short-cut across a field, thirsty for the scent of the sea. A tide of uneasiness washed through him.

His master had sent him to fetch Meggy's sister from the moss. *Tell her Meggy's ill*, he'd said, though it was clear to anyone that Meggy was already dead. *For fear of alarming her*, he'd said. Rannie had protested. After all, the poor woman would find out the truth soon enough. But Rannie wasn't the master. He didn't make the decisions. Like a good servant, he did as he was bidden, though the lie still lay bitter on his tongue.

Memories, unbidden and unwanted, stole into his thoughts. He tried to will them away. Like waves on a stormy beach, they returned to harass him: John Lovie's deep blush when Rannie had told him that Meggy was ill; his stories of Mary Smith, the poisoner of Dundee. His strange talk of physic and laudanum and arsenic.

Rannie shivered. His loyalties were torn. He was a simple farm-boy. He wanted nothing of doubt or suspicion. He hurried to his father's house, where the demands of the young ones would leave no room in his head for these fears. He would return in the morning; the corn and the neeps and the cattle wouldn't let up on their demands just because a servant girl was dead. The widow would need him, and so would her son. For now, though, he would try to forget Meggy.

What quantity of jalap would cause purging, John Lovie had asked *... and what would cause death?*

Chapter 33

Tuesday 14 August 1827

The instant the doctor-in-training had declared Meggy dead, Widow Lovie had flung open the door and window to let her soul escape into the evening sky. If the evil spirits were lurking, waiting to obstruct Meggy on her journey to Heaven, *she* would not be the one to let them have their way. She opened the door to the closet to allow Meggy's soul free passage to the cottage door. Meggy's mother had been too stunned to act. It had been left to the widow to attend to the rituals.

She had taken the milk from the kitchen, poured it upon the ground in the yard and cast the butter out after it. She had scooped water from the pail and sprinkled it upon the chairs and upon Meggy's clothes. She had placed two candles on the kist by the body and taken a taper to the fire to light them. She had tipped salt onto a plate and placed it upon Meggy's chest. And all the while, guilt had roped itself around her. She had given up on Meggy; she had given up on God. But she hadn't wanted Meggy dead; she'd never dreamed of *that*.

Henrietta, Meggy's mother, had sat and watched her attend to the rituals. Jean – red-eyed, red-haired and red-nosed – had risen, finally, from her grief to stop the clock. The cottage had fallen into deathly silence.

John had gone out to see their neighbour James Walker, the square-wright, to ask him to build Meggy a coffin. Little John Yule had gone to his father's home. The women sat still in the kitchen, with the dead girl in the open closet bed where they could keep an eye on her.

A chill breeze washed in from the sea through the open cottage door. Jean shivered, took off her shawl and wrapped it around her mother's shoulders. The widow, noticing, stoked the fire. She dared not shut the door lest Meggy's spirit be trapped. It'd had hours to escape, but there was no telling what Meggy would do – she had been wayward in life and might be just as contrary in death. It was best to be cautious.

The silence! It was too much. Henrietta shivered in spite of her shawl, and the widow, on edge, went to John's room to fetch a blanket to wrap around the bony shoulders. Jean sat beside her mother with fists clenched.

When the pallid square of light in the window turned grey, the widow said, 'I'll sit with her. Go home.'

Jean, mutinous, shook her head.

The widow clucked in annoyance. 'Your mither needs rest. Take her home while there's still light.'

At this, tears sprang from Henrietta's eyes and Jean, sighing as if repentant, wrapped an arm around her mother's shoulders.

'You *will* sit with her?' Jean said, pale eyes anxiously darting to her sister.

'Of course I will,' she said tightly.

Still Jean wavered. Impatient, the widow rose and took Henrietta's hand. It was as cold as the dead girl's. 'Go on,' she said. 'I'll take care of her.'

Jean rose slowly, held out both hands to her mother and drew her to her feet. The pair shuffled out of the door, arms around each other's waists, leaving the widow alone in the dim cottage with Meggy. She sighed, glad to be rid of the women and the weight of their grief. Her own sorrow was hard enough to bear. The salty breath of the sea swirled into the kitchen through the open door; she turned her back to it, dragged a creepie stool into the closet and sat by Meggy's bed.

It was impossible to think of Meggy as dead, with the candlelight animating her features. At times she appeared to be smiling; at others, frowning in anger. The widow crouched on the stool and steeled herself against the long night ahead.

Part Two

Chapter 34

Wednesday 15 August 1827

Futteret Den

In the morning, Alex Rannie helped John Lovie shift Meggy's body from the closet onto the master's bed.

It was right that the girl should lie on the best bed in the house, in the best room where the visitors could see her. It was the traditional thing to do – the respectful thing. But as he leaned over John Lovie's bed with the body in his arms, Rannie's skin prickled. He couldn't rid himself of the image of Meggy emerging from that same bed into the kitchen, hot and dishevelled. The lewdness of her laughter: *I'll go to bed wi' you!*

Now she lay cold in John Lovie's bed.

Her face was white and dull. Drained of life, it wasn't especially pretty. She would not have aged well, Rannie supposed, had she been given a chance. He found himself mourning her. It was as if death had exposed the true Meggy, and he wished he'd liked her better when she was alive.

She didn't look as if she'd suffered, although he knew she had. Her face showed nothing of the agonies she'd endured in the hours leading to her death. *I should have been kinder.* Remorseful, he closed his eyes and said a quick, silent prayer. When he opened them, John Lovie's gaze was upon him. Rannie blushed, and then squared his shoulders. What right had Lovie to judge him?

'I'm going out to Meggy's cousin, Mrs Grant,' Lovie said. 'Meggy's mother has given me a letter for her to send to Meggy's sister Ann.'

Rannie nodded. 'There will be visitors today,' he said, unnecessarily, folding Meggy's hands across her chest. The posture made her look pious and wholly unlike Meggy. He straightened her arms again and placed them by her side.

The widow came in, carrying two candles. Their light made deep gullies of the lines in her face. The mistress had not slept all night. She had sat up to guard Meggy's body, as was the custom. He felt a twinge of guilt. Duty had driven him back to the cottage at first light, but he'd been glad to escape from it the previous evening. The old woman had had no such respite. He watched as she leaned over the dead girl, placing a candle carefully each side of her.

'My mither will take care of things,' Lovie told him as he backed out of the room.

Can't get away fast enough. Rannie moved to the door and watched his master bitterly as he strode across the fields.

'You might as well tend the neeps,' the widow said wearily to Rannie.

'Aye,' he said, and his shoulders relaxed. To be out in the fresh air, away from this gloom! It was all he wanted.

'But don't ... don't shovel the earth. Not until she's buried.'

'Of course!' He would respect the traditions, as was only right. It was the least they could do for poor Meggy.

He hurried through to the entryway and almost collided with Jean McKessar, who was coming in with her mother. Rannie dipped his head at the women as he skirted around them and out into the yard.

***

'Mrs Lovie,' Henrietta croaked, and the widow clasped the old woman's hands. She ushered Meggy's mother and sister into the but. There would be no more sitting in the kitchen with the stink of the closet so near. From now until she rested in the earth, Meggy would host her visitors in the best room.

The widow watched anxiously as Henrietta stared frankly at the body of her daughter, lying in the cavern of John's box bed. Jean was clenching her fists and oozing tears. The candlelight cast changing shadows upon the dead girl's face.

Widow Lovie was babbling again. All night she had watched the light and shadows flicker across Meggy's face. All night she had suffered, alone by the dead girl's side. Reliving the events of the day, almost delirious with fatigue and stricken with guilt. *What should I have done? Might the girl have lived, if only I'd acted differently? If I had sent for the doctor the moment Meggy's pains began? Or the moment I found her face-down in the yard?* And yet ... Meggy had been young and vigorous; how could she have known the decline would have come so fast? How could she have known?

Still – the signs had been there. Lying face-down in the dirt, unresponsive: that wasn't normal. She should have sent the boy for the doctor. She should have alerted Meggy's mother. If Henrietta had known how poorly the girl was, she'd surely have sought help. No use pretending that she wouldn't have. And John had known Meggy was sick; why hadn't *he* told Henrietta? He'd had the opportunity. He'd let her walk by, ignorant. Four times.

John. Why hadn't he spoken? The worry made her sick. John had come in late last night after he'd seen Walker about the coffin, and he'd gone straight to his bed. She would have liked him to sit by her, to comfort and reassure her – maybe even to take a shift at Meggy's side and let her rest. But no, he'd gone straight to bed, leaving her alone with her thoughts.

She asked Meggy's mother and sister to sit as she trudged into the kitchen to cut chunks of stale bread for them. She brought tea and bread back to Henrietta and Jean, but neither was hungry. They sat in dull grief in her home, looking at Meggy, looking at each other, looking at her.

The cottage still stank of vomit. She should have scraped the mess off the floor, but she'd forgotten to do it. The sand she'd sprinkled on it hadn't really done the trick. Bile rose in her and she swallowed it down. She handed a plate of bread to Henrietta, who stared at it but didn't seem to know what it was for. Jean reached over and took it. She held it in her lap and fingered a piece of bread, but didn't put it to her lips.

***

Later in the morning, John returned. A plump, well-dressed woman bustled in with him: Meggy's cousin, Mrs Grant. Widow Lovie knew her by sight; her husband was a well-known businessman. A hat dresser, if she remembered rightly.

'Poor Meggy,' Mrs Grant said, clutching Henrietta's hands. 'John told me the news. I sent a note to her sister, like you asked me to.'

Henrietta shed fresh tears. John strode about the room like a preacher. His presence made the room smaller and got on the widow's nerves. *Sit,* she urged him silently, but he didn't.

'It's a heavy affair,' Mrs Grant went on. She was a talker, a woman with too many opinions. She took the bread that the widow offered and nibbled upon it. 'John's friends did Meggy wrong,' she said, 'with all those speeches against her.'

Henrietta stared blankly at her. 'What speeches?'

'Oh, all that gossip about Meggy and John,' Mrs Grant said. 'My cousin Meggy was wronged.'

She saw John's nostrils flare. *There'll be trouble,* Elspet had said. She was glad Elspet hadn't come. *I told you so,* she'd be saying. Not with her tongue, but it would be there in her eyes. *I told you so. Trouble.*

142

'What gossip?' the widow said, aware of the acid in her own voice. Mrs Grant glanced at her and at John, who turned his back. She could tell by his stillness that he was listening.

'Oh – it was nothing.' Mrs Grant lowered her voice. 'There was nothing in it.'

***

Jean stood and sighed. She ached from sitting still so long in the Lovies' parlour. She rolled her shoulders and stamped her feet. She wasn't used to inactivity. She'd dreamed of it often – a day in bed, an hour to sit on the shore gazing out to sea – but inertia, it seemed, didn't agree with her after all. Sitting here in the gloom was numbing. Years of cutting moss and spinning and weaving hadn't trained her for the tedium of death.

The room was full of old women and a dead sister and a brooding man. She paced, adding her restless energy to John's. She drifted to the kitchen, where she caught sight of a kist in the corner: Meggy's. She darted to the trunk, shaken from her lethargy. The lid was open, and she knelt to inspect the contents. Meggy's blouse lay on top, carelessly tossed, encrusted with mud and stained in the armpits. Jean lifted the shirt and pressed it to her face; it smelled stale: of sweat and peat fires and body odour. Then there was her skirt – dark wool – stained and stinking. Jean put it aside carefully. There was a petticoat underneath, a bonnet, a spare shift and some flannel undergarments. That was all.

'Is this all of Meggy's?' she asked Widow Lovie, who had followed her to the kitchen.

'That's all she had,' the widow replied. It was pitiful; one tiny trunk for all her sister's worldly possessions.

143

Chapter 35

Wednesday 15 August 1827

Futteret Den

I n the afternoon, Meggy's brother Jimmy appeared in a whirlwind, flinging open the door and bringing gusts of sea air and light in with him. Widow Lovie blinked at the onslaught.

'I heard this morning,' Jimmy blustered, standing broadly in the passage between but and ben, legs apart and plough-roughened hands on his hips.

'It's true,' Jean wept, what was left of her composure shattered, it seemed, by her brother's stormy entrance. 'Meggy's dead.'

'That's not all I heard,' Jimmy McKessar said. 'There's a report abroad that she was poisoned.'

Poisoned!

'No—' Henrietta cried.

'Poisoned!' Jean gasped.

The widow's head pounded. 'Who says?'

Jimmy didn't answer. He turned and pointed a shaky finger at John, who had ceased his pacing. 'What do *you* say, John Lovie?'

John regarded him steadily. 'I dinna ken about poison.'

'Why would our Meggy take poison?' Jean said, shaking her head. 'I doubt it, Jimmy. This report of yours – it can't be true.'

Widow Lovie clasped her hands together and pressed her knuckles against her dry lips. She tried and failed to put her thoughts in order. Mrs Grant's eyes were so wide they were in danger of falling from her head; even she, it seemed, had been shocked into silence. Meggy lay stiff in the box bed. This can't be happening, thought the widow.

Jimmy McKessar shrugged and held his ground. 'It's what they're saying.'

'*Who* says it?' Jean persisted. 'What would they know? My sister had no cause to end her own life.'

'Maybe …' Jimmy hesitated. 'Maybe she took poison *without knowing*.'

Silence fell again, and, with it, a cold twist of dread.

'Someone *gave* it to her?' Jean whispered.

Jimmy shrugged again and turned his palms up. 'I dinna ken. It's what people are saying.'

Jean's chest was heaving. She wiped her eyes with a bony wrist and turned to her mother. Henrietta was panting, hands to her breast, looking as if she might faint. Jean pulled her chair closer, hunched upon it knee to knee with Henrietta, peeled her mother's hands from her breast and grasped them in her own.

At length, Henrietta's breathing slowed. She withdrew a hand, cupped her daughter's cheek and spoke at last. 'We must ask a doctor to inspect her.'

John turned away. 'Of course.'

'Of course,' Widow Lovie echoed. 'We should send for a doctor.'

'I would not like a doctor to open her body,' Henrietta added, glancing furtively at Meggy, as if afraid Meggy might have misunderstood her.

'Of course not!' Jean said.

'I expect a doctor could tell, without opening the body,' John said. 'A doctor might tell by looking at the tongue.'

The body. *The* tongue. Not *her* body. Not *Meggy's* tongue. John wouldn't look at the dead girl in his bed; hadn't glanced at her all afternoon. She was his mother; she noticed these things. She didn't want to, but she noticed.

'I would not like the body to be opened either,' John said quietly. 'It might show ... things about Meggy that her mother would not want revealed.'

Widow Lovie caught her breath, glanced up and met John's gaze. Pale blue eyes, a perfect mirror of her own. Even steeped in anguish, she could not help admiring him. The strong jaw, the fine cheekbone, the wide, red lips, the dark lashes. Her love was a torment.

'A doctor's report would clear the innocent,' she whispered. 'Or bring in the guilty.'

Chapter 36

Wednesday 15 August 1827

Futteret Den

Late in the afternoon, Mrs Grant rose and said she would go home. Not as bumptious as she'd been earlier in the day – subdued now, sagging.

Jimmy McKessar leaped to his feet and said, 'I'll walk with you.'

He was handing his cousin her wrap when John said, 'Come and fetch Dr Jamieson with me.'

Widow Lovie saw the look that passed between Mrs Grant and Jimmy McKessar. Her John was standing there smiling at them, calm and affable as ever, but the pair of them had frozen.

'Come,' John said, pushing between them and striding to the door.

Like lambs, they followed him. What else could they do? Grants and Lovies and McKessars had lived side by side for generations. Suspicion and fear had no place between neighbours; this talk of poisoning was some mistake that would soon be righted.

Widow Lovie struggled to her feet, stiff from hours of sitting by Meggy's body. She limped to the door after them, suddenly desperate to inhale the fresh air that had washed into the cottage as they left. She stood at the door and watched them striding across the yard. John turned to wave; the misty gloaming had given his cheeks a sheen, as if he'd been weeping.

They walked towards the turnpike road, past the hayricks and out of sight. It was a mile and a half to Dr Jamieson's home in Fraserburgh. *She* would have gone with John if he'd asked, despite her aching hips and knees; she'd have welcomed a chance to escape the stifling cottage and breathe the drizzly air all the way to town. She'd go anywhere with him. She'd go anywhere to clear this up. She closed her eyes and thought of the sea. The herring season had been good, and the Broch would be smelling of fish from the curing yards now. The fishwives would be striding about the town with creels on their backs, and the fishermen would be out on the water, setting their nets for the night, as if nothing had changed.

She went back in and prepared herself for another long evening.

***

It was dark when John returned. He'd been gone for hours; the guests had all left, thankfully, and she was alone again with Meggy.

'You're still up,' he said.

She'd never heard his voice so flat, never seen his eyes so dull and tired. The firelight glistened on his wet hair, on the beads of damp on his jacket, made shadows under his cheekbones.

'Where's Dr Jamieson?' she said. 'What happened?'

He let out a long, slow sigh as he sat. 'We got to Dr Jamieson's. He didna seem too pleased to see us. We interrupted his supper, I think – we could smell the meat.'

'What did he say?'

'I told him Meggy had died. He knew already – he said his apprentice had told him. I said there was a report going about ... that she was ... poisoned.'

Poisoned. She shook her head, eyes on John.

'Jimmy asked him to examine his sister's body, but the doctor said he couldn't do it without a warrant.'

'A warrant?'

'Aye. He told us to get a warrant from the baillie.'

'From Baillie Chalmers? At that hour?'

'Aye, Mither.' John was starting to sound annoyed. She pursed her lips and waited while he passed a hand across his face and sighed. 'So we went to Baillie Chalmers' house,' he went on, 'only first we called in to fetch Mr Grant.'

'What does Mr Grant have to do with it?' she asked, but she needn't have. She could imagine the scene: two farmers and a woman turning up at the grand home of the baillie late in the evening, asking for a warrant, with the suspicion of poison hanging about them. Lewis Chalmers was known to be a fair man, but he was an important man for all that, and a busy one. Lord knows, his servants might have turned them away.

'I dinna ken,' John said. 'I suppose James Grant is the kind of man the baillie would trust.'

She nodded. Mr Grant was a town-dweller with clean nails and clever speech – a dependable fellow, a man capable of smoothing the way with the authorities. Mrs Grant would have enjoyed the opportunity to parade his status in front of John.

'So we fetched him, and we all walked to the baillie's home.'

'Did he let you in?'

'Aye, he was kind.'

Any other day she would have asked him what it was like inside the home of such a grand man, but it seemed wrong to talk about such things while Meggy lay dead under her roof.

'And did he give you a warrant?'

John, leaning forward, rested his elbows on his knees and his chin in his hand. The firelight lengthened the shadows that his eyelashes cast upon his cheekbones, and her heart ached.

'He said that if all parties wished for an inspection, there was no need for a warrant.'

'Och!'

'He said we should go straight back to Dr Jamieson. So we did, but Jimmy left us; he had to collect things for the funeral.'

'And what did Dr Jamieson say? Why did he not come back with you to inspect the body?'

A bitter smile flickered across John's face. 'The doctor said, "Well, it's too late tonight." He said he'd do the inspection tomorrow.'

'Tomorrow! But Meggy's to be buried tomorrow.'

'He said he'd come in the morning, with Dr Coutts.'

'He'll need to come early,' she muttered.

'You should be abed, Mither,' John said, looking at her properly for the first time since he'd come home. He got up and bent to kiss her on the cheek, startling her. The damp wool of his jacket smelled rank, but she closed her eyes to breathe him in.

'I'll never sleep,' she said.

Chapter 37

Thursday 16 August 1827

Futteret Den

The chesting was held at the Lovies' home.

Widow Lovie put a coin in the coffin to pay the ferryman and closed her eyes in prayer.

James Walker, the square-wright, had built the coffin, and Meggy's mother and sister had rested her in it. Walker and John had placed the coffin upon a row of chairs in the but. Meggy lay there silently while her mother arranged the curls about her face and Jean smoothed out Meggy's white linen shroud with wind-chapped hands. The widow watched as Jean bent her frizzy ginger head over her sister, taking in every curve, every curl, every inch of white skin for the last time.

John had set planks of deal upon blocks of wood around the perimeter of the but to serve as seating. Last night, before he'd escaped to his father's home, Alex Rannie had set up a deal table in the centre of the room and placed upon it a bowl of clay pipes and tobacco. A candle flickered in the morning gloom.

Meggy's brother, Jimmy McKessar, blew in. He went straight to Jean and squeezed her hand. They looked down mutely at their sister.

The small room hummed with conversation. People streamed in through the door. They came and peered at Meggy and touched her body and clucked their tongues. Mrs Urquhart, the Wills, the Scotts, junior and senior. Little John Yule was still at his father's home. John Lovie stood by the door with his brother James, shoulder to shoulder.

Mr and Mrs Grant bustled in; Mrs Grant sat with the women while John gave her husband whisky. Grant ambled to the table, picked up a pipe, filled it with tobacco and lit it from the candle. Behind him, another neighbour strolled in with his whisky and took up a pipe. The air was heavy and sweet with smoke. Someone was reading from the Bible.

The widow was finding it hard to talk; she'd barely slept since Meggy's death and was caved in with worry. She sat in a corner, watching the stream of guests crowding into her home. Now and then, feeling a call to some sort of duty, she stood, but the effort of edging around so many people was too great, so she sat again with her eyes down and hands clasped. John was sidestepping around the guests, always moving. She raised her eyes each time he passed.

It was steamy inside, away from the freshness of the wind. The neighbours were whispering. A young girl – a local servant – was holding court. 'I passed by on the day she died,' she was telling her audience, who huddled close. 'I heard someone coughing and vomiting in the corn yard.'

'Did you see her?' old Mrs Scott said.

The girl shook her head. 'She was behind the hayricks.'

'It's a bad business,' Mrs Urquhart said. 'I sat with her just after she died. Her hands and feet were cold already. Her nails were blue.'

'Have you heard the reports?' the young servant girl whispered, loudly enough for the widow to hear across the room. 'They say she took poison.'

The hum about the room fell into silence at the girl's words, and the guests shifted their gazes to their feet. The men puffed at their pipes and swigged their whisky. Widow Lovie stared dully at the floor.

The clopping of horses outside broke in.

'It's Dr Jamieson,' said John, bolting through to the door.

There were voices outside, firm and authoritative. Instructions being issued and horses harrumphing. The door opened and two well-dressed gentlemen marched through the passageway into the room. They removed their hats and gazed about.

'Dr Jamieson.' The widow rose stiffly and reached for the hats. 'And Dr Coutts. Thank you for coming.' She glanced through the door, expecting John, but he did not come back in. She left the door ajar for him. She could hear him outside, murmuring to the horses.

James Grant strode across the room to greet the medical men. 'I'm glad you came in time,' he said. 'She's to be buried soon, and I half-expected you would not ...'

Dr Coutts's eyes strayed to the coffin. The guests fell back, clearing a path to Meggy. The doctors went to the coffin and looked down at the dead girl.

'You say there are reports of poison?' Dr Coutts said.

'Aye,' Henrietta rose to put a bony hand on the younger doctor's arm and then, seeming to remember her place, quickly withdrew it.

'We will need to open the body,' said Dr Jamieson.

'No!' Jean sprang to her feet.

'NO!' Henrietta grasped Dr Coutts's arm again, whimpering. 'You'll not open poor Meggy's body!'

Cut into Meggy? 'No,' the widow whispered.

Meggy's brother put an arm around Henrietta's shoulders and prised her claw from the startled doctor's arm.

'But you invited us here,' Dr Jamieson protested with a frown.

'We thought,' Jimmy McKessar said, as the hubbub subsided, 'that an *outward* inspection might tell if she died by poison.'

The doctors looked at each other and turned back to the dead girl's mother. 'It can't be done,' Dr Coutts said. 'We'd have to open the body.'

The voices rose again, loud and urgent. The widow looked out the door. John was standing there still, holding the horses' reins, listening.

'You'll not open Meggy's body,' Henrietta said, clutching her hair.

Dr Jamieson sighed. They were all glaring at him, a wall of resistance.

'Well then,' he said stiffly, taking the hat from the widow's outstretched hand and clamping it back on his head. 'We'll bid you a good day.'

He turned on his heel and strode out the door with Dr Coutts in his wake.

Chapter 38

Thursday 16 August 1827

FUTTERET DEN

By the afternoon the room was stuffy with tobacco smoke and body odour. The village folk were lined up tightly upon the deal seats like rows of corn. The din of two dozen whisky-soaked voices and the smoky air were giving Widow Lovie a headache. She longed to lie down somewhere dark and breezy, somewhere far away from Meggy McKessar and her family.

She closed her eyes and tried to remember a time when she had felt peace. Memories came and she dismissed them. They were all imperfect or, at best, fleeting: the pleasure of Meggy's company beside her in the kirk ruined by the Chessor girl; a good harvest offset by dread of the coming winter; the joy of a daughter's marriage spoiled by the prospect of losing her. Where was happiness? She thought of the silkiness of Elspet's wean – the downy head, the fringed half-circles of his sleeping eyes. The innocence of him. How lucky he was, to be unconscious of the world's troubles. Perhaps there could be no peace once there was awareness. The thought was depressing.

Mr Grant and Jimmy McKessar handed around a corn sieve piled up with biscuit, and John poured the rum. It was nearly over. Then Meggy's brother cleared his throat and called for silence, and the noise died. The widow pressed the heels of her hands into her eye sockets. Dimly, she heard Jimmy McKessar, his voice thickened with whisky, inviting the guests to touch the corpse for the last time before the coffin was sealed.

155

The braver folk rose first. The rustling of skirts and shuffling of feet replaced the earlier buzz of conversation as they filed past the coffin to take in a last glimpse of Meggy. The widow stayed in her seat with eyes closed. She didn't want another look. She heard padding feet, murmured prayers, now and then a cough, a sniff, a sob. She heard the lid being screwed shut, and the grunt as the men lifted the bier. She opened her eyes to see Meggy's brother and uncles carry it out through the door. She stood heavily and kicked one of the chairs upon which the coffin had rested until it toppled to the floor. The remaining guests followed suit. When she was satisfied that all the chairs in the room had been upended, she joined the procession as it filed out into the grim light.

Chapter 39

Thursday 16 August 1827

KIRKTON

There was a small gathering at the cemetery at Kirkton. Meggy was to be buried without fuss, as was the custom.

John Brown had steeled himself to bury her – Meggy, whom he'd known since she was a wean. He tried not to look at Henrietta, who was clinging to Jean's arm like a withered vine. Meggy's brother hunched beside Mr Grant and a smattering of neighbours. John Lovie and his black-clad mother were there too, standing apart.

John Brown was sober, and his usual good cheer was nowhere in sight. His son, Peter, had dug the grave with him. At Brown's age, the work was back-breaking, and he was grateful for Peter's help – but mostly, at a time like this, it was good just to have a loved one near. At least Meggy had died in the summer and she wouldn't have to wait for the ground to thaw – that was something. The earth lay open and waiting for her.

A damp breeze carried the cries of gulls in from the shore. The men lowered the coffin into the pit, and clods of soil thudded onto it as Brown and his son scooped and tossed the earth. Brown had buried many a young woman before her time. Some of them he'd known; many he had not. Meggy had been almost like a daughter. All that promise, all that beauty and charm, all that spirit: gone. He scraped and shovelled and thudded, and piled layer upon layer of earth upon her, until the ground was level and Meggy was no more.

Chapter 40

Friday 17 August 1827

FUTTERET DEN

'**J**ean,' said Widow Lovie.

'I've come for Meggy's trunk,' Jean said shortly; she had no heart for small talk. The widow held the door wider and let her inside.

She pushed into the kitchen and made for the kist in the corner. The room was empty without Meggy in it. It still smelled of her, though – of her death. Through the open door to the closet, Jean saw on the floor the patch of sand that covered the contents of Meggy's stomach. The widow still hadn't cleaned it up. She'd been sleeping in there, amid the fumes of Meggy's last digested meal, on the bedding that the girl had sweated and died in. This, from a woman who thought her son too good for a McKessar. Jean did not bother to hide her disgust.

The widow hovered behind her and offered tea, but Jean ignored her. She squatted, opened Meggy's trunk, brushed a hand over the folded clothing in it, then closed the lid.

'Is there anything else?' she asked.

'You can check the closet,' the widow said. She seemed to have shrunken in the last few days. Up close, Jean could see whiskers on her chin. Above the black of her widow's weeds she was grey: face, hair, lips. The only colour was in her eyes – like her son's, winter-sky blue. She wouldn't raise them to Jean's. Jean didn't care; the widow's worries were not her concern.

Jean stood up and bustled to the closet. The smell hit her, but she didn't flinch; it was Meggy's smell. Her dying smell. She lifted her

158

skirts and stepped over the sand-coated vomit. The bed was small and lumpy, heaped with blankets. She pushed the bedclothes aside and saw a handkerchief crumpled beneath the blankets. Jean picked it up, remembering; she'd found it on the day of Meggy's death and had intended to keep it, but she'd forgotten about it until now. The smell of it was vile; it was crusted together with her sister's vomit.

'You'll want this too,' the widow said, hovering outside the closet door. She held out a wrap. 'The wrap Meggy was wearing on the day she ...'

Jean swallowed hard and nodded. She took the wrap from the widow's hand and draped it over her arm. She withdrew from the closet into the kitchen and knelt by the trunk to put the wrap inside but hesitated as the smell of bile overwhelmed her. She inspected the wrap; it was Meggy's fancy one – too extravagant for a servant girl. There was a frill about the neck that gave her a pang. She'd noticed it that day they'd walked along the shore together to their aunt's place. Jean had envied her for it. *Oh, Meggy ...*

Jean sighed. 'The frill is slidery with her vomit.'

'You can use our washing tub.'

Jean rose and took Meggy's fouled items out of the cottage to the washing tub on the other side of the corn yard. It was a relief to get out of the stinking air.

A bucket of water from the well sat next to the tub; the widow must have fetched it earlier. Or maybe she'd sent Alex Rannie or the little boy; fetching the water used to be Meggy's job. Jean hoisted the bucket and sloshed water into the tub. She flung the handkerchief and wrap into the water and swirled them about. Rage boiled in her. *Why Meggy?* Her sister had been joy itself. Bold, playful, trusting. Too beautiful for her own good. Too young.

Why hadn't the widow fetched a doctor? Why hadn't her son called Meggy's mother? He'd had the opportunity. Four times Henrietta had passed the Lovie farm that day – *four* times, and they'd only alerted her on the last, when it was too late. Jean scrubbed with bare hands, feeling with disgust the water turning the dried vomit into slime. It was gummy and stubborn. She emptied the dirty water onto the ground and it splashed onto her skirts. She tipped a little more from the bucket into the washing tub.

After all that Meggy had done for that family. Jean dipped the handkerchief into the fresh water and scrubbed. The eyes she'd made at John Lovie. The promises he'd sworn to her, through his actions if not his words. How could he have let her suffer so long? How could his mother have sat by and watched her die? Meggy had always said the widow was kind to her. Meggy had been too trusting.

The slime wouldn't come out. The bucket was empty, so Jean trudged to the well to fill it. She carried the rattling, sloshing bucket back to the washing tub and threw the wrap and the handkerchief in one last time. Her hands were red by the time she finished scrubbing. What was the point? She'd never wear the wrap. She'd never use the handkerchief – not now. Maybe her sister Ann would find a use for them.

When she finished, she went back to the house. Someone had put Meggy's trunk into a handcart outside the door for her – John, perhaps, or Alex Rannie. The widow was still in the kitchen and her son was leaning against the dresser. He stood up straight when Jean entered. Unlike his mother, he had no trouble meeting her eye.

'Jean,' he said easily. He looked well-rested. Jean smelled oats; John had just eaten his brose. He hadn't lost his appetite, then.

'I've heard a report,' she said, 'that you bought poison from Mr Officer.'

She hadn't planned to say it, but John Lovie was looking so smug – so pleased with himself – that she couldn't hold the words back. She wanted to rattle him. But he barely flinched. She watched him closely, shaking with rage; his eyes flickered to his mother and then rested back on hers. They were blue and steady, fringed with black; sweet and cold. He didn't speak.

Jean faltered. 'My ... my mother is going to ask Mr Officer.'

John Lovie shook his head. 'Jean,' he said. 'Why should your mother go to such trouble? Hasn't she had trouble enough?'

'Aye. She's had trouble enough.'

'Tell her to wait till Tuesday next,' he said, placing a hand on Jean's arm. Jean drew back, but Lovie didn't seem to notice. 'Then I'll go to Mr Officer along with her.'

'My mother will do as she pleases,' Jean said, trembling. Then she flung a glare at the silent widow and backed out of the door.

***

At midday, Alex Rannie came in from tending the turnips to eat his dinner. There was tension in the air. He'd seen Jean McKessar leaving the cottage and wondered if she was the cause of it. Lovie was going out as the farmhand came in, but it seemed he barely noticed Rannie, such a foul mood was on him.

The widow was clattering about in the kitchen. The brose was already made; the master had eaten his share, and the cold leftovers sat congealed in the plate for Rannie. He sat on the deece and wolfed it down.

'What did Jean McKessar want?' he asked through a mouthful of brose.

'Meggy's things,' the widow said. 'She said ...'

'What did she say?'

'Nothing.'

The widow looked pained, clutching at her belly as if she was about to vomit.

161

'You're not sick?' Rannie said, alarmed.

'No.'

Not my business. He ate in silence, and the widow put before him a cup of milk. He nodded his thanks and slurped from it.

'On the day Meggy died ...' the widow said slowly, her back to Rannie, 'I went out and found her in the yard—' she broke off and shook her head. 'When you were at breakfast. I think she had been purging there.'

'Purging? In the yard?'

'Aye.' She nodded, turning to face him. 'I found her lying there, face-down in the yard.'

Rannie was mute, thinking of Meggy's suffering. He lowered his spoon and rubbed his eyes with a rough hand. He couldn't get the image of Meggy's misery out of his head: Meggy, vomiting in the closet, easing her bowels in the yard. She hadn't even made it to the midden to ease nature, or hadn't cared to. *I never was so unwell before*, she'd cried.

He pushed the bowl aside. The widow would eat the rest. Or maybe not; Rannie hadn't seen her eat in days. It wasn't his problem.

He emerged from the cottage and went out into the yard. It made him sick to the stomach to think of Meggy groaning and straining there. The poor, suffering lass.

He strode about, scanning the ground. There in the small yard, by the high stone wall, were three deposits of excrement. He bent to examine the first; it was unmistakably human. Meggy's. Bile rose in his throat. It was Meggy's shit he was looking at. Three piles of it: one thin and unformed, as if affected by physic; the other two dense and solid.

The enormity of what had happened weighed upon him. Meggy – bold, bright-eyed Meggy – had suffered and died. Three piles of shit were all that was left of her.

Chapter 41

Saturday 18 August 1827

Futteret Den

Widow Lovie rose at dawn as usual and fuelled the fire. John and Rannie were in the fields. Wee John Yule was at his father's home; she had thought it best to remove him – for now – from the place of death. She prodded the fire and found that the cavorting of the flames cheered her slightly. The last week had been unsettling, and she longed for a return to routine. She longed, more than anything, for peace of mind.

Life, until now, had asked little from her but duty. She'd had no choices to make; her days had been a series of prescribed steps. There were chores to be done, and she'd done them. She'd been expected to marry, and she'd married. Children had come – happily – but without any planning on her part. She'd raised them according to custom. She'd put up with hardship – slim harvests, back-breaking labour, snow-bound winters, her husband's fists – without ever dreaming pointlessly of alternatives. She had made her bed and she had lain in it.

She was not a philosopher. She wasn't interested in doubts or regrets. But the events of the past week wouldn't leave her alone. The cottage's emptiness was like a reproach; she found herself unusually troubled by the solitude.

She grabbed two buckets and clanked out with them into the bright morning. She hooked them to the yoke and rattled to the well. One by one, she attached the buckets to the rope and lowered them into the well until she heard the splash, then turned the handle to haul them back up, full. It was a familiar old routine; before Meggy, fetching the water had been *her* job. Perhaps now Futteret Den would be restored to the days before Meggy had flounced into her life. There was guilty comfort in the thought.

But as she hauled the buckets out of the well, her old bones creaked against the strain. How much easier life had been with Meggy there to share the load, after all.

What now? Would John replace her? *Will we have another pretty maid in our home?* Her mouth dried up at the thought, although she knew she'd soon sorely need the help. The pains that were worsening daily, spreading from her knees to hips, ankles, hands and back, told her so. But what girl would come to them now? If the rumours of poison got out, who would come near them?

She hurried back to the cottage with the buckets sloshing, wrested them from either side of the yoke, deposited them in the kitchen and went outside again. She didn't bother with tea; she'd eat and drink with John when he came in for breakfast – if he came in – if she could work up an appetite.

Instead, she went straight to the byre. The lowing of the cattle was soothing. The widow took a stool and placed it beside a beast, hushing it gently. She rested her forehead against its side and breathed in the familiar scent.

The previous day, she'd come upon John and Rannie by the barns. Rannie had been sweeping out the stables while John sat and cleaned the horses' gear. From a distance, it was a charming scene, an echo of happier times.

John had looked up when she approached. 'There's talk of suicide,' he said.

Rannie dropped the broom. 'Nay! Meggy would never!'

Never! Her hand flew to her mouth. Suicide was a terrible sin – the worst kind. She hated to think of Meggy committing such a crime. The girl had had her share of faults: she had teased the young farmhand and provoked them all with her shirking ... but *suicide!* Never. Meggy would never have done such a thing. The idea was appalling; she had pushed it from her thoughts.

Now alone in the byre, she wrapped her hands around the teats and pulled. Jets squirted into the bucket: tug, squirt, tug, squirt, tug ... the rhythm should have been comforting – like the well-worn prayers she recited in the kirk – but her heart refused to settle. If only John would talk. But he wouldn't – at least, not to her. He shared no more of his mind with her than did this cow whose milk she was extracting. At least the cow gives me milk, she thought bitterly.

And then she chided herself for her disloyalty. John gave plenty. He worked to keep her in comfort, day after tedious day, and never once did he grumble about it. He gave her food and shelter and company.

And love? Her heart thudded. Was she loved? She'd never wondered such a thing before; she had assumed it, she supposed, as a mother's right. Why doubt it now? All this worry – all this *thinking* – was driving her mad.

The moaning of a cow brought her back to her senses. Her mind had been wandering, her nonsense distracting her from the job at hand. 'Fool,' she muttered. She stood, carefully shifting the bucket away from the cow she'd been milking. The groaning was coming from a black hummel stirk. She edged around to the complaining beast, which exhaled a long, low moan and turned a leery eye at her.

There was a rattling at the door and the shuffling of boots. John came into the byre with Rannie.

'What is it?' John asked. 'We heard a bellowing.'

'She's got a sore belly,' she said.

John ambled over to the stirk, squatted and placed a hand on its side. His blue eyes shone in the dimness of the byre, and she had to turn away from the hurting of her love. The way he looked at those cows! She moved aside and fetched a tonic, pouring it into a spare bucket for the cow. She passed the bucket to John, who held it to the stirk's mouth. She stroked its neck while John guided the beast's head patiently into the bucket.

They listened as it gulped. There was no other sound. There was peace and calm in the byre, and John was smiling beside her.

***

Jean McKessar saw John Lovie across the field; he was hoeing the turnips, his sleeves rolled up, arms strong, streaked with sweat and dirt. She strode towards him, flapping like a scarecrow. She trampled the seedlings, not caring, and stood before him with her hands on her hips. He didn't look up. He thrust his hoe into the soil, put his head down and kept up the rhythm.

'John Lovie,' she said, moving right in front of him so it was impossible for him to wield the hoe without stabbing her in the foot. Her chest heaved with emotion. 'You bought *poison* from Mr Officer.' She spat out the word *poison* as if she could taste it on her own tongue.

John Lovie stood tall and planted the hoe in the earth, keeping a white-knuckled grip on the handle. His face was in shadow, the bright sun behind him blackening it.

'I did not buy any poison from Mr Officer,' he said, enunciating slowly as if he had rehearsed the words. 'I never saw any poison and I know nothing about it.'

Jean bit her lip. 'But—'

Lovie threw down the hoe and groaned like a beast. His passion, so out of character, so unexpected, startled her. She stepped back and stumbled on the uneven ground.

Lovie roared, 'I would rather have put a knife to my own heart than have given Meggy anything to injure her!'

Trembling, Jean crossed her arms over her chest. 'Mr Officer would not have lied ...'

Lovie grunted, picked up the hoe and passed a hand over his face. He took a deep breath and fastened blue eyes upon her. She stepped back again; his composure was more chilling than his rage.

'Some other person might have gone to Mr Officer, using my name,' he said, calm now, 'and bought the poison, and blamed *me* for it.'

Jean glared at him, furious. Lovie stared back.

'Well then,' she said with a wobble in her voice, 'I suggest you get one man and I'll get another, and we'll go together with them to Mr Officer, and he can point out to us who it was that bought the poison.'

Lovie's hatred wrapped around her. She forced her gaze to hold his; it seemed to her that a man's treachery *should* show in his eyes, but John Lovie's were inscrutable.

'It would be better to wait some time,' he said in the voice of a reasonable man. 'I hear tell that the body may yet be disinterred.'

Chapter 42

Saturday 18 August 1827

ABERDEEN

Reports of the unexplained and premature death of a young servant girl at Percyhorner had reached the procurator fiscal, William Simpson, in Aberdeen. There were rumours of poison abroad. It was Simpson's role to investigate sudden or suspicious deaths in the county, and the reports interested him greatly.

The dead girl, Margaret McKessar, was not much younger than his own wife. Her sudden illness and the rapid onset and escalation of her symptoms rang alarm bells. Suspicions of suicide had been raised – and now there were even uglier rumours circulating about her employer and the purchasing of poison, and whispers of that word almost too awful to speak: *murder*.

Simpson read the reports and considered carefully. It was up to him to investigate and decide whether a crime might have been committed. Whether to prosecute or not was *his* decision.

He had no wish to blacken the names of any innocents, but this case wouldn't leave him alone. As the son of a Fraserburgh minister of religion, Simpson was conscious of the disadvantages of the lower classes and anxious to see them treated justly, whether they were the victims or the accused.

Simpson had been five years in the role and was eager to deserve his substantial income. He had a reputation to build, a young family to support. He pondered the case carefully. It appeared that the girl had been hastily buried. This was the usual practice in the country, but it was a pity. She would have to be exhumed.

He made up his mind. He would leave for Fraserburgh first thing in the morning. Meantime, he would instruct Baillie Chalmers to arrange the disinterment – immediately.

Chapter 43

Saturday 18 August 1827

THE GRAVEYARD

The gravedigger Brown's customary merriness had long deserted him. Burying Meggy had been a grim enough affair, but to dig her up again ... he'd had to fortify himself with a generous swig of whisky.

He plunged his shovel into Meggy's grave. The soil had not had time to settle and was loose and friable; Meggy had been at rest for only two days. Brown's son, Peter, worked beside him, and again the old man thanked God for him. Again and again they stooped and thrust, stood, swung and flung the earth away from Meggy's grisly nest.

An early drizzle had been swept away by a breath of salt air that rolled straight in from the sea, bearing with it the weeping of gulls and long-dead sailors. The men sweated and grunted as they worked.

A small group of gentlemen hung back and watched with wooden faces. They were the medical men: the senior doctor, Jamieson, his colleague, Dr Coutts, and the young apprentice, Thomas Bisset. Two other apprentices fidgeted beside them.

James Grant, whose wife was a cousin to poor Meggy, stood by the grave and watched in silence. The procurator fiscal had appointed him to see that the men followed correct procedure, but it was clear from his frown that he would rather have been anywhere but here.

'Ghouls,' Dr Jamieson said, cocking his head at the crowd that had gathered in the old churchyard. His colleagues murmured in agreement. The knot of onlookers was growing. Some of the bolder folk

170

were edging closer, hoping for a better view. They were scattered amongst the headstones, wide-eyed, grey-faced, ragged, hungry.

Brown and his son were shoulder-deep in the grave. They plunged and swung, plunged and swung. Brown heard the buzz of chatter swell above ground; the spectators were getting excited.

There was a thud. They had reached the coffin. The crowd fell silent.

Brown shouted, 'Now!' and ropes were lowered. Brown and his son climbed out, sweating and mud-streaked, the men strained at the ropes, and the coffin arose from the earth like a shipwreck recovered from an ocean of mud.

The gentlemen huddled closer to the coffin, screening it from the greedy eyes of the bystanders. Dr Jamieson threw a glance over his shoulder. 'We must get her away from them,' he said.

'The outhouse,' Brown replied, and the doctors nodded.

Grant, looking as if he might vomit, led the way. The gravedigger and his son carried the coffin, one at each end, towards the barn of a farm building that backed onto the churchyard. Dr Jamieson followed close behind with Dr Coutts, Thomas Bisset and the other young apprentices. The onlookers trailed behind, elbowing each other aside for a glimpse of the coffin. Grant hurried into the outhouse ahead of the gravediggers to clear a benchtop for Meggy's body. The doctors came in after him and shut the door against the crowd.

'Here will do,' Grant said, and Brown nodded. He gave orders to his son, and they lowered the coffin to the ground. A draught sneaked in through the cracks of the barn, breathing damp chill onto the back of Brown's sweating neck as he bent over the coffin. Doctors Coutts and Jamieson stood back. Thomas Bisset and the young apprentices folded their arms. Brown unscrewed the lid and then, with a swift turn of the wrist, levered it open.

Grant gasped and put a hand to his nose. Peter's brow creased in disgust and Brown shot him a warning glance; he rearranged his features. Together they reached into the coffin to haul poor Meggy out. Her shrouded body *whumped* as they placed her on the bench. Brown folded back the shroud and rested his eyes on Meggy's face one last time before surrendering her to the doctors. Her face was bloated and ashen – not like Meggy at all.

He stepped aside to let the doctors move in on the body. Like vultures they flapped about her. His hands were shaking – from the drink or from emotion, he couldn't tell. The doctors struggled with Meggy's shroud, sending gusts of sour air through the room as they undressed her. Then she was naked, swollen like a maggot.

Dr Jamieson took his scalpel and sliced a neat vertical line down the girl's abdomen. Dr Coutts prised the edges of the opening apart, while Bisset held a bowl in readiness. Dr Jamieson reached into the abyss of Meggy's belly with a length of yarn. The stench of her decaying innards fouled the air.

'Tying off the stomach,' Jamieson explained to the apprentices, 'to stop the fluids from leaking out.' When he had finished tying, he applied his knife into the gash again, drew out a dark, slimed mass and dropped it into Bisset's bowl.

'The stomach,' Jamieson said. Bisset covered the basin with a cloth.

Jamieson reached back inside the cavity and withdrew another distended organ. Jamieson's and Coutts's eyes met over the body.

'The uterus,' said Jamieson, blinking. 'Complete with foetus.'

Chapter 44

Saturday 18 August 1827

M r Officer was just about to close the drugstore for the day when the door rattled and one of the local farmers strode in. Officer knew the man slightly; it was John Lovie's brother-in-law, George Yule. His boy worked as a cattle-herd on the Lovie farm. Officer's scalp prickled. The Lovie case had been dogging him in recent days, and he wanted none of it.

The men greeted each other warily. Yule was a stocky fellow, slow and heavy, with the stoicism of a man who had spent his life steeling himself against nature. An Aberdeenshire farmer: tough and pragmatic. Only none of his experience with lean harvests or sick cows or inclement weather would have prepared him for the horror and suspicion that faced him now.

'Have you heard the result of the inspection on the body?' Yule enquired stiffly, without preamble. Only a fool wouldn't know whose body he referred to. John Officer replied that he had not. He didn't ask to hear it; he didn't wish to know. He busied himself with his preparations for closing, making clear his desire to end the conversation.

George Yule ignored the hint. 'It's been reported in the country,' Yule said, 'that my brother-in-law bought arsenic from you.'

Officer stiffened. 'That might or might not be the case,' he said after a pause. 'If I am examined by the judiciary, I will tell the truth.'

Yule gazed at Officer with eyes so clear and candid – a farmer's eyes – that Officer felt himself blush. 'I don't wish to give you any information on the subject,' he muttered, turning away.

'I asked my brother-in-law about it,' Yule persisted. 'He denied that he bought poison from you.'

Officer shrugged.

'He said he'd not been in your shop since the beginning of May harvest this summer,' Yule said. 'He said he called in then to enquire about a scythe.'

'I do not recollect Lovie calling in about a scythe,' Officer snapped. 'Goodbye, Mr Yule.'

Chapter 45

Sunday 19 August 1827

Fraserburgh

William Simpson arrived in Fraserburgh early on Sunday morning. He took a carriage to Dr Coutts's house and sprang up the steps to the modest front door. Doctors Jamieson and Coutts were waiting for him.

The gentlemen ushered him into the chamber where the dead girl's organs lay. Dr Blaikie of Aberdeen was already there.

'Good day, sir,' Blaikie said, rubbing his hands.

Simpson nodded. 'Doctor.'

The procurator fiscal had mixed feelings about Patrick Blaikie's presence. Blaikie was a well-known figure in the medical world – an ambitious man from a successful and powerful family. His career, thus far, had been glamorous; he had served as a medical officer in the Royal Navy and had the distinction of being on board the ship that had exiled Napoleon. He lectured on anatomy at Marischal College in Aberdeen and boasted his own dissecting room. Only the previous year, he had taken up a controversial post as a lecturer at the Aberdeen Infirmary, against protests from older physicians who saw no need for clinical lectures in Aberdeen when medical students could just as well take their degrees in London or Edinburgh. They were not impressed by the ambitions of a young upstart like Blaikie, however clever or well-educated he might be.

But to Simpson's mind, Blaikie's opponents underestimated the man. The doctor was single-minded and astute, and determined to make his mark in the medical world. To date, he seemed to be succeeding.

'Shall we begin?' Dr Blaikie said. William Simpson noted his eagerness with some revulsion. He wasn't bothered about the doctor's ambition, and he had faith in his skill and experience, but he had one reservation about the doctor: he was known to be a resurrectionist. One of the growing cohort of medical men who procured the bodies of the recently dead to use for anatomical research. His presence here gave Simpson the creeps.

'Of course,' Simpson replied. 'There is no reason to delay, though natural scruples, of course ...'

But he put his scruples aside. The case was an extraordinary one, and therefore extraordinary diligence was required. Doctors Jamieson and Coutts were respected local surgeons, but they weren't experts when it came to chemistry. The procurator fiscal was not going to leave anything to chance; his investigation would be as thorough and scientific as it needed to be. His personal feelings were immaterial. This investigation must be done by the book. He relied upon the expertise of a man like Dr Blaikie.

Meggy's stomach and uterus had been preserved in Dr Coutts's house since the previous night. After the disinterment, Mr Brown and his son had returned the eviscerated body to its coffin and lowered it back into the grave. The doctors had moved from the barn to the adjacent farmhouse by the churchyard, one of the apprentices carrying the cloth-covered basin containing Meggy's stomach and uterus. They had waited there, the medical men and the dead girl's organs, through the long afternoon, until twilight crept in and the disappointed herds outside trudged back to their dreary lives.

At dusk, Dr Jamieson and the three apprentices had gone, leaving Dr Coutts alone in charge of the grim specimens. When darkness had driven the last of the thrill-seekers home, Dr Coutts had stepped out with the farmer, and the pair had walked with the bowl of Meggy's parts for the mile back to Dr Coutts's home in Fraserburgh. Dr Coutts had locked the grisly cargo in a chest and secreted the key upon his person.

Now Dr Coutts unlocked the chest and removed the covered basin of Meggy's organs.

'What do we have?' Dr Blaikie rubbed his hands.

'Young woman, twenty-two,' said Coutts. 'Sudden onset of vomiting and death five days ago. To all outward appearances, the body was in a good state of health. The circumstances are suspicious.'

Dr Coutts placed Meggy's organs upon the table. William Simpson stepped back; this was not his domain. He was here as a witness, to prevent any accusations that investigations had been improperly done. He shared none of Blaikie's enthusiasm for anatomical study.

The medical men showed no sign of the tension he felt. He was glad he'd been spared the business at the graveside, though. Viewing the organs here in Dr Coutts's rooms was one thing, but seeing a freshly unearthed body would have been quite another. The absence of the girl's body, Simpson supposed, made it easier to set human sensibilities aside and view the organs simply as scientific specimens.

'Uterus,' said Dr Jamieson. 'Pregnant.'

Dr Blaikie nodded. The pregnancy was obvious even to Simpson; the uterus measured eight inches in length. The surgeons gathered around as Dr Jamieson raised his scalpel and sliced into Meggy's womb. Inside was a curled-up baby, small but perfect.

'A girl,' said Dr Coutts.

'Four to five months,' added Blaikie, prodding the tiny limbs.

'The stomach,' said Dr Jamieson, and Coutts cleared the butchered womb and the foetus away.

The stomach sat in a bowl on the table before them. 'Normal size, no obvious pathology,' Dr Jamieson said. 'The knots I tied at both ends yesterday to seal in the contents are intact.'

'Some patches of inflammation on the external surface, particularly near the cardiac orifice,' Dr Blaikie observed. He nodded to Dr Coutts, who cut through the twine at each end. Then he incised the stomach and laid it open. Dark fluid poured from the fleshy sac – almost two cups of it. Shreds of dark-coloured material floated in the liquid. Dr Coutts poured the fluid into a separate container.

Dr Blaikie poked a finger into the organ. Simpson watched in disgust as he probed and stroked the interior of the stomach. 'No hard or gritty particles,' Blaikie said.

Instructed by Dr Blaikie, Dr Coutts measured out five ounces of rainwater. He poured it into the bowl containing the stomach, rinsed the stomach, and tipped the putrid water into a glass jug. The men bent closer to examine the cleaned-out organ.

'The villous coat is easily detached from the muscle,' Dr Blaikie remarked. He sliced off parts of the stomach and frowned in concentration as he turned them this way and that. Then he pushed the stomach aside and turned his attention to the two jugs of liquid: one containing the stomach contents; the other, the rainwater in which the stomach had been washed.

'Test the liquids,' Dr Blaikie said.

'For arsenic?' Dr Jamieson asked, and Blaikie nodded.

Dr Coutts placed the two containers onto the table. 'We'll need a third container filled with a solution of rainwater and arsenic,' said Dr Blaikie. Dr Coutts fetched another jug, poured rainwater into it, opened a small packet of white powder, tipped it in and stirred.

Dr Blaikie nodded his satisfaction. 'Now,' he said. 'We'll need fresh containers – small ones – for testing each.' When the glasses were all lined up, Dr Blaikie filled three with a small portion of each of the three liquids. Then he opened his bag and took out a selection of bottles. 'We shall test each of these with the three samples.'

The men watched attentively as Dr Blaikie added a drop of limewater to the glass of arsenic solution.

'Note that when limewater is added to arsenic,' Blaikie explained, 'a white precipitate appears. Now,' he went on, 'we'll see what happens when we add limewater to the fluids we took from the stomach.'

They leaned in eagerly as Blaikie dropped the powder into the samples of liquid.

'Nothing.'

The men drew back, disappointed. 'But the test is not definitive,' Blaikie said.

His colleagues nodded and looked to Blaikie for further instruction. 'We'll repeat the test with the other substances,' he said, and Dr Coutts busied himself with the preparation of further samples for testing. Methodically and carefully they poured and tipped and stirred, holding their breath as they watched the powders and potions dissolve into Meggy's swirling fluids.

'Inconclusive,' he said, when they were done.

William Simpson sighed.

Dr Blaikie glanced at him, as if surprised to find him still there. With a reassuring smile, he said, 'That's not the end of it. We'll also need to inspect the body for any signs that natural disease might have caused her death.'

Doctors Jamieson and Coutts looked at each other in dismay. Meggy had already been returned to the grave. She'd have to be dug up ... *again*.

Chapter 46

Sunday 19 August 1827

FRASERBURGH

Alex Rannie had been making himself scarce since Meggy's death. His father needed him to help prepare for the harvest, he told himself, but the truth was that Futteret Den frightened him. He helped out there most days, but he hadn't slept at the cottage again. The widow unnerved him, with her straight-backed silences and her pale eyes. He pitied her. The weight of it, knowing that Meggy had slipped away under her own roof, and no kin there to help or comfort her. No wonder she kept to herself. So Rannie did what he could, but he stayed outdoors as much as possible. The beasts and the neeps were his friends; he shunned all others.

Rannie was walking along a Fraserburgh street when a familiar figure approached. James Walker, square-wright, a neighbour and friend of the Lovies, was hurrying towards him. Rannie stopped and waited for him to cross the street.

They greeted each other, and Rannie waited for Walker to speak. The square-wright shifted from one foot to another, panting lightly from his exertions.

'How is Widow Lovie?' Walker asked, keeping his gaze on the horizon beyond Rannie's shoulder.

Rannie shrugged. 'I keep out of her way.'

'It's a sorry business.'

'Aye.'

'I made her coffin, you know – the McKessar girl,' Walker said. 'Your master came to see me that evening – the day she died – to ask me to make it. A sad business. He told me her illness came on all of a sudden.'

Rannie folded his arms and looked away. Because it was a Sunday, the town was quiet but for the shrieking of gulls and the occasional clopping of hooves upon cobbled streets. Here and there, people were going about their business. How lucky they were, to have no knowledge of Futteret Den, no memory of Meggy's dying sounds.

'He said she was well enough early in the morning, but she was vomiting all through the forenoon,' Walker said.

He sighed. 'Aye, that's right.'

Walker glanced at Rannie, then at his boots. 'He said there'd be reflections amongst her friends that ... that his people didn't think she was so ill, that they didn't call in her friends to see her before she died.'

'It was sudden,' Rannie said.

'Well, then.'

Was Walker counting him, Rannie, as one of John Lovie's 'people'? Surely not.

Walker said, 'Today I was at George Yule's place, borrowing a newspaper. While I was there, your master came in.'

Rannie waited.

'He said that the doctors dug up Meggy's body yesterday.'

'I heard the same.'

'I told Lovie a report was going around that he'd bought arsenic from Mr Officer in Fraserburgh.'

Rannie caught his breath. 'What did he say?'

'George Yule answered for him. He said that he saw Mr Officer last night, and Mr Officer denied that John had bought any poison, but—'

'Then that's an end to it.'

'But—'

'I have errands to run, Mr Walker. Good day to ye.'

Chapter 47

Sunday 19 August 1827

Fraserburgh

Meggy's corpse lay upon Dr Coutts's dissecting table, this time sporting a crudely stitched incision from ribs to pubis. Brown had lain her there tenderly with shaking hands. Inured as he was to death and decay, the matter of Meggy McKessar had become a recurring nightmare for him. The horror seemed to have no end. His tongue shrivelled for want of whisky.

Meggy had been almost kin to John Brown. He remembered her as a wean: such a bright little thing, blessedly ignorant of the lifelong suffering that the loss of a father would bring. And her mother, Henrietta, crushed doubly by her husband's departure and the mystery of his absence – trebly, by the demands of a fatherless daughter. Brown had pitied them – the whole family: the tragic mother; the defenceless child; the brother, trying so hard to be the man of the family; the fierce older sister. How would they survive now, with Meggy gone?

Like so many others before them had done, he answered himself with uncharacteristic bitterness. Death could come at you when least expected, he knew only too well. He'd seen young men cut down in the French wars, women perishing in childbirth, babies expiring from hunger, wizened mariners drowning at sea. Death was daily fare in his line of business, but still, Meggy's sudden end had shocked him, and to have to bear her recurrent unearthing and witness her decay was ... well, it was an abomination. If John Lovie was responsible for this, then may God torment his conscience for every one of the undeserved days he lived yet on this sorry Earth.

Shaking, Brown retreated from the doctor's home and tottered to the nearest public house.

***

William Simpson watched uneasily as the doctors turned their attention to the cadaver. This time they were opening her fully, sawing through ribs, prising apart her chest cavity. They bent over her, inspected her heart, lungs, liver, spleen, kidneys, bladder and bowel.

'The viscera appear natural,' Dr Jamieson remarked.

'Indeed,' said Dr Blaikie. 'But perhaps the poison – if it exists – has become entangled about the valve of the colon. Dr Coutts, would you boil some water?'

Dr Blaikie took a knife and excised the top of the colon, slicing it up while Dr Coutts set a pot of water to boil. When it was bubbling above the fire, Dr Blaikie put the pieces of bowel into the pot. They continued their inspection of Meggy's insides for twenty-five minutes while the chunks of colon boiled in the pot. Then Dr Blaikie fished the pieces out of the water to subject them to further tests with his potions.

'Nothing,' he said, after he had applied his various chemicals and inspected each result in turn. 'No traces of arsenic.'

'And yet ...' the procurator fiscal spoke up.

'And yet.' Dr Blaikie frowned. 'The circumstances ...'

The men stood together in silence, thinking.

'We'll send her stomach and its contents to Edinburgh,' Dr Blaikie concluded, 'for further investigation.'

Simpson nodded. Dr Coutts poured the remaining liquids into two separate phials and sealed and labelled them. He gave one to Dr

Blaikie and the other to William Simpson. He also placed the sliced-up stomach into separate phials, sealed them, and handed one to Blaikie and the other to Simpson. It wasn't over yet.

Chapter 48

Sunday 19 August 1827

FUTTERET DEN

Elspet blustered in like a gale from the sea.

The widow, hunched in her armchair by the hearth, did not stir.

'Is it true?' Elspet said, squatting at her feet. 'Is it true that John's been arrested?'

The widow rested her chin on her hand and tried not to hear Mary Yule's wailing.

Elspet deflated into the spare armchair – John's chair. 'It's true, then?'

Mary sniffed. 'My husband has gone to the Broch for news.'

Elspet shook her head as if trying to clear it. She searched about for something to say. 'Where are they holding him?'

'At the inn,' Mary said.

'Not the gaol, then,' Elspet said quietly. 'That's something.'

'I suppose you're pleased,' the widow sat up sharply and glared at Elspet. Her daughter's eyes were bloodshot. 'Meggy brought us trouble, just as you said she would.'

'Mither!' Elspet said, but for once she seemed unable to speak more.

'All will be well,' Mary whispered. 'My husband will see to it.'

Chapter 49

Monday 20 August 1827

Fraserburgh

The Saltoun Inn stood three storeys high on the perimeter of Saltoun Square, in the heart of the Broch. Alex Rannie had hurried there when he heard the news of his master's arrest. John Lovie's misfortune would be a trial for the widow, and Rannie had felt it his duty to help where he could. He had set aside his misgivings, then, and borrowed one of his father's horses so that he might get the encounter over as quickly as possible.

The inn was something of a landmark, a stately meeting place for respectable folk. That the messenger-at-arms had chosen to hold Lovie in custody here was a good sign, Rannie thought. If the law had really thought him a foul murderer, wouldn't they have thrown him into the gaol under the town hall, where the stocks still stood outside as a reminder of bygone days of cruel and summary justice?

Rannie tied the horse's reins to the post outside the inn. He knocked the soil from his shoes at the grand entrance and went in, cap in hands. He felt dirty and clumsy, and wished he could be anywhere but here. He followed the hallway down to the parlour, where a maid greeted him politely. Rannie asked about John Lovie, stumbling upon the word 'prisoner'. The maid took him up creaking timber stairs to the bedrooms. The hall was dim and smelled of furniture polish.

Rannie knew immediately in which room Lovie was captive, for there was a man stationed outside the door. It was the messenger-at-arms: one of the Milnes, though in his distress he couldn't re-member which. The man stood and greeted him.

'I want to speak to my master, John Lovie,' Rannie said.

The messenger-at-arms nodded affably and jangled a key. He un-locked the door and pushed it open into the prisoner's room.

John Lovie was seated in a straight-backed chair by the window, the light behind him. 'Aye, aye, Rannie,' he said, smiling and rising in greeting.

The room was small and neat, light and comfortable.

'What is to be done?' Rannie blurted.

Lovie shrugged. 'It's a misunderstanding that will be soon settled.' He waved a hand around the room – the bed, the washbasin, the curtained window. 'I'm comfortable, as you can see.'

Rannie took a deep breath. 'I've heard rumours,' he said, and the look that John Lovie shot him – eyebrow arched, eyes steady – stilled his tongue.

'I've come to ask for your instructions about the farm,' Rannie said after an awkward pause to inspect his fingernails. They were filthy.

John thanked him with a nod. 'My brother-in-law George Yule has been here with the same purpose,' he said. 'He will take care of the grounds in my absence.'

'Aye, then,' Rannie said, the weight lifting from his shoulders.

'Rannie,' John Lovie said, fixing him with his blue-eyed stare. 'If you are examined about this business, you should tell the truth.'

'I will,' Rannie said.

But what *was* the truth?

Chapter 50

Monday 20 August 1827

Futteret Den

For Widow Lovie, the biggest shock came when word arrived that John was to be taken to the Tolbooth at Aberdeen. Until that point, it had seemed that order and normality *must* soon return. George Yule had warned her that John would be transferred to prison – the messenger-at-arms had told him so – but she hadn't believed him. It hadn't seemed possible.

'The Tolbooth!' she cried, clutching the back of her chair.

'Sit, Mither, and be calm,' Elspet said, taking her arm and trying to guide her onto the chair.

She snatched her arm away. 'How can I be calm? How can I sit?' she wailed, but she folded herself into the chair nevertheless, wrapping her arms around herself.

Mary was weeping loudly. 'That terrible place!'

'It may not be as bad as they say,' Elspet said faintly.

The widow's throat was too constricted to reply, but she glared at her daughter. She knew about the Tolbooth. People said that the gaolers kept it squalid on purpose, so as to discourage folk from committing crimes. That vile and stinking dungeon.

She moaned, pressing her wet face into her apron. She'd known hardship and loss before, but *this* – this business had unmoored her. She'd been a smug fool, a wretched ingrate. She hadn't realised how contented she'd been, or should have been. Six children grown to adulthood, a long-term tack on the farm, a roof that didn't leak, healthy cattle, a team of horses, and a son who cared for her: all those blessings she had failed to count. Gone now, and what if her own complacency was to blame?

She hadn't always wanted a quiet life. As a girl, she'd loved the sea for its wildness, its unpredictability. She'd loved it best after a storm, when waves would tear at the beach, snatching driftwood and rocks and stranded fish back into its belly. She'd loved its vastness and its power. Now, though, she wondered how she could ever have admired it. So pitiless it was. She felt, now, as if the ocean had come ashore and seized *her*; she was sinking and drowning. She wanted nothing but peace. *Peace, God help me.*

Mary Yule sat beside her, damply – annoyingly – clutching her hand, while Elspet paced about the kitchen with her baby squirming upon her shoulder. Where once there had been Meggy and John and the dour farmhand and the wee boy, now there was only a broken old widow, two grieving farmwives and a fussing wean. Where there had been passion and spirit and humour and warmth, now there was only misery and death.

'They'll want to hang him,' she said, setting off another of Mary's howls.

'Stop it,' Elspet remonstrated, whether to her mother or sister, it was impossible to tell.

'He's innocent,' the widow said, staring Elspet fully in the eye, daring her to contradict, knowing she would not. 'My boy is innocent.'

Elspet thrust out her impressive jaw and shifted the baby to her other shoulder and did not speak.

'Innocent!' she hissed again at Elspet, who was burying her face in the doughy warmth of her baby. Taking comfort from her child. A mother's love, the widow thought bitterly. When all else failed, a mother's love was all that remained.

Chapter 51

Tuesday 21 August 1827

Aberdeen

L ate in the summer they took him to the Tolbooth at Aberdeen.

The prison could be seen from afar, its spire rising, spear-like, into the evening sky. The grim chamber grew closer as the carriage, bearing its manacled prisoner, rumbled into Castlegate. The carriage stopped in the broad square, between the elaborately carved hexagonal Mercat Cross – where once Jacobite rebels had proclaimed the Young Pretender king – and the imposing sandstone façade of the Tolbooth Prison.

Twilight cast shadows upon the stark planes of the building. A crenellated tower – from which rose the spire – was flanked by a broad, rectangular wing on each side, three storeys high. A double staircase wound from the street up to the base of the tower, its two arms meeting at the arched door.

If John Lovie's sojourn at the Saltoun Inn had been comfortable, the situation was about to change. He was led in handcuffs up the stairs to the wardhouse, past a sundial bearing the motto *Ut umbra sic fugit vita*. As flies the shadow, so does life. With a guard at each side, he clanked along the stone corridor and up a narrow spiral staircase.

The newcomer's wretchedness was a drop in the ocean. For two hundred years, prisoners had shuffled along these flagstones with leaden hearts. Two centuries of woe. The county folk had grown up with stories about the Tolbooth; they were legendary. Some were merely ghoulish fables of ghosts and revenge and despair; exaggerated fantasies, invented for whisky-fuelled fireside entertainment. They were the sort of stories that Meggy had been fond of telling in the evening, while the widow knitted and John Lovie smoked and the loons drank it all in.

But some of the stories were true. It was said that when the Laird of Strathbogie had declared Bonnie Prince Charlie king in the uprising of 1745, he had ordered the doors of the Tolbooth to be cast open, and all the prisoners had poured out of their cells to the joyful ringing of all the town's bells. But then the Duke of Cumberland had ridden into town and posted troops on the tower to watch out for the Jacobite rebels, and when he had quashed the rebellion, he had brought them back to the Tolbooth to be interrogated.

The prison had an even darker side that was spoken of in whispers in the county. There were stories of corrupt merchants and magistrates who had conspired to steal children in broad daylight and secrete them in the Tolbooth before selling them as slaves in the Americas. It was said that the ghosts of the children who perished in custody could still be heard in the Tolbooth, keening for their lost parents.

Two hundred years of suffering – and on it went. A new courthouse had been built, and wings had been added and renovated. But the wretchedness remained.

The warder rattled his massive key in the lock, swung the iron-bound door open, and thrust the prisoner into his cell. Broken men lined the stone floor, fouling the air. An iron bar stretched from one end of the cell to the other. The prisoners hunched against the walls with legs outstretched and ankles shackled to the bar. Tiny window slits, high in the wall, let in the feeblest of light.

Somewhere in a nearby cell, the exciseman and forger Malcolm Gillespie languished, waiting for fate to catch up with him.

Into this scene of despair, John Lovie was cast and bound.

Chapter 52

Wednesday 22 August 1827

FRASERBURGH

At Fraserburgh the twenty-second day of August, eighteen hundred and twenty-seven years; In presence of Lewis Chalmers Esquire Baillie of Fraserburgh, and one of His Majesty's Justices of the Peace for the county of Aberdeen.

Compeared Margaret Watson, or Lovie, residing at Percyhorner (also called Futteret-den, Mains of Phingask, or Burnside) Parish of Fraserburgh or Parish of Pitsligo, and county of Aberdeen, Widow of George Lovie, Farmer, who being judicially examined declares that her son John Lovie lives in family with her. – that Margaret McKisser or McKessar came to their service at Martinmas last – that the witness and her son John are both Tacksmen of the ground, and her son manages out of doors and the witness in the house ... That since Whitsunday last, the family consisted of the witness, her son John, Margaret McKessar, Alexander Rennie and her Grandson John Yule – that for Breakfast, Pottage was generally made in the kitchen by McKessar and the servants and John Lovie partook of them in the kitchen and afterwards, John and McKessar would get a cup of tea from the witness in the other room of the house, this tea being made by the witness for her own breakfast. That McKessar slept with the witness in a closet off the kitchen. That the witness had no reason to think that John and McKessar were too strong together nor that McKessar was with child.

***

'She complained of thirst,' Widow Lovie said. 'I made her some strong tea and took it in to her.'

The baillie nodded, smiling. She warned herself not to be taken in by his kindly air. Lewis Chalmers was part of the system that was trying to hang her son, and he would trick her into incriminating John if she wasn't careful. His solicitousness had caught her off guard. She had to tread warily.

'And then?'

'She vomited it up.'

Despite herself, the widow yawned. More than a week since Meggy's death, and she'd hardly slept. She felt a hundred years old. It had been a long day; the baillie had taken her, step by plodding step, through the events of that dreadful morning already, and she wondered how much more of it she could take. Her thoughts strayed – as always – to her son, rotting in the Tolbooth. She'd sent money for his food; she hoped he'd received it, but she had no way of knowing. At night when she lay on her straw mattress, she could think of nothing but John crumpled up on the flagstones of the prison floor. The thought of his misery was more than she could bear.

She had never in her life done so much talking. She had told the baillie about Meggy's attack of dysentery three weeks ago and had recounted in minute detail her own movements on the fatal morning: how Meggy had tended the fire, fetched the water and yirned the milk, how she had milked the cows herself. How she had found Meggy lying face-down in the yard. So much detail. Why did it matter? It wouldn't bring her back.

But the baillie wanted more.

She went on. 'At about one o'clock she complained of thirst again and I took her more tea. She sat up in bed and drank it.'

'Did she vomit again?'

'No, she fell back. I thought she had fainted.'

'Is that when you sent for her mother?'

'Aye. I saw Meggy's mother going along the road, so I sent my grandson for her, and she came immediately. And after she came in, Meggy breathed a little and then died.'

'Did anyone else see Margaret McKessar during her illness?'

She thought for a moment. John had done his best to avoid seeing her, scurrying to the but with his tea. And Rannie? He had been lurking in the kitchen and must have heard the terrible noises from the closet, but had he actually laid eyes on Meggy while she was dying? She shook her head. 'No.'

'Did you ever observe her to have difficulty breathing?'

'No.'

'Did you touch her before she died? Did she feel cold?'

She looked up, puzzled. Was the baillie accusing her of mistreating her servants? The fire was always lit and the servants were well clothed. She resented the implication. And yet ...

'Her hands were cold,' she said reluctantly. It was a terrible thing, to tell a lie; she couldn't do it – not yet. Not while God was her judge. 'I didn't feel any other part of her.'

The baillie nodded mildly. His inscrutability was getting on her nerves. 'Was there any cold sweat upon her?'

'I didn't notice any.'

'What was the colour of her lips?'

She closed her eyes and tried to remember. She saw Meggy, lying back on the closet bed in her rumpled white shift, her brown curls in a tangle. She heard Meggy's moans and smelled her vomit. It was dim in the closet. She couldn't remember the colour of her lips.

'I dinna ken.'

Baillie Chalmers rested his elbows upon his desk and his dimpled chin on his fingertips. 'How was McKessar the previous night?'

Meggy, eating her potatoes, humouring William Park, throwing glances at John. Warm in the bed beside her. She remembered *that* clearly. 'She was well. She slept beside me in the closet and was quite well.'

'Mrs Lovie,' the baillie said cautiously, leaning in to her with gentle eyes, 'Did you ever hear Margaret McKessar talk about making away with herself? Did you ever hear of her purchasing drugs?'

'Never!' she cried, half rising. The thought, ever since John had suggested it, had gnawed at her. It sickened her. And yet ... if Meggy had died by her own hand, then she could not have died by John's. And if the court saw that it was so ... she put a hand to her head, stricken. Would it be a contest, then, between Meggy's soul and John's life?

'Had any of your son's cattle been unwell in recent times?' the baillie hammered on.

'Cattle?' She sat back again, bewildered by the change of subject. The air knocked out of her, she sagged against the back of the chair. 'Cattle?'

Lewis Chalmers nodded.

'Well,' she said, wishing she knew the rules of this game, 'I believe there was a stirk that had a swelling in the back about a month after Whitsunday last. It was ill for a day or two.'

'A stirk? Did your son ever rub its back with anything?'

'Rub its back? He might have done.' Or had Milne bled it? It was hard to remember, with so much work always waiting to be done. Why would she keep track of what cows were bled and what were rubbed, which beasts had vermin and what needed feeding? That was John's work. 'There was a calf unwell too, with vermin on its back. He might have rubbed it with the same kind of stuff.'

'When was this?'

'Like I said, the stirk was about a month after Whitsunday.'

'And the calf?'

She rubbed her temple. It had started to throb. 'I dinna ken. About a week after that, I suppose.'

'I see.' He tilted his head and smiled. 'So, perhaps late June or early July?'

The widow shrugged. 'I dinna ken.'

The baillie smoothed his thick dark hair back from his high forehead and said, 'Mrs Lovie, did you *see* your son rubbing the cattle?'

She considered, frowning. Had she seen it? 'No,' she said at last.

'How did you know that your son rubbed the cattle?'

'John *told* me about it.'

'I see,' the baillie said again.

He said it with an eyebrow raised. What did that mean, *'I see'*? What did he see? Did he think she was lying? Did he think *John* was lying? John wouldn't have lied to her about rubbing the cattle, would he? *Why didn't I pay more heed?*

'Have there been any other sick cattle?' the baillie was asking.

She said more firmly, 'Only at the end of last week, a black cow was unwell with a sore belly.'

'Did your son rub it with anything?'

The widow shook her head and regretted it; the movement aggravated the growing ache in her head and neck. 'He only gave it a drink of oil.'

'Mrs Lovie, have there been rats or mice on the farm since Whitsunday?'

'Rats? I might have heard some, once,' she said, warily. 'I caught two in a trap.'

'Has anyone laid poison for the rats about the farm?'

'Not lately,' she said. 'Not to my knowledge.'

The baillie's voice was mild, but she noticed the narrowing of his eyes. It frightened her. What was she saying? If only she knew which words would hurt John and which would save him.

'When was poison last laid there?' Baillie Chalmers asked.

'It would be more than a year ago,' she said, her voice husky. 'I put it in the kiln barn myself. But I didn't see that it killed any vermin.'

She watched as the baillie's pen scratched away. With all this talk of vermin, his bright, dark eyes and whiskers and his long face put her in mind of a rat. She had to stop herself from letting out a sob of laughter. It was no use getting hysterical.

'My son is a good man,' she said suddenly.

The baillie looked up, surprised. 'Has he taken any physic since Whitsunday last?'

Didn't you hear me? she wanted to shout.

'A few times, I think,' she said with a dismissive wave, stung.

'When was the last time?'

'Oh.' She sighed. John had said something about jalap. 'I believe it was about three weeks ago. He took some jalap.'

'I see,' Baillie Chalmers said again, and his pen scratched the paper. No, you don't, the widow thought, irritably. You don't see.

'Was this about the time that McKessar had the dysentery?'

'I suppose it was. I suppose it was just before that occasion.'

'Did she suffer from dysentery on the day she died?'

She covered her face with her hands. 'In the forenoon she arose a few times from her bed and went out a little,' she croaked through her fingers. 'She *might* have been easing nature. I don't know if she had dysentery.'

The baillie bent his head over his papers. The widow closed her eyes and listened to the sound of the pen scratching like rats in the kiln barn. She could not comprehend any of it. Was she being accused of wrong-doing? Was Meggy? And why had they put John in the Tolbooth?

'Mrs Lovie, can you read and write?'

'You know I cannot.'

Baillie Chalmers nodded. He cleared his throat and read her declaration aloud. It felt odd, to hear her own words coming from his tongue. They sounded wrong, though she knew they weren't.

'... all which is truth, and that she cannot write,' he concluded, placing the document on the desk and glancing up at her.

'Yes, yes.'

'Thank you, Mrs Lovie.'

This was a dismissal, at last. She rose on stiff legs. 'Baillie Chalmers, do you have a son?'

A pause. 'I have two small boys.'

'Then you know what it is to love a child.'

For a moment it seemed that he would not respond. She felt she had achieved some small victory as she lifted her chin and turned to leave. Then the baillie's voice arrested her.

'Henrietta McKessar knows it too,' he said. 'Remember that, Mrs Lovie.'

Thomas Hodge, keeper of the courthouse of Aberdeen, who resided in that establishment, received a message from the procurator fiscal William Simpson a day or so after the investigations into Meggy's organs had been completed in Fraserburgh. His instructions were to make a wooden box and paint the address 'Adam Rolland Esq Crown Agent Edinburgh' upon it. Thomas Hodge did as he was asked, and a short time later, Simpson visited the courthouse in person. He was bearing two glass bottles, each sealed and bearing a label. The procurator fiscal drew Hodge's attention to the seals. On inspecting them carefully, the keeper agreed that the seals were intact and bore the impression 'W.S.' While Simpson watched, Hodge carefully packed the two bottles with coarse flax into the custom-made box, screwed down the lid and tied up the box with rope. Carrying the box, Hodge walked with Simpson to the mail coach office, where Hodge arranged for it to be taken to Edinburgh.

It was a grisly business and an unusual one, even for a man in his station. He had no doubt that he would know the box again if he saw it.

Chapter 53

Thursday 23 August 1827

ABERDEEN

At Aberdeen

The 23d day of Augt 1827 Years

In presence of Alexander Dauney Esq L.L.D.

Sheriff-Substitute of Aberdeenshire

Compeared John Lovie Farmer in Percyhorner, parish of Fraserburgh or parish of Pitsligo and County of Aberdeen unmarried, aged 42 years, who being judicially examined declares that a young woman named Margaret McKessar entered to the declarant's service at Martinmas last and continued in it up to the time of her death which took place on Tuesday ...

—From precognition against John Lovie for the crime of murder

***

'Mr Lovie, you are facing serious charges of administering poison to Margaret McKessar on the fourth of August and the thirteenth or fourteenth of August, causing her death. Anything you say may be used against you,' said William Simpson, 'and you may decline to answer. Do you understand?'

'Aye,' said John, favouring William Simpson with a mild smile. The procurator fiscal was surprised at Lovie's composure; it was almost as if the prisoner was trying to put *him* at ease.

Lovie had spent two nights in the Tolbooth. His skin was grey and stubbled, and he reeked with the stink of a man who had spent forty-eight hours stewing in his own sweat. Simpson was familiar with the cells; they were hot and crowded, and the air was thick with body odour. And yet when the warder had delivered Lovie to the office, the prisoner had appeared unperturbed. He had smoothed his hair with a greasy palm, drawn back his shoulders and seated himself comfortably.

Simpson gestured to the gentleman by his side, an elegant old man with a high forehead and a receding chin. 'This is the sheriff-substitute, Mr Dauney.' The old man raised his heavy-lidded eyes to Lovie's. 'In the absence of the sheriff, who does not reside in Aberdeenshire, Mr Dauney will hear your declaration. The seriousness of the charge against you means that the case will be heard in the High Court if it comes to trial.'

'Of course.'

'The Circuit Court will be in Aberdeen in late September, so we're anxious to expedite the investigation,' Simpson explained.

'As am I,' replied the prisoner.

Simpson regarded him curiously. John Lovie was leaning forward with his elbows on the desk and his hands clasped earnestly. They were rough, meaty, labourer's hands. There was nothing dangerous in his appearance.

'These other two gentlemen,' Simpson gestured to the two smartly dressed men sitting at a discreet distance from the desk, 'are here to witness your declaration.'

'I understand, sir.'

The chamber was cool and calm. Its dark wainscoting and heavy polished furniture made it possible for Simpson to ignore the chaos and squalor of the cells above, though they were never far from his consciousness.

'If I'm satisfied that there's enough evidence against you, you'll be indicted and tried at the Circuit Court. Rest assured that you'll be entitled to legal advice if the matter proceeds. You will be furnished – free of charge – with legal assistance throughout the proceedings.'

John Lovie raised an eyebrow. 'Free?'

'The Scottish legal system is a matter of pride for our country,' Dauney said.

Lovie smiled at the old gent. Simpson frowned. Granted, Dauney was inclined to pomposity, but Lovie, he felt, had no right to be amused at his expense. The sheriff-substitute was a wise old bird who, despite his pretentions, lent the proceedings gravitas.

'In a case of such *seriousness*,' Simpson said, 'if you should plead not guilty, you may apply for a senior advocate. The dean of the Faculty of Advocates would assign an experienced man to your case ... and he would be obliged to serve you.'

'I am not guilty.'

'In that case ...'

'Let us proceed,' said Dauney.

The procurator fiscal settled back into his leather-padded chair and cleared his throat. It annoyed him that the prisoner seemed more at ease than any of them, with the possible exception of Dauney. Dauney, meanwhile, had dipped his pen into the ink and was waiting to begin.

'How long had Margaret McKessar been in your service?' Simpson asked.

'She came to me at Martinmas last, and she continued in my service until her death.'

'Did you have carnal connexions with her?'

'No.'

'Did she ever tell you she was with child?' He eyed the prisoner closely. 'Did you know that a female foetus of about four months old was found in her womb?'

'No.' Lovie shook his head. 'I never heard such a thing until now. She never told me she was with child, and I had no suspicion of it.'

Simpson tried to catch Dauney's eye, but the gentleman's head was bent over his papers. Lovie's expression was impossible to read. If indeed the prisoner had only now learned of McKessar's pregnancy, he was doing a remarkable job of hiding his surprise.

'Did you see Jean McKessar on the day after her sister died, and did Jean McKessar question you about her sister's being with child?'

'She never said anything about Meggy being with child.'

Lovie's gaze was steady. He might have been sizing up the grass, deciding whether it was ready to cut. He was so sure of himself. Simpson shifted uncomfortably; he was accustomed to hearing lies, but rarely did a man lie so affably and with so mild and cool an eye.

He changed his approach. 'Did you buy jalap from John Officer a few weeks ago?'

Lovie nodded. 'I bought it once. I cannot tell you exactly when.'

'Why did you buy it?'

'I bought it as a physic for myself. One of my horses had run away with a cart and thrown me down. It rubbed the skin off my back and shoulders.'

'How did you take the jalap?'

'I took it – one fourth part – mixed with cold water for my hurt.'

'Where did you drink it?'

'In my own house.'

'Did anyone see you drink it?'

Lovie shrugged, turning up his palms. 'I cannot say.'

'Did you take it on medical advice?'

'No. I took the jalap of my own accord and not by anyone's advice.'

Simpson steepled his fingers and frowned. 'Did you take anything else for your injury?'

'I also took a dose of salts, about two weeks after taking the jalap. I bought the salts out of Mr Officer's shop about two weeks after I bought the jalap. Nothing else.'

Simpson suppressed a sigh. The case against Lovie had appeared straightforward, but he could see now that it would not be so. The glibness of Lovie's replies needled him. What if the prisoner was telling the truth?

'What did you do with the remainder of the jalap?'

'I threw it out of the door of the house.'

'Did anyone see you throw it out?'

'I cannot say.'

'Did you ever give the jalap or the salts to Margaret McKessar or any other person?'

'I did not.'

'Do you recollect that when you bought the jalap from Mr Officer's shop that you enquired about poison?'

'No.'

'Did you *ever* go to Mr Officer's shop to buy poison?'

A faint line appeared between Lovie's brows, but he quickly erased it. 'A few days before Meggy's death, I went to Mr Officer's shop and asked for some stuff to kill vermin,' he said smoothly. 'Mr Officer asked if the stuff I wanted was for killing vermin on sheep, and I told him it was for killing rats and vermin upon black cattle.'

Simpson looked up sharply. Cattle? Lovie's account didn't add up. Simpson was no farmer, but he'd been interviewing witnesses all day and he'd learned a thing or two about using arsenic about the farm. He made a note to check John Officer's evidence again. Was Lovie lying? It was impossible to tell.

Simpson questioned him further about the poison. In what form did he buy it? Was the word 'poison' written on it?

'The shop boy took down the poison at his master's orders,' Lovie said. 'He gave it to me in two small paper parcels. I didn't notice whether the word "poison" was written on them.'

Simpson leaned forward. 'On that occasion, was the word "arsenic" used by you or by Mr Officer or the shop boy?'

'I don't recollect,' Lovie said, raising his shoulders and wrinkling his brow with an apologetic smile.

'What was in the parcels?'

'A whitish powder.'

'What did you do with the poison?'

'I took it home and mixed a little more than half of it with cold water in a saucer, and then rubbed the backs of my cows with it—'

'How many cows are there?'

There was the slightest hint of exasperation in the prisoner's shrug. 'Four cows, a black hummel stirk and a black hummel bull calf. They were all afflicted with the vermin.'

'When and where did you rub the backs of the cows?'

'In the byre twixt seven and eight in the evening.'

'Did anyone see you rub the cows?

'Only my mither.'

'Only your *mother*.' Simpson paused, meeting Lovie's eye. He reminded himself of his duty to remain impartial, but his scepticism was threatening to reveal itself. In his profession he dealt often with lies, but still it was not always easy to identify them. 'No-one else can confirm this, then? Not your servant, Alex Rannie?'

'No.' Lovie ran a hand through his hair. 'Rannie was away at his father's.'

'Did you tell Rannie you had rubbed the cattle?'

'No.'

'Did *anyone* else know that the cattle were afflicted with vermin?'

'Only myself, the young cattle-herd, John Yule ... and my mither.'

'I see,' said Simpson. 'Strange, don't you think, that Alex Rannie knew nothing about the vermin?'

Lovie shrugged.

Simpson sighed and let it drop. 'Did you use all of the mixture on the cattle?'

Lovie shook his head. 'No.'

'What did you do with the rest of it?' Simpson asked.

'That same evening, I mixed the rest of it with milk, put it in the same saucer, and put the saucer upon the couples of the kiln barn, and upon an old sieve, so that the rats in the barn might drink it and be killed.'

'Did anyone see you do this?'

Lovie paused. 'No.'

'And what was the result of this action?'

'The next day, I took down the saucer and found two dead rats lying on the sieve beside it.'

'What did you do with those rats?'

Lovie hesitated. 'I threw them into the cow's dung-hill, before the barn door.'

'And what did you do with the mixture in the saucer?'

'That same evening, I threw it into the kitchen fire, washed out the saucer and put it back in the house.'

'Did anyone see you do this?'

Lovie frowned. 'No-one saw me throw away the rats,' he said. 'My ... mither ... saw me empty the stuff into the fire.'

'Your mother. No-one else?'

'No.'

'And you told *no-one* else about the rats?'

'No.'

'Was there any of the powder left over?'

'No. I used it all up in mixing the stuff for the rats.'

The interrogation went on. Each time Simpson thought he had gained an advantage, it slipped away again. He wanted to shake the man. Would anything unsettle him? John Lovie remained inscrutable, while Simpson's frustration grew. When he had run out of questions, he still had no real answers. What, then, was the truth?

Simpson leaned back in his plush chair and folded his arms.

'Are we finished?' Lovie asked.

'Yes,' Simpson replied shortly. 'Mr Dauney?'

Dauney stopped writing, picked up the document and read it aloud. John Lovie listened with his head slightly bowed and lips curved; he might have been listening to music. Dauney finished and placed the paper before the prisoner. Lovie glanced at it and shook his head. His eyes flicked to Simpson's and slid away. There was something secret there that quickened Simpson's breath. Hatred? Fear?

Dauney sighed elaborately and seized the pen again. He dipped it in the ink and, with a flourish, applied it to the paper.

> On the foregoing declaration having been distinctly said
> over to the declarant, he says, that he is satisfied that what
> it contains as being all truth; but that altho' he can write
> his name he declines to sign it.
>
> Signed Al Dauney
> W. Simpson, James Mackie, Geo. Cockburn, witnesses
>
> *—From precognition against John Lovie for the crime of murder*

Chapter 54

Thursday 23 August 1827

ABERDEEN

Dr Patrick Blaikie opened the door of his Aberdeen surgery to the crisp morning air and ushered two colleagues inside. Blaikie lived and worked in a large and austere townhouse in the sloping lane of Castle Brae. Beneath the shadow of the old castle, his home lay just a short walk from the squalor of the docks and overlooked the harbour, a reminder of his days as a naval surgeon.

The men bustled inside the doctor's surgery. They removed their hats and coats, hung them upon the hall stand and followed Dr Blaikie down the stairs to his dissection room in the basement.

'Gentlemen,' Dr Blaikie began, placing a phial of liquid onto the dissecting table. It was labelled and sealed with wax bearing the impression 'W.S.'. 'Here we have the liquid obtained from the stomach of Margaret McKessar in Fraserburgh on Sunday 19 August. It was handed to me by William Simpson, procurator fiscal for the county of Aberdeen, whose initials – you'll see – appear on the seal.'

The gentlemen leaned in to inspect the phial. The elder, Patrick Forbes, straightened up, looked down his long nose and nodded gravely.

'I note that the seal is intact,' he said, and turned to his younger colleague for confirmation.

'Excellent work, Dr Forbes,' the younger gentleman said, with a twitch of the lips. Dr Forbes responded to the sarcasm with a gentle smile.

Dr Forbes raised his eyes to Dr Blaikie's. 'And there is a suspicion of arsenic poisoning?'

Dr Blaikie nodded. 'But the tests we conducted at Dr Coutts's residence in Fraserburgh were inconclusive. That is why we thought further investigation from gentlemen with your expertise would be invaluable.'

Dr Forbes acknowledged the compliment with a nod. 'My brother-in-law and I are happy to be of service.' Then his eyes twinkled. 'And of course, young William relishes any opportunity to spend time in the laboratory rather than with his students at Marischal.'

'All right, then, Forbes,' Dr Knight said with good-humoured impatience. 'Let's not delay.'

'Of course,' Dr Forbes said. 'First, I suggest we add water impregnated with sulphuretted hydrogen gas to a sample of the fluid and observe the colour produced.'

Dr Knight rubbed his hands together. 'Right.'

The two gentlemen chatted as Dr Blaikie prepared the solution.

'Ready,' said Dr Blaikie. Dr Knight broke the seal on the phial, releasing the stink of Meggy's stomach contents into the air. Dr Knight poured a sample of the fluid into a small glass cup, then Dr Blaikie added some of his solution. The liquid immediately turned golden yellow.

'Now,' Dr Forbes went on, and his voice was deep with excitement, 'let us add the same solution of sulphuretted hydrogen gas to a solution of arsenious acid in water.'

They prepared the second solution carefully.

'The circumstances of the death were highly suspicious,' Dr Blaikie said. 'As you can understand, I thought it vital to consult the best men in the field ...'

Dr Forbes nodded. Blaikie expected them to be meticulous in their testing, for the stakes were high. A false positive could send an innocent man to the gallows. On the other hand, if poison was in Margaret McKessar's stomach contents and they missed it, they might set a murderer free. Even worse, sloppy procedure could invalidate the results.

When the solutions were ready, Dr Knight picked up two glasses, one in each hand. He raised them with a smirk and clinked them together as if in a toast. Then he poured the sulphuretted hydrogen gas into the arsenic.

The solution turned golden yellow.

'Well, well!' Dr Knight exclaimed.

'Well, well, indeed,' Dr Forbes murmured.

Chapter 55

Saturday 25 August 1827

FUTTERET DEN

'I've a warrant from the sheriff,' said John Milne through the small opening in the doorway.

'What warrant?' Widow Lovie said, holding the door fast and peering through the crack with one eye. The messenger-at-arms waved a paper at her. 'What use is that? I can't read it.'

Brown, the gravedigger, who had been waiting behind Milne, stepped around him and addressed her. 'It's a warrant to search your property,' he said, looking past her into the house. The way his watery eyes shifted about, avoiding hers, made nausea swell in her chest.

She narrowed her eyes. 'Why would you search my property?'

The two men exchanged glances. Milne cleared his throat. 'The servant girl was poisoned,' he said.

'I know that!' she retorted. The news had spread quickly in the village. 'You'll not find poison here, if that's what you're thinking.'

'Be that as it may,' Milne said. 'We've a warrant to search.'

'Uh!' she huffed, stepping back into the gloom and dropping her hands by her sides. Let them open the door themselves. She wouldn't make their job any easier. She crossed her arms as the men pushed the door open and clattered into her home. Lips compressed and eyes slitted, she watched as they stomped into her kitchen.

Milne crossed to the dresser and ran a hand along its surface. He picked up the plates on the shelves one by one, turned them over and replaced them carefully. The men nosed about the room, turning

John's newspapers over, sifting through her knitting, crouching to open the drawers under the deece. Brown poked about the hearth, lifting the lid of the pot that bubbled above the fire and dropping it back with a thud. He bent over the ledge by the hearth, fussing with the pots upon it.

'It's just tea,' she said as he raised the kettle to his lumpy, purple-veined nose. He ignored her. There was a small chest of linen; Milne opened it and unfolded each item. He shook down the blankets and left them in a heap on the floor.

Brown opened the case of the clock, disturbing the pendulum. It was her pride, that clock; it showed that the Lovies were better than their neighbours.

'Have a care!' she cried, and Brown mumbled an apology.

Milne picked up the ceramic milk jug from the small table and swirled it around, sniffing.

'You can't have any,' she said, and he gave a wry, one-sided smile.

'Nothing in here,' said Brown.

'Try the closet.'

She'd cleaned Meggy's vomit from the floor at last, but a faint smell lingered. It was dim in the closet, but she didn't offer them a candle. While she hovered, they pulled back the blanket – unwashed since Meggy's death – and ran hands along the mattress. They peered underneath the bed and checked the cracks in the walls. They found nothing.

'The other room?' Milne asked Brown, and he nodded.

Widow Lovie followed them into the but, where John's bed lay empty. He wasn't there; he was locked up in the Tolbooth. The reminder caused her physical pain. The thought of John in a dismal cell – lonely, hungry, humiliated. She squeezed her lids shut, tried to steady her breathing. The men turned John's bed over, feeling every inch of the mattress. They opened his trunk of clothing and took each article out and probed its seams and pockets.

'There's nothing here,' the gravedigger said to the messenger-at-arms. 'No poison. No drugs at all.'

'I told you!'

Milne turned a cold eye to her. 'We're not finished,' he said. 'Where's the dung-hill?'

'What do you want with the dung-hill?'

'Show me the dung-hill, Mrs Lovie.'

She pushed past them, back through the passage and out the door. Anger burned in her throat. Where was John? Why had he left her to deal with this mess? It was Meggy's fault. Elspet had been right: Meggy had been nothing but trouble. Damn that girl. Damn that Chessor girl with the red hair, too. Nothing but trouble – all of them.

'Here,' she said, waving a hand at the dung-hill.

'Thank you,' said Brown.

'We'll need a fork and shovel,' said Milne.

'Should've brought your own.'

Milne regarded her coolly. 'Don't you want to see justice done for your servant girl?'

Justice be damned, she thought, but she went to the barn and fetched a fork and shovel. She stood with hands on hips and watched them sift through the dark, loamy pile. At least the stink of manure on Milne would disgust his wife tonight.

'What are you looking for?' she asked, when the men had scrutinised the heap for half an hour.

Milne's face was sweat-streaked and grubby. 'Rats,' he said.

'Rats?' This was a surprise. The baillie had asked about rats. 'What for?'

'Never mind,' Milne replied.

When they had sifted the whole heap, Brown stood, pushed back his grey hair with a filthy hand and said, 'There're no rats here.'

A look of triumph passed between the men. 'Not even one,' Milne confirmed.

'So what?' the widow demanded. The brightness in their eyes had nothing to do with their exertions. Dread gripped her insides. 'What does that mean?'

'Never mind,' Milne said again.

Chapter 56

Monday 27 August 1827

FUTTERET DEN

Widow Lovie was still smarting from the search of her property two days later when the procurator fiscal knocked on her door. Alex Rannie was in tow. Rannie! He'd been keeping himself apart ever since Meggy's death, and now here he was keeping company with the men who were slandering poor John.

They stood at the door, and Rannie wouldn't look her in the eye. *Is he too good for us now?* She would get rid of him – only she couldn't. He was fee'd till October – and besides, she needed him. It was hard enough keeping the place in order, with Meggy dead and John in prison and all the neighbours keeping their distance.

William Simpson invited himself in, and she had no choice but to oblige. He didn't seem like a bad man; there was something gentle in his voice and eyes, though looks could be deceiving. She clenched her teeth. It was no use trusting people like him.

She showed Simpson a chair only to give herself an excuse to sit as well. She'd already milked the cows, yirned the butter, fetched water from the well, fed the horses, made brose for her grandson and tea for herself, swept out the kitchen and started kneading dough for the bread – and it wasn't yet mid-morning. It was a warm day, and she was clammy with sweat. Her back and knees and hands ached. Her head was dull; she hadn't slept much since Meggy died. There were still so many chores to do, and she didn't know when she would do them if the procurator fiscal was going to waste her time, but the opportunity to sit – even for a minute – was a relief.

She didn't offer Simpson tea, and he didn't seem to expect it. He cleared his throat and peered searchingly into her face.

'I'd like to inspect the yard, Mrs Lovie,' he said. 'The doctors want to test Margaret McKessar's excrement for arsenic. Alex Rannie tells me that she may have purged in the yard on the day of her death.'

'*Did* he?'

Rannie was slouching against the door jamb, his head down. It hurt, somehow, that he wouldn't look her in the eye. It made her ill, too, to think he'd been discussing Meggy's private business with strangers. But then, did it really matter? Could Meggy care? *Will it make a difference, how many nails they put in my son's coffin?*

She raised her chin and turned away. '*He* can show you where,' she said.

They went out, Rannie leading. The widow stayed in her armchair. Who cared if the bread didn't get kneaded? She was so bone-weary, she could hardly sit upright; she leaned her elbow on the arm of the chair and rested her head in her hand. Her neck was too feeble to hold up the weight of her head. She heard the men's voices outside in the yard. She imagined them scraping up the piles of Meggy's shit from the ground. Disgusting. To Hell with them, she thought. To Hell with Meggy.

She was still sitting there when they came back. With her eyes closed, she willed them to leave. But the voices grew louder, and the men re-entered without knocking. She raised her head and noticed that the procurator fiscal was holding a leather satchel. Her nose flared as she realised what vile samples were inside it.

'I'm told the girl vomited on the floor of the closet,' Simpson said.

'I cleaned it up.' No city lawyer would accuse her of poor house-keeping.

'Still,' he said. 'I'll need to see the site.'

She sighed and pushed herself upright. Every joint creaked. She limped to the closet and pointed to a dark patch on the floor. 'There.'

'Thank you.'

'I don't see what use it is,' she said, as Simpson crouched and scraped away at the earth. 'I cleaned it up.'

'Nevertheless, the doctors might find it useful.'

Rannie was still lurking in the doorway. She saw him from the corner of her eye, but she ignored him.

'Mrs Lovie,' the procurator fiscal said, emerging from the closet, 'I'm afraid you and Mr Rannie will have to come to Fraserburgh for further questioning.'

'Oh!' she exclaimed, and put a hand to her face, feeling tears ooze through her knotted fingers. 'Why must I?'

'I'm sorry, Mrs Lovie.'

Alex Rannie took her black wrap from the back of the chair and draped it about her shoulders.

'Mrs Lovie,' he said, in a voice thin and shy, almost tender. 'I saw the master at the inn ... when he was in custody there.'

Her heart shuddered. She stopped with her hand on chest and her eyes streaming.

'I went to get directions from him ... regarding the land.' He waited for her to respond, and when she didn't, he went on. 'He told me ... that if I am examined, I should tell the truth.'

She kept her eyes on the floor.

'I *will* tell the truth, Mrs Lovie,' he said.

It wasn't clear whether he meant it as a comfort or a threat.

Chapter 57

Monday 27 August 1827

EDINBURGH

Some 170 miles south of Fraserburgh, a coach rattled through the busy streets of Edinburgh and drew to a halt outside the grand stone building of the university. Adam Rolland, agent of the Crown – a gentleman – stepped down from the coach, bearing a small wooden box, tightly roped. He strode up the stone steps flanked by tall columns and through the door to the lobby. Dr Robert Christison, the city toxicologist and professor of medical jurisprudence and police, was expecting him.

The doctor greeted the Crown agent and took the box from his hands, his fingers twitching with anticipation. Having signed his receipt of the package and farewelled Rolland, Dr Christison took the box into his laboratory. He placed it upon a table, cut through the ropes and picked up a screwdriver to unfasten the screws that held the lid down. The lid came open and he peered inside. There, nestled upon a bed of flax, were two sealed glass bottles, each labelled with the impression 'W.S.'.

Dr Christison, satisfied, carefully took the bottles from the box and settled to work.

Chapter 58

Monday 27 August 1827

FRASERBURGH

Fraserburgh 27th August 1827

The said Margaret Watson or Lovie, being further examined declares, that William Park a neighbour supped in the witness house on the evening before McKessars death, – and he went away after supper. That from the time William Park went away up to the time when McKessar died <u>no stranger, nor any of the neighbours was within the witness house, –</u> That on the Monday there were <u>potatoes for supper</u> and John Lovie and William Park and Margaret McKessar all partook of them. That the potatoes were all boiled in the same pot, but these three, in eating them, ate from separate dishes. – That the witness did not partake of any of the potatoes, but took a little porridge for supper. That the witness did not see her son <u>rub any of the cattle; nor see him make any mixture to do so, nor see him empty any stuff</u> into the fire. That she does not recollect what they had for dinner on the Monday. That her son John got a hurt driving out the turnip dung, and in consequence he took physic once or twice, – the first time immediately after the hurt and the second at some time thereafter: but she cannot mention the time. That she does not know if her son took any physic about the day before McKessars death or not. All of which she declares to be truth and that she cannot write.

A. Dauney

Chapter 59

Wednesday 29 August 1827

Edinburgh

Dr Robert Christison bent over his desk, and his extravagantly coiled whiskers swung forward, casting shadows upon the page. He lifted his pen and drew his heavy brows together.

Report by Dr Christison, he wrote. *Edinburgh, August 29, 1827.*

His frown deepened as he began. *I certify that, on the 27th instant, I received from Adam Rolland, Esquire, Crown Agent, a box, enclosing two bottles duly sealed and labelled, and which were described as containing – the one a part of the contents of the stomach – the other, the stomach itself of Margaret McKessar.*

The notes he had taken during his investigations of two days earlier lay in a neat pile upon his desk. He paused, resting his pen in its holder to flick through the papers. The notes were hardly necessary, as the details were fresh in his mind – but Dr Christison preferred to leave nothing to chance.

He read carefully, pressing his thin lips together. The stomach, according to his notes, had shown patches of red on its inner surface. Interestingly, at one end the interior had been dusted with fine, bright yellow particles. His records showed that after inspecting the stomach, he had turned his attention to the bottle of fluid: nine and a half ounces of opaque, thick, reddish-brown liquid with a trace of dirty, greenish-white powdery sediment resting at the bottom.

Dr Christison set his notes back onto the desk and resumed his writing. His pen scratched the parchment as he described his investiga-

221

tions: the decanting, washing, boiling, mixing with various substances, filtering, drying and crystallising.

Then he straightened, settled the pen in its stand, and re-read his account. Satisfied that it was clear and complete, he dipped his pen into the ink and bent his head over the desk once more.

From the foregoing experiments, he wrote, *I am satisfied that oxide of arsenic existed in the contents of the stomach transmitted to me.*

Sighing, he continued: *Signed R. Christison, M. D., Professor of Medical Jurisprudence & Police in the University of Edinburgh.*

Chapter 60

Thursday 30 August 1827

ABERDEEN

While Dr Christison had been conducting his experiments in Edinburgh, 130 miles away at Dr Blaikie's surgery in Aberdeen, Doctors Blaikie, Forbes and Knight had continued their tests on Meggy's stomach contents. On Thursday 30 August, they convened for the fourth and last time.

They worked throughout the long day, dropping samples of fluids into glass tubes and heating them, sniffing them and holding them to the light to examine the results. A strong garlicky odour, produced by the boiling of certain substances, hung about in the stuffy room. The scientists' commission had demanded intense concentration, and they looked forward to its conclusion with a mixture of fatigue and excitement.

By Thursday evening they were done.

Dr Blaikie sat at his desk to begin his report. The evidence the doctors had found was significant, and Blaikie was acutely aware of the gravity of the situation. He rubbed his weary eyes, flexed his fingers and began to write. Doctors Knight and Forbes looked silently over his shoulder as the young doctor scribbled. When Blaikie had completed a paragraph, Forbes bent closer to read and nodded.

'Good. Now let me dictate.' His voice droned on as Blaikie put his pen back to the paper: *... a portion of the same fluid was boiled ... mucilage separated ... solution of nitrate of silver ... filtered ... no precipitate*

... a drop of ammonia ... a yellow precipitate which gradually turned black, and had all the character of arsenite of silver, was produced.

'Let me see?' Dr Blaikie handed over the script. Dr Forbes read it, his lips pursed and high forehead creased. He nodded his satisfaction and handed the paper back to his colleague.

'*Third*,' Forbes went on, '*When portions of this precipitate were mixed with black flux in a glass tube ...*'

He continued to dictate as Blaikie wrote. Knight stood with hands clasped behind his back, listening.

Forbes waved a hand. 'Write down the dates of our experiments, that is, the 23rd, 24th, 27th and 30th instant ... yes, that's right. A considerable portion of each of those days. Oh, and, of course'—he jabbed an index finger at the paper—'don't neglect to write that when we were not present in the rooms in which the experiments were conducted, the doors of the apartment were sealed ... and that the seals were always found intact on our return.'

Blaikie's pen scratched some more. When he had finished, he raised bloodshot eyes to the professors.

'*And this*,' Dr Knight added, indicating with a nod that Dr Blaikie should resume, '*we certify on soul and conscience.*'

Satisfied, Dr Blaikie handed the document to his colleagues to sign.

'Well done,' said Dr Knight, and turned to his brother-in-law. 'Forbes, would you dine with us tonight? Jean has been asking for news of the children.'

Chapter 61

Early September 1827

T he wheel of the handcart squeaked as Jean McKessar trundled it along the shore. The high-tide mark was littered with clumps of sea-ware. Jean stopped, stooped, swept up an armful of the slick ribbons and deposited it in the cart. She had been collecting for hours, and her back ached.

Collecting sea-ware was normally her mother's job, but Henrietta was indisposed. Her health had been fragile since Meggy's death. Jean did what she could to ease her mother's way, but it was hard. Most able-bodied folk were working in the fields now that the corn harvest had begun. Harvest time brought with it an avalanche of chores, and Jean had found herself spread thinly. The bitterness of overwork and loss was wearing her out.

The air was mild and tangy and the sea deep blue, like an evening sky. The beach was dotted with fishing folk. The season had been kind to the herring trade, and a fishy stink from the curing yards hung about on the breeze. Fishing nets dried like cobwebs upon the beach, and the fishermen swarmed about them, inspecting and mending them and calling to each other in salt-roughened voices. Fishwives scuttled to and fro with creels upon their backs.

What would it be like to live their lives, to drift from port to port, chasing herring? To owe one's livelihood to those silvery treasures of the deep – to depend upon the mercy of that great, capricious beast: the sea? Her whole life, Jean had existed alongside these fisher-folk, their lives parallel, never intersecting. How different her life might have been if her father had been a fisherman and not a labourer. If he hadn't been a soldier. If he hadn't gone missing.

She piled more sea-ware onto the cart, and the salt stung the cracks in her work-worn hands. She missed Meggy. She missed her sister's optimism; Meggy had always kept them lively. She had been brash and brazen and unpredictable, cruel in one moment and kind in the next. Trusting, arrogant, *stupid* Meggy. Jean had once wondered whether her sister's guilelessness was a virtue or a fault, but now she knew only too well. Poor Meggy; how she'd overestimated her own charms.

Out in the harbour, sails of fishing vessels fluttered. Beyond them was the open sea, criss-crossed by the paths of a thousand emigrant ships ferrying anxious souls to foreign lands. How adventurous those travellers were – and how brave! How must it feel, she wondered, to take that first step into such an uncertain future? She paused, staring at the horizon. She couldn't imagine taking that gamble. What did this say about her character? Was it a lack of courage that kept her chained to the familiarity of home, miserable as it was – or was it an excess of imagination? Were those emigrants to the colonies more daring than she, or simply more desperate?

Then, of course, there were the involuntary emigrants: the convicts, transported to some far-off Hell on Earth. Jean's thoughts turned, as they had too often lately, to John Lovie. Maybe he would be sent to the colonies. More likely he would hang. She thought with satisfaction of her sister's murderer languishing in the Tolbooth at Aberdeen, and found pleasure in imagining him chained, beaten and starving. She hoped that his suffering had already outstripped Meggy's. She hoped that he would hang.

A woman had been hanged as a murderess in Forfar in the summer: a woman from Arbroath named Margaret Wishart. They said she had laced her sister's porridge with arsenic. Her sister had been blind and pregnant with an illegitimate child, and rumour had it that the father had been Margaret Wishart's sweetheart. The blind victim, even while stricken from the poison, had given birth to a son, and both mother and child had died after three days of suffering. Margaret Wishart, the dead woman's sister, had maintained her innocence right up to the end. There were people who had believed her – and believed her still. They said that she had gone to the gallows with dignity and grace.

John Lovie also claimed to be innocent. He was even denying his connexion with Meggy – the *liar*. He was fighting the charges against him, prolonging the suffering for Meggy's family. Jean hoped he would admit his guilt before he swung. She wanted to see him beg for God's mercy. But he wouldn't – of course, he wouldn't.

Thousands had turned out to watch Margaret Wishart hang. Would they do the same for John Lovie? She didn't care whether his execution was witnessed by hordes or by none. So long as he was put to death, Meggy would be avenged, and Jean would be satisfied. It was all she asked; there was nothing else to hope for.

Her cart was full. She wheeled it westward and tramped across the beach towards the grassy flats, leaving a trail of footprints from the water's edge to the dunes. Grasping the handles with wind-chapped hands, she trundled home to her mother.

Part Three

Chapter 62

Thursday 27 September 1827

THE TRIAL BEGINS

Summer bled out. Its dying breath wafted in from the sea, sighing through the cracks around windows and doors and into the dim interiors of the farm cottages. The grain harvest was well underway, and the labouring men and women were preparing for the cooler months: making ropes, repairing steadings and byres, cutting peat from the mosses. The herring season was over, and the fishermen had drifted south to carry on their trade in warmer waters.

In Aberdeen, news had blown in that John Lovie was about to be tried. The story was a sensation. Folk of all stations from all corners of Aberdeen and beyond converged upon the courthouse, looking forward to a day's amusement. In Castle Street, beneath the Gothic tower of the Tolbooth, they wove between horse-drawn carriages and street vendors and frock-coated businessmen, bustling under the high arch into the narrow confines of Lodge Walk. Some glanced up at the granite walls, thrilling at the knowledge that a murderer languished somewhere beyond them.

They elbowed their way into the lobby of the courthouse. A grand staircase led them up to a large vestibule on the first floor, where Gothic architecture gave way to Greek, and the stateliness of the chamber with its Doric columns and high ceilings subdued the more feverish amongst them. They filed into the gallery, where the public seating formed the arc of the semicircular courtroom.

The prisoner's mother, clad in her widow's weeds, sat nervously in the throng. Mary Yule sat on her right, her face blotched and damp. The widow felt sorely the absence of Mary's sweet boy, John Yule, who had been taken aside by his father to the witnesses' rooms somewhere at the northern end of the courtroom. James slouched on her left. He was twitchy and distracted – making no secret of his wish to be anywhere but here – but she took heart from his presence just the same. With the neighbours now so wary, she had to be grateful for any show of loyalty that came her way, no matter how small.

The public continued to pour in, and the widow and her son and daughter had to slide along the bench seats to allow others to squeeze in beside them. The hubbub was frightening. So many strangers, eager to turn her suffering into entertainment! She might have hated them for it if it weren't all so surreal. The laughter, the greedy eyes, the open mouths. It was hard to believe it was really happening – that John's life was at stake. Hard to believe that for these people, the suspense was a lark. Her boy's life was at stake – his *life*! Today, the court might decide to kill him.

Elspet hadn't come. The courthouse was no place for a wean, she'd told her mother, and she'd had no choice but to agree. They'd parted with tears; there had been no sign of *I told you so* in Elspet that day – only worry and grief. The widow now felt the lack of her daughter so keenly that she doubled over and wrapped her arms around her bony, aching self.

Mary clasped her hand and stroked it. Irritated, she itched to snatch her hand back, but she resisted for fear of upsetting Mary. People were looking at them. She didn't know them; they were Aberdeen people, not her Fraserburgh neighbours – although even some of *them*, she knew, had travelled the forty miles to enjoy John's distress. Traitors, all of them.

People were looking at them and whispering behind cupped hands. How did they even know who she was?

'They hate us,' she muttered.

'No, Mither,' Mary whispered back. 'They don't know us.'

Was that the truth? It was so hard to tell. It didn't matter anyway. What mattered was whether John would live or die; that was all that mattered.

Outside in the street, earlier, she had caught a glimpse of the McKessars: Henrietta, stooped and frail, propped up by her furious, frizzy-haired daughter. Jean's eyes had sliced into her like scythes. She'd looked away, Jean's anguish too much to bear.

Something was going on at the front of the courtroom now. Robed and wigged men were sweeping in. In the gallery, people scrambled for seats; there was more shuffling along and squeezing in and exclaiming as toes were trodden on and ribs were nudged by stray elbows. They were farmers and shopkeepers and toffs, all looking forward to a day's sport. The body odour and smell of sweat-caked jackets was suffocating.

Then there was pounding, and the racket settled to a hum, and people craned necks and held their breath.

Two men in scarlet robes and long white wigs sat upon a raised platform at the head of the courtroom. The widow's heart staggered; these were the judges, Lord Pitmilly and Lord Alloway. She didn't know which was which. One, the older and fatter of the two, was a smug-looking gent with large puffy eyes and a jutting lower lip. The other had thin, smiling lips, a big nose and chin, and surprised-looking brows. These were the men who would steer John towards his fate. Their faces were already etched into her memory.

A familiar face caught her eye. 'That's him!' the widow hissed, pointing at a small, genial-looking man in advocate's robes. 'That's Mr Cockburn!'

'John's lawyer?' Mary craned her neck to see.

'It's him,' the widow repeated. 'It is. I saw him last night when your husband and I came to the courtroom. *He's* the one who wouldn't hear us out!'

'He's an important man,' Mary said, licking her lips.

'Important! What's *important* is my son's life.'

'Mr Cockburn will surely save him,' James said, quietly so the people around them couldn't hear. 'He was Mary Smith's lawyer.'

'Who is Mary Smith?' the widow asked irritably.

'The poisoner from Dundee,' James said, then shook his head and corrected himself. '*Alleged* poisoner. Tried for the murder of her servant girl.'

She remembered. 'The servant who was pregnant by Mary Smith's son?'

'Aye. That's the one.'

'And *he*'—she jerked her head at Cockburn—'*he* got her off?'

'More or less,' James said.

'What do you mean, "more or less"?' she said, but James did not reply.

Henry Cockburn had a long, pale face and sweet, melancholic brown eyes, like a cow's. *He* was the man upon whom John's life depended. She peered at him, seeking reassurance. How could such a man save John?

She turned to her son. 'James,' she urged. 'Go and speak to Mr Cockburn. Tell him that I want to testify!'

'Mither!' Mary's eyes widened. 'Don't be mad!'

The widow closed her eyes, despairing. 'But why won't he let me testify?'

'You know why, Mither,' James said through gritted teeth. 'George Yule spoke to Mr Cockburn's agent last night.'

'But ...'

'George *told* you what he said.'

She snatched her hand from Mary's clammy grasp. 'I want to tell the court that John is a good man.'

George Yule hadn't begged hard enough. She wanted to stand up in the courtroom and convince them all of John's virtues, but the agent had told Yule that Mr Cockburn had no intention of calling her. Her testimony would 'not be in John's interests,' he'd said. This she couldn't understand. She wanted to tell the jury how hardworking John was, how reliable and kind; how he'd never raised a hand or even a voice to her. She wanted to clear his name. She'd even lie for him, if only she knew the right lies to tell. God help her.

'The jury wouldn't believe you,' James replied, stubborn. 'They'd assume a mother's words are influenced by her natural affection.'

'Phht.'

'Mither ... leave it be. George said it's lucky the Crown hasn't called you as a witness.'

'The *Crown*?' She couldn't comprehend. Testify against her son?

James bit his lip. 'It's not usual ... but George said the prosecution can compel a mother to give evidence against her son if it wishes to.'

She was flummoxed. 'But why would the prosecution wish to call me?'

James hesitated, shifting uncomfortably. 'He said that ... in some details ... your evidence contradicts John's.'

His words took a moment to sink in.

'Mither,' said Mary, reclaiming her mother's limp hand.

'No,' she whispered, chilled. 'No.'

***

Looking at his lawyer was one thing, but it was a far harder matter to look at John. She forced herself to do so, fearing she would find a broken version of her son. But there he was in the dock, hale as ever. A little paler, a little thinner, perhaps, but far from defeated. He was reclining in his seat, alert but calm. Was he smiling, even? Bless him. Love made her eyes water.

As the courtroom held its breath, Widow Lovie noticed the other wigged and robed gentlemen in front of the judges. She gripped Mary's arm, suddenly desperate for physical support.

'Those men,' she said. 'They're the ones who ...'

The prosecution.

Mary caught her breath. 'They're young,' she said.

She was right. The man who was trying to kill John appeared to be only in his thirties at most. Pompous-looking, with a broad forehead and whiskers. Beside him was an even younger man, looking like a boy in his father's robes. A flutter of hope stirred; pitted against Mr Cockburn, what harm could these mild-eyed gentlemen do?

Through the chamber, a sonorous voice chanted.

'John Lovie, farmer, charged with administering, or causing to be administered to a pregnant woman, poisonous or deleterious drugs, with intent to procure abortion, and with murder, or with one or other of those crimes – in so far as, *one*: upon 4th of August 1827 (Saturday), he did, within the house occupied by him at Percyhorner, otherwise called Futteret Den, or Burnside, or Mains of Phingask, parish of Fraserburgh and county of Aberdeen, administer, or cause to be administered, in some way to prosecutor unknown, to Margaret McKissar or McKessar, his servant, a young woman then in a state of pregnancy, a large dose of jalap, or of some other poisonous or deleterious drug, in such a quantity as to produce, shortly after she had swallowed the same, a violent purging, and seriously endanger the foetus or unborn child of the said Margaret McKissar or McKessar; and all this he did with intent to procure abortion in her. *Two*: farther, upon 13th of August (Monday), or on 14th of August (Tuesday), he did, in place aforesaid, administer, or cause to be administered to the said Margaret McKissar or McKessar, in some way unknown, a quantity of arsenic, and she having swallowed the said arsenic, was in consequence thereof shortly after taken violently and dangerously ill, and languished until the afternoon of the 14th of August 1827, when she died.'

'He didn't,' she whispered.

James frowned. 'Hush, Mither.'

Her skin prickled. James was embarrassed to be there. With death waiting to seize his brother, what James felt was *embarrassment*! She leaned away from her son, closer to Mary, momentarily distracted from the proceedings.

'Not guilty,' John's lawyer said, drawing her back.

There was more scrabbling about, indistinct voices saying things she could neither hear nor understand. Men coming and going.

'What are they doing?' she whispered.

'Shhh!' someone behind hissed, and her face burned.

She started to turn, to give him a tongue-lashing, but Mary put an arm around her. 'They're selecting the jury.'

Men filed through: farmers, scrubbed and dressed in their best trousers and waistcoats. Someone was dipping his hand into a bowl and pulling out papers, chanting names. James Findlater at Old Castle of Balvenny. Theodore Gordon of Overhall. Peter Falconar, farmer, at Collarsgreen. Macduff Fyfe, residing at Glasshaugh. William McCombie of Easterskene Common. James Falconar, farmer, Kinermony. Ferguson Simpson, farmer, Mains of Pitlow. James Smith, farmer …

On and on, until there were fifteen.

Five gentlemen and ten farmers. She tried to study their faces; her old eyes struggled to make out the detail, but she saw enough. They looked like solid, honest men. Was that good or bad? What type of person would take a kinder view of John: a jury of misfits, or these pillars of the community?

The jury – John's judges – stood and raised their right hands. An official chanted, 'You fifteen swear that by Almighty God, and as you shall answer to God at the great Day of Judgement, that you will truth say and no truth conceal, so far as you are to pass on this assize,' and the jurors droned, 'I do.'

'Give me strength,' the widow whispered, to Mary and to God. Just let it be over, she thought, and then quickly checked her prayer. If it was over, and not in John's favour? Better this torment than the noose.

Mary held her right hand, and James the left.

'It's beginning, Mither,' Mary said. 'It's beginning.'

Chapter 63

William Simpson's Testimony

The people fell silent and craned their necks as the procurator fiscal settled himself in the witness stand. Suspense buzzed through the gallery; the people were looking forward to a good show.

The widow, with her cheeks burning, raised her chin and glared at William Simpson. Hatred pierced her. *He* was the cause of all their problems; *he* could have stopped it all if he'd had the inclination. But then, she felt the same surging of bile when she thought of any of them: John Milne, the messenger-at-arms who had ransacked her cottage; Mr Officer, who had told vicious tales about poison; Baillie Chalmers, who had ordered Meggy's exhumation; and Mr Brown, who had buried Meggy three times and twice dug her out. Henrietta and Jean McKessar, whose accusing stares ran through her like blades. Alex Rannie, who saw everything in black and white when, really, the whole world was shrouded in grey. Meggy.

William Simpson's right hand was raised, his soft, white, uncalloused office-worker's palm turned to the gallery. 'I swear by Almighty God, and as I shall answer to God at the great Day of Judgement, that I will tell the truth, the whole truth, and nothing but the truth, in so far as I know, or shall be asked on this occasion.'

The young prosecutor stood to face his witness. The widow strained to see him better, squinting her ancient eyes. He was fresh faced, with wild side-whiskers and a small, full-lipped mouth.

'What is his name?' she whispered to James.

'Archibald Alison,' James muttered. 'Now hush, Mither. Listen.'

She directed all of her hatred towards the pleasant-looking Archibald Alison, whose mildness only fuelled her rage. The mob leaned forward as he addressed the witness. They were not to be disappointed, for the case got off to a grisly start. The prosecutor opened by quizzing the procurator fiscal about the examination of Meggy's corpse.

'The uterus was opened,' William Simpson said, as coolly as if he were discussing the slaughtering of a beast, 'and the four-month-old foetus of a girl was found.'

How the crowd loved that. A hum went up and heads bobbed and swivelled. The widow tried to keep her eyes on the witness but found her gaze sliding away.

And there, across the aisle, a red-haired girl. Not a girl, but a woman: a woman with pale skin and a frown of concentration on her dainty profile. Helen Chessor. If it weren't for her, she thought. Nothing had been right since Helen Chessor had walked into John's life. The fishing folk knew that red hair brought bad luck. They were right. She'd blighted them all.

As Simpson described the extraction of the stomach contents, the crowd leaned in with open mouths. 'The stomach and its contents were bottled and sealed in my presence,' he said. 'Dr Blaikie took the stomach to Aberdeen. I saw it later in Dr Blaikie's hands with the seal unbroken, and I had it and another bottle containing half of the stomach contents transmitted to Edinburgh. I had Mr Hodge make a box to transmit it to Edinburgh by coach.'

Mr Alison strode to a table upon which a wooden box and other items sat. He picked up two large bottles and raised them high. Gasps swept across the courtroom. In one bottle was a greyish chunk of meat; in the other, brown fluid.

'Are these the bottles containing the stomach and stomach contents that you sent to Edinburgh?'

Meggy's insides.

'Yes,' said the procurator fiscal. 'That one'—pointing—'is the stomach. And the other contains half of the stomach contents. My seal is on the bottles.'

The prosecutor replaced the bottles on the table. With a flourish, he swept up the wooden box in both hands and held it high. 'Is this the box in which you transmitted them to Edinburgh?'

'It is.'

Mr Alison, pressing his hands together, announced that he'd finished with the witness and resumed his seat. Mr Cockburn – John's advocate – sprang forward. The widow, realising that her knuckles were sore from clenching, spread her fingers and wiped sweaty palms upon her skirt. It was warm in the courtroom, but the blood running through her was cold.

John's lawyer approached the witness with his head cocked and a mild half-smile upon his lips.

'Mr Simpson,' he began. 'Can you say with certainty that this is the very same bottle that you transmitted to Edinburgh?'

'Yes, I can,' Simpson said. Mr Cockburn nodded and regarded the witness silently, patiently. Simpson shifted. 'Well,' he said, after a long pause. 'It looks exactly like it.'

'*Looks* like it?'

'It bears my seal.'

'The seal is only hung on it by a string, is it not?'

'It is ...' Simpson opened his mouth, shut it, opened again. 'The doctors were concerned that in affixing a seal to the tubes, the heat might have cracked them. They affixed the labels instead – very firmly – with twine and then enclosed them in a sealed parcel—'

'Ah,' said Cockburn. 'Is it possible that the string might have been slipped off one bottle and put onto some other of the same dimensions and appearance?'

'I wouldn't think it likely.'

'But not impossible?'

A heartbeat. 'Not impossible, no, but—'

'Thank you, Mr Simpson.'

Chapter 64

Alex Rannie's Testimony

All eyes were upon Alex Rannie. He sweated in the witness box. Not for the first time, he wished he'd never heard of Meggy McKessar.

He knew the widow was in the courtroom, but he couldn't bring himself to look at her. He'd tried to do the right thing by her since her son had been put away, though the very thought of Futteret Den gave him gooseflesh.

The months he'd spent at the Lovies' farm now seemed like a bad dream. He could hardly remember the living Meggy; she'd been replaced in his memory by a corpse. His life at the farm with Meggy, the widow, her son and grandson – all had turned into a ghoulish drama for the entertainment of the public. It made his sickened heart race.

John Lovie was in the dock. Rannie sneaked a glance at him, hoping the prisoner wouldn't notice, but Lovie caught his gaze and held it. Despite his weeks in the Tolbooth, Lovie looked fresh. His self-possession sent the blood to Rannie's head, made it pound in his ears. The hide of him! Hell would be too good for John Lovie. Poor, poor Meggy.

'I swear by Almighty God, and as I shall answer to God at the great Day of Judgement, that I will tell the truth, the whole truth, and nothing but the truth, in so far as I know, or shall be asked on this occasion,' Rannie repeated after the judge. *And, by God, I will.*

Mr Alison led him through the tale of Meggy's death. Damn, he was sick of it. He had told it all to the baillie a month ago – every detail. Over and over.

The prosecutor prompted him. 'Mr Rannie,' he said, in a voice so benign that it unnerved him, 'did you, during your time in the pannel's service, ever see or hear rats or mice or other vermin about Lovie's farm town?'

'No, sir,' said Rannie, relieved to begin with a simple question. He had a ready and confident answer for it. 'I never did.'

'I see,' the whiskered gentleman replied. He paused, head tilted. Rannie began to sense the steel beneath the young prosecutor's mild manner. I would not like to be his target, he thought. 'Did you ever hear John Lovie or his mother speaking about rats being about the farm town, or about laying poison for them?'

He shook his head, adamant. 'No, I did not.'

'Ah,' said Mr Alison, with a kindly smile to the jury. Rannie glanced at them. Fifteen men, mostly farmers. He hadn't paid them much heed until now. He chided himself. These were the men who would decide. What power they had! It made him tremble to think of it. They were men just like him.

They were all looking at him: the jurors, the lawyers, the judges, the crowd.

'I beg your pardon, sir?'

'I asked about your master's cattle.'

'He has four cows, four stirks and four calves.'

'Since you joined the household at Whitsunday, have any of the cows had any illness or vermin that were treated by rubbing with any substance?'

Rannie shook his head. 'No.'

'Not ever?'

'Well, there was a stirk that had something the matter with it – I think it was the houk.'

'When was this?'

When was it? He had held the beast's head and sung to it while Milne bled it and the cattle-herd watched in wonder. 'I think it was more than a fortnight before Meg – Margaret McKessar – died. Alexander Milne bled it. And then there was a sick cow *after* Meggy – Margaret – died. I saw John Lovie and his mother give it something to drink.'

At the mention of the widow, Rannie glanced at the gallery, caught her eye and froze. Her hatred shook the breath out of him.

'Mr Rannie—' the prosecutor's voice broke through. 'Mr Rannie, I must ask you to answer the question. Did the cows require rubbing?'

'No,' he rasped, swallowed and tried again. 'No. I never saw anything rubbed into any of the cattle.'

'Did you ever hear your master say that he had got anything to rub into their backs?'

Rannie shook his head again. 'No. I never did.'

'Did you ever see anything that might make you think the cattle would need anything to cure vermin?'

'No.'

'Did you ever see any dead rats lying about on the dung-hills or any other place about Lovie's farm?'

'No, I didn't.'

'How often do you see the dung-hills?'

'I see them every day.'

'How often do you go into the kiln barn?'

Puzzled, Rannie said, 'Every day.'

The prosecutor smiled his encouragement. 'Did you ever see any saucer or old sieve in the kiln barn?

'No, sir,' Rannie said, sneaking a quick glance at his former master. John Lovie stared back, unblinking.

'Did you ever hear of any saucer or old sieve being in the kiln barn?'

He gazed into the faces in the courtroom, confused. 'No.'

The prosecutor changed the subject. 'Tell me, Mr Rannie, about the injury John Lovie suffered during the summer.'

'The injury?' Rannie frowned. 'Oh! A beast ran off and my master was hurt.'

'What was his injury?'

'Some skin was rubbed off his shoulder. It wasn't severe.'

'When was this?'

Rannie rubbed his chin. 'It was in June,' he said.

'More than two months before Margaret died,' Mr Alison observed, with a glance at the jury to make sure they were attending. 'Did John Lovie take any physic for his injury?'

'N ... no,' Rannie replied. 'I know that he took some salts as physic, before he got his hurt ... but I never heard that he took any physic for that hurt.'

Mr Alison nodded, satisfied. Rannie was dimly aware that something he had said had pleased the prosecutor. He didn't know what it was.

'Did you ever suspect any intimacy between the prisoner and the deceased?' the lawyer changed direction again.

All ears in the courtroom waited for his answer. Rannie licked his lips. He could feel John Lovie's eyes upon him. The widow's eyes, flaying him.

'Uh ... not at first,' he said. 'But there was one day we were driving out the turnip dung, and the widow Lovie was away. John Lovie went to his bed, and Meggy went to him.'

A murmur rippled through the gallery.

'Where were you at this time?' the prosecutor said, smiling, tapping his finger to his cheek.

'I was in the kitchen.'

'How long did the deceased remain with John Lovie?'

'I cannot say.'

'And then? What did she do?'

Rannie blushed. He fixed his eyes on his feet. He mumbled, not wanting the widow to hear his words. He remembered Meggy's heat. Her hot breath on his cheek. 'She came out into the kitchen. I said, "Is that how you do?", and she said, "I'll go to bed wi' *you*." '

There was a tittering from the gallery. His ears burned.

'I see. And what did you reply?'

'I told her, "I don't want you." '

Muffled laughter.

'Mr Rannie, do you recollect any conversations you had with John Lovie about poison?'

'Aye,' he said, heavily.

'Will you tell the court, please, Mr Rannie?'

He took a deep breath. 'One day before Meggy ... died, my master and I were out hoeing – potatoes or turnips, I don't remember – and John Lovie said, "Do you know what would produce abortion?" I said I didn't know. We had a long conversation about it.'

The courtroom buzzed. Rannie wiped the sweat from his brow with a sleeve. The judge pounded his gavel. When the uproar had ceased, Mr Alison continued, mild and avuncular.

'Can you tell the court that conversation?'

Rannie shrugged. 'I don't recall the exact words. He asked me if I knew how much jalap would kill, and how much cure.'

'Cure?'

'I didn't know what he was driving at. I supposed that he was asking what would poison, and what cause a woman to part with a child.'

Rannie wiped his palms upon his trousers. He could not look at John Lovie in the dock. 'He also asked if I knew how much laudanum would make someone go to sleep. I told him I warranted that Saty would know.'

'Who is this Saty?'

'He's a man ... a kind of prophesier.'

'Go on.'

'I told him that I'd heard of this man, but never saw him.' The words started pouring from him. 'John Lovie told me one morning that he'd dreamed he gave me two glasses of whisky and one of laudanum. This is how he used to start these conversations about poison. And one morning, when we were hoeing turnips, he asked me if I knew of a white kind of stuff – a poison. I answered, "I suppose you mean arsenic." Then he said he supposed Mr Officer or Mr Massie in Fraserburgh kept it for sale, and I said aye .'

'When was this conversation?'

'I don't recall. It was more than a week before Meggy's – Margaret's – death.'

'Might it have been a month before?'

'I dinna ken. I entered into Lovie's service at Whitsunday last. It was sometime after that.'

'I see. And, Mr Rannie, did these conversations not strike you as odd?'

Rannie hung his head. 'I suppose I thought nothing of it at the time.' The prosecutor smiled reassuringly at him. 'It was only later ... when I heard she died so suddenly, that I ...' He looked up and glared at the prisoner in the dock. John Lovie smiled back at him. 'It was even before any report got abroad that she had been poisoned, that I recalled these conversations, and they struck me ... and made me think that John Lovie had been trying to get clear of Meggy's child. You see, everyone knew that Meggy was with child.'

Mr Alison, waiting again for the hubbub to subside, cocked his head and smiled pleasantly.

When he resumed his questioning, he fell back onto more comfortable ground, probing Rannie about the day that he and Meggy had both been stricken with dysentery. There was some to-ing and fro-ing about the timing of the incident. Rannie had dined at Lovie's. John Lovie had eaten with him, and Rannie thought they'd had potatoes. He'd taken salts for his bowel complaint. It was the day that he went to his father's, he confirmed. The second Saturday before Meggy died.

The crowds shifted, restless. They were fanning themselves and squirming in their too-cramped seats; Rannie registered this dimly. He supposed they wanted more spice but was disinclined to provide it. Then Mr Alison returned to the day of the death, and the crowd was still, listening and watching.

'I rose at six. Meggy was up about the same time.'

'How did she seem?'

He shrugged. 'In her usual health.'

'And then?'

'The master desired me to fetch a drill plough from the neighbour, so I went.'

'And when did you return?'

Rannie scratched his head. 'It was about seven.'

'Did you see your master then?'

He nodded. 'I met him when he was coming from his house. He was about three hundred yards from the house.'

'When did you hear that Margaret was unwell?'

'I came in for breakfast at about half past eight. The old woman told me that Meggy was sick.'

'Where was the prisoner at this time?'

'I left him working in the fields.'

'Did you tell him that Margaret was sick?'

'I told him after my breakfast.'

'When was that?'

'I was at breakfast for better than a quarter of an hour, and then I went back to the fields and told my master that Meggy was unwell.'

'What was his reaction?'

Rannie wiped a sleeve across his mouth. 'His face went red,' he said, 'but I don't remember if he said anything.'

'When did the prisoner go back to the house?'

'He went to his breakfast at about half past nine.'

'Did he see Margaret McKessar then himself?'

'He didn't say if he saw her. He told me he'd heard her vomiting. He said, "Meggy is no' well" and said if she did not soon get better, she would not be long in this world.'

'How long did you remain in the fields?'

'I worked till dinner time – past one. I left the master in the field when I went in to dinner.'

'Did you see Margaret McKessar's mother when you were in the field?'

'Aye,' Rannie said. He shifted and gripped the railing of the witness box. 'I saw her more than once. She was driving ware past from the seashore.'

Mr Alison narrowed his eyes and leaned forward. His voice was soft. 'How close was Margaret McKessar's mother to the prisoner?'

'She was very close at hand.'

'Did John Lovie see her?'

Rannie glanced at Lovie nervously. 'He would have seen her if he had looked that way.'

'Did the prisoner speak to her?'

He shook his head. 'No, sir. I did not hear him hollo out anything to her. In fact, he said ...' He broke off and glared at John Lovie. Anger flooded through him. 'He told me *not* to tell Meggy's mother that she was ill.'

Hisses, surging through the courtroom, brought heat to his cheeks.

'Mr Rannie, please tell the court the events in the hour or so before Margaret McKessar's death.'

'I went to dinner. Widow Lovie and the boy Yule were in the house. I could hear Meggy in the closet off the kitchen, retching and groaning. I thought she must be in pain. She said that after I'd done with my dinner, she wished I would tell her brother and sister Jean to come and speak to her. She said, "I never was so unwell before." '

'Did Mrs Lovie hear her say this?'

'I don't think so. During dinner, I heard the widow tell the boy to fetch Meggy's mother. But by the time I'd done with my dinner, she was dead.'

'Did you see the prisoner's mother give her something to drink before she died?'

'Aye. Meggy wanted water. Widow Lovie took her something to drink. I don't know what it was.'

'I see.'

He caught the widow's eye in the crowd. She looked stricken. *I don't know what it was*, he'd said. The weight of his words hit him. Did she think he was accusing *her*? *Was* he accusing her? His legs felt boneless; nothing made any sense. He wished he could sit. He passed a hand across his eyes.

'Mr Rannie, please answer the question.'

'I ... I beg your pardon?'

'What did you do after Margaret died?'

'The widow told me to go and tell John. I met him as I was going out, and I told him that Meggy was either dead or close to it. He told me to tell her sister she was ill, but not to say she was dead, for fear of alarming her.'

'Mr Rannie, did you ever speak to Margaret McKessar about her pregnancy?'

'Aye,' he lowered his eyes. That day they'd walked together along the turnpike road, and he'd carried Meggy's basket of warm bread, and she'd teased him gently ... and then he'd said *I've noticed things about you*, and she'd stepped back from him, angry. The sun had been harsh on her, turning her skin sallow and ugly. 'I heard rumours she was with child. I taxed her with it some weeks before her death.'

'Did she confirm the rumour?'

'She didn't confirm it,' he said. 'But she didn't deny it either.'

'Did you ever speak of her pregnancy with the prisoner?'

'Aye.' Heat surged through him again. 'I did. I told him that I thought Meggy was with child, and he said, "I do not think that." But he didn't seem surprised.'

'Mr Rannie,' Mr Alison said, slowly and carefully. 'Did you ever hear of anyone from your household going to Fraserburgh to buy anything for the cow that was bled?'

'No.'

'Did you ever see any dead rats in the dung-hill?'

'No.'

'Did your master ever caution you or anyone else that poison had been set about the place?'

He shook his head vigorously. 'I never heard him caution anyone.'

'Thank you, Mr Rannie.'

He thought it was over. Trembling engulfed him: legs, hands, chin. But then John's lawyer was standing and leering at him through the haze. It wasn't over, after all; would it ever be? He closed his eyes and breathed.

'Tell me about the night before Margaret McKessar's death,' the lawyer with the undertaker's face was saying.

Through gritted teeth, Rannie said, 'I was at the shoemaker's.'

'When did you return?'

'I don't know. Sometime before nine.'

'Did you dine at the house?'

'Aye,' he sighed. He'd been through this before.

'What did you eat?'

'I had potatoes. The others had already supped. I suppose they had potatoes too.'

'Who gave you your supper?'

'Meggy did.'

That evening, he'd walked from the village through the syrupy gloaming along the turnpike road. The twilight sun had turned the hayricks on either side of the road into mounds of gold, and the summery breeze – of grass and sea and earth – had ruffled his hair. He remembered feeling light. He remembered turning off the turnpike road towards the cosy little Lovie house, seeing the smoke puffing from the chimney, and thinking of the cattle shuffling about in the byre and Meggy and the widow clattering in the kitchen, and feeling as if he was coming home.

He remembered seeing John Lovie strolling towards him with the neighbour, William Park. He remembered exchanging greetings with the men out in the honeyed evening. John Lovie and the neighbour had continued along the turnpike road, and Rannie had gone on to the cottage. It was just as he'd pictured it from without: the air smoky and dim and warm; Meggy humming in the kitchen and the widow sitting in her armchair with her knitting on her lap. 'You'll want supper,' Meggy had said, and she had given him a potato and a smile.

The fresh air and the walk from the village had made him hungry, and he'd wolfed the potato down. He remembered Meggy clanking the pots and pans in the kitchen in her cavalier way, and he remembered her glances at the door. She'd been waiting for her master's return.

She'd been bright and brittle, falsely cheerful. Rannie had felt embarrassed for her. He regretted that now.

'Was John Lovie there?' His master's lawyer asked.

Rannie shook his head. 'Not at the cottage, not when I came in. He'd gone out with the neighbour, William Park. I met them on their way. He came back in a little later.'

'What did he do when he returned?'

'He went to bed in the but end of the house.'

'Did he sleep alone?'

A pause. 'Aye,' said Rannie.

'And what were you doing at that time?'

'I went to bed in the kitchen.'

'And where were Margaret McKessar and the widow Lovie?'

'They went to bed too.'

'Where did they sleep?'

'In the closet off the kitchen.'

'I see. And is there any communication between the closet and the room where Lovie slept?'

'N ... no,' he said slowly. 'Not directly. Only through the kitchen.'

'I see,' said Cockburn again, smiling. 'And did you hear John Lovie arise at any time during the night?'

'No.'

'Did you see John Lovie give anything to McKessar, either that morning or the previous evening?'

'No.'

'Did you see her take anything on either of these occasions?'

'No ... well, just before she went to bed, I saw her take a drink – twice – out of the water bucket in the kitchen.'

'Could she have mixed anything with it herself?'

'No!' Rannie cried, alarmed. 'She was in my sight all the time. She didn't mix anything with it.'

'Hmm,' said John's lawyer. He paused for effect, raised an eyebrow at the jury. Rannie's face felt hot. He wished the lawyer would come out and ask him directly if he thought Meggy had taken her own life, so that he could swear she had not.

'Did you ever see anything particular by John Lovie towards McKessar in respect to what she ate or drank?'

'No,' he said shortly.

'In the Lovies' household, is there any distinction kept between master and servant in regard to eating?'

'No.'

'Do you eat from the same dish?'

'Sometimes. Sometimes not.'

John Lovie's lawyer blinked his hooded eyes at Rannie and gave a slight smile. He felt as if he might faint. The courtroom was stuffy and his head was in a fog. All these questions! He was only a labourer. He didn't know whether his words had saved his master or condemned him. He didn't know whether he wanted John Lovie to be saved or condemned. All his views of right and wrong had been battered and scattered about like the corn at threshing time. He thought of Meggy, cold and stiff and white. And John Lovie, placid in the dock. And the widow, out there in the gallery, with eyes that were shredding him into ribbons.

Chapter 65

William Park's Testimony

After Alex Rannie's sensational testimony, William Park's was an anticlimax.

Widow Lovie's heart was so bruised she could barely look at Park. The crowd was slow to settle. Lords Pitmilly and Alloway pounded their gavels, and she forced herself to breathe and focus on their neighbour up there in the stand. Even from a distance, she could see that his forehead was glistening with sweat. He must have been wondering how he had arrived at this position. *Well, aren't we all?* Head down, eyes up, he scanned the courtroom – looking for a sympathetic face, she supposed. Seeing none, he turned his attention to the prosecutor.

Mr Alison asked William Park to recount the events of Monday 13th of August.

'I supped at John Lovie's house,' he began. 'We supped between six and seven. I stayed till near eight.'

'Was Margaret McKessar present?'

He shrugged. 'She was whiles present and whiles absent.'

'What was her health?'

'She seemed in good health.'

'And her spirits?'

He shrugged again. 'She seemed in good spirits.'

The prosecutor dismissed him. The widow leaned back and watched him scurry from the courtroom.

Chapter 66

John Yule's Testimony

The clerk of the court called the next witness to the stand. It was little John Yule. A hush fell as he tiptoed through the door at their right and into the courtroom. Widow Lovie's heart clenched. People glanced at each other and then at their shoes, shamefaced. They'd come for a spectacle, but they hadn't counted on being party to the harassment of a child. The widow, observing the embarrassed coughs and hunched shoulders in the gallery, felt vicious. See, she thought. See what you're doing.

Her little grandson's head could barely be seen above the witness stand, and there was some delay as officials fetched a box for him to perch upon. The boy was tiny up there. Mary had said she'd washed his face, but there would be a ring of dirt around his neck; the widow couldn't see it, but she knew it would be there. His eyes were so blue that they looked bright to her, even from this distance, even with her old eyes. He was frightened, she could tell, and so he should be. It wasn't every day the law called upon a child to hang his own uncle. She wanted to push her way to the stand, shove the rabble aside, take the boy in her arms. Her heart strained towards him. If they took her John away, who would she love? This boy, so unlike her John, and yet so dear. The thought should have consoled her, but it didn't.

The child's father had objected to his court appearance, but he'd had no say in the matter. The law allowed it, and what right had a poor farmer to protest? The law said that a child under fourteen was unable – from a 'defect either of education or intelligence', they said – to understand the solemnity of the oath, but that was no help to the poor loon. The court could still examine him, it seemed, so long as the lawyers only asked questions about facts that could be readily understood by a small boy. There would be no oath and no Bible, but the seven-year-old would be publicly grilled just the same.

He was speaking in a voice high and clear. If you closed your eyes, she thought, letting her lids drop, you could pretend he wasn't afraid.

'Tell me what happened on the day Meggy died,' said the young prosecutor.

She opened her eyes to glare at him. John's tormentor was sharper than he had at first appeared. Beneath his amiable manner, she saw, were unbending principles. He was young, clean and diligent. And hatefully *righteous*. What would *he* – from his high position – know of hardship and suffering? What would *he* know about the shades and subtleties of truth and fairness and justice and right and wrong?

'I was at my father's house the night before,' John Yule piped up. 'I got up betwixt six and seven and came to Grannie's place.'

'Did you see Margaret McKessar that morning?'

'Yes, sir. Meggy brought me my pottage. She was crying.' A murmur in the courtroom.

'What time was this?'

'About eight o'clock, sir.'

'When did you see her next?'

'I saw her standing outside, at the gable of the house. I saw her vomit twice.' The boy's head bobbed above the rim of the witness stand. His blue eyes combed the gallery. Searching for his family, she supposed.

'Over here,' the widow whispered, willing the boy to find her.

Mary dug fingernails into her arm and sniffed. The widow shifted to ease the pressure of Mary's grip. If only Elspet were here; Elspet's fierceness would have given her heart. The boy couldn't find them in the crowd. He gave up, visibly deflated, and returned his attention to the prosecutor.

'Did you see her take any food that morning?' Mr Alison persisted smoothly.

'No, sir.'

'Did you see Margaret McKessar again that morning?'

'No, sir. But I went back into the house and Meggy was in the bed, and I heard her vomit.'

'Was Widow Lovie in the house at this time?'

The boy was silent.

'Your grannie,' Alison prompted gently. 'Was she in the house?'

'Aye,' he said. 'She asked Meggy if she was getting better, and Meggy said no.'

'What did you do next?'

'I stayed in the house a while and then I went to work in the fields.'

'What time did you return to the house?'

'Betwixt one and two, I think. Grannie said that Meggy was still sick and bade me fetch her mother.'

'Did you see John Lovie – your uncle – in the house that day?'

'No, sir.'

'Have you ever heard or seen rats at the farm?'

The boy hesitated, seeming disoriented by the change in subject. 'Like I told Baillie Chalmers. Once I heard a noise at my bed head that might have been rats or mice. I told Grannie and she said she'd set the rat trap, but she didn't do it, and I never heard them again.'

Widow Lovie raised a hand to her mouth. The memory came back to her now. The boy's complaint had given her a start at the time, for the old folk said that noises heard in bed at night foretold a death in the household. The death watch, they called it. She had pushed the thought aside and forgotten to set the trap. Bile rose in her throat. If only she'd remembered. If she'd remembered, she might have had a rat to show the prosecutor, and if she had a rat for the prosecutor, he would know that John's poison had been intended for *it* and not for Meggy ... but had the noise really been rats, after all? Or had it been death lurking in the night, spying, preparing, waiting to snatch Meggy to its breast? And if it was death ... was it waiting for John too?

'Did you ever hear or see rats or mice on any other occasion?' the prosecutor said.

'No, sir.' The boy seemed pleased; you could hear it in his voice. Here was a question he could answer with certainty. *God help him.* He smiled in the general direction of the gallery, possibly hoping that his smile would find its way to his mother, wherever she was. Mary made a small noise – something between a moan and a cough. James, on the widow's left, shifted in his seat. He was angry; she could sense it. Why? Which particular detail angered him? There were so many to choose from. She hardly knew her youngest son. She'd given all her attention to John. And for what? John was still a mystery to her.

'Did you ever see any dead rats in the dung-hill?'

'No, sir.' The boy finally found her eye in the crowd. She could make out his smile – just – but she could also sense confusion in his voice. What, after all, had rats or mice to do with Meggy's death? The widow forced her lips into a smile, and the boy turned back to his tormentor.

'You are John Lovie's cattle-herd, are you not?'

He stood taller. 'I am, sir.'

'Did you ever see John Lovie rub anything into a sick cow?'

'No, sir. There were no sick cattle,' he chirped, seeming confident now. 'Well, not so sick that they needed anything rubbed into them.'

Stupid child! She breathed deeply, slowly, with eyes closed. No sense blaming the innocent. The boy had been told to tell the truth. If he sent his uncle to the gallows, it would not be his fault. She would love him anyway. She would love him all the more, for he would need protection from the knowledge of what he had done. He would need forgiveness.

'Well,' little John Yule said, 'a black cow was sick of a sore belly after Meggy died, but we never rubbed nothing into her. My uncle gave her a drink of oil and she got well.'

'Have there been any other sick cows?'

'There was a hummel stirk had the houk, sir. Alex Milne bled it and it got better.'

'Did anyone rub anything into that cow?'

'No, sir. No-one rubbed anything into any cow.'

She buried her face in her hands and wept.

Chapter 67

Mrs McKessar's Testimony

The crowd had been subdued during the boy's testimony, but as soon as he stepped down and was swallowed up by the throng, excitement mounted again. Widow Lovie stood, anxious for the boy. Where was he? Mary Yule, with a face of thunder, was elbowing the crowd aside. She'd pushed her way through the mass of bodies to find her son and take him away. George Yule was beside her, looking uncomfortable in his best shirt and waistcoat. Mary pulled little John Yule through the horde towards the side of the courtroom, back out to the witnesses' waiting rooms. It was a treat to see Mary so steely. The widow strained to watch their retreat, but her view was obscured by the hateful crowd.

'Way to treat a child,' James muttered, mopping his brow with his sleeve.

He was all she had in the courtroom now. He wouldn't be any use to her; she might as well be alone. It was only James's sense of duty that had brought him to Aberdeen at all. He was conscious of what he owed his brother, she knew – John had raised him, after all. Even before George had gone to his Maker, it had always been John. James owed him love and loyalty; that's why he was here. But it didn't suit him to be there – it didn't suit him at all. James had been trying to make a name for himself in the Broch. He'd been talking about buying into the fishing trade, getting himself a boat or two, doing business. The right connexions were important. An association with a murderer

– or an alleged one – could be disastrous. John's predicament would be inconvenient for his brother, the widow supposed. She didn't care. She didn't give a damn about James's convenience.

She looked at his slumped figure – so elegant, so forlorn – and softened. He was there, and that was something. But what she really needed was her daughters: Elspet and Mary, and even Jean, the eldest, whom she rarely saw though she lived a stone's throw away. *What has happened to our family?*

Little John Yule had cast a searching glance in his grandmother's direction as he'd scuttled out the door, and she'd seen how frightened he really was. His hair, slicked down earlier by his mother, stood up like straw.

'Bless you, wee one,' she whispered, knowing how damaging his testimony had been, bleeding inside for her son and grandson.

'Hush now, Mither, the judge is trying to speak,' said James.

The judge – the slimmer one with the big nose and chin – was pounding the bench with his gavel. His mildness had vanished; his thin lips had caved in upon themselves. One by one, the voices fell silent, and the rabble squeezed back into their seats. As the judge lectured the people about courtroom behaviour, James whispered to his mother, 'Henrietta is next.'

He was right. In the melee, she hadn't noticed Meggy's mother being ushered to the stand. Emaciated, black-clad and stooped like a question mark, Henrietta shuffled to the front of the courtroom. She raised her head and faced the people with her brows arched and lines like canyons crossing her face. Widow Lovie's mouth dried up. Henrietta had aged a decade in the last month; she could see it even from this distance. She fought back an urge to wail.

Henrietta was talking, but her voice was too feeble to be heard. The judge asked her to speak up. Henrietta cleared her throat.

'I said that John Lovie used to call on Margaret before she became his servant. *I* wanted her to go into another man's service at Martinmas, but *she* wanted to go to John Lovie.'

'Did you know she was with child?'

Even from that distance, the widow sensed the heat in Henrietta's face. The twitching of her caved-in cheek.

'I kent,' she said.

A murmur rose amongst the crowd. Rage boiled in the widow's chest. She closed her eyes; she couldn't look at Henrietta, couldn't look at anyone.

'I taxed her with it.' Meggy's mother was speaking clearly now.

'What did she say?'

'She said, "Wait till you see." '

'Did you ask her if John Lovie was the father?'

'Nay,' Henrietta said. Then, leaning forward, she added, 'I did not, because I had no doubt of it.'

The murmur swelled, and outrage surged through the crowd. Widow Lovie felt that it was directed at her. She didn't care if it was; she would absorb it all – the fury, the hatred, the vitriol – if she could only divert it from her son. The judge pounded his gavel again and the noise gave way to silent hostility.

It was hard to concentrate on Henrietta's words, although the woman's voice was gaining strength. She was saying something about Meggy, about a headache, about how the girl had visited her mother to get a coal to light her master's pipe. Then she was talking about that awful day: the day that Meggy had died.

'I was carrying sods from the Bro—Fraserburgh, and ware from the shore,' she said. 'I went past John Lovie in the field four times. *Four times!*'

'What was the time, Mrs McKessar, when you passed John Lovie in the field?' the prosecutor asked.

'Well,' she said, getting louder and shriller. 'The *first* time was between seven and eight. I had two miles to go to the shore and the same to return, and I had to fill my cart. So it would have been near eleven when I came back. I passed him on my way to the shore again between eleven and twelve. It was when I was coming back the fourth time that the Yule boy called me in.'

The widow heard hisses from the gallery, though the judges were keeping them to a low buzz with their threatening frowns. No-one wanted to be thrown out of the courtroom; no-one wanted to miss the highlights of the show.

Why didn't John Lovie tell Meggy's mother she was ill? they all wanted to know. *Why didn't Widow Lovie fetch her?* Some of them were turning to look at her. They knew who she was; they'd worked it out. Glaring openly, not even bothering to hide their muttering behind cupped hands. She bit her cracked and trembling lip. Why *hadn't* she fetched Meggy's mother? God knows, if she could have the time again, she would have. For all the good it would have done.

There were more questions and more answers. The same questions, the same answers. The same five hours, relived again and again and again. The same memories. Meggy in bed, with only a shift on her. Her hands cold. A napkin full of vomit on the bed. Thomas Bisset, the doctor's assistant, coming from Fraserburgh, finding Meggy already dead.

Yes, Henrietta told the prosecutor, she was at the chesting and funeral.

'Did you see your daughter's body again after it was lifted?' he asked.

A shudder rocked through the courtroom at the thought.

'Nay,' she replied faintly. 'I did not.'

The prosecutor paused to let the jury reflect upon the mother's suffering. He turned back to the witness, poised for his next question. How she hated the arrogant tilt of his chin.

'Mrs McKessar,' he asked, and the confidence in his voice turned the widow's insides to porridge, 'did you ever find any medicines or powders in your daughter's belongings?'

Henrietta shook her head. 'I looked through my daughter's trunk when it was brought home. I didn't find any medicine or powder in it.'

'How was your daughter's state of mind in the days before her death?'

A collective intake of breath. Here was the critical question again: did Meggy take her own life? The courtroom was silent.

'My daughter was in her usual spirits for some time before her death.'

There was movement up the front: judges nodding, wigged people speaking in wealthy voices, gowns flapping. Henrietta's eyes were like stones, her brows lowered but chin high. Even the question mark of her spine had straightened a little.

Had Meggy been in good spirits? The widow pressed her knuckles into her eye sockets. She couldn't remember. Every time she thought about that morning, it played out differently. Sometimes she thought about how it should have been, and confused that version with how it really was. She was sick of thinking about it. The evil never went away, no matter how she looked at it, or away from it. If anyone asked what sort of spirits *she* was in, she'd give them an answer that would make their spit curdle. Not that anyone would ask.

And yet, low as she was, would she ever take poison? She couldn't imagine being driven to such lengths, not with the threat of eternal damnation pressing upon her. To what depth would a woman have to sink, then, to take her own life?

James dug an elbow into her side. 'It's John's lawyer's turn.'

Henry Cockburn was standing before the courtroom with his hands folded, smiling kindly at the witness. 'Did you tell John Lovie that your daughter was dead?'

'Aye,' Henrietta said warily.

'What did he say?'

'He said, "Good God" or "Oh my God" or something like that.'

'Then what did he do?'

'I said it was a strange thing for no doctor to be sent for, whether she was ill or dead. We proposed it, and John said he would go for a doctor, and he did.'

'When did he return?'

Meggy's mother shrugged. 'I dinna ken. Maybe in an hour.'

'Did the doctor come?'

'Aye. He tried her mouth with a candle and he felt her pulse, but there was no life.'

'What did you think of the proposal to examine the body for poison?'

'I objected to it at first,' Henrietta paused. She turned, for the first time, to look at the prisoner. Her cheek twitched wildly. 'For I thought it would do John Lovie harm.'

Lovie looked back at her, clear-eyed. The witness drew a ragged breath. Her voice, when it came again, was cracked with grief. 'I did not suspect poison.'

Chapter 68

Jean McKessar's Testimony

'Yes, I heard the report that she was with child,' Jean said.

Her fingers gripped the rim of the witness box. 'I taxed her with it. She neither denied nor confessed it. She told me'—here she paused and leaned forward to emphasise her words—'she said that John Lovie would marry her.'

She withdrew again, flaring her nostrils and breathing deeply to savour the thrill that rippled through the courtroom. She lifted her chin to glare at Lovie. He gazed back mildly. How she hated him.

She kept an eye on Lovie as she answered the questions, as if to pin him there, afraid that he would escape. She gave her answers mechanically. She had already told it all to the sheriff-substitute and she didn't have to think about her replies. But with each telling, the venom grew. Sometimes, it felt as if the hatred would swell up so fully that it would burst, like the fermenting stomach of a dead beast left too long in the field. She tried to keep her voice steady. Hysteria would not help her dead sister.

'It was Alex Rannie who told me that my sister was very ill and wanted me,' she said. 'But I went to my sister and found her *dead*.' Not ill, but *dead*. Hands cold, nails blue, breast still warm.

She had told all of this to the procurator fiscal and the sheriff-substitute: about the sand on the floor where Meggy had vomited, and the vomit on Meggy's handkerchief. She had relived it all a thousand times. Despite her best efforts, the words still came out angrily. Rage had been building, day by day, since her sister's death. She watched John Lovie sitting there, all fresh and handsome despite his weeks in the Tolbooth, and she wanted to dig the chipped fingernails of her work-worn hands into his eye sockets and gouge those cornflower-blue eyeballs right out of his well-chiselled head. She wanted to stab him, spit on him, pierce him through with a pitchfork, throw him under the hooves of an enraged bull, set him alight.

That a man like John Lovie could ruin a girl like Meggy! Even before he'd poisoned her, he had destroyed her. Poor, foolish Meggy.

The lawyer was asking about Meggy's vomit-soaked handkerchief. Jean remembered washing it in the widow's tub. She could still feel the sliminess under her fingertips.

'I did not think anything particular of the vomiting in the handkerchief until I washed it and found it hard to get out,' she said. She should never have washed that handkerchief. 'I suspected nothing at the time.'

What evidence might that dried-up mucus have held? Gone now, washed clean by Jean's scrubbing. But the prosecutor wanted to move on from the subject of Meggy's handkerchief.

'Did John Lovie object to the body being opened?' Archibald Alison asked. His dispassionate tone – 'the body' – startled and subdued her.

'Aye,' Jean said, and her voice was heavy with regret. 'He objected to it being opened because she was with bairn. He worried that it would be known. And I also objected, for the same reason.'

'What did your mother say?'

'John Lovie wanted me to tell my mother to object, but I didn't need to; my mother didn't want Meggy's body opened either.'

Jean leaned forward again, clenching her jaw and glaring at John Lovie, trying to bore holes in his face.

'I never blamed my sister for being with child,' she said, sorrowfully. 'I thought it was John Lovie's, and I thought that he would have taken charge of it. He told me that if I had taken her away, he would have taken Meggy back.' Then she paused and turned to the jury. 'He said that I should not long have it in my power to say anything against her.'

A commotion buzzed through the courtroom. Jean watched, her face hot with emotion, as her words echoed about the chamber. *What had John Lovie meant by those words?* She had asked herself, night after night, the very same question, ever since Meggy's death.

'Did you ever ask the prisoner whether Margaret had spoken to him about the child?' the prosecutor enquired.

'Aye,' Jean said. 'I asked him.'

'And what did he reply?'

'At first,' she replied slowly, 'he said, "I dinna ken." But later he said, "*Maybe she had.*"'

Chapter 69

Mary Will's Testimony

The judges announced a break. *A break?* The widow wanted to scream. The torture was to be prolonged. A break, so that John's tormentors and those vultures in the gallery could breathe fresh air and eat and drink and gossip and speculate. Oh, she could imagine the gossip. *Was he guilty? Would he hang?* And: *Did his mother know?*

James ushered her outside. His hand was on her elbow, but his eyes were off in the middle distance.

She wrenched her arm from his grasp. 'Thinking about your own reputation,' she said, 'when your brother's life is at stake.'

'It's the farm,' James said, his face flushing. 'It's the farm I'm fretting about.'

In John's absence, it had been a struggle to get through the corn harvest. George Yule and James had done their best – and even Alex Rannie had briefly lent a hand, though his presence had been a torment for them all – but they had crops of their own to attend to. Harvest time was drawing to a close, but at Futteret Den they were lagging behind. The neighbours had declined to help. William Park, old Mr Scott, the Milnes: not a peep from any of them. And this season had promised such plenty! The previous year had been a bad one, and the landlords had allowed their tenants indulgences. John had hoped to make up the arrears with this year's harvest. If only Meggy McKessar hadn't come along and thrown so much trouble in their way.

'John won't thank us for neglecting it,' James said with a stubborn pout.

'John will be home himself soon enough to finish the hairst,' she said. He didn't reply. His doubt made the blood pound in her ears.

Stop it, she told herself, breathing deeply. James was looking out for her, and she'd do well to remember that. He found a seat for her in the square and tried to make her eat the bread and drink the ale he had brought. She couldn't manage it. No doubt her abstinence annoyed him, much as he tried to hide it. James ate, and the sight of his Adam's apple bobbing up and down as he swallowed nauseated her.

People were milling about everywhere on the Castlegate. Smiling, sweating, gleeful people, enjoying the drama. The trial would give them something to talk about for weeks. Years, maybe.

She couldn't see Henrietta or Jean, and she was glad of that. She thought of Jean's blotched face, her bloodless lips as she had stood there and told her lies. The lashless eyes that made her look unhinged. She guessed that Jean and her mother were inside, protected by the law. She hated them, but she didn't wish them ill – if they'd only leave John alone.

James was chewing loudly, and she suppressed an urge to snap at him. She turned away and gazed up the street. A familiar figure was weaving its way through the crowds towards her: Mary.

They embraced. The widow's arms wrapped around her daughter, feeling the narrow frame, the ribs, the fragility of her. Her daughter. She kissed the pale moon of her face and wept into her neck.

'How is my grandson?'

'He's all right,' Mary said. 'He's got the jitters, but his father will calm him.'

'You came back.'

'Aye,' said Mary, with a wobble in her voice. 'I couldna leave you.'

'Or *him*,' the widow said. 'You couldna leave *him*.'

'Aye,' Mary said, without conviction.

They went back in with their damp hands clamped together. James trailed behind. Then they were back in the noisy chamber – back in the air that was rank with afternoon sweat and fear. They found seats again, closer to the front. She was glad to see that they were unrecognised by their new neighbours. The crowd swallowed them up.

Then the judges were pounding again, and the hubbub subsided, and the people turned their faces to the dock, where John – strong, unblinking John – sat, gazing back at them. She could see him better from the new vantage point. He was still sitting tall, still calm and mild-looking. Her John.

The clerk was calling a woman to the witness stand. The widow didn't catch her name.

'Who is she?' she whispered to Mary. She felt better now, with her daughter back at her side.

'Shhh!' said James.

Mary whispered, 'Her name's Mary Will.'

Widow Lovie craned her neck. The break had revived her, and she was afraid to miss a single detail. She saw a grey-haired woman, open-faced, clean, thin and frail in the black garb of a woman in mourning.

'What is your relationship to the deceased?' the young prosecutor was asking.

'Margaret McKessar was my niece,' the woman said. 'Her father – God rest him – was my brother.'

Meggy's aunt. Widow Lovie had sent her fresh-baked bread once, when Meggy had gone to visit.

'When did you last see your niece, Mrs Will?'

'I saw her on the second Sunday before her death,' the woman said in a clear, sweet voice. 'She came to see me on a visit of condolence.' She turned to the jury. 'My son had died.'

A wave of sympathy washed through the courtroom; the widow felt it with alarm. This pious, motherly woman – the jury would love her. What would she say? *Lord, let her show mercy.*

The prosecutor cleared his throat, and she steeled herself. 'What passed between you and your niece on that day, Mrs Will?'

A pause. Then the woman said, 'Meggy spent about two hours at my cottage. Then she went away home, and I walked with her part of the way.'

'How did she seem?'

'She seemed ... distracted. I reminded her that when my brother set off for India with the regiment, I promised I'd help her mither look after her. I think that prompted her to confide in me.'

Confide! Widow Lovie's heart pounded. *What did she confide?*

The prosecutor had the same question. 'What did your niece tell you, Mrs Will?'

'Meggy confessed to being with child.'

'She confided in you about the child?'

'Aye. She asked me if I'd heard that she was with child, and I told her I had not.'

'Did she name the father of her child?'

'She said the child's father was the master, John Lovie.'

'What was her state of mind when she delivered this news?'

Mary Will hesitated. 'At first, she seemed fine. She said that she would be married to John Lovie in a fortnight.'

Married. There it was again. The girl must have been spreading her lies all over the county – not just the sister but the aunt had heard it as well. Widow Lovie glanced at her daughter. Mary was round-eyed and appalled. James huffed, almost as if in amusement, beside her. It was an absurd notion, that John might marry a quine so far beneath him; she saw that now. John had said nothing about marriage. The girl had been fooling herself. Fooling herself, or telling barefaced lies. And at the back of her mind, a deeper truth niggled – a truth she hadn't wanted to dwell upon: John *couldn't* have married unless he admitted to Helen Chessor's child and paid the kirk – and if he'd done as much, how could he have afforded to marry?

'But before long'—the Will woman hadn't finished—'she was in tears. She told me that John Lovie was good to her, and that she had no doubt he would continue to be so if his friends would let him be. She said his friends had been sore against her ever since they knew she was with child to him. She said that his sister Elspet was against her. She said that Elspet was saying she should not be allowed to stay at John Lovie's house, whatever should be the consequences.'

Elspet! The blunderer. So word had got to Meggy.

'I see,' said the prosecutor. 'Mrs Will, how did you hear that your niece had died?'

The witness turned to face the prisoner. 'On the day after Meggy's death, I happened to be in Fraserburgh and a woman there told me.'

'And how did you react?'

'My first thought was ... that Meggy had suffered injustice at John Lovie's hands.'

Chapter 70

Alex Rannie's Retreat

Alex Rannie did not return to the courtroom after he had given his evidence. Instead, he scuttled out of that evil hall as fast as his legs would take him – away from the muggy heat, the body odour, the hungry eyes. He strode across Union Street, making for the docks. The cries of seagulls and the smell of salt air drew him on.

Out on the street, people were going about their business. They were pushing carts and mounting carriages and strolling about with their coat-tails flapping, and none of them turned a head in his direction. The fishy breeze, growing stronger as he approached the quay, was a balm.

He had no wish to hear the verdict. He didn't want to know whether John Lovie would hang, though he supposed the news would reach him soon enough, whether he wanted it or not. He had said his piece and wanted nothing more to do with it. Nothing more than to forget the whole sorry business – to forget his strange master and the tortured loyalties of his frosty-eyed mother. To forget the poor wee cowherd. Forget Meggy.

As soon as he was able, he would ride back to Pitullie on the horse he'd borrowed from his father, and he would put the horrors of Aberdeen out of his mind. Before long Martinmas would be upon them and he would find a new position. In the meantime, he'd help his father on the farm. And he'd be choosier with his next position.

Or perhaps he'd learn a trade and turn away from farming altogether. The earthy stink of manure held no charm for him now; he could not sniff it without thinking of Meggy, the damp curls clinging to her cheek, the curve of her hip, the way she'd looked at John Lovie. Better the sharp smell of fish on the shores of Fraserburgh, or better still the clean tang of fresh-sawn timber. James Lovie was making a name for himself as a carpenter, moving further and further away from the land. Folk said he would soon be in business by himself. Why couldn't he, Alex Rannie, do the same? It was all in the hands: strength and dexterity, a sensitive touch; that was what a carpenter needed. His hands were well attuned to the flesh of the beasts and the heft of the plough – and surely, with time and devotion, they could learn the ways of an adze and a chisel.

Besides, what future was there in a labouring life? Aye, he could progress to a richer master and a bigger farm, always bettering himself – but where would it end? The best he could hope for was a long-term tack on a farm like Futteret Den and a life like John Lovie's: always at the mercy of the weather, always praying to make the rent. And if he was lucky enough to find a wife, there would be bairns to feed, and all on a farmer's unreliable earnings.

A wife! His thoughts strayed to the neighbour's girl, Fiona. Fiona, standing forlorn at the feeing market in her sister's boots, turning away for the shame of it all; Fiona, grown strong, pious and practical. They'd grown up together, more or less. But she'd turned into a woman since he'd left his father's house.

Rannie raised his face to the sun and sucked in the fishy air. For him, the trial was over. It was time to start again.

Chapter 71

William Massie's Testimony

Inside the courtroom, the trial went on.

'He came twice into Mr Officer's shop,' William Massie said. John Officer's young apprentice addressed the prosecutor in a frightened squeak. His Adam's apple bobbed and dipped up and down his pimply neck as he swallowed. 'First at the beginning of August ... or maybe late July. He asked for an ounce of jalap and got it. He said it would be a good dose; I asked him if it was for a beast, but he said it was for a person.'

'*Liar!*' Widow Lovie cried. *No, no!* Why all these lies? If only they would let her speak, she would tell them all the truth. That John was a good man, in spite of everything. That she loved him, she loved him, she loved him.

'Hush, Mither!' Mary said.

A few people turned to scorch her with their eyes, but not many had heard her. She thought she had screamed it, but it seemed that her cry had come out only as a whisper. In any case, the vultures in the courtroom had ears only for the shop boy's slander.

Her head was pounding. Massie's words hit her temples like hammers: jalap – purgatives – rats – poison – arsenic – *nux vomica* ... what was all this nonsense?

'He came back about eight days later – it was a few days before Margaret McKessar's death – and said he would take the poison now, as he was very much troubled with rats. Mr Officer was there that time.'

The boy's ears were red – bright red, like a robin's breast. A bad-luck robin, portent of trouble with the law. Would praying help? If she prayed right here, in the courtroom, would God hear? If she promised to give thanks to Him every day; if she promised never to miss a Sunday service? If she vowed to try, every day, to bring John back into the bosom of the church? Would He have mercy?

The shop boy was talking about half-ounce packages of arsenic, and how much they cost, and how many packages there were, and whether they were labelled. What did it matter? She rubbed her thumping temples. What did any of it matter? Meggy was dead. Hanging John would not bring her back. It was hot in the courtroom, but her hands were cold. Cold and stiff, just like Meggy's.

'Did the prisoner give any other reason for wanting arsenic?' Mr Alison asked in his deep, resonant voice.

Massie shook his head. 'No, sir. Only rats.'

'Did he say anything about vermin on black cattle?'

'No, sir.'

'Do you ever sell arsenic to any customer who you do not know?'

'No, sir,' the boy shook his head vigorously. 'Mr Officer has expressly forbidden me to sell any poison to folk that I don't know.'

'Did you sell arsenic to anyone else at that time?'

'No, sir,' said the shop boy. 'Only to John Lovie.'

Chapter 72

John Officer's Testimony

'Do you know the pannel?' Mr Alison asked the witness.

'Aye,' John Officer replied, nodding at John. 'I have known John Lovie personally for the last fifteen years.'

'Is it true that you sell arsenic?'

'It is,' he admitted. 'But only to those I know personally, and who I know to be of good character.'

John Officer looked relaxed in the witness box: calm, confident and self-assured. He was a tidy man, a man who clearly liked order. He spoke dispassionately; he would not care whether John lived or died. Widow Lovie's stomach clenched.

'Did you ever sell arsenic to John Lovie?' the prosecutor asked.

Mr Officer stared frankly at John as if studying a museum exhibit. Unlike the other witnesses, he looked unafraid. 'It was either on the Friday, or the Saturday before Margaret McKessar died. John Lovie came into my shop. The shop boy William Massie was there with me.'

'Was there anyone else in the shop?'

Officer shook his head. 'Just Massie and me.'

'Go on.'

'Well,' he said, 'Lovie came straight in and said to me, "Give me some of that stuff." I asked, "What stuff?" and Lovie said, "For killing vermin," and I said, "What kind of vermin, is it rats?" and Lovie said yes.'

'And then?'

The spectators held their breath and leaned forward so as not to miss a word. Widow Lovie found herself doing the same.

'And then, I asked if it was arsenic he wanted. Lovie said yes, and I asked him how much. He said he didn't know. I told him that if he hadn't many rats, three pence worth would be enough.' John Officer paused as if for dramatic effect, and then turned to face the gallery. 'He said,' he went on, 'that to make the dose effective, he'd take sixpence worth.'

Her cry was drowned out by the whooping of the crowd. Mary wrapped an arm around her shoulders. The people had been restraining themselves for too long; nothing would hold them back from sharing this moment of outrage. It took a full minute of furious gavel-pounding for the judges to get the courtroom under control. In the meantime, John Officer waited, unruffled, in the witness box.

'What did you do next?' Mr Alison asked, once the racket in the gallery had settled.

'Well,' Officer continued. 'I keep the arsenic in a safe place, by itself, made up in packages of three pence worth. Each package contains about half an ounce. My shop boy, Massie, took two of these packages from the place where the arsenic is kept. I wrote the word "poison" on the packages, and the boy gave them to John Lovie.'

'Did you *see* Massie give the packages to Mr Lovie?'

'Aye.' Officer nodded confidently. 'Aye, I did.'

'Are you quite certain that when John Lovie called and bought the arsenic from you, the word "arsenic" was used? Are you *quite* certain that Lovie *knew* that it was arsenic he was getting?'

'I am quite certain.'

'And are you quite certain that John Lovie saw the word "poison" written on the packages?'

'I am. I pointed out the word "poison" on each of the packages. I warned him to be careful with it, to prevent an accident.'

'And he explicitly told you he wanted it for killing rats?'

'Aye, he did.'

'He did not mention that he wanted it to treat black cattle?'

Officer shook his head. 'He did not say he wanted it for any other purpose. Your Honours'—he turned to address the bench—'arsenic may be rubbed on sheep that are infected with vermin because they don't lick their sores with their tongues, but it can't be used to rub the sores of black cattle. The cattle will lick their sores and be poisoned by it.'

'Indeed,' said the prosecutor. 'Did you instruct Lovie on how the poison was to be used?'

'I asked Lovie how he was going to mix the arsenic, and he said, "with meal".'

'Mr Officer, does John Lovie come often into your shop?'

The witness shook his head. 'Nay. Although, on the day of the girl's funeral, my shop boy Massie told me that John Lovie had called in to the shop some days before, when I was out. He said that John Lovie was asking him about poison then.' Officer turned to the judges again. 'That's how Massie knew what John Lovie was talking about on the day he bought the arsenic – when he came in and asked for "that stuff". He knew Lovie wanted arsenic because they had discussed it before.'

Lords Pitmilly and Alloway nodded their wigged heads.

'Have you ever, on any other occasion, sold poison to John Lovie?' the young whiskered prosecutor asked.

'No,' Officer insisted, turning again to the judges. His obsequiousness was starting to grate upon Widow Lovie's nerves. 'I have not.'

'In what form was the arsenic you sold to John Lovie?'

'It was a white powder.'

'From whom did you acquire the arsenic?'

'I think I bought it from the Apothecaries Hall at Glasgow.'

The prosecutor cleared his throat. 'Mr Officer, in your statement to the baillie, you claim that George Yule, brother-in-law to John Lovie, called in to question you on Saturday the 18th of August after Margaret McKessar's body was exhumed.'

'That's right,' the witness said.

'What did he want?'

'He said it was reported in the country that Lovie had bought arsenic from me. I told him that I did not wish to give him any information on the subject. Mr Yule said that he'd questioned John Lovie, and that his brother-in-law had denied that he'd bought poison from me. He said Lovie told him he'd not been in my shop since the beginning of May harvest this summer when he called to enquire about a scythe.'

'Do you recall John Lovie enquiring about a scythe?'

A pause. 'I do not.'

'Is William Massie your only shop boy?'

'Aye.'

'And is there anyone else in Fraserburgh who keeps arsenic?'

The druggist shrugged. 'As far as I know, I'm the only one – except maybe for Dr Coutts or Dr Jamieson.'

'Thank you, Mr Officer.' Mr Alison peered at the man in the witness stand with eyes sharp and insistent. Widow Lovie gripped the edge of her seat. She was beginning to recognise that cocky tilt of the prosecutor's chin – the way he tipped his head back to look down that roman nose with those slitted eyes – and to fear it.

'One more thing. Did you know Margaret McKessar?'

'I did not.'

'Could you have sold poison to Margaret McKessar?'

'I did *not* sell poison to Margaret McKessar,' John Officer said firmly. 'I only sell poison to people I know. I did not know Margaret McKessar. I did *not* sell poison to her.'

Chapter 73

More Testimonies

The parade of witnesses was endless. Widow Lovie lost count. She watched helplessly as, again and again, they stood to condemn her son.

James Walker – John's neighbour, the wright who had made Meggy's coffin, John's *friend* – stood in the witness stand and addressed the courtroom.

'I saw John Lovie at his brother-in-law's home on the Saturday after Meggy died. I called in to borrow a newspaper, and John Lovie arrived soon after.'

'His brother-in-law? Do you mean George Yule?' asked the prosecutor.

'Aye.'

'And what conversation did you have on that day?'

'George Yule's wife asked me what news there was in the country, and I told her I had heard that the doctors had dug up Meggy's body the day before. And then ... and then I told John Lovie that reports were going about that he bought arsenic from John Officer.' Walker looked down at his shoes. 'And so I told John ...'

'What did you tell him?'

'I told him ... that he should take the south road. That he should fly.'

He ducked his head as if to dodge abuse from the gallery, but the crowd was silent.

'What did he say?'

'He told me he would not know poison if he saw it. He said he'd never bought any poison in his life.'

***

Her son-in-law, Alex Milne, told the courtroom that he had bled Lovie's cow when it had the houk. This was fully two weeks before Meggy's death, he said. He did not recollect having bled any other beast of John Lovie's this season.

'What is the houk?' the prosecutor asked.

'An inflammation of the back that causes the hide to become bound.'

'Does it produce vermin?'

A pause. 'It does not.'

But later, when John's defence pressed him: '*As far as I have ever heard*, it does not.'

***

A stocky young man took the stand; he looked familiar. The widow squinted.

George Byth was his name, he said. *Ah!* Byth had once been in service at Futteret Den. He'd left to become a square-wright in Fraserburgh with Thomas Brebner. He'd fattened up since then.

'I saw John Lovie going into Mr Officer's shop in the afternoon of the Saturday before McKessar's death,' he said. 'We exchanged a few words, but I was leaving the shop and did not stay to hear what he wanted.'

'When were you in the Lovies' service?'

'It was for half a year, two years past Whitsunday last.'

'Did you ever see rats about Lovie's farm town?'

'No, I never saw any rats.'

***

John Milne, the messenger-at-arms, told the court that he had searched Lovie's house and dung-hill but found no poison. Neither had he found a single rat, dead or alive. Widow Lovie burned with the memory of it.

With Brown the gravedigger, Milne said, he had searched the whole of Fraserburgh to ascertain whether poison could be purchased anywhere besides John Officer's shop, and found that it could not.

'I had the prisoner in custody at the Inn at Fraserburgh,' he said, 'when his brother-in-law George Yule came to see him. Yule came to make arrangements for the farm in Lovie's absence.'

'Did they speak about poison?'

'Aye. George Yule asked Lovie if he had bought poison from John Officer, or anything else that might have done McKessar harm.'

'What did the prisoner reply?'

'He said that he had not.'

***

James Grant stood to say his piece. *The fancy hat dresser.* His suit was clean and new, his whiskers neatly trimmed. He clasped his soft hands over his plump belly and told the court that he had known the deceased for ten years; she was a cousin of his wife's. He had seen Meggy's body in the coffin and was certain it was hers. He had seen Meggy buried and then unburied again. He had seen her body opened. He could confirm

286

that the body lifted from the grave was Margaret McKessar's, and that the stomach extracted from it was hers as well.

'In the evening before the funeral,' he said, 'my wife had been out at the Lovies' home. When she left, John Lovie and Meggy's brother James McKessar went with her. There had been talk of poison, so they called in to Dr Jamieson to ask him to examine the body, but he said he'd need a warrant. They came to me, and we walked together to see Baillie Chalmers.'

Grant paused, and the prosecutor asked him how John had seemed on that occasion.

'He seemed very low in spirit. On our way to the baillie, he asked me – several times – if a body would swell if it had got poison.'

***

Then there was John Brown, the gravedigger. The jolly beadle, everybody's friend. He stood in the witness box and dabbed his forehead with a handkerchief, and the tremor in his hands was plain to see, even with the widow's poor eyes. Yes, he said, he had searched the house and the dung-hill. No, there were no rats.

'I knew Margaret McKessar well,' he said. 'I stayed in the same house with her for a time.' The court was silent but for the rasping of his voice. 'I buried her and I disinterred her, and I delivered her body to Dr Jamieson. And I buried her again ... and I took her up again. I buried her three times.'

***

The prosecutor produced witness after witness; so many that it seemed he barely needed to concentrate on the task at hand. Even Thomas

287

Bisset, the apprentice doctor who had come too late, had something to say. He had been called to the prisoner's home to see a woman, he said. Dr Jamieson being out, Bisset went in his place. It was about three in the afternoon. He had felt her pulse – twice – and found her dead. He had seen her body disinterred and examined.

The attention of the crowd in the gallery had drifted – she could sense it. The heat and repetition were making them drowsy, and John's lawyer had sat through this parade of witnesses without raising an eyebrow. She wanted to give him a shove.

But at last – *thank God!* – Henry Cockburn roused himself.

'Mr Bisset,' he said, and his voice was sharp, like a gust of sea air, 'who was it who fetched you when Margaret McKessar was dying?'

'It was John Lovie,' he said.

It wasn't much, but it was something. Widow Lovie hung onto that.

Chapter 74

The Medical Evidence

By the time Dr Jamieson was called to testify, the mob was dull and lethargic. It had been a long day indoors, but still, they couldn't drag themselves away. Entertainment like this was hard to come by.

Dr Jamieson spoke of how he and Dr Coutts had gone to the churchyard and watched John Brown scoop Meggy's body from the grave. Mr Alison asked him to read his report of the autopsy, and Dr Jamieson unfolded a document and cleared his throat. The crowd leaned forward.

'The uterus was about eight inches in length,' he read, 'containing a female child nearly perfect, except in size, with the usual appendages belonging to a foetus during the end of the fourth or beginning of the fifth month. It appeared to be healthy. On inspecting the stomach, we observed on its internal surface a few patches of inflammation. On opening it, about a pound of dark-coloured fluid, mixed with shreds of the same colour, and having no particular smell, escaped.'

Here was the grisly detail they'd been waiting for. Widow Lovie put her hands over her ears.

'Mither,' Mary whispered, and her mother turned away from the staleness of her breath. 'Come outside.'

But she couldn't go out. She didn't want to hear it, but she couldn't go.

It went on and on. The descriptions of Meggy's insides and the tests they had done.

When Mr Alison had finished, Mr Cockburn began his attack. She dropped her hands back in her lap and held her breath.

'Who asked you to open Margaret McKessar's body, Dr Jamieson?'

The doctor frowned. 'It was the prisoner, John Lovie.'

'Ah,' said John's lawyer. 'How did John Lovie approach you?'

'He called upon me. We met in the street, and he asked me to open the body. He said a report had gone abroad that the woman had been poisoned, and that he wished to clear himself. I understood this to mean that he wished me to open the body.'

'How did the prisoner seem when he asked you this?'

'He appeared very anxious about it.'

'Thank you, Dr Jamieson.'

***

Dr Blaikie was called next. He read out his report, explaining in painful detail his experiments on Meggy's stomach. Unbelievably, people were yawning. How she would have loved to have the luxury of boredom. The doctor's words – sulphuretted hydrogen and arsenious acid and filtration and precipitate and alliaceous smells – fell beyond her ken, and it didn't feel fair that such foreign words should be weightier than any words had ever been. Folk trusted words like these, though they could not understand them; they were beguiled by them. They were beguiled in the way that her mother had once been by the superstitions of old. These scientists were the new prophesiers.

After Dr Blaikie came the prosecutor's trump card: the Edinburgh authority, Professor Christison of Edinburgh College.

Mr Alison began with chitchat to introduce him. It seemed that he wanted the jury to believe the professor had the final word on the cause of Meggy's death. On the prosecutor's prompting, the Edinburgh doctor recited his long list of qualifications. Mr Alison wanted the court to know that Christison was an expert in chemistry and toxicology with a particular interest in poisons; that he was a rising star in the world of medical jurisprudence. *Jurisprudence? What gibberish is he talking?* Here, Widow Lovie thought, was a man who knew all about test tubes and Latin but nothing of hardship or death or the heartbreak of love.

The professor explained to the court that he had been frequently called upon to conduct experiments to determine the presence – or not – of arsenic in the human stomach. He had been a key witness in the recent trial of Mary Smith.

'Smith,' she whispered to James. 'That Dundee woman.'

James nodded vigorously. 'Aye,' he said. 'Same doctor, same lawyer for the defence.'

'Same prosecutor,' Mary said, eyes round in her sweat-beaded face, squeezing her mother's arm. 'And *she* got off! Mither, they found Mary Smith not guilty.'

'It was *not proven*,' James corrected her. 'It wasn't *not guilty*.'

'Still,' said Mary. 'Still.'

Widow Lovie leaned forward and fixed her eyes upon Dr Christison. He looked something of a dandy, with his thick, glossy brown hair curling above the ears and cascading down on each side into whiskers like ringlets. But she wasn't fooled; the small eyes were intense, the brow heavy and serious.

'I received a phial contained in a box, with an unbroken seal and a label,' the professor was saying. 'I recognise it as the exhibit you have shown me. I analysed the contents and drew up a report, which I will read to the court now.'

The gentleman opened a document and began to read. 'Edinburgh, 29th of August 1827. I certify that, on the 27th instant, I received from Adam Rolland, Esquire, a box, enclosing two bottles duly sealed and labelled, and which were described as containing – the one a part of the contents of the stomach – the other, the stomach itself of Margaret McKessar ...'

The professor rattled on as if delivering a lecture to a hall full of medical students. It meant nothing to her. When he had finished, the prosecutor thanked him and paused to allow the jury to absorb his words. They had been beyond the comprehension of most in the courtroom: chemical names and processes foreign to folk who knew only of the hay harvest and the fishing trade. The professor was a young man, but he had authority, there was no mistaking it. He was the sort of man a lay person would trust. It was now up to the prosecutor to tease out his words, to help the witness translate his jargon into the language of an Aberdeenshire farmer.

'Professor Christison,' Mr Alison said, 'might the symptoms of Margaret McKessar's illness have been produced by arsenic poisoning?'

'Indeed,' the professor replied. 'Her symptoms correspond exactly with the effects of arsenic.'

Mr Alison threw the jury a meaningful glance.

'But,' Professor Christison cut in, 'they might also be produced by natural disease such as cholera.'

A murmur spread around the room. The judges raised their gavels and it subsided.

Mr Alison opened his mouth to speak, but the professor interrupted. 'Of course,' he explained, '*that* disease does not prove fatal in this climate in so short a time. And of course, in the case of cholera, no arsenic would be found in the stomach.'

Apparently mollified, the prosecutor nodded. 'What then, in your professional opinion, was the cause of Margaret McKessar's death?'

'It is my decided opinion,' Christison said clearly, 'as a professional man, judging from the contents of the stomach, that the deceased died of arsenic poisoning.'

The jury – and the spectators – had seemed hypnotised by the weight and mystery of the medical reports. They were beginning to sag in their seats. Even Widow Lovie was losing concentration, losing hope. The lawyers vied to bring them back to life, but on whose side would they rally?

Before the defence could lay John's case out before the jury, Mr Alison had one final shot. He called Dr Coutts to the witness stand. 'Dr Coutts,' he said, 'on whose order was Margaret McKessar's body disinterred?'

'It was disinterred at the order of Baillie Chalmers,' he replied.

'Not on John Lovie's order?'

'No, it was *not* on John Lovie's order.'

Chapter 75

The Declaration

Jean McKessar had been waiting to hear John's defence.

It would be hard to bear, but she needed to hear it just the same. She had slipped into the back of the gallery and stretched up on her toes to see over the heads of the crowd. Her mother was resting in a side room, taking comfort from the presence of her remaining children. Jean should have been with her, but she couldn't help herself. Listening to Lovie's defence was like picking at a scab.

He wasn't going to speak for himself. His lawyer, Mr Cockburn, stood to read the declaration aloud to the courtroom. The audience was silent, spellbound. This was it, she supposed: the part they'd all been waiting for. What would the monster say in his defence?

'John Lovie, Farmer in Percyhorner, parish of Fraserburgh ...' Mr Cockburn began.

In the centre of the gallery was an inscription: *Servate terminos quos / Patres vestri posuere.* It meant nothing to Jean; she knew nothing of Latin and in any case she couldn't read. Earlier, a court official had seen her frowning over it.

'It means "Keep the boundaries which your fathers set",' he had told her. He'd meant to be helpful, but she still couldn't see the sense in it. Maybe one had to have a father to understand. Her and Meggy's father had disappeared when they were children; he'd signed up and gone to India, and all they'd had from him since was in the form of a few shillings from the kirk: 'poor relief'. Except that there never was any relief.

Keep the boundaries which your fathers set. John Lovie would have been the father to Meggy's child: the little girl who had never been allowed to take a breath. Boundaries! Jean snorted. *He* had observed no boundaries. *He* had disregarded every principle of decent behaviour. He'd crossed the line into lechery, deceit, betrayal, and cold-blooded murder. The court would do better to advise 'keep the boundaries which your *mothers* set'. If it were so, then perhaps one might have faith in justice.

'The declarant never had any carnal connexion with Margaret McKessar,' the lawyer said. 'Nor did the said Margaret McKessar ever tell the declarant that she was with child. He had no suspicion of it, and he never heard of her state until informed in court that a female foetus of about four months old was found in McKessar's womb after her death.'

Jean McKessar shook her head, hissing her breath out through clenched teeth.

'On the day after her death, the declarant saw her sister Jean McKessar at the declarant's house ... He denies that on that or any other occasion Jean McKessar questioned him about Margaret being with child.'

Jean balled her fists. If she could have thrown a brick at him, she would have done.

'A short time ago,' Cockburn continued, 'the declarant bought some jalap at John Officer's shop in Fraserburgh ... the next evening, he mixed about one fourth part with cold water and took it as physic to himself. He took the mixture because he was injured after his horse ran away with his cart and threw him down. The declarant drank the mixture in his own house, but he cannot say if anyone saw him doing so.'

Of course he can't, she thought, as the lawyer droned on.

'The declarant, immediately after drinking the jalap, threw the remainder of the mixture out of the door of his house, but he cannot say if anyone saw him throw it away. He never gave any of the jalap to Margaret McKessar or to anyone else.'

The lies kept coming. *He cannot say, he cannot say.* The declarant didn't remember asking the shop boy about poison when he purchased the jalap. He only remembered asking at Mr Officer's shop, later, about poison for killing rats and vermin upon black cattle. He remembered buying two small paper parcels; he did not remember seeing the word 'poison' written on them. He did not remember the word 'arsenic' being used by Mr Officer, William Massie, or himself. He did not know what substance he was purchasing.

He claimed, on the day of the purchase, to have mixed some of the contents of the parcels – whitish powder – with cold water in a saucer, and to have used it to rub the backs of his cattle.

'The declarant rubbed the mixture on the cattle in the byre twixt seven and eight in the evening. The only person who saw the declarant do so ... was his mother.'

His mother. Jean scanned the gallery and found her easily. Even from behind, from a distance, Widow Lovie's black-clad figure was unmistakable. There was such stillness about her. Head high, shoulders square. She had turned slightly towards her daughter, and Jean made out the strong angles of her cheekbone and jaw. Meggy had always spoken of the widow fondly. Jean saw, in her mind's eye, Widow Lovie sitting rigid by Meggy's body in the stone cottage. Even then, in the warm glow and flicker of the candlelight, the old woman's eyes had been cold.

Lovie's lawyer was saying something about sick cattle – something about a cow with the houk. There seemed to be some confusion about whether the beast had been bled or rubbed with a mixture. Or had there been two separate occasions: a bleeding and a rubbing? No-one seemed to be sure. Everyone had a different story, and no-one could remember dates. But why would they? Every day was the same as every other. Until now. Would that confusion go in Lovie's favour, though, or against him?

Cockburn was telling the court some story about the mixture Lovie had used on the cattle, saying that Lovie had put the leftover mixture on a saucer in the kiln barn to kill the rats. Had anyone seen him do it? No, of course not. Neither had he told anyone about it. The next day, according to the defence's story, Lovie had found two dead rats lying beside the saucer and thrown them onto the dung-hill. The remaining mixture he had thrown into the kitchen fire. No-one, of course, had seen him throw away the rats. Those rats that no-one had been able to find. And no-one but his mother had seen him toss the remaining mixture into the fire.

It seemed to Jean as if there was no-one in the courtroom but herself, John Lovie, and his mother. She stared at the widow, searching for a reaction. There was none – not a flicker.

And again: 'No other person but the declarant, his mother, and his cattle-herd, John Yule, knew that the cattle were infected with vermin.'

There followed John Lovie's account of the night before Meggy's death, when the neighbour William Park had supped at the cottage. Jean listened intently, trying to capture every word and hold it in her memory. She imagined her sister dawdling about in the kitchen in her breezy, lazy way, boiling the potatoes, setting them before her master and his friend, sitting at the round table by the fire, bending over her own plate, eating and drinking and smiling.

And then, the terrible day. He arose at six in the morning, Lovie's lawyer declared on his behalf, 'and went ben to the kitchen. Then he lit his pipe and went out to put his horses to the grass.' He worked by the well, about a hundred yards from the house, shearing grass for his horses' supper. He did not go into the house until breakfast time, between nine and ten o'clock.

'The only time he saw Margaret McKessar that morning was when Rannie was out fetching a plough. She came out of the house to ask the declarant when he wanted his breakfast. He was some fifty yards from her when she called out.

'Rannie went in for his breakfast before the declarant, and afterwards he returned to work in the field with him … but the declarant does not recollect that he said anything about Margaret McKessar being unwell.

'When the declarant went in for his breakfast, his mother told him that Margaret McKessar was unwell, but he did not see McKessar.' He paused, stared at the jury. 'His mother did not say what ailed her … and she did not tell him the extent of McKessar's illness.'

How could the widow bear it, listening to her son's lies?

Lovie's words must be like knives into his mother's back. *She did not tell him the extent of McKessar's illness*; in other words, if he hadn't called for the doctor, it was his mother's fault. Jean might have pitied the widow if she didn't hate her so violently. She had only to think of Meggy, pierced through with pain and begging for her loved ones, and any pity she might feel for the old woman shrivelled to dust.

After Lovie had breakfasted, his lawyer told the court, he had worked in the turnip field until dinner time. Rannie had gone in for dinner first and come out to tell his master that Meggy had fainted. Lovie claimed to have run into the house on hearing the news, and there he had come upon Henrietta and the widow Lovie in the closet. He had known Meggy was in the closet bed, but he hadn't seen her.

'The women told the declarant that Margaret had fainted, and so he rode into Fraserburgh to fetch Dr Jamieson, but the doctor was out. Instead, a young apprentice of the doctor's went with the declarant to his house. By the time they got there, Margaret McKessar was dead.

'The declarant does not recall telling Rannie that Margaret McKessar was unwell when he returned from his breakfast to the field. He does not recall telling Rannie that he had heard her vomiting while he was in at breakfast.'

Then the lawyer faced the jury and told them how, a day or two after Meggy's death, rumours of poisoning had reached Lovie's ears.

'The declarant saw Jean McKessar at his house twice after Margaret's death'—Jean's heart pounded—'but the declarant does not recall any conversation with her about poison.'

He could not 'recall' any of it: not her charging him with the rumour that he had bought poison from Mr Officer, not his denial, not his feeble theory that some other person might have gone to Mr Officer and purchased poison in his name.

It was surreal, listening to John Lovie's version of events; it was like looking at a poor painting of a landscape instead of the real thing. The generalities were there, but the detail was all wrong. Jean exhaled slowly, realising her mistake in choosing to hear Lovie's account. She'd hoped he might say something to make her feel better. She hadn't known what that something might be, but, somehow, it had seemed *he* was the only one with the power to make sense of Meggy's death. Now she knew: there would never be any sense in it.

'Since Margaret's death the declarant has spoken to his brother-in-law George Yule twice; but he does not recollect that George Yule asked whether he had bought poison from Mr Officer; nor does the declarant recall denying to George Yule that he had bought poison.'

Jean shook her head slowly and turned to march from the courtroom. She couldn't bear to hear another word.

Chapter 76

Margaret Lovie

'His mother did not say what ailed her ... and she did not tell him the extent of McKessar's illness.' There was a moment during John's declaration when Widow Lovie had felt as if she was being buried in a blizzard: frozen, airless, blinded. It came back to her again: the sounds of Meggy's groaning and retching coming at them from the closet, and John retreating from the kitchen to the but. 'Meggy's ill,' she had told him, and Meggy's cries had said the rest. But John had hurried away.

'In some details,' Mr Cockburn's agent had told her son-in-law, 'Widow Lovie's evidence contradicts her son's.'

She had tried to disbelieve the lawyer's words. Now she knew them to be true. She struggled for air. Where had John's version of events come from?

He sat in the dock, blue-eyed and innocent. Calm. She remembered, wildly, her mother's stories of changelings. The fair-folk, it was said, stole beautiful children away and left fairy babies – flawed replicas – in their place. You could tell that your child was a changeling if he sickened suddenly or grew deformities or altered his behaviour. The fair-folk stole the babies to give to the Devil in payment of a tithe. Sometimes they stole as a punishment. Who was this handsome man in the dock that everyone said was her son – a changeling? She gritted her teeth. The fair-folk didn't take grown men. Not even beautiful ones.

She closed her eyes and steadied her breath. *Memory plays tricks on you – everyone knows it. Different people see with different eyes.* A tale told by a child would sound different coming from its father, and any two gossips telling the same story varied wildly in the particulars. Ask any old man to reminisce about his youth, and his wife would contradict him. It was only natural. Mistakes, false memories, faulty recall: they signified nothing.

They signified nothing, but the blizzard still threatened to engulf her. She was submerged, and she didn't know how she would ever dig herself out.

Mrs Lovie hadn't always been a widow. She'd been a bride once and, before that, a girl. Margaret Watson, she was back then: a farmer's daughter. Born at Pitsligo and raised in a two-room stone cottage a mile from the sea – raised between the cries of gulls and the groaning of cattle, between the tang of the ocean and the warm reek of livestock. Raised like every child she knew, with a brood of siblings, a work-worn mother, a taciturn father, and the broonies and the fair-folk.

She had never learned to read or write. You didn't need to read to milk a cow, and the bread would rise whether you could sign your name or not, as long as you had kneaded it right. She wondered, now, as she sat in the stuffy courtroom, whether in lacking an education she'd missed something after all. If she'd learned to read, might she have understood something about this other world she had never seen before, this world of lawyers and declarations and courtrooms and prison cells and oaths and lies? And if she understood it, might she have a better chance of saving John?

Then again, John could read and write, and look where it had got him.

Her childhood seemed idyllic to her now. Never mind the work or the worry about getting through the winter. Never mind the daily rising with the sun – or before it – to do the milking; never mind the endless chores. There had always been Sundays, spent in worship, and there had been evenings by the fire with her brothers and sisters, when she could forget about the holes in her shoes and the growling in her stomach.

The fair-folk and the broonies had always been there too; they had raised her alongside her mother. She closed her eyes and thought of her mother, whose fear of offending 'themselves' had guided every word and every action. Those unseen forces still whispered their lessons and warnings in Margaret Lovie's ears, though reason told her to ignore them. And anyway, who was she to doubt? Those sweet-toothed, hairy, easily affronted broonies were well known to cause trouble. Broken crockery, sick livestock, infant deaths – any of these could befall a family if one of them incurred a broonie's wrath.

What precautions had she forgotten to take? What had she done or not done to have brought this calamity upon her family?

She shuddered. She'd tried so hard! Despite herself, she'd absorbed her mother's lessons; she'd done what she must to appease the authorities in her life: the fair-folk, her mother, and God. She'd thrown salt over her left shoulder when it was spilled, she'd milked the cows and fetched the water without complaint, and she'd prayed every day of her life. What had she missed? Whom had she offended? The fair-folk – or God?

She could never have imagined her life would have come to this. How could she? Once, long ago, the future had seemed hopeful. Once, she knew, Margaret Watson had turned heads. Not a beauty, but fair enough, she liked to think. People had thought her proud. They had often mistaken her silence for self-assurance.

Some men had found her intimidating, she knew, but George Lovie hadn't. She'd known him forever and had taken it for granted that they would wed. George Lovie: a good-looking man who didn't fawn or flatter, a man of action, a hard worker and a good provider, a no-nonsense salt of the earth. The hard drinking and the heavy fists were traits she'd learned about later.

They had married at Pitsligo, in the church where their families had worshipped for generations. Up to that day, Fraserburgh was as far as she had ever ventured. She was at home on the land, didn't like to leave it. Even Fraserburgh, with its tall buildings and its pubs and curing yards and horse-drawn carriages and fishwives marching single file along the cobbled streets, was too busy, too closed-in. And Aberdeen? It was another world altogether: a world of noise and bustle and the stink of too many people. *Give me open fields, unbroken skies, gulls, the moans of cattle.* Aberdeen! How she hated it now.

What would George have made of all this? Would he have stood by John? Of course he would. She shook her head. Nothing was clear to her anymore. She could hardly remember her husband; the details had faded. Her marriage had been tolerable, she supposed. George had been no better and no worse than most husbands. She tried to think of him fondly, but the only feeling his memory stirred was sadness – sadness for the loss of him, and for the opportunities not taken. For the words they'd never spoken and the affection they'd never shown. But what use were words? Life was chores and rituals and children. There was so little to say.

What if she had married someone else? But if there hadn't been George, there wouldn't have been the children. How proud she'd been of her children, as if breeding was a skill.

The children. Everything always came back to them. To John. From the minute she had first held him, her love had been like a wound that would never heal. Her bonny child, blue-eyed like her, and perfect.

John hadn't liked it when Jean had been born so soon after him, usurping his position. But she hadn't really usurped him. There was only ever one John: the listener, the watcher. Folk always wanted John to like them. After Jean had come Mary, and then George, Elspet and

James. But when George had gone and died, it had been John who had kept the farm going – thriving – while his father rested in the grave.

Let them say all they wanted about John, but *she* wouldn't listen to a word.

She was so tired.

She had lived too many years, too many winters. Until now, nothing had ever changed – not the seasons, nor the routines that the seasons dictated. The sowing of neeps in June, the oats in March. The hay harvest in July and the grain in September. The ploughing and turf cutting and thatching and the endless repairs to the tools and the byre and the cottage.

But no; things *had* changed. While these patterns of her own life went on, the world had shifted around her.

The lighthouse had been built at Kinnaird Head. The herring trade had grown and taken over Fraserburgh. The military had come and gone, swept in and out by a wave of patriotism during the wars with the French, taking Meggy's father with them. A new pier had gone up at the northern end of Fraserburgh Harbour and, later, another in the south. The town had grown. George had died. John had bought more cattle. Margaret's children had become adults and married and left the home.

Except for John. John had stayed, despite the best efforts of the women who had tried to lure him away. Through his father's moods and illnesses and death, and through the ups and downs of the harvests, John had stayed. They'd never been at odds, she and John. She'd never had cause to scold him; never had cause to doubt.

Oh, John. *Everything* had changed, but her love for him had not.

Chapter 77

Mr Alison's Summing-up

'Gentlemen of the jury,' Archibald Alison said. 'You have been chosen from your peers to administer the great tradition of justice of which our country is rightly proud. Our noble and independent judicial system ensures that all men and women receive a fair trial, and that the families of victims like the unfortunate Margaret McKessar have the satisfaction of a proper investigation into the crime. You, gentlemen, have not only the profound honour of witnessing our justice system in action but the distinction of playing an active part. The exercise of your rights as jurymen is a privilege. It is also a solemn duty. The discharge of your responsibility will have consequences, both to yourselves and to the public.

'Gentlemen of the jury, you have heard evidence from a multitude of witnesses. I would gladly spare you the trouble of hearing further remarks upon the evidence. The case before you, however, is a heinous one, and a crime has been committed that warrants a capital punishment. I am bound, therefore, to draw your attention to the leading points of evidence.'

He drew a breath – deep and gusty. Widow Lovie drew in a breath with him. 'The crime with which the pannel is charged is the most reviled in our country,' he said. 'The premeditated murder of an innocent girl by her master – an older man upon whom she relied as a neighbour, a friend, a protector. To convict a man of so shocking a crime, and to condemn him to death, the court ought to rely only on evidence that is clear and tangible. In such a case as this, however, the evidence can only be circumstantial. You must trust the evidence you have heard here today and rely upon the direction of the court.

'First, consider: did Margaret McKessar die from poisoning? As to this question, you have heard the evidence of not one but *six* learned gentlemen – one of whom is the highest authority on such matters in the country. You have heard in great detail the pains these medical men took to examine the stomach and its contents – tests conducted in three different laboratories, by three different sets of experts, on several different occasions. You have heard of the scrupulous measures they undertook to ensure that every test was conducted accurately and securely. You have heard that these gentlemen independently concluded that arsenic was present in the deceased's stomach. You have heard Dr Christison testify to having little doubt that Margaret McKessar's death was caused by arsenic poisoning.'

The prosecutor paused, clasping his hands upon his chest and casting his heavy-lidded gaze upon the jury. The jurymen stared back.

'The next question you must ask yourselves,' Alison went on, 'is this: *who* administered the poison?'

He took a step towards the jury, leaning in to them urgently.

'Was the poison administered by the hand of the prisoner? Or, as defence will ask you to consider, was it administered by Margaret McKessar herself? I ask you to examine these two possibilities in the light of the evidence.'

A pause as he stepped back. The jury exhaled audibly.

'Let us look first at the evidence of Alex Rannie,' the prosecutor went on. 'A fellow servant. A man who worked daily with the prisoner and lived in close proximity to both prisoner and victim, he was privy to the comings and goings and private conversations of both. He has *nothing to gain* by accusing his master unfairly – on the contrary, he stands to lose his position, whether or not the prisoner is convicted.

You must accept that his evidence is disinterested and fair, *and* it is well-informed.

'Alex Rannie has given us accounts of alarming conversations that took place between his master and him. He has spoken of John Lovie's frequent references to poison and has shown us that the pannel was preoccupied with the question of ridding a woman of an unborn child. He told the court about the prisoner's musings about how much poison was needed to part a woman from her child, and *how much to kill.*'

Widow Lovie screwed up her eyes, trying to read the expressions of the jurymen. Their faces were blurred at this distance. There might have been nods. In the gallery, people whispered, their heads bobbing.

'In stark contrast with the prisoner's denial of carnal connexions with Margaret McKessar, Alex Rannie gave evidence of their clandestine liaisons. Other witnesses – even the deceased's own mother and aunt – have corroborated Rannie's words about their relationship. Several witnesses knew that the girl was pregnant, and the medical examination confirmed it. The girl told her aunt that her master had promised to marry her. And yet the prisoner has denied all relations with her and all knowledge of the pregnancy. What are we to make of these denials?

'Consider, now, the evidence of the druggist John Officer and his apprentice. These witnesses testified that the prisoner purchased jalap and arsenic from Mr Officer's store. Immediately after Lovie purchased jalap – a known purgative – from the shop boy William Massie, both Margaret McKessar and Alex Rannie were stricken with purging. Then, nine or ten days later, immediately after the prisoner bought arsenic from Mr Officer, Margaret McKessar was seized with an attack of vomiting and died in agony, *showing all the signs of arsenic poisoning.* It would be naïve to see these events as coincidence.

'Mr Officer and William Massie both maintain that the poison they sold to the prisoner was clearly marked with the word "poison", that the prisoner knew it was arsenic, and that they cautioned him most emphatically against carelessness and misuse. And yet the prisoner – who is perfectly able to read and write – claims that he neither noticed the word "poison" on the packages nor knew what particular substance he was purchasing. To his neighbour James Walker, to Jean McKessar, Henrietta McKessar and George Yule, he denied having bought poison at all – a claim which has been shown to be false.

'The prisoner can provide no adequate reason for purchasing poison. He insists that he bought the jalap to treat his wounded back and shoulder. Yet no other witnesses – except, according to him, *his mother* – saw him take physic for his injuries. He also claims that he bought arsenic for the purpose of killing rats and vermin upon black cattle. Both Mr Officer and William Massie denied any mention of black cattle; in fact, Mr Officer has told the court of the inadvisability of rubbing cattle with arsenic.' At this, there were nods from farmers amongst the jurymen. 'It is laughable,' Alison continued, without the slightest hint of mirth on his narrow, downturned lips, 'to think that a farmer with the pannel's experience would make the mistake of using such a poison to treat vermin on his cattle – a poison that might easily kill them.

'And what of John Lovie's claim that the poison's purpose was to rid his farm of rats? We have heard that there were *no rats* at the Lovie farm! Only one witness has reported the presence of rats: a seven-year-old boy; a child whose tender age precludes his understanding of the solemnity of the oath; who has given his evidence today under declaration because he is too young to be sworn in under oath. Even this boy only claims that he *once* heard noises from his bed at night but neither *saw* any rats nor heard them again. The most thorough of searches of the dung-heap, where the prisoner claims to have thrown the poisoned rats, failed to find any trace of them.'

The prosecutor shook his big whiskered head wearily.

'The prisoner's statements are contradicted by *all other witnesses* on all of these counts. He had no honest reason for purchasing poison and he has lied about the circumstances of the purchase. He tells us that the only person who claims to have seen him rubbing any cattle with any substance is his mother. Likewise, the only person who he claims could corroborate his story of killing rats is his mother. He says that after rubbing the cattle and killing the rats, he threw the remainder of the poison into the fire – and who was the only person to see him doing so? His mother! He says that no-one knew that the cattle were infected by vermin but his little nephew – and, again, *his mother.*'

'Mither,' said James. 'Take some ale.'

He was thrusting a flask at her. The world was falling away, turning to liquid, vanishing into a fog. There was something bitter in her mouth, something wet spilling down her chin. She didn't drink; she had no desire for the drink. The drink had been George's refuge, but never hers. She swallowed, unwilling, and coughed, and turned her head away to bury it in her hands.

Oh John, John.

'Gentlemen,' John's would-be executioner continued, 'I ask you to consider how unlikely it is that John Lovie alone has told the truth ... and that *all* the other witnesses are lying. John Officer, William Massie, Alex Rannie, Mary Will, Jean McKessar, Henrietta McKessar and the others have told one story, and the pannel has told another. Which version is the truth?'

Eyes closed, face cupped in her hands, the widow was burning, hot and cold. Details came to her: the sweat soaking her armpits, the softness of Mary's hip against hers, the coughs and rustlings of the crowd, the creaking of boots, the hardness of the wooden seat, the smell of the courtroom – of polished wood and hot, damp humans.

'And if the prisoner did not administer poison to Margaret McKessar,' Alison said, 'then *who did*? The defence will ask you to believe that the girl died by her own hand. And yet the evidence shows us that she had no reason for self-murder. Several witnesses have testified as to her health and good spirits. The defence will argue the contrary. They will suggest that she was in despair upon finding herself with child. But, gentlemen, I ask you to consider this: *Margaret McKessar had no reason to despair!*

'Whether John Lovie intended to marry McKessar or not, she *believed* that he would. She told her aunt as much. She told her aunt that her master would do right by her – that they would be wed in a fortnight. Even on the evening before her death, the neighbour William Park observed her to be in good spirits. Margaret McKessar *believed* that John Lovie would marry her. Believing this, why would she have taken her own life?

'Others, however, knew differently about John's intentions. Even if the prisoner himself was inclined to wed, his family was against it. But he wasn't inclined. Margaret McKessar's mother and sister had both cautioned her against taking a position with John Lovie, knowing him to be of doubtful character. The prisoner denies any connexion with the girl; he had no intention of taking responsibility for her or her child. He sought to procure an abortion, and when it failed the first time, he tried again. But the second time, he did not trouble himself with caution; either the poison would rid Margaret McKessar of the child, or it would kill her. Either consequence would satisfy him. He did not care. *He did not care!*'

John, her little boy, bonny like the Chessor woman's son. Always so easy, so independent, so cool. Slow to anger. Never any bother or fuss.

She pressed her fingertips into her eye sockets. Alison's words kept coming.

'When the girl fell ill, her tormentor worked on in his fields, indifferent to her sufferings. Her mother walked past him *four* times and he said *not a word* about her illness. He let Henrietta McKessar walk by in ignorance, denying Margaret McKessar even the comfort of her mother's presence in her dying hours. Neither did he seek medical assistance for his servant, unwilling as he was to see her recover. Such was the prisoner's callousness.

'Gentlemen, the pannel's case is a tangled mess of contradictions and lies. On the other hand, the case against him is consistently supported by the evidence of more than twenty reliable witnesses. The pannel has been shown to have lied about his relationship with the deceased, his knowledge of her pregnancy, his purchase of poison, and the reason for the purchase. The most likely truth is that, determined to remain a bachelor, John Lovie sought to abort Margaret McKessar's child without her knowledge or consent. Having embarked on that course, he progressed from one step to another, until, having failed initially in his purpose, he committed murder. That he possessed the means for her murder has been proven – which, gentlemen, is the most significant piece of evidence in a trial of this kind.

'Gentlemen, the pannel is a man of some standing in the farming community. He was employer to an innocent, fatherless woman, and should have been her protector. Instead, he took advantage of his position of power over her, secured her trust and affection, and seduced her. Thinking only of his own selfish needs, he refused to acknowledge or take responsibility for her unborn child. Some might argue that his crime was that of attempting to procure abortion. They might protest that this was a lesser crime. Gentlemen, I remind you this is *not* the case. I remind you that in the advanced stage of pregnancy, procuring abortion is itself a capital crime.

'I remind you also that arsenic was the cause of Margaret McKessar's death – *arsenic*, a deadly poison. No man could administer arsenic without full knowledge that the likely outcome would be death.

'Gentlemen of the jury.' The prosecutor gazed intently down his roman nose at the jury, while the sweat trickled like blood from an open wound down the widow's rigid back. 'You have sworn by Almighty God that you will truth say and no truth conceal. Yours is a task of the highest privilege and it bears the weight of the highest duty. Consider the fate of the poor deceased servant girl, so sorely abused by her master. In light of the evidence of his callousness, perfidy and deceitfulness, you have no course but to *find him guilty*.'

Chapter 78

Mr Cockburn's Summing-up

Margaret Lovie was strangely calm. The damage was done; hope was gone. As the prosecutor spoke, she'd seen the nods and murmurs of agreement from the gallery. The spectators had convicted her son. They wanted him dead.

She'd always seen herself as a good woman. She'd been an honourable wife and a dutiful mother. She'd never shirked in her chores nor overcharged for her butter – not once. She fed her servants well. She paid the rent on time. She neither swore nor drank. She took care not to walk under ladders and she touched wood if a white cat crossed her path.

And she had always paid her respects to God. Would He, then, show her son mercy? She doubted it. He'd shown none to Meggy. Why would He favour John, who had refused to submit to the kirk's discipline? No; all hope was lost. She was like a hollow log, sitting there in the courtroom, emptied out, worm-eaten, stiff, dead.

Her son's champion, the smooth-cheeked, wigged lawyer with the cow-like eyes, hadn't given up. He was on his feet and speaking with such confidence and zeal that she almost felt sorry for him. She sighed. *He might as well try, if he has the energy for it.*

'The crime of which the prisoner is accused is of a most vile and abhorrent kind,' Cockburn began. Nods rippled through the gallery. Aye, it was a terrible crime. They leaned forward, silent, hostile and fascinated. What could this man possibly say to make them doubt John

Lovie's guilt? Let him try! What sport it is, thought Margaret Lovie. What sport.

'If the case is proved against the pannel,' Henry Cockburn went on, 'there are no limits to his iniquity. But if it is not, he has been most cruelly maligned. You, gentlemen of the jury, must decide whether to permit my client to live free as an innocent man, or condemn him to death as a murderer.

'The prosecution asks you to proclaim that John Lovie – an honest farmer of good character against whom his alleged victim never uttered a word of complaint – did *twice* secretly administer poison to her in a callous attempt to end her life, only succeeding on the second attempt. You have been asked to believe that he was *so* determined to rid himself of Margaret McKessar that he administered poison indiscriminately to the members of his household, causing violent illness not only in his alleged lover but also in his blameless farm labourer. The prosecution is asking you to believe that John Lovie was such a heartless and manipulative monster that he would impregnate his servant girl and then casually murder her rather than take responsibility for her child. That when he knew she was dying, he failed to seek medical help in a deliberate attempt to thwart her recovery.'

The spectators set their jaws and narrowed their eyes. Yes, they believed it! They *did* believe it – that John Lovie *was* such a heartless and manipulative monster. They wanted it to be so! They wanted blood. She had thought herself beyond feeling, but grief and despair now flooded through her again.

'Gentlemen, you have heard in ghastly detail the story of a young woman whose life was cut short in the most dreadful way. It is only natural that the revulsion you feel on hearing of her suffering should inspire a desire for justice – or even revenge. I must warn you to *resist* the temptation to rush into a judgement that is shaped by your emotions rather than by the hard evidence before you. Do not be tempted by your natural inclination to punish the prisoner, simply because he is the one upon whom suspicion has fallen. Be conscious of the enormity of the alleged crime – if a crime has indeed been committed – but be warned that no man should be sent to the gallows by suspicion alone.

'The pannel is a hardworking, honest farmer whose family has been well known and respected in the district for generations. Mr Officer, the druggist, affirmed the prisoner's good character himself when he stated that he never sold poison to a man whose morals he did not know to be sound. Mr Officer has known the pannel for *fifteen* years and never had reason to doubt his integrity. In selling the poison to the pannel, Mr Officer – himself a pillar of the community – demonstrated his faith in the prisoner's good intentions. We have heard the pannel's servant, Alex Rannie, describe his master as a fair and decent employer. Even Margaret McKessar's aunt, Mary Will, admitted that the deceased had spoken of John Lovie's kindness to her. *Not one* witness has produced evidence that John Lovie *ever* showed Margaret McKessar anything but kindness.

'The pannel is, in fact, a devoted family man, having faithfully supported his aged mother for many years since the death of her husband, and having provided employment and lodging to his seven-year-old nephew. In all his forty-two years, John Lovie has never displayed any predisposition to violence. Are we really to believe that this man could have callously murdered his servant?

'Let us now consider the chemical evidence. While I have the greatest respect for modern science and for the esteemed medical men whose tests have so excited the prosecution, I urge you to interpret the results with caution. Science is ever developing, and what is held to be true on one day may be proved false the next.

'We have seen alarming contradictions in the results of the various tests conducted in this case. The first tests, conducted by Drs Jamieson, Blaikie and Coutts in Fraserburgh, failed to detect any arsenic in the deceased's stomach. Later tests by Dr Christison in Edinburgh and Drs Forbes, Knight and Blaikie in Aberdeen did suggest the presence of the poison. So which test do we trust? Dr Christison, who is undoubtedly one of the highest authorities in the land, tells us that the first tests conducted in Fraserburgh are less reliable than the later tests performed in Aberdeen and Edinburgh. And yet, not so long ago, those initial tests conducted in Fraserburgh were the very tests relied upon by such experts in chemistry as Dr Christison. How many people have been wrongly convicted in the past on the evidence of these flawed tests? And might not the more "reliable" tests conducted by our Edinburgh and Aberdeen experts be found *unreliable* in future? Can we truly put such complete faith in such an inconstant "authority" that we would condemn a man to death on its word?'

Was that a shift in the mood? Margaret Lovie looked wildly about her. There were raised eyebrows and heads tilted in contemplation. There were also flared nostrils and mutinous glares at Cockburn. What of the jury? She craned her neck, trying to read their faces, cursing her aged eyes. Mary's clammy hand was on her arm again. She shook it off. She cast an eye sideways at James, but he was inscrutable, like his brother.

The lawyer cleared his throat and continued. 'The procurator fiscal, William Simpson, has described in some detail the measures he took to seal, label and transport the portion of stomach and stomach contents to Edinburgh for examination. And yet, despite these measures, he was unable to declare categorically that the bottle whose contents were examined in Edinburgh was the *same* bottle that he sent from Fraserburgh. Even the procurator fiscal admitted that it was possible that the seal and label could have been taken off and put onto another bottle. Not likely, granted, but *possible*. And gentlemen, I must remind you that if you have even the *slightest* trace of doubt that a lethal quantity of arsenic was present in the stomach of the deceased, you *must* give the prisoner the benefit of that doubt.

'Just supposing, then, that arsenic was indeed the cause of Margaret McKessar's death ... we are then faced with a serious difficulty. How and when was the poison administered? The pannel is accused of administering poison with intent to procure abortion, or to murder, on two occasions: first, on 4th August, and second, on either 13th or 14th August.

'Let us look, then, at the first occasion: Saturday 4th August. The prisoner is accused of having administered a large dose of jalap, or "some other poisonous or deleterious substance or drug", with intent to procure abortion. So was the substance jalap or "some other poisonous substance"? There is so little evidence, chemical or otherwise, to prove that *any* poisonous substance was administered to Margaret McKessar on that day, that the prosecution is unable even to identify that alleged substance. It would be an outrage to condemn a man to the gallows on such a vague charge.

'And is it not strange that the servant Alex Rannie was afflicted with the *same* condition on the *same* day that Margaret McKessar was stricken with purging? Are we really to believe that John Lovie was so determined to rid the girl of her unborn child that he would endanger not only *her* life but the life of his other loyal servant as well?

'Consider, gentlemen, another alternative. Consider the simple possibility that these two young servants were simultaneously stricken by some natural illness – one from which they both quickly recovered. The simplest explanation is often the true one, and in this case, the simplest and most likely explanation is indeed that the two servants were visited by some natural ailment.

'Now consider the second occasion upon which my client is alleged to have secretly administered poison to Margaret McKessar – in the hours just prior to her death. This was alleged to have happened on the night of Monday 13th August or the morning of Tuesday 14th August. And yet, we have heard clear statements from several witnesses that show it was *impossible* for anyone to have slipped poison into the deceased's food or drink at those times without her knowledge. On the evening before her death, the Lovies' neighbour, William Park, supped with John Lovie, his mother and Margaret McKessar. He testified that all of those present ate potatoes boiled *in the same pot*. The milk they drank was even from the same dish. Alex Rannie testified that John Lovie went to bed alone that night at his end of the house. We heard that there is no communication between the closet where McKessar and Mrs Lovie slept and the room where Lovie slept, except through the kitchen. Rannie himself slept in the kitchen, and he *neither heard nor saw John Lovie arise at any time during the night.* He could not have entered the kitchen to tamper with any food or drink without disturbing Rannie. We can only conclude that John Lovie did *not* enter the kitchen!

'No-one, in fact, saw John Lovie give anything to McKessar, either on the morning of her death or on the previous evening. McKessar had an undisturbed night and was perfectly well when she arose on the morning of the 14th. No-one saw McKessar eat or drink anything before she became unwell. John Lovie was out working in the fields by the time she arose that morning. How then, could he possibly have administered poison to her that morning? He had no opportunity at any time on the evening before or the morning of her sudden illness.

'The prosecutor can provide *no evidence* that John Lovie or anyone in his household administered poison to Margaret McKessar; he cannot even provide any *theory* as to how or when the poison was administered. To find John Lovie guilty of murder, we must first accept the suggestion that arsenic was found in the stomach and, second, prove that it was he who purposely put it there. The first premise is by no means proven, as we have already seen. Putting those doubts aside, ask yourself: if arsenic *was* the cause of death, is there any real evidence that John Lovie was responsible?'

Henry Cockburn's eyes swept the courtroom. The unsettled murmuring that had washed through fell to silence. He transferred his gaze to the jurymen, who shifted and blinked.

'Suspicion has fallen upon John Lovie not from any firm evidence,' he declared, 'but as a result of unfounded rumour. The court has heard young Alex Rannie's stories about the conversations between him and his master that led him to suspect murder. These alleged conversations, as he reported them, were of an alarming nature, and yet – if the witness is to be believed – he thought *nothing* of them at the time they took place! It was not until *after* Margaret McKessar's horrible death that this young servant suddenly recalled his master's bizarre questions about poisons. Does that not strike you as odd? Any man who would discuss poisoning a person with another man, and then purchase arsenic, administer it to his servant and expect to get away with it must be a simpleton. John Lovie does not strike me as a simpleton.

'Did any other witness ever hear the prisoner talk of poisoning another human? Of course not – because such conversations never happened! How strange if the accused had multiple casual conversations about abortion and murder with his *servant* but not with any other of his many friends. Are we really to believe the stories of a well-meaning but misguided youth, lately traumatised by the ghastly death of his fellow servant – stories that have been corroborated by *no-one*? Alex Rannie's testimony is nothing but the product of an overactive imagination. The case against my client has been built upon nothing but rumour and malicious gossip. It is your duty, gentlemen of the jury, to weigh up the facts laid out before you and to exclude the influence of rumour and hearsay from your deliberations.

'Gentlemen of the jury, you have a duty to acquit my client if you can admit the slightest possibility of innocence. You must acquit him if there is the slightest possibility of another explanation for Margaret McKessar's death.

'Ask yourself this: *if* arsenic was the cause of her death, could the poison have reached the unfortunate girl's stomach by any other means than by her master's hand? Ask yourself: is there any possibility that the wretched girl took her own life?

'Margaret McKessar was a young, headstrong and passionate woman in a delicate situation – unmarried and with child. We have heard her aunt Mrs Will's testimony that less than two weeks before her death, her niece wept about her condition. Her niece, rightly or wrongly, believed that John Lovie's friends and family were attempting to turn him against her. Yes, as Mr Alison pointed out, the neighbour, William Park, reported that the girl was in good spirits when he saw her on the evening before her death. I ask you, gentlemen, which of the two witnesses is more likely to have been privy to the young woman's emotional state: a male neighbour and friend of her employer, or her own beloved aunt? Is it not likely that she put on a brave face when supping with William Park on the evening of the 13th of August, but revealed her emotional anguish to her aunt nine days earlier?

'Margaret McKessar did not – as the defence would have us believe – lack a motive for self-murder. Did she have the opportunity? We have heard that McKessar was alone in the cottage early in the morning before she fell ill. *She* had the opportunity, where *no others* did, to administer poison to herself.'

Mary's hand was on her arm again, moist and clawing. Her heart thumped. She was afraid to hope.

'We have heard no proof that John Lovie knew his servant was pregnant, or that she had ever charged him with the paternity. We have only hearsay. If Lovie did not know of her condition – and he swears he did not – then he had no provocation either to abort her child or to murder her. If he *did* know she was with child, and if she had alleged that the child was his, this is still not evidence of his guilt. There is a vast leap from unchaste conduct to murder.

'Aspersions have been cast upon John Lovie and his mother for failing to notify the deceased's mother of her illness and failing to seek medical assistance until it was too late. This was an error of judgement that, no doubt, the pannel and his mother regret. His – and his mother's – mistake must not be misconstrued as evil design. Margaret McKessar had been violently ill less than two weeks earlier and had recovered without medical intervention. No-one had any reason to expect that this episode would be different. She was a strong, healthy young woman. There is scant evidence that the pannel even knew the seriousness of her illness. He was out working in the fields all morning and saw nothing of Margaret McKessar. He only knew what others – his mother and Alex Rannie – reported of her illness, and saw no reason for alarm. When it was suggested that a doctor should be fetched, John Lovie went promptly and willingly to fetch one.

'He also went willingly to seek medical examination of the body when rumours of poisoning reached his ears. It was not the prisoner who objected most strongly to the opening of the body, but the *family of the deceased*. When, after the burial, the order to exhume the body was given, the pannel made no objection. He co-operated with authorities from first to last in the investigation, hoping to clear his name.

'Much has been made of the purchase of arsenic and other poisons from Mr Officer's shop. Gentlemen of the jury, there are farmers amongst you.' Here, Mr Cockburn turned to the jurymen with palms up and brows raised. 'You *know*,' he implored, 'you *know* the havoc that vermin can wreak upon a farm. There is a simple reason that a farmer might purchase poison, is there not? To rid his farm of vermin. This was, of course, John Lovie's stated reason when he bought the poison from John Officer, and we have no reason to doubt it. Some witnesses have denied the presence of rats on the farm, but young John Yule – a guileless child – has admitted to hearing them. What are the chances of such a farm being free of rats? Quite low, I would expect.' Murmurs in the gallery, nods from the jury. 'Just because Alex Rannie says he wasn't aware of them does not mean they weren't there.'

'Gentlemen, I ask you to consider the conduct and situations of both parties in this case: the deceased and the accused. On the one hand is a troubled young woman who has found herself in an intolerable situation: poor, unmarried and pregnant. On the other is an honest, hardworking farmer who supports his widowed mother and was a just and generous employer to three servants. John Lovie had no opportunity to poison his servant girl and there is nothing in his character or behaviour towards her that suggests he might have had cause. His only mistake was in seeking help too late. He has co-operated in investigations and has never acted in any way that suggests he had anything to hide.

'I beg you to consider: what is the most probable explanation for Margaret McKessar's death?

'Gentlemen of the jury, I remind you that murder is a capital criminal offence. In cases such as these, you *must not* convict unless the pannel's guilt can be *proven*. To convict, you must believe that his innocence is an *impossibility*. If you have *any* doubts as to the pannel's guilt, you must acquit him.

'The so-called "evidence" against my client is mere rumour and speculation, full of contradictions and ambiguity. The prosecution has been unable to produce one shred of firm evidence. Gentlemen, such a case merits a verdict of *not guilty*. And yet this tragic case has no answers. Should you find yourselves unable to exonerate the prisoner fully, you must at the very least return a verdict of *not proven*.

'Gentlemen of the jury,' Cockburn concluded, 'I trust you now to perform your solemn duty, as you have sworn to do before God.'

323

Chapter 79

Lord Pitmilly

The mood had turned; Margaret Lovie sensed it. A wave of doubt had washed aside hatred and vitriol. The people shifted in their seats, restless and confused. They were dissatisfied; they preferred certainty. Black or white, the way farming folk liked it. They mopped sweating brows with stained handkerchiefs, nudged roughly at neighbours whose elbows were too close to theirs, rubbed at cricked necks and strained eyes.

It wasn't over. One of the judges – the thin-lipped one – was getting ready to address the jury. She could hardly hear him over the pounding of her heart.

'Which one is that?' she whispered to James.

'Shhh,' he said. 'Lord Pitmilly.'

The judge's speech was an anticlimax, though; he had nothing new to add. His role, it seemed to her, was to string out the proceedings – to prolong the suspense. To keep the restless crowd on the edges of their seats, wanting more. She had never been to the theatre, but this, she guessed, was theatre at its most powerful.

The judge summed up the evidence – again! – with maddening precision. How many more times, she wondered, must she hear the story of Meggy's death? How many more voices would tell it? And how many versions of *John* would there be? John: the faithful son, the brother, the farmer, the friend, the master, the lover. How many more? The father? The murderer?

Lord Pitmilly's voice was deepening; he seemed to be coming to an end. He reminded the jury of the significance of the pannel's testimony, and – to Margaret Lovie's dimly felt gratitude – pointed out the evidence in his favour.

'I remind you,' he counselled the jury, 'that where any doubt might arise in your minds, the prisoner should have the advantage of that doubt. I leave it entirely to you, gentlemen, on your taking into view all the circumstances of this extraordinary case, to determine on which side the preponderance lies.'

And then the jurymen rose and filed out of the room, and she was left with nothing but her own despair.

Chapter 80

The Jury's Deliberations

The jury was out for half an hour. Margaret Lovie hadn't the energy to rise, but James insisted. He made out that it was for her sake, but it was really for his own. She could see that inaction was driving him to distraction; he needed to move. He told her that she should take some air, and – lacking the strength to resist – she followed him out onto the street. Mary was holding her hand and trembling.

'Mr Cockburn spoke well,' Mary said. 'I think we have hope.'

She shrugged. She raised a hand to her temple. 'I have a headache.'

'Have some ale,' James said, but she shook her head.

'Nay! No ale.'

They were out on Castlegate, where citizens, uncaring, crossed to and fro. Gulls cried. People spilled out from the courtroom, excited by the scandal of it all. Chattering loudly, pleased to be in the fresh air, glad for the opportunity to stretch and mingle and gossip. Glad of the salty breeze that cooled their sweat-dampened clothes. Stretching stiff backs, flexing knees, laughing.

A red-haired woman was staring at her. She groaned. She waited for the woman to move, but she seemed unable. Margaret Lovie dropped Mary's hand and pushed her way through the throng to stand before the redhead.

'I suppose you're enjoying this,' she said. Helen Chessor's eyes grew wide. 'I suppose you can't wait to see him hang.'

Helen Chessor put a hand to her forehead and breathed deeply. When she dropped her hand and spoke, her voice was harsh. 'Is that what you think?'

'You're here for the spectacle.'

'No. I'm here for the truth. Better to face the truth than spend my life hiding away, wondering what folk are saying about my son's father.'

Her instinct was to contradict, for the hundredth time, the woman's accusation, but what was the point? Instead, she said, 'Truth! There's no truth being spoken in there.'

Helen shook her head and turned away, not bothering to answer. Margaret Lovie grabbed her arm. Helen turned back, shook the claw off her arm. 'You think I *want* him to hang?'

'Aye,' she said. 'Don't you?'

'He deserves to hang,' Helen said hotly. 'But do you really think I'd want my boy to be known as the son of a murderer?'

Margaret glared at her, wordless.

The woman shook her head and cast her a look of pity. 'You can't save him now, Mrs Lovie.'

Chapter 81

The Verdict

It was a relief to re-enter the anonymity of the courtroom after the brush with Helen Chessor. The woman's hatred had shaken her badly; it had re-awoken – painfully – a shame that she had thought buried. She followed James in and took a seat, feeble as a foal.

The excitement in the air was palpable, though it didn't reach Margaret Lovie. She was too wrung out to feel it.

The jurymen filed in and took their seats. The judges made their endless announcements. The foreman stood. Margaret Lovie was dimly aware of the sweat that glued her palm to her daughter's. Aware of Mary's trembling flesh on one side and James's muscle on the other.

'We have reached a unanimous verdict,' the foreman was saying.

The courtroom held its breath.

'Not proven,' said the foreman.

***

Gasps eddied through the gallery. Feet stamped, voices rose in shouts and sobs and protests, and gavels pounded.

'Not proven?' she pleaded. She craned her neck to look at John; he was sitting unmoving as the commotion raged around him. '*Not proven?* What does that mean?'

'It means they're releasing him, Mither,' Mary said, weeping. 'It means he's free.'

'He's not free,' James said, pressing a hand to his forehead. His face was flushed, and he spoke loudly, harshly. 'They're releasing him, but he won't be free. Look at them! Look at the crowd! They want him to hang. Look at the jury! They think he's guilty too, or they'd declare him innocent. They *think* he's guilty, but they can't *prove* it.'

She was hot and cold and panting. John's lawyer was nodding and smiling, his satisfaction evident. The jurors looked glum and shifty-eyed. John stood, running a hand through his hair, half-smiling, getting ready to re-join life.

'He's not free, Mither,' James rasped. 'He'll never be free.'

Epilogue

MARCH 1829

Futteret Den

Margaret Lovie stood at the door and peered into the fog. The turnpike road was hidden beyond the grey curtain.

'It's bitter out,' she said. 'No-one will be about.'

John laughed softly at her shoulder. 'A good day for errands, then.'

She nodded. 'I'll come along with you,' she said. 'My boots need mending and I canna wait longer.'

'Will the cobbler see you, though?'

She blushed and shrugged. 'He might, if ...'

'If *I* don't show myself.'

She nodded.

John sighed. 'All right, then.'

She pulled her shawl tight about her shoulders and they stepped out into the yard. The sky was olive green and threatening sleet, and a briny ice-wind washed in straight from the sea. They walked down to the turnpike road and marched together, leaning into the wind, towards the Broch.

After a short silence, she spoke. 'Will you hire a new hand at Whitsunday?'

'You know we canna afford it.'

'But how will we manage?'

John shrugged. 'No hand would work for us, even if we *could* pay.'

She had nothing to say to that. Rannie had long since deserted, and the only hands who would work for them now were the occasional lame ones, the old and the crooked, the men nobody else wanted. Even *they* were few. Her mind wandered. Alex Rannie had wed, she'd heard. Turned his back on the land and taken up carpentering or some such. Good luck to him.

She looked sideways at John, whose eyes were fixed on the road ahead. He didn't like to talk about their troubles. They trudged in silence, until she spoke again. 'Can we make the rent, then?'

'Can you sell the butter?'

'No-one will buy it.'

'*Still?* Well, then.' He bowed his head and she saw the muscles working in his jaw.

'What, then?' she heard the whining in her own voice and hated it.

'What, then?' He stopped and turned to her. 'I'll tell you what, Mither. Milne won't bleed the beasts when they're ill, so more of them will die. Walker makes excuses when I want to borrow his plough, so I canna sow half the seed I should. I canna even *ask* to buy poison, so rats will eat the corn. You ask me *what, then?*'

'Oh, John.'

'I canna even buy a drink at the inn.' He kicked a stone and then cursed. 'And now I've put another hole in my boot, damn it!'

'John!' she said, but this time it was a warning. Up ahead loomed the figures of a woman and child. By the time they came into focus, it was too late to avoid them. Her heart hammered in her chest.

John exhaled slowly. 'Never mind, Mither.'

The figures approached and grew clearer, the woman strolling, the boy skipping. The light chatter of the woman's voice filtered through the mist to them. She hadn't seen them yet; she was occupied with watching the boy. When the young woman drew closer and saw them, not twenty feet away, she stopped dead.

'Gweed day tae ye, Helen,' John said.

Helen reached for her son's hand. The boy nudged closer to his mother's skirts and stared up at John curiously.

The wind ripped at Helen's skirt and hair. She was staring at John with her mouth open. Hazel eyes, bad-luck red curls escaping from her mutch cap, pale skin blotched with emotion. She drew the child close and wrapped an arm around his shoulders.

Margaret Lovie dropped her gaze down to the boy. She'd seen little of him over the years, though they were neighbours, for she never ventured out if it could be avoided – and only then in harsh weather when most decent folk could be expected to stay indoors. She eyed the boy curiously, despite herself. Now that he had shed his baby fat, his resemblance to John was striking. Dark-haired, blue-eyed, tall for his age and well-formed. Cocooned by his mother, he was humming, smiling at the widow, not a care in the world. Sweet, like John had been as a child. Like John had been, back when he was innocent.

'I hear you've wed, Helen,' John said. 'I wish you—'

Helen Chessor spat. The wind took her saliva, aimed at John, and sprayed it upon Margaret's sleeve instead. She didn't flinch; she couldn't take her eyes away from her grandson. Helen blushed and turned sharply aside, dragging her bewildered son after her as she skirted around them and scuttled down the road.

John looked at the spittle on his mother's arm, but neither of them made a move to wipe it off. The wind would dry it. They trudged on in silence along the road to Fraserburgh. She remembered that her knees and back ached, that her hands were chapped and swollen, that her left boot was worn through at the heel and the cobbler might refuse to mend it. She hunched against the wind.

'I have to leave,' John said at length. 'Give up the lease. I can't stay.'

'No!' The wind thinned her voice to a whine. 'Things will settle.'

'They won't settle.'

It had been on a day much like this that Meggy had come to them. A black day. Sometimes her hatred for Meggy outstripped her sorrow. Meggy had destroyed them all; she had plotted to take John away – and she might yet get her way.

'You know how bad it is,' John said.

She did. People crossed the road to avoid them.

'I might just as well have gone to the gallows, like Gillespie,' he said.

'Don't say that. Gillespie was guilty. He got justice, like you did.'

'Huh.'

'Huh?' she said, stopping again and tugging at his arm. 'What do you mean by that?'

She remembered when John had read the newspaper story about Gillespie's trial aloud to her. The man had been tried for forgery on the very day after John's trial, by the same judges who had tried John's case. She hadn't wanted to hear about Gillespie; she'd had enough of courtrooms. But John had been so pleased about his own escape back then, he'd crowed about Gillespie's fate. He'd read the article sitting in his armchair by the fire while he smoked his pipe. She could still see the look on his face: triumphant.

And Lord Alloway's words to the convicted prisoner? John had read *them* too. 'Do not waste the few remaining days of your time upon earth in vain hopes of a pardon, but apply yourself earnestly and diligently to a preparation for another and a better world into which the greatest sinner may hope to enter, if sincerely repentant of his crimes, and resting his faith and salvation upon the merits of our blessed Redeemer and Saviour.'

She shuddered. Gillespie had pleaded guilty and gone to the gallows repentant. He'd gone to a *better world*.

But there was no repentance in her son. There would be no better world for him.

John was smiling, as if his remark about the gallows had not run through her like a spear. She swallowed, licked her lips and forced herself to speak. 'Where will you go, then?'

He shrugged. He was still handsome, though there was more grey in his hair than black now. 'South, I suppose. Someplace where they don't know me.'

Her heart was breaking. 'But what will you do?'

'Plenty of farmers could use a labourer.'

'From tacksman to farmhand,' she said bitterly.

'Aye.'

'And what about me?'

He turned back to the road and kept walking. 'Mary and George Yule will have you, I dare say. Or Elspet.'

Mary! Elspet!

There was nothing more to say. She marched on beside her son, head down, charging into the wind, while fine needles of sleet stabbed at her face.

***

December 1863, St Cyrus Poor-house

SUICIDE OF A SUPPOSED MURDERER. The *Edinburgh Evening Courant* of Saturday has the following paragraph: – A few days ago an old man, named John Lovie, about the age of eighty-four, an inmate of St Cyrus Poor-house, put an end to his existence by cutting his throat with a razor. He had been complaining on Monday, and on that account retired to bed earlier than usual, and while there he committed the dreadful act. He had been for nearly forty years in the parish. He is believed to have been the John Lovie, farmer at Futteretden, near Fraserburgh, who was tried before Lords Pitmilly and Alloway at Aberdeen, in the autumn of 1827, for the murder, by arsenic, of Margaret McKessar, his servant girl, who was pregnant by him. Notwithstanding that the evidence was as clear as circumstantial evidence could be, the jury deliberated for half an hour, and saw fit, to the utter amazement of all who had listened to the trial, to return a unanimous verdict of not proven. 'The jury,' says Mr Alison, in his book on criminal law, 'misled by the eloquence of the late Lord (then Mr) Cockburn, found the libel not proven, but the court were of opinion that the case was clearly made out.' Lovie was never heard to refer to this murder while in the poor-house; but perhaps it may have been the cause of his sad end.

—*The Banffshire Journal*, 22 December 1863

Glossary

baillie – municipal magistrate

bairn – young child

bide – to stay

breeks – trousers (breeches)

the Broch – Fraserburgh (colloquial)

broonie – (brownie) – a mischievous, easily offended creature from
Scottish folklore

brose – type of uncooked porridge, made of oatmeal. The oatmeal is
mixed with boiling water and allowed to stand.

but-and-ben cottage – traditional two-room humble cottage found in
Scotland. Typically the 'but' was the kitchen and the 'ben' the 'good
room' or parlour, but in Aberdeenshire in the period during which
this novel is set, the opposite appears to have applied.

byre – cow shed

chiel – young man (a boy in his late teens or early twenties)

chesting – a ceremony in which the deceased person is placed in the
chest/kist (coffin) before the burial. Also known as a 'kisting'.

compeared – interrogated, questioned

creel – wickerwork basket, especially one used to hold fish

creepie – low, three-legged stool

deece – type of settle (see below) used in Aberdeenshire. It has a small
hinged table attached to the middle of the seat backrest, with space

for sitting on each side. The table can be flipped up and out of the way, so the deece can double as a bed.

dinna ken – don't know (past tense: didna ken)

fair-folk – fairies

fee/feeing market – hire. Labourers were fee'd at hiring (feeing) markets, generally for six-month terms

fleam – handheld device used for bloodletting

gweed day tae ye – greeting: 'good day to you'

hairst – harvest

heritor – landowners who contributed to the upkeep of the parish church and had considerable authority and status

houk – disease of cattle (also howk, heuck or heugh) that makes them hide-bound and causes inflamed eyes

hummel – cow without horns

kirk – church

kist/kisting – chest, trunk or box; also, a coffin. The 'kisting' or 'chesting' is a ceremony in which the deceased person is placed in the kist (coffin) before the burial.

laird – landed proprietor (landlord)

loon – boy or young man

mutch – white cap with a frilled border, worn by married women

neeps – turnips

pannel – accused person in a criminal action from the time of their appearance in court

pottage – thick soup or stew, made of leftovers – sometimes boiled herbs, roots and vegetables, or sometimes oatmeal, like porridge

precognition – witness statement

quine – girl

settle – long timber seat used for sitting on during the day and sleeping during the night. *see also*: deece

skaffie – Scottish fishing boat

square-wright – carpenter

steading – service building or area of a farm

stirk – young heifer or bullock, kept for slaughter not for breeding

tack, tacksman – lease or tenancy (tacksman: leaseholder, tenant)

tatties – potatoes

wean – baby

yirn – to curdle milk (also yearn or yurn)

From the Author

Three Times Buried is closely based on a true story. I have neither in-vented characters nor changed names (except for Alex Rannie's wife's name – for the story didn't need another Mary!). All of the significant events (and some of the less significant ones) are founded on real events, though of course the thoughts, motivations and feelings of the characters spring from my own imagination.

Most of my information about the events surrounding Meggy McKessar's death came from the precognitions (witness statements) and trial notes, which are held in Register House, Edinburgh. The in-troductions to witness statements are transcriptions of small segments of these. Contemporaneous newspaper reports were also extremely helpful.

Official historical accounts, however, only provide limited infor-mation: names, ages, occupations, places of residence. For some of the more prominent citizens (doctors, lawyers and judges), physical descriptions, portraits and character sketches exist – and I have relied upon these when they do – but for the ordinary folk, they do not. I have, therefore, taken the liberty of inventing these details. All I know of John Lovie's appearance is that he was 'rather a good looking man, of mild aspect and demeanour' (*Morning Chronicle*, 3 October 1827), who remained impassive throughout the trial. As far as possible, I have inferred personalities from the witness statements (I have no doubt that Meggy was a sassy young lady). Some of the dialogue in this story has been taken directly from witness statements, but much of it is my own invention.

A brief word about but-and-ben cottages. Readers who are familiar with these humble Scottish homes might view my depiction of the ben as the kitchen and the but as the best room as a mistake. Usually the but is the kitchen end of the house and the ben is the best room, but it seems that historically, the opposite applied in Aberdeenshire. The precognitions make it quite clear that at Futteret Den, the kitchen was indeed described as the ben end of the house and John's room – the best room – the but.

The case of John Lovie was a notorious one in its time. So infamous was the case, and so strong the feeling against him, that a folk song was written about the story. The lyrics of the song, 'John Lovie', written by one 'Mrs Taylor', may be found in *The Greig-Duncan Folk Song Collection*, Volume 2, published by Aberdeen University Press in 1983.

A final note: recent DNA tests of descendants suggest that Helen Chessor's son was indeed fathered by John Lovie.

Acknowledgements

Many people and organisations have helped me research nineteenth-century Aberdeenshire farming life in general and the John Lovie story in particular. It was my brother-in-law, Geoff Smith, who alerted me to the story of his ancestor John Lovie. His fascination for the subject and his thought-provoking questions have fuelled my enthusiasm. I'm grateful to Geoff for transcribing copious notes and sharing his family history research with me. I'm also grateful to my 'man on the ground', Jim Gardner, for conducting valuable research in Edinburgh and obtaining copies of documents on my behalf.

I'm indebted to many people for answering my deluge of questions. They include the staff of National Museums Scotland, particularly at the National Museum of Rural Life, and particularly Marion Lawton, Rachel Chisholm, Dorothy Kidd and Elaine Edwards. I am also grateful to Professor Marjory Harper of the University of Aberdeen, who helped me with details about nineteenth-century Aberdeenshire; Professor John Finlay of Glasgow University, who advised me on aspects of historical Scottish law; and Reverend Douglas Galbraith, whose assistance with historical church matters was invaluable. The staff of the National Records Scotland have also been extremely helpful.

When the Covid-19 pandemic forced me to cancel my plans for a research trip, Bob Clark from Auchindrain Township patiently answered my many questions about but-and-ben cottages, the diet, and the social customs in early nineteenth-century Aberdeenshire over the phone. Leona Skene, with her local knowledge of history, geography and language of Aberdeenshire, also provided valuable guidance to improve the authenticity of my story.

I would also like to thank staff from the Aberdeen City and Aberdeenshire Archives; Jennifer Pape from Aberdeen's Tolbooth Museum; staff from the Special Collections Centre at the University of Aberdeen; David Oswald, Local Studies Librarian at Aberdeen City Council; and the librarians at the National Library of Scotland. Thanks also to the Fraserburgh Old Parish Church staff and Sheila Watt for information about gravesites. Thanks to Karen Dustman for sharing her research on the Chalmers family, and for her gracious support of my work. Any errors are my own.

Editor Michele Perry and amazing author/editor/friend Tara East gave me valuable feedback on early versions, for which I'm very grateful. Many thanks also to the meticulous and methodical editor Charlotte Cottier, who picked up the errors that had somehow made it through to the hundredth draft, answered my questions patiently and gave my manuscript a special polish.

And finally, thanks to Steve, Lucy and Eddie, for making the world a better place.

Other Books by Jane Smith

Non-fiction:

One Free Woman
Ship of Death: The Tragedy of the 'Emigrant'
Captain Starlight: The Strange but True Story of a Bushranger, Impostor and Murderer – re-released in 2024 as *The Killer's Game*
Australian Bushrangers non-fiction series

Children's books:

Carly Mills, Pioneer Girl series
Tommy Bell, Bushranger Boy series

www.ingramcontent.com/pod-product-compliance
Lightning Source LLC
Chambersburg PA
CBHW071919130726
47909CB00014B/2079